Dedalus Europe 2013
General Editor: Mike Mitchell

Barbara

Jørgen-Frantz Jacobsen

Barbara

Translated by W. Glyn Jones

With an introduction by William Heinesen

Dedalus

Dedalus would like to thank The Danish Arts Council's Committee for Literature and Arts Council England, London for their assistance in producing this book.

Published in the UK by Dedalus Limited,
24-26, St Judith's Lane, Sawtry, Cambs, PE28 5XE
email: info@dedalusbooks.com
www.dedalusbooks.com

ISBN printed book: 978 1 909232 30 3
ISBN ebook: 978 1 909232 58 7

Dedalus is distributed in the USA by SCB Distributors,
15608 South New Century Drive, Gardena, CA 90248
email: info@scbdistributors.com   web: www.scbdistributors.com

Dedalus is distributed in Australia by Peribo Pty Ltd.
58, Beaumont Road, Mount Kuring-gai, N.S.W. 2080
email: info@peribo.com.au

Publishing History
First published in Denmark in 1939
First published by Dedalus in 2013

Translation copyright © W. Glyn Jones 2013
Introduction copyright © William Heinesen 1939

The right of W. Glyn Jones to be identified as the translator of this work has been asserted by him in accordance with the Copyright, Designs and Patents Act, 1988.

Printed in Finland by Bookwell
Typeset by Marie Lane
This book has been printed on Ensolux Cream wood-free paper.

The Author

Jørgen-Frantz Jacobsen (1900–1938) spent his early childhood in his native Faroe Islands, then proceeded to high school and university in Denmark. He worked as a journalist for the newspaper *Politiken*, but in 1922 fell prey to the tuberculosis that led to his early death.

He worked to the very end, and while *Barbara* was his only novel, it was preceded by a work entitled *The Faroes, Nature and People*, which has the dual quality of being informative and a work of considerable beauty. Although written in Danish, his work is intensely Faroese.

The Translator

W. Glyn Jones read Modern Languages at Pembroke College Cambridge, with Danish as his principal language, before doing his doctoral thesis at Cambridge. He taught at various universities in England and Scandinavia before becoming Professor of Scandinavian Studies at Newcastle and then at the University of East Anglia. He also spent two years as Professor of Scandinavian Literature in the Faeroese Academy. On his retirement from teaching he was created a Knight of the Royal Danish Order of the Dannebrog.

He has written widely on Danish, Faeroese and Finland-Swedish literature including studies of Johannes Jorgensen, Tove Jansson and William Heinesen.

He is the the author of *Denmark: A Modern History* and co-author with his wife, Kirsten Gade, of *Colloquial Danish* and the *Blue Guide to Denmark*.

W. Glyn Jones' many translations from Danish include *Seneca* by Villy Sorensen and for Dedalus: *The Black Cauldron, The Lost Musicians*, *Windswept Dawn*, *The Good Hope* and *Mother Pleiades* by William Heinesen, *Ida Brandt* by Herman Bang and *My Fairy-Tale Life* by Hans Christian Andersen.

He is currently translating William Heinesen's last novel *The Tower at the Edge of the World*.

Introduction

When Jørgen-Frantz Jacobsen died in March 1938 at the early age of 37, he left behind the manuscript for this book. Jacobsen had previously been known to the Danish public as the author of two books on the Faroe Islands in addition to a large number of articles in the newspaper *Politiken* on Faroese, Icelandic, Norwegian and other Scandinavian subjects, and through these articles he achieved a reputation as a gifted and original journalist with a distinctive style, a man who tackled his material with authority and complete honesty, but writing in an artistically fascinating, *amusing* manner.

Jørgen-Frantz Jacobsen was born in 1900, the son of a grocer in Tórshavn in the Faroe Islands. He was of an out-going and positive nature and was gifted in many fields, and people rightly had great expectations of him. He would undoubtedly have been able to make an important contribution both as a scholar (historian) and as a politician if stubborn ill health had not prevented him from developing to the full extent of his ability. This illness, tuberculosis, already made its appearance when he was only twenty-one years old, living as a student in Regensen, the hall of residence in Copenhagen, and it made its mark on the rest of his later life. For long periods he was condemned to being bedridden and passive, but his courage and his spirit were never subdued. As soon as a temporary relief gave him back his freedom, he threw himself into the active life that suited his temperament. He took part in politics, became acquainted with a great number of people and conditions, undertook studies and journeys, fell in love – and all the time devoting himself to the writing that had been a compulsion for him ever since childhood. He undertook demanding tasks and exposed himself time after time to over-exertion, which again led to relapses and once more tied him to his bed. "The organ is strong enough," he would say, "but the church can't stand it." And as he approached maturity the church became ever weaker, though the organ remained just as indomitable.

Jacobsen also occupied himself with literary activities from his earliest youth. He wrote some poems, some short stories and plays, and he left hundreds of poetical letters and reports often in the form of elegant descriptions of nature and travel accounts or in the form of memoirs.

He started on the novel *Barbara* in 1934. His illness had by then taken a complicated and dangerous course. Most of the book was written while he lay ill in bed, often under conditions that least of all could be expected to predispose a man to productive work. But it was not in Jacobsen's nature to break down. He was absolutely invincible, and he met every adversity in a manner that could only be described with one word: heroic. No one ever heard Jørgen-Frantz Jacobsen complain at the really quite unusually harsh fate that was his. On the other hand, he often expressed his gratitude to life, with which, as he put it, he had always been on good terms and the gifts of which he did not intend to subject to suspicion. "Simply all these Faroese mountains and valleys: Kirkjubøreyn, Reyðafallstind, Sjeyndir – and all that music: Bach, Mozart, Beethoven, Ravel or Carl Nielsen! Yes, and then Kingo, Bellman and La Rochefoucauld!" as he exclaims in one of his letters.

Four months before his death he wrote to a friend: "Don't you be bothered about my Mozartian view of life... my strength lies in my not striving for happiness and well-being but for better or for worse being in love with my own fate." During a catastrophic bout of his illness which, as he well knew, would necessitate a difficult and dangerous operation, he wrote these stoic and ironic words: "This is a trial, but if you want the good, you must accept the bad as well. If I die, you will be able to write on my grave: Here lies one who had many human experiences and was always harmoniously happy. He finally even managed to experience a touch of the molestations of old age."

As will be clear, Jørgen-Frantz Jacobsen was not prone to either the pretentious or the mystical. On the other hand, his view of life was characterised by *humour*, a humour of a certain honest and pithy kind, often containing a touch of wormwood in the manner of harsh criticism and self-irony and always linked to the respect for life and its immediate realities, which he rated more highly than any sort of unconstrained and dishonest metaphysical ramblings.

The material for the novel *Barbara* is taken from a Faroese legend, "Beinta and Peder Arrheboe", which builds on a foundation of historical events. The beautiful, but evil parson's wife, Beinta, who has been married several times and is the cause of her husbands' misfortune and death, is traditionally seen as a virtually demonic female figure, a vampire who is evil for the sake of being evil. The *Barbara* who is the subject of Jørgen-Frantz Jacobsen's novel is also in her way a jinx and a vampire, but she is portrayed in such a way that we understand her, come to be fond of her and finally to feel sorry for her. She is neither demonic nor mystical, but in all her paradoxical womanliness, all too human. The same applies to the book as a whole. It takes place at the time of Frederik the Fifth (1723–66), though this is no archaic portrayal, but, one might say, a modern one, and Jacobsen builds throughout on his own experiences, not on reading and literary studies. It is a book about life and youth, a portrait characterised by archness and charm, by humour and poetry, but also containing a touch of irony and an undercurrent of melancholy. It was written by a man who was still young and resilient in spirit, but whose body was already broken and aged – a man who in spite of all his troubles and painful experiences never grew bitter because, "for better or for worse" he was genuinely in love with life in the form in which he had found it.

William Heinesen

Fortuna

The lights in the Royal Store buildings in Havn were almost blown out by the wind each time there came a gust. Occasionally, it could be as quiet as the grave. Then the heavy timberwork would start to groan, and the gale again caught the brown tarred wooden houses in its stranglehold. There was a pitiful wailing in every corner; the warehouse shutters tore and struggled in their iron cramps; the turf roofs danced in turmoil like wild flames, and the surf cast itself heavily on the stony promontory of Tinganes and enveloped all Tórshavn in a shower of salt and rain.

In the storehouse, Ole the stocking buyer and Rebekka's Poul were busy sorting jerseys. They sat in the small circle of light provided by a lamp. Otherwise, the warehouses lay in darkness. But several folk were assembled in the shop.

They had received news. A boat that had been out fishing to the east of Nolsoy had seen a ship. They thought it was the *Fortuna*, which was expected from Copenhagen with goods for the Store. But she could not get into the harbour in this weather. The fishing boat had made the shore at the last moment before the storm broke.

The men stood around, idly discussing this ship. They were Tórshavn men – *Havn* men, as they were known – at one and the same time soldiers at the Redoubt, porters in the Royal Store and fishermen far out at sea when the weather was suitable and the commander would allow them to go. They were leaning over the counter. The tallow candle shone in their flaccid faces and their sullen, red-ringed eyes. They were spitting and yawning in a generally miserable manner. The news was turned over like a plug of chewing tobacco. Gabriel, the storekeeper, was standing at his desk behind the counter. He occasionally looked up from his accounts and made a small contribution to the conversation.

Were there two or three masts on this ship? Oh, two masts. Yes, it would probably be the *Fortuna*.

Katrine the Cellar fought her way into the Store. The gale was right on her heels like some evil spirit. Then the door slammed to. She timidly wished everyone a good evening, cowed by all the commotion she had caused. The men spat at a slightly greater distance and acknowledged in this way that they had noticed her. They were not particularly grand – neither Springus, Niels the Punt, Samuel the Hoist nor the Beach Flea. But they did not approve of female interference in a strictly factual discussion on seafaring. Katrine also fully understood this. For a long time she stood there meekly and was only Katrine the Cellar. Or rather: for the time being she hardly existed. But her eyes were watchful and determined. She had her little war to wage. So when Gabriel at some stage, almost by chance, caught sight of her, she was there straight away: "God bless you, Gabriel, will you let me have a jug of syrup this evening."

She cautiously pushed the jug forward on the counter.

"What the hell are you doing out here again now? Haven't you been out here once before today buying both flour and oats?

"God bless you! Just so the children can have something to drink this evening."

12

"Oh, go to blazes," shouted Gabriel furiously. "Why the devil can't you buy everything at the same time?"

"We couldn't take more on account this morning, you know. But now Marcus has had such a good day's fishing."

"Do you think I haven't anything else to do but stir the syrup barrel every time Marcus catches a tiddler?"

Clearly showing his irritation, he went over to the barrel, bent his fat back and filled the mug with the thick syrup. Katrine watched him excitedly. It was taking such a long time. If only he didn't change his mind half way! Gabriel groaned and swore gently. Finally, he straightened his back and flung the mug across the counter: "There!"

He took her shopping book and made a note in it. Katrine left. The men spat.

Gabriel was easy-going by nature, but somewhat self-important on account of his position. He had a big, full mouth that actually bubbled with kindly impudence. Idleness had made him fat, and during the hours he spent every day behind the counter in the store, he had grown accustomed to gossip. He was a king to his customers and he supplied corn and sugar, snuff and sarcasms to the small fry on the other side of the counter.

And now all this talk about the ship started to weary him.

"Oh," he said suddenly, addressing Beach Flea: "I suppose you didn't see any pilot whales today?"

Beach Flea spat. He had got the message. Now it was his turn to be teased. He turned his head left and right, quickly and spasmodically, and his eyes wandered cautiously over the scene. Were they laughing at him?

"Pilot whales? Who sees pilot whales in November, if I may ask?"

"I thought perhaps *you* did. You see pilot whales when no

one else does."

That story was never going to be forgotten. Beach Flea had once mistaken a flock of eider ducks out on the water for pilot whales. In his excitement he had sounded the alarm and caused a good deal of bother. Others had been guilty of similar mistakes. Was it worth bringing up so many years later? He was furious every time anyone referred to it.

The men laughed. Beach Flea stared them out, giving each of them a bad-tempered, hurt look as he tried to think of what to say. He stopped at Samuel the Hoist: "Well, you are not the one to talk, Samuel. At least I've not been found asleep on my job in the Redoubt while a pod of pilot whales was swimming right in front of my nose! That was you!"

"Me?"

Samuel's mouth was quite rigid with hurt and amazement. "Me?"

The entire gathering chuckled. That story was just as well known. Samuel was the only one who refused to accept it. There were hints of fury in his eyes and he was ready to erupt. He studied the miserable Beach Flea. What was this he was daring to accuse him of?

They gently banged on the counter. Gabriel was in his element. He had set things going now. He made the odd serious, extremely factual remark that greatly stimulated the fighting spirit. A turning point in the struggle came when Beach Flea suddenly – as though on some sudden inspiration – got hold of the expression *bamboozler* and flung it out. He didn't know what it really meant. The result was silence. Samuel the Hoist straightened his back and stared at Beach Flea:

"Me, a bamboozler?"

Nor did he know what a bamboozler was. But that did not make the accusation any less offensive. Something had to be

14

done.

"No!" he exclaimed with composure and much dignity. And then he set off. Everyone watched in amazement. He went behind the counter! In between barrels and sacks, right over to Gabriel's desk. And there he stood.

"No, *you* are a bamboozler," he roared banging his fist down on the account books with a resounding thump. He gave Beach Flea a look that was enough to unnerve him. Then he returned to his place, all that long way, like a man who has done his job well.

Beach Flea's eyes fluttered wildly. He had been hurt.

"I? I? Am I a bamboozler?"

Could that possibly be true? He stood open-mouthed.

"No," he said decisively at last, full of regained conviction: "It's you, you, yes *you*!"

He threw off his clogs and went behind the counter, went right over to the desk and banged on it, saying in a tearful voice: "*You* are a bamboozler."

Then he went carefully back to his place again and put on his clogs.

If Samuel the Hoist had been amazed the first time the accusation was flung out, he was no less surprised when it was repeated. He had in general a rare ability to feel amazed at the evil in the world – and to encounter it with fortitude. But in this case a protest *must* be made.

Then he went calmly to the desk again, took up a position there, aimed and fired like the soldier he was. The desk groaned: – "No! *You* are a bamboozler!"

Beach Flea ducked a little. Again this worrying flank attack. His head jerked warily, to the right and to the left, and he squinted watchfully through irate eyes. No, this was more than he could countenance. Clogs off. Off to the desk. He, too, was a soldier and knew how to make a direct hit. He would show them. He put all his tousled and hectored spiritual force in his wounded glance and all his physical strength into his angry fist: – "No! *You* – are – a – bamboozler."

He screamed this last word and accompanied it with three small extra shots, a salvo on the desk. Then he went back again. Victorious, he put on his clogs. Now, Samuel had got what he deserved.

Samuel was upset by this brutal attack. But he gradually more or less regained his composure. He got going again, still a little bowed, but with a new tragic grandeur. And so they went on. The other men shrugged their shoulders in enjoyable neutrality. They kept their hands in front of their mouths, but their eyes were alive, attentive and amused. Thank heaven it was not they who were in the firing line.

At first Gabriel did not like the natural forces that had been unleashed on his desk at all. But he gradually came to sacrifice his dignity on the altar of amusement. At least he had got them going pretty damned well now. He was itching to see the outcome, and his stomach quietly moved out and in. And the men of *Havn* dutifully went on with the comedy to the satisfaction of his lordship. Finally, he took up a position at the counter and organised them a little by virtue of his official capacity. No one was allowed to go in and bang on it until the other had come out.

Gabriel was that sort of a man. A virtuoso at playing on people's weaknesses, working them up against each other and getting them to reveal the most secret and most foolish aspirations of their hearts. What did these poor folk want out there in his store? No, life at home with the womenfolk in the smoke from the peat fires and the wailing of infants was probably no more fun. Out here there was at least a scent of cardamom and other spices, indeed there was also the view of a barrel of brandy. And then there was the news. Reflections of the world.

And something could happen, of course.

The door had once more been opened to the storm and the din. No one had noticed it during the confrontation – it was probably some woman or other. Now they all saw that the new arrival was Barbara, the judge's daughter.

Everything was different all of a sudden. Even Gabriel was different. Beach Flea had stopped in the middle of the word bamboozler; his fist fell like some idiotic accidental shot on the royal desk. There he stood, in his stocking feet, Oh Jesus, putting on an act!

It was not that Barbara enjoyed any particular respect. She spoke kindly to the ordinary men and was never haughty. But when, on an evening of storm and wind, the sun suddenly shines on the circle of men...

"Have you any silk ribbons that I could buy?" came the sound of her voice.

"Silk ribbons." Gabriel pulled himself together. "Oh, silk ribbons."

Barbara, the sun, suddenly developed a knowledgeable wrinkle between her eyes, pouted and started to choose and reject. Beach Flea very cautiously tiptoed out to his place, but – Barbara's skirt was hiding his clogs.

"But we shall be having some more silk ribbons tomorrow," said Gabriel. A gleam came into his eyes.

"Tomorrow?"

Her voice suggested amazement.

"Yes, or the day after."

"What do you mean?" Barbara's voice suggested still more amazement but at the same time bordered on laughter.

"Oh, do stop it, Barbara," said Gabriel affectionately: "Don't try to kid me that you are the only person in the whole of Tórshavn not to know that the *Fortuna* is off Nolsoy."

"God knows..."

Barbara became obstinate, and indignation started competing with the slight laugh that rose in her throat.

"Aye," Beach Flea intervened now, standing with his legs apart and making explaining movements with his hands, "we saw it, Tommassa Ole and Marcus the Cellar and Samuel the Hoist and me, while we were out fishing this morning."

Barbara suddenly let the sun shine on Beach Flea.

"Did you? Then why is she not coming in?"

Beach Flea was bathed in light and felt honoured and he eagerly shook his head. "No, there's no getting into the harbour here in this weather."

"Oh no, of course."

"And haven't you heard of the new Vágar parson, who's on it either, Barbara?" asked Gabriel.

"Of course I know that a new parson's coming for Vágar."

She sounded a little irritated and abandoned the silk ribbons.

"Aye, as I say," Gabriel went on, "when the ship arrives tomorrow or the day after, you can have all the silk ribbons you want. But I suppose that'll be too late?"

"What do you mean?" Barbara was again somewhere between being insulted and smiling.

"Nothing. I simply mean that'll be too late to bedeck yourself for the parson. Because then he'll already *be* here."

The men looked at Gabriel in amazement. He was certainly Barbara's cousin. But to taunt her in just the same way as he taunted anyone else...! They gave her a furtive look. There she stood in the golden candle light with a smile on her lips. Not at all angry. It was almost as though she felt some subtle delight in the revelation.

Then she turned towards Niels the Punt, with her voice full of delight: "Is your little daughter better, Niels? I will come round with something for her tomorrow."

She went towards the door and started to push it open. Beach Flea, who had got his clogs on meanwhile, sprang across to help her. There was just a trace of a smile in his angry face after she had gone. They were probably all smiling a little. Something in her laughter as it rose in her throat seemed to float there like some melodic sound in the scent of cardamom. A vision had come and gone. The shabby men had become reverential.

But then Gabriel broke the silence: "This is a bit bloody thick! I'll swear that she'll be going down tomorrow to entice the new parson when he comes ashore just as she did with Pastor Niels and Pastor Anders when *they* arrived."

There was outrage in Gabriel's voice.

Oh of course. They all knew that story. Barbara was already the widow of two parsons, Pastor Jonas on the Northern Islands and Pastor Niels on Vágar. Pastor Niels had died only a year ago. A third, Pastor Anders of Næs, with whom she had been betrothed in between, had had second thoughts in time. *He* had not suffered a tragic fate. It was said that Barbara had brought about the deaths of both the men to whom she had been married. There had been a lot of talk about this in various places in the islands, and some people had called her *evil Barbara*. But that was probably mainly in the outlying villages. Those who knew Barbara said that she was not *evil* by any means. And as for the people of Tórshavn, her fellow-townspeople, she had never been at cross purposes with them. On the contrary. But Gabriel simply had to find something scornful to say.

Ole the stocking buyer and Rebekka's Poul came in from the warehouse with their lamp. They had finished. And it was time now to go home for supper. All the men broke up and tramped out among the pack houses, over Reyn, past the church and home to their huts.

Gabriel was suddenly alone in his shop. He was a big man, a king to his customers, and now everyone had heard that he could even go as far as to taunt Barbara. But it hurt Gabriel a little somewhere or other deep down inside. He was only human. And in his merchant soul, too, there resided a hidden touch of folly. It was nothing. Perhaps it was simply a little dog howling at the moon when no one could hear it. He was all right; he had his wages and he earned a little extra. And he would probably be made manager one day. Or perhaps even bailiff, for he had good contacts. And as for his lonely state, there was always Angelika, who came to him in his lodgings when he wanted her to. Everything was well organised; he managed well. But now there was this cousin Barbara, who had been married to two clergymen. She had celebrated weddings with far more men; he was well aware of that; he was bright, and nothing went unnoticed. It was a disgrace to the family and a source of scandal in general. But if things came to that pass, why had she never celebrated a little wedding with *him*? It was such an obvious thing. It could surely be arranged quite easily.

But now this new parson was coming.

The little dog inside Gabriel started howling pitifully with its snout right up in the air. Then he suddenly had an idea. He exploded in a little whistle: Of course!

When, shortly afterwards he was in the manager's office with the keys, his plan had been laid.

Barbara

"Where have you been, Barbara Christina?" asked Magdalene, the judge's widow, somewhat coldly and testily. She had been sitting by the bureau in the best room going through some old things.

Barbara was cold and more or less wet through after being caught in a shower. "You are always at that bureau, mother. Why don't you stay out here in the hearth room, where it's warm?"

"Good heavens, I have put some peat in the stove."

"Yes, but it doesn't give off any heat, as you well know."

They ate their supper in silence. Then the mother returned to her fine room with the bureau and the two poor miniatures hanging on the whitewashed walls. "Don't you think your father might have kept some money hidden in a secret compartment in the bureau?" she asked in the doorway.

"You ask that question every day. I don't believe that story any longer. If there were any, we would have found that compartment long ago."

When Gabriel knocked on the door and entered an hour later, he found Barbara dressed in a woollen petticoat and sitting close to the fire. A pair of stockings had carelessly been thrown down just as she had pulled them off. She was sleepy and tired, and the arrival of her cousin awoke no feelings of femininity in her.

Magdalene came in from the sitting room and asked her nephew what news he had. "Don't sit like that," she said, turning to her daughter. "You could put some more clothes on."

"Oh, Gabriel's no stranger," said Barbara sullenly.

No, Gabriel was no stranger. He could sit here and see her white arms and neck – as a matter of course, too much of a matter of course. That was the trouble with it. Her skin was uniquely lustrous. Could that be because she had been in the tub?

It was not long before Magdalene went back again. But Barbara yawned.

"Barbara, would you like some silk ribbons and clothes and that sort of thing?" asked Gabriel in a voice that was suddenly confidential in tone.

Barbara started; her eyes suddenly sprang to life and her voice took on a warm tone: "Have you got some?"

"I might be able to get something for you."

"Where? Where?" Her entire body had suddenly come to life; her face shone in radiant, almost comical anticipation.

"You mustn't say a word about it," said Gabriel.

"Of course not," she shouted impatiently; she was trembling, radiant and secretive. That little laugh of hers rose in her throat.

"I have quite a lot out there in my place," whispered Gabriel.

"Do you mean that? Out in the store. Shall we go straight away?"

It took only a moment: a chest was opened, a drawer pulled out, and Barbara was again in skirts and shoes with a scarf around her neck and deeply complicit. Gabriel was a little taken aback, and his mouth relaxed.

At that moment, Suzanne Harme, the bailiff's daughter, arrived.

"Isn't this fun," burbled Barbara: "What do you think? I'm going over to the Store with Gabriel to look at some silks and dresses that he has there. Isn't that exciting? It's so nice you came."

That was not what Gabriel was thinking. A great hope sank within him. Bloody hell!

"Over in the shop?" said Suzanne. She seemed to shudder

a little. She was dark and elegant. She wrinkled her forehead.

"Isn't it just so exciting?" Barbara repeated.

"I don't know. Now, this evening? Won't it attract attention? And father's the bailiff, you know."

"You don't usually bother very much about that," Gabriel burst out. "But we can manage perfectly well without you, you know."

"Oh no." Barbara didn't agree.

"Well, father has an office in the Store," said Suzanne. "And what if we are caught, Gabriel?"

"Oh. Don't you think the bailiff's ever sold a yard of material? What about that time the Dutch East-Indiaman was here? But in any case the bailiff's office isn't up there in my space – at least not this evening."

"Mother, I'm going across to Suzanne's for a while," Barbara shouted as they went out. They made their way through Gongin in pitch darkness. The rain was gusting malevolently, both from above and below. They groped their way forward and had to tread very carefully.

"But this is smuggling," Suzanne determined.

Barbara uttered a deep laugh. Exciting. She had to take Gabriel's arm. Gongin was the only continuous street in Tórshavn. Otherwise just a few odd alleyways between the scattered houses and huts, *Skot* as they were called, often so narrow that there was scarcely room for two people to pass. They reached the top of Reyn, Reyn, where the school, the parsonage, Reynegaard, and the church stood. They went across the churchyard. Behind the church, in Church Alley, was the entrance to the shop, the northernmost of the buildings belonging to the Royal Store. Gabriel put a huge key in the lock. The pitch darkness, the sudden silence and the heavy air felt oppressive to the two young women as they stepped into

23

the blackness of the warehouse. Gabriel felt his way forward, finally found a lamp, struck a light and lit it. They ascended a steep staircase and crossed the long loft. Their shadows fluttered across the creaking floor planks. The withered roots of the grass on the roof hung down here and there between the rafters. Suzanne shuddered and clung to Barbara.

They went into Gabriel's lodging over in one of the gables. It was a small room with alcoves, a wall cupboard and chests.

"Do you never come across Master Naaber here?" asked Suzanne in a voice suggesting mirth mixed with anxiety.

"Master Naaber – who's that?" asked Gabriel.

"Don't you know? No, of course you weren't born here. All the people of Tórshavn are frightened of him. He is supposed to haunt the lofts out here in Tórshavn at night."

"I've never seen him."

"He wears a black, pointed hood and talks to himself. And when he looks at you, he has yellow eyes."

Gabriel didn't like to hear this. He started to light some candles, making rather a noise as he did so.

"Haven't you seen the *Council* either?" Suzanne went on.

"The Council, what are you talking about?"

"Yes, the Council." Suzanne's eyes opened wide. "The seven men. They meet in one of the buildings – I don't know which – and sit at a long table."

It was beginning to run cold down Gabriel's spine. Suzanne was carried away with her own words. Her face was just a little distorted. Her voice was low and tense: "Several people have seen them. They sit there quite silently and write and write and seal letters."

"Be quiet," shouted Barbara vehemently. A shudder went through her and she gave a rather weak smile.

"You're crazy," said Gabriel.

They all fell silent. The weak light from the candlestick quite failed to penetrate into all the corners in the little room. Bare woodwork, dark from age, could be glimpsed through the magic wrought by the gloom. Suzanne's eyes were still curiously radiant. But then Gabriel started to unpack, and colours blossomed from mysterious hiding places. The little room was suddenly transformed, the oppressive feel broken. Greedy female hands grabbed after the materials and spread them out; white fingers ran through crackling silks; the poor furnishings were bathed in light and radiance. At first there was nothing but silent wonderment and shining eyes. A hushed springtime had been created beneath Master Naaber's turf roof – it rose mound-like on four planks; the two women sat spellbound.

Gabriel, shopkeeper and lover, played his cards intelligently; he did not waste his trumps, but went about things in a matter-of-fact manner and allowed the drama to develop like a firework display. The occasion was his. He did not break the silence, but simply let one miracle take place after the other.

"But Gabriel," said Suzanne in a sudden fit of reason, "where did you get all this?"

"Do I need to tell you? I haven't stolen it."

"You must have been dealing on the quiet with some sly Dutchman or Englishman."

Gabriel made no attempt to deny that. It sounded quite good. The truth was actually that it was one of the Royal Store's own skippers he had been working with.

"And you have silk stockings as well," exclaimed Barbara in amazement and delight.

"Goods are power," thought Gabriel. He suddenly had a vision of Barbara's wet woollen stockings that had lain by the fireplace, all drab and ordinary. He thought he had made a splendid trick and made another bid: "Just look here."

He took a pair of brocade shoes out and placed them beside Barbara's feet, which were all dirty with mud from the street.

Both women were wide-eyed. Barbara drew her feet back, a little embarrassed by the contrast, but a moment later she wanted to try the shoes. Gabriel had no objection to this; indeed he even wanted to help her, knelt down and removed her shoe. Barbara's foot was simply in a coarse woollen stocking, but never mind about that – small and supple as it was it fitted perfectly in the fine shoe; indeed the shoe was, if anything, too big. Oh, that blasted Suzanne! Why had she come? Suddenly, Gabriel saw a dizzying perspective of what lost opportunities the moment held. He had so many things that Barbara would perhaps not have been unwilling to try!

His heart was thumping. And then it happened that his bright intellect suddenly let him down. He took out a fine garter. Would Barbara like to try that as well?

Barbara almost gasped and she looked at Suzanne. Then she laughed and said affably: "But a garter isn't something to try on, Gabriel."

Suzanne looked up, slightly confused, with a brief wrinkle on her brow, and then, with sudden enthusiasm, said, "Let me try those shoes."

Barbara rose. "What would a dress in this stuff look like?" she asked, starting to drape herself in some flowered material.

"Now, if I had a skirt like this and then these shoes," said Suzanne, shaking her foot a little under a length of silk.

"Oh, just look here," exclaimed Barbara enthusiastically. She pulled something out of the pile and held it up to the light.

Gabriel tried to join in, but they did not listen to him. And suddenly it was clear to him that his wares had completely put him out of the picture. The two women had launched themselves into an intoxicated discussion about clothes; they selected and rejected, felt and tried. Barbara's eyes were shining; she was shouting with delight; she was becoming more and more beautiful in her enthusiasm for beauty.

"I think I had better have my dress off," said Suzanne.

"I think I will, too," said Barbara.

Their dark costumes were wet and shapeless from the rain and made the fine garments damp when they tried them on. Suzanne had already started to undo her bodice when her eyes caught sight of Gabriel:

"Oh, Gabriel, go and leave us alone for a bit, will you?"

"Oh, that's not quite fair," said Barbara.

Suzanne directed a thoughtful, searching look at Gabriel. Then she came to a conclusion: "No, we can't have you in here looking at us."

And Gabriel went.

By chance discovered in his own room and thrown out like an unwelcome dog! He was furious. This was his splendid, great plan. And here he was standing out in the desolate loft. They had probably already forgotten him in there. He went backwards and forwards with his lamp, angry, but also really uncomfortable. Master Naaber! The gale had increased and lay like some unceasing, superior pressure on the building – an inexhaustible song of a thousand voices in torment. He reached the other end of the loft, by the Chapterhouse and looked out through the small window. The west bay was covered in spume and the froth shone through the darkness. The Chapter – were they now sitting at the counsel table somewhere or other in the Royal Store buildings? Perhaps no more than a few yards away. That confounded girl Suzanne – producing that story just this evening. *She* was not going to have to sleep alone in this building tonight.

He went back to his own door. Women and chattering inside. Barbara's laughter, fancies and exclamations. Suzanne's rather deeper and more prudent voice. No, in there they were deaf to storm and surf. They were not turning the hourglass; they were not counting the passing hours. Least of all did they take notice of Gabriel's beating heart and burning desire. He was but a shadow in a loft. But in there it was summer. They were gorging themselves on clothes and trinkets and colours. He could imagine the rustling and crackling of the materials. Indeed, he would swear they had taken off every stitch of their homely woollen clothing. They were two butterflies sunning themselves in this fantasy, wrapping themselves in red and gold and blue, in airy calico and heavy silk – *his* wares. They were dressing up and filling themselves on vain delight.

It was a very long time before the women thought of letting Gabriel in again. By then they had chosen what they wanted. It was actually Barbara who had come to buy from him, although the other was also to have a little. And what did it cost?

Gabriel, lover and merchant – he *had* been thinking, under certain happy circumstances, to tell Barbara that it would cost her almost nothing. But now he was angry and reeled off some stiff, almost exorbitant prices.

The unexpected happened in that Barbara paid without query, in cash from a purse – wantonly, in silver. A sacrifice on the altar of beauty.

Gabriel blushed.

Suzanne had not been prepared for buying, so she needed credit. And was given it willingly – the finest lady in town.

Then Gabriel had to show them out. No thank you, they wouldn't have any wine; it was getting late now, Suzanne thought. And Gabriel understood that he ought not to have waited so long with this trump.

Barbara

As they were going through the long loft, Barbara said quietly and kindly to Gabriel: "I tried your garters after all."

Was that supposed to be a consolation? A strange consolation, it must be said. And yet, in the way in which it was uttered it almost sounded like an expression of thanks. Was it true, as people said, that no one paid tribute to Barbara without receiving some sort of reward?

But Gabriel did not pay homage to her. The bitch! Parson's tart. He knew a thing or two.

The women took leave of him in the churchyard. He went back through the graves, past the church. Barbara's coins were still in his sweaty hand. Now he would soon be able to buy some land. But the little hound in Gabriel howled. Then he entered the dark, empty building to join Master Naaber and to enjoy a lonely bed.

And while the storm lay over the town like a nightmare, two women, cunning and suspicious, filled with experience and with a rich booty, crept through the driving rain in the alleyways, back to their homes.

The Widow in the Benefice

"Of course, you know there is a widow in the benefice?

The speaker was the country's bailiff.

The new Vágar parson, Pastor Poul Aggersøe, knew that. It was not something that had preoccupied him much at all. Most clergymen dealt with that problem in a very practical manner and married the widow. But he was made of less pliable material. He had not thought of marrying at all and it irritated him when others did so on his behalf.

He was sitting in the Tórshavn parson's parlour, surrounded by people who wanted to hear news from the outside world. He had had to tell them about battles and about generals, about King Frederick of Prussia, whom no one could conquer, and about King Louis of France, whom no one could disturb in his debauchery. Everyone was in something of a state of excitement at the news, both the judge, the bailiff, the manager of the Royal Store and the commandant. They went to and fro and stepped over the high threshold between the parlour and the study. The women said nothing – with the exception of old Armgard, the old law speaker's widow, and her sister Ellen Katrine, the woman with the crutches and the happy face. She was of the opinion that no one could be compared with Marlborough, who had been alive when she was a young woman.

Pastor Poul sat observing all these completely unknown

people in whose midst he had landed. The world was still rocking for him. He had been sailing for four weeks. For the past two days, the ship hove to in a severe gale off a black, sharp island called Nolsoy. At last, the weather had settled early this morning, and they had sailed in.

There were still remains of nocturnal darkness in the air when the *Fortuna* dropped anchor. The air was raw and snow showers were moving slowly across the shabby greensward in the mountains. A weather-beaten, black, wooden church tower rose above a few clumps of houses. This was Tórshavn. Everything was so fusty. The people who appeared beneath the eaves were weak and pale in the pallid morning. Pastor Poul had felt almost as though he had landed somewhere in the underworld when he stepped ashore on the rocks at Tinganes. But as he went up towards the Royal Store buildings he saw two beautifully dressed women standing amidst a crowd of curious people in the entrance. He noted one of them in particular. She was fair and tall, so elegant as she stood there seemingly taking no notice of him.

Throughout the entire dark, rainy day he had been mixing with people he did not know. He still did not have a clear impression of them; they were large shadows speaking a semi-incomprehensible language; a spinning wheel was whirring somewhere or other in the house; the withered grass from the roof hung down in front of the windows; there was a grey view across the East Bay to the Redoubt on the other side, where the flag was flapping. But it was all accompanied by the memory of the woman he had seen. He could forget her for long periods, but she was nevertheless there all the time – like something sweet, a glimpse of light, a consolation.

But now the bailiff obviously wanted to talk mainly about that widow in the benefice.

Augustus Harme, the bailiff, was Danish; he was a big man, rubicund and slightly sweaty. His voice was smug, quite charming, but always didactic, always expressive of superior knowledge. He was constantly clearing his throat and he allowed himself plenty of time for the process. He took a pinch of snuff and let his listeners wait until he was ready to make a statement.

"Yes," he said, "perhaps you also know that this widow is the daughter of the late judge Peter Willumsen Salling. She is not old, only twenty-eight, I believe."

"Don't you go praising Barbara Christina," came a stern voice from behind some knitting. "She is nothing but a jade, and everyone knows that." This intervention came from the law speaker's widow. She was a woman with a big nose, and her eyes were as sharp and cold as those of a sea bird.

"I don't commend Barbara," said the bailiff. "But neither do I do the opposite. I simply believe our young parson should be given an insight into the circumstances."

"Then, in that case you would do better to tell about her goings-on than about her age," replied Armgard, placing her clenched fist on the table: "about everything she has done in her twenty-eight years..."

"I don't know, I don't know," the judge said now. "I don't think one can call Barbara a jade. She has her faults, which are easy to see. But can she help that? There is not really a drop of evil blood in her."

"Well, what about you, Johan Hendrik? You have spent a lot of time in that house and been on close terms with the old judge. You must be the right person to say something about these things."

"That's correct, Armgard. I've known Barbara since she was a child. But you know no more about her than the gossip you have picked up from other people."

"I know the truth. I know how both Pastor Thomas and Pastor Niels died."

Judge Johan Hendrik Heyde said no more. He stroked his chin thoughtfully. There was something nervous, something dubious about his tall, slightly stooping figure. He was always like that. A man of honour, wiser than the others, far too wise to be strong. But he was capable of dry, caustic sarcasm, for which reason he was also respected, indeed feared.

Like his brother, the Tórshavn minister Wenzel Heyde, he was considered to be among the best Faroese citizens. They were members of an ancient family, a family in which there was foreign blood in plenty, but which was firmly rooted in the country. Otherwise, the two brothers were very different. The judge was tall and thin, the minister short and thickset. The judge was sceptical, the parson unctuous. And while there always simmered a furtive dislike of his Danish-born colleagues – the bailiff and the head of the Store – Wentzel was filled with an equally surreptitious and equally consuming urge to please them and to be in their company. So Pastor Wenzel was also content now he had them in his living room. The great bailiff, the witty head of the Store with all those amusing stories and the distinguished wife, Madame Mathilde, who said little and was probably anaemic, but who could giggle and swoon in a very distinguished manner.

The conversation had flagged for a time among all these people. Once the news had been exchanged, there was no longer anything really to unite them. But in the study there was a covert focal point that repeatedly persuaded the men to exchange shrewd glances. They were restless. They wandered back and forth and crossed the threshold. It was probably not exclusively on account of Barbara that Armgard was knitting so irately and excitably. She had smelt a rat, and she was annoyed. The same applied to the other women. It was always like this when a ship had arrived.

Samuel Mikkelsen, the law speaker, rose and made an excursion into the study. For this bulky, immovable man this was almost a whole journey. And it took him a long time. Armgard grunted angrily when she saw her nephew, her husband's successor, fill the entire doorway with his huge back. But her sister, Ellen Katrine, had a conspiratorial glint in her eyes. She lay reclining on a bench and made a cheerful sign in the air with her crutch: "Oh, this world, this world!"

The new parson later remembered all this very clearly indeed. But at that moment he did not really understand it. Not until he was discreetly invited by his colleague Pastor Wenzel were his eyes opened to the fact that there was French brandy to be had in the study.

Nor did he understand all this about the widow Barbara – the fact that a fresh breeze had caught the limp sails of the conversation when the bailiff mentioned her name.

The law speaker returned from the study, large and serene, but with some indeterminate sign of renewal about him. He had a big, wavy full beard. He resembled the god Jupiter. But his eyes were calm and gentle. They usually radiated a fine, almost tender smile.

He sat down without immediately saying anything. Then his gentle voice made itself heard: "What Barbara was like in her first marriage I will leave unsaid, although I have heard some strange things about it. As for her second marriage, I think I can say that she was not a good wife. But to maintain that she was responsible for Pastor Niels' death – I think that is unjust, for it was an accident."

Armgard snorted. "Accident! In that case there have been a

lot of accidents in Barbara's life. And they have always come at a remarkably convenient time for her."

Ellen Katrine stretched on her bench and raised her crutch almost as a signal: "You be quiet, Armgard, and let Samuel speak. He knows better than you after all."

Samuel sat looking at his small hands. He rarely said very much. Everyone watched him in anticipation. He had never before said anything about Barbara. But he must know all about her. His official residence, Stegaard, was in Sandavág, only a good mile from the parsonage of Jansegærde, where Pastor Niels and Barbara had lived.

"I don't understand Barbara. When she came west to Vágar with Pastor Niels, no one could doubt that she adored him. Everyone spoke well of her, and for my part I can't but say that she was quite angelic in her actions and her personality."

"*Angelic!*" The sea bird, old Armgard, looked sharply at her nephew: "No, by God, Samuel." Her fist approached the table top again: "If everyone else failed to be so wise, *you* at least should know that being an angel on the outside is not the same as being an angel on the inside."

The law speaker smiled. He hesitated a little. But no one interrupted, so the way was clear for him. It came deliberately, with an infinitely small touch of indulgent irony: "Well, Aunt Armgard, you are rather hasty in your judgement. But that was not exactly what I was going to say. She was *no* angel at heart. But that does not necessarily mean that she was a devil, for that was not her nature. I think she wanted to be good to everyone. She went down to the ordinary people when they returned from fishing; she went to fetch peat, which is not exactly customary for parsons' wives. And she took part in dances – something that was probably not to the liking of Pastor Niels.

"Good heavens," said Ellen Katrine: "taking part in a dance is surely no great sin even for a parsons' wife."

"No," the judge intervened. "If you were the parson's wife, Aunt Ellen Katrine, and went to a dance, I do not think it would result in any sin either."

"Oh, Johan Henrik, do for once refrain from your insolent remarks." She waved her crutch at him. Her expression was at once pompous and playful.

There was a glint in the law speaker's gentle eyes, though it lasted only a fraction of a second. Then he went on: "It might well be that Pastor Niels would have felt safer with another wife. I am not saying that was Barbara's fault. But the fact was that when Barbara joined the dance, *everyone* joined the dance, both men and women."

"No one is going to understand that," said the parson's wife, the hostess, Anna Sophie. "It is not always so easy to be Barbara at a dance."

"If Barbara herself had understood that, she would have kept away from the dance," said Armgard. And this time she thumped her fist down heavily on the table.

"I wonder whether it was always so much fun sitting at home evening after evening in Jansegærde with Pastor Niels and his dusty books," said Anna Sophie suddenly with passion.

"Oh, what a world this is," exclaimed Ellen Katrine, thoughtfully sketching in the air with her crutch.

But Pastor Wenzel Heyde, the unctuous little parson, looked disapprovingly at his wife. With deeply dimpled cheeks, she was cheerful and buxom.

"But tell me one thing," said Ellen Katrine: "Was Barbara not fond of her husband?"

"I can assure you," said the law speaker, "that I do not recall having seen a wife treating her husband in such a fond manner as during the first time I knew them. She always wanted to have him with her and to help him with everything. And when he was away, she always missed him. And he probably missed her as well. He always refused to spend the night with us at Stegaard. Even in the worst weather he would always ride home to her in the evening – in rain, sleet or frost. And throughout their entire marriage, incidentally, the situation remained that she could not tolerate being neglected by him. And this was where their first disagreements came in – I believe, by God, that she would hardly allow him to write his sermons."

"Aye," said the judge: "When Barbara is in that mood she is capable of being jealous of God in heaven Himself."

The law speaker smiled: "Yes, but she was quite prepared to allow herself what she refused to allow her husband. For *she* frequently neglected *him*. It was difficult to understand. I am convinced she *did* want to do well by him. But Barbara simply can't control herself. She does exactly as she wants at any given moment: if there was a dance she wanted to take part in, then she would go to it. God knows, I think she often felt terribly sorry for her husband. But she still went. And then she quickly forgot him. And it was just the same if there was anything exciting going on here in Tórshavn, Barbara absolutely *had* to take part. She would often spend weeks or even months here, as you all know who live here."

"There's no denying that," said the storekeeper.

The law speaker gave him a searching look for a moment: "As to how she behaved here – you know that better than I do."

"We were not able to help – hmm – were not able to help noticing this and that," said the bailiff.

"Aye, we did indeed," said the storekeeper.

The judge gave him a sarcastic look: "Well yes, you showed

a certain interest in all that yourself."

"Well, I made sure that Melzer on the *Jubilee* went off in a different direction. I suppose you have no objection to that?"

Johan Henrik Heyde had no objection. He simply looked even more sarcastic.

"Well," the law speaker went on, "Barbara didn't behave as she should even at home on Vágar. It soon came out, although she went about things very carefully. I won't sit here and retail everything I have heard, and much of it is probably only gossip. But there are various men to whom she has shown friendship."

Armgard had long remained silent. Now she burst out: "From all I hear, Samuel, the woman you are talking about is a *hussy*."

The storekeeper gave a little whistle: "No, a parson's wife."

"God forgive me," said Samuel Mikkelsen: "she is as correct and distinguished in her conduct as a queen. And friendly and kind to everyone. As Anna Sophie said a moment ago, it is not all that easy to be Barbara. Everyone flocks around her. She is such a person as tempts everyone and she is tempted herself. I often think that she is like a child."

"A good child yes, twenty-eight years old, parson's wife and the biggest whore in the country," said Armgard.

"Now, now," said the judge. "And Samuel is right after all. A child – though admittedly a dangerous child."

"Oh, what a world this is! Yes, everyone has a story to tell. But tell me, what was the parson like, Samuel?"

"I can tell you, Aunt Ellen Katrine, that Pastor Niels was a particularly decent and upright man. A peaceful character. He gave in and tried to close his eyes to things. As I say, she was fond of him, but as time went on his meekness started to irritate her. Then he tried to put the boot on the other foot and stand up to her. But that only made her defy him. They fought each other. She is even said once to have thrown a candlestick at him. Then everyone started to feel sorry for the parson. The servants especially took his side. And conditions in Jansegærde gradually became more and more confused."

The law speaker's voice was deep and rural. He was almost reminiscent of cows gently lowing in their stalls, or of stable doors creaking on their wooden hinges. The words he spoke were simple and almost naive. But his Jupiter-like face reflected a restrained play of kindliness, satire and wisdom.

"Then there was one day," he continued, "when Barbara was particularly unreasonable towards Pastor Niels – while everyone was listening. She heaped him with derision and words of scorn. The good man didn't know what to do. He tried to calm her down, but that only made her more furious. Finally, she hit him. They had a servant called Kristoffer, an enormous fellow. This was too much for him. He suddenly went across and took hold of Barbara and carried her out of the house."

"Did a servant take hold of the parson's wife?" asked Madame Mathilde.

"Yes."

"Good heavens. What did she say?"

"What could she say? He carried her out as though she were a little child. She is said to have looked somewhat surprised. Only when he had got behind the house with her did she start to be worried. But she wasn't big in his hands. Then he took her and put her head first down into a barrel intended for liquid manure. And there he left her."

"Is it really true that he did that?" asked several of the listeners.

"Kristoffer himself told me," said the law speaker.

Madame Mathilde was a little overcome and needed her

smelling salts. "Good heavens, if it had been me, I would never have shown myself to people again."

"It is said not to have looked particularly seemly," said Samuel, smiling as he contemplated a life which occasionally took a dramatic turn. "All the servants had followed them. I think they were rather taken aback."

He smiled again, just a little: "Well, it isn't often you see a parson's wife in that position."

"Who helped her to get out?"

"Kristoffer knocked the barrel over and then she crawled out herself."

"I suppose she didn't exactly appreciate that bit of humble pie?" the judge asked.

"She was furious. She turned all the servants out of the house for the rest of the day. Poor Pastor Niels caught it in the neck and had to help her to get herself cleaned up. They say he had to carry eighteen tubs of water to her from the river. It was summer, Saturday afternoon. His sermon the following day at Midvág was as you would expect. But when the servants came home that evening Barbara was just as comely and pretty as usual and acted as though nothing had happened. Kristoffer came to me and gave himself up. I assumed that neither Pastor Niels nor Barbara wanted a court case out of it. And nor did they. So I kept Kristoffer in my service and from him I learned a great deal about what went on in Jansegard."

There was an amazed silence. Knitting needles were all that was heard.

"Oh, so that was the queen you were talking about," said Armgard after a time.

"She is a queen nevertheless," said the law speaker. "Three days after this I had to come to Tórshavn by boat. Barbara came and asked whether she could come with me. But then I actually said that I couldn't take her. I don't otherwise like to refuse help. And this seemed to be a matter of amazement to her. Aye, that's what Barbara is like."

"It is really strange that that story has not made Barbara look more ridiculous than is the case," remarked Pastor Wenzel. "One would think that even the most beautiful woman would be completely humiliated and impossible after that."

"No, but why not the exact opposite?" said the judge.

"Ugh, no," exclaimed Madame Mathilde.

"It shows how clever she is," thought Anna Sophie.

"Oh, what the hell," explained the store manager. "She simply made sure that people had something else to talk about, for it was not long then before she killed her husband."

"It was almost six months after all this," the law speaker corrected him quietly. "It was in November. Pastor Niels had been with us and preached in Sandavág Church. It had been thawing and then it had rained, but during the day a hard frost set in and all roads and paths were covered with ice. Pastor Niels wanted to ride home as usual that evening. We tried as best we could to persuade him not to go. But he was not to be persuaded. He insisted. Fed up with him as Barbara probably was, she still would not accept that he left her alone in the evening."

"So the minister rode off," continued the law speaker, "and everyone knows what happened then. At Midvág sands the horse stumbled on a slippery rock, and Pastor Niels fell and broke his leg. They say that Barbara was very kind to him at first and looked after him so tenderly that it looked as though they were fonder of each other than ever. But then it apparently started to be too monotonous for her. The minister made good progress and had reached the stage where he could sit up with his bad leg stretched out over a chair. One day, one

41

of the servants came in and said that some boat was putting in at the landing place. "It's probably some men from Tórshavn," he added. Barbara, who had been sitting with Pastor Niels, flew up and rushed across to the window – that's what she is like, of course – and she inadvertently overturned the chair with the result that the minister's damaged leg was knocked to the ground and broken for the second time. Then they took the minister to the surgeon barber here in Tórshavn. But he simply made a mess of it. The result was gangrene, and Pastor Niels didn't get over that."

"Yes, Samuel," said Armgard. "And the widow went into deep mourning."

"I don't know how deeply she mourned, but she certainly mourned, as everyone could see."

"Of course she mourned," said the judge. "Barbara is no monster. But she does forget confoundedly quickly, I will grant you that."

"I think I am probably right when I say she really *is* like a child."

"Oh, stop all that nonsense. All you grown men in charge of the country and its inhabitants! Just fancy letting yourselves be dazzled like that. A child! A real baggage, I say, the way she behaves, playing up to everybody."

Armgard was incensed.

"Tell me," said Anna Sophie, "have you ever been in Barbara's company?"

Armgard scowled.

"She is so beautiful," said Anna Sophie.

"She's a dangerous woman," said Bailiff Harme with great dignity.

"Yes," said Pastor Wenzel. "As the hymn says: 'fairest flower has poisoned juice'. Barbara can be as charming as she likes, but Christian people must still disassociate themselves from her deeds."

"She ought to be locked up," said Armgard scornfully. "She is a danger to everyone around her and she leaves behind nothing but disaster. It ought to be possible to put her away for adultery."

"Well," said Johan Henrik, shrugging his shoulders. "In that case there are perhaps quite a lot of others who should be put away as well. As far as I have understood the world."

"Oh yes, God have mercy on us," said Ellen Katrine, crippled but amused on her bench.

"No, let the Lord deal with Barbara," reasoned Johan Hendrik. "She is simply made in such a way that almost any man, indeed any living being that sees her likes her. And she feels that in every instance however small, even if it is just a dog looking admiringly at her from a corner."

"Well," wondered Anna Sophie, "can she help it? That is woman's nature."

"Yes, indeed," Johan Hendrik continued eagerly. "And she has become so much a woman that it is a necessity for her that everyone, even the least and the most unworthy, should admire her. Everything in her must conquer over all and has done so to this very day. Everyone must love her. And she will love everyone. But that's where it goes wrong for her. She can't manage that."

"I simply don't know what you mean when you talk like that," said Armgard.

"I think it is all very right and wisely put," said the storekeeper, "but it can all be put in words that are far shorter and more comprehensible. Barbara is simply lecherous through and through. That is quite simply my opinion."

At that moment there came the sound of women's voices

from the hearth room and two young women appeared. Pastor Poul started: it was the two beautiful women he had seen in the entrance to the Store.

"Blast and damnation!" exclaimed the commandant. He was so drunk and amazed that he remained in the doorway to the study holding his bottle for everyone to see.

That remained his sole contribution to the discussion, and no one noticed it, for all eyes were suddenly turned on the newcomers, who enhanced the room with their beautiful dresses, the scent of their powder and their laughs and smiles.

"Talk of the devil..." said Bailiff Harme.

"Were you talking about us?"

"About you, Barbara, yes," said the judge in a serious voice and with a hidden little smile.

That seemed to please and flatter her; she looked down and laughed, modestly and happily.

But Pastor Poul was as though turned to stone.

The two young women went around and shook hands with everyone. Barbara Salling was fairly tall and fair haired; her mouth was large and red, her teeth beautiful. She carried herself with natural charm and with courtesy to match. Suzanne Harme was of a more delicate figure and had a far more beautiful face. But her intelligent eyes were outshone by the lively and quickly changing quality of Barbara's, while her sonorous voice seemed monotonous beside all the remarkable modulations in her friend's voice. It was like a rainbow of enchanting sounds that had suddenly made its appearance in the midst of the dry conversation.

The new Vágar parson rose and in some confusion made himself known to the widow in the benefice. He was surprised and dazzled. Barbara shook hands with him without taking much notice of him, but her natural manner was so perfect that it had the effect of calming him. Indeed, calm descended on everyone. The law speaker smiled up from the quiet depths of his kind nature; Pastor Wenzel was friendly, though with some reservation on behalf of Heaven; Anna Sophie was elated and the storekeeper's gallantry bordered on the officious. But his anaemic wife, Mathilde, sat there agog, devouring Barbara and her every movement and expression with eyes radiating the wildest demons of curiosity. Yet no one noticed that, for everyone noticed only Barbara.

But Barbara noticed Armgard's knitting and was very interested.

"It's not a jersey... oh, a scarf, or is it a shawl?"

And the pattern was very interesting. Armgard had to explain how it was going to turn out, pointing with her knitting needle.

"That will be lovely." Barbara's eyes adopted an expression of lively anticipation as to how old Armgard's scarf would look when at last it was finished.

Armgard's face took on a look of contentment; a smile started to spread across her shrunken lips; the stumps of her teeth appeared in an expression of pure friendliness, and she finally looked at Barbara with as much tenderness in her eyes as can conceivably under any circumstances be expected of a seagull. The two of them carried on a conversation about knitting and purling.

From her bench, old Ellen Katrine wanted to get a proper look at Barbara. She had never spoken to her before; she lived on a large farm in the interior of Esturey and so was rarely to be seen in Tórshavn. She held the young woman's hand for a long time: "Oh, so this is Barbara; that's what you look like." Her old eyes radiated courteousness.

Barbara was somewhat overcome by all this scrutiny; she

looked down and she looked up; there was something almost comical in her uncertainty. She blushed.

"Aye, well," the old woman finally said, "you are pretty, as I had expected. God bless you. Oh dear, oh dear..."

Barbara's errand was only to ask the bailiff whether the *Fortuna* had brought any letters for her mother. She had looked for him in vain in his office. There they had told her that he was out in Tórshavn somewhere. She had persuaded Suzanne to come with her. Now, thank goodness, they had finally found the bailiff on Reyn. But the bailiff informed her that there was unfortunately no letter for Mrs Salling, Well, there was nothing else, and so the two women left.

The judge greeted Barbara in a certain ironical tone that they had both come to agree on viewing as a form of affectionate banter. She answered him with a glance that could be interpreted as saying, "Yes, you are the only one who really understands me, and you appreciate me." He rather liked that. But who could know? Perhaps she also thanked the storekeeper for his gallantry with some glance that made him feel that he was the only one, that he was the real one.

Aye, Barbara probably had sweet secrets with everyone – greater or lesser secrets.

"Isn't she lovely," said Ellen Katrine. "It could well be that you are right in what you all say, but are you really sure that Pastor Niels was the husband for her?"

"No," said the judge with a little smile, "but who is?"

He stroked his chin thoughtfully, as was his custom. There had been a lot of going to and fro in the study. The law speaker had been there again and was going around slowly in a process of profound and quiet self-renewal. Outside, it was growing dark and rain was falling. The men agreed to go down to the store and look at the wares. It looked as though it was going to be a thirsty evening, a very thirsty evening. Armgard's needles were again knitting angrily at the pattern that had awakened Barbara's excitement and expectation for a brief moment.

This was Pastor Poul's first day in Tórshavn.

Happiness on Account

The rain continued.

Pastor Poul Aggersøe went for the occasional stroll in the streets, but found nothing that could raise up his heart from the feeling of melancholy into which it had immediately sunk at the sight of this dark and desolate town.

He had not expected to feel like this, for he was not otherwise inclined to hang his head. He was usually a cheerful person, and in his life so far there were many points from which his heart could derive strength even in solitary moments. While a student and after graduating from Borchs College he had gained a great deal of respect for his ability in the field of theology, something about which he was suitably pleased. He was aware that something was expected of him in the world of theology, and his very despatch to the Faroe Islands he had seen to be an important mission. No, he was not one of these hungry boys with a third class degree who were only considered suitable for some small parish in Finmark or in Greenland. The bishop in Copenhagen had personally sent for him and *asked* him to apply for the parish of Vágar. It was not going to be prejudicial to him – no, he would be called to other parishes after this. But the bishop had pointed out to him that the clergy in the Faroe Islands were in a bad way and that in addition he had received complaints from the islands' dean, Anders Morsing. He was hoping now that by sending one or two of the best of the young clergy he would be able to introduce them to support the good clergy there and serve as examples to be followed by the poorer ones.

When, after his conversation with the bishop, Poul Aggersøe had emerged into the street again, the late afternoon sunshine had just caught the tall, gilded spire of the Cathedral Church of Our Lady. It rose from one level to another, square and closed at the bottom, octagonal further up, still blossoming and striving upwards, one element growing out of the other, untiringly and vertiginously reaching for the heavens until, finally, like the top note in an aria, it ended in a long point and a bar holding three resplendent crowns 350 feet up in the air. It was a magnificent sight, a majesty in which he delighted every day, and he suddenly realised how difficult it would be for him to leave Copenhagen. For although really a country dweller, he had increasingly fallen in love with this city, where he found all the things that gladdened his heart.

He had a liking for festivities and splendour as well as for honour. He would listen with delight to the playing of the organ and the singing in church, but he was also fond of drama and opera. And he had participated in masquerades, too, although he had had his doubts as to whether this was a suitable pursuit for a man who was preparing to serve the Lord. For he did intend to serve the Lord, although he honestly often felt that his fiery, passionate nature, alas, was far too much a thing of this world.

But he was young and had so far found it easy to agree with God. Indeed, God helped him; He had given him rich gifts, graciously strengthened him in zeal and ability and led him far in learning. And this call to the distant Faroe Islands could only be seen as a further distinction, for it was no ordinary call, but rather to be seen as a steep step on the ladder of grace which

– although at the moment rather a burden to him – would later help him further on his way.

The very fact that it was a burden could only encourage him all the more. Was he perhaps a soft, weak, indolent person? Not at all. He had strengths that he would like to test. Admittedly, he had not hitherto seen the preaching of the Word to be something for which he was suited. He was much better fitted for learning. But it was ultimately not so much in order to preach as to reinstate peace and calm and good customs that he was being sent, and in truth he did not intend to spare himself. What he achieved was to be heard as far away as the bishop's palace in Copenhagen.

And at the same time he was not going to forget that any honour coming to him was due solely to God. In this way he fired his spirit, and when, the following day, he attended divine service in the cathedral and the entire splendid congregation sang Kingo's great hymn "Farewell, oh world, farewell" his heart swelled as never before, and with a mind filled with fervour, he took leave of the splendour and glory of the city to travel to the distant Faroe Islands as a soldier of the Lord. Indeed, his breast was afire when he left the church to the jubilant play of the organ pipes. The rays of the sun were refracted to bristle unevenly between the huge columns in the tripartite chancel. Gloriously elevated he emerged into the crowd at the foot of the tower. At that moment, his will was as upright as the spire high above his head reaching out and stretching to heaven.

But he had not heeded a tiny thought that insidiously entered his heart at that moment. The thought that it was not *everything* in the city that was holding him back with the same force and that there was also something that turned him away a little. This was Lucie Gemynther, the highly regarded daughter of an affluent merchant.

He had for a time found her particularly pleasing, and he had thought that this might perhaps go far. But then, Lucie herself had become far too engrossed with the same thought – indeed she had shown herself to be so deeply in love that Poul Aggersøe had started to turn away from her. For she bothered him with her constancy and with her feelings, which quickly developed for him into a melody he knew only too well. He reproached himself for it, but it was all too clear to him that he did not love her. For she was like an ivy seeking to twist its way up him as though round a tree trunk and to cover him completely with her devotion. But he did not want that. He only wanted to be himself, Poul Aggersøe, and felt the affection of others to be a burden and a limitation.

Lucie wept the day he left, and he was happy and relieved when the ship had passed the toll booth and he could no longer see her. The voyage went well and they only encountered stormy weather at the end when they were approaching their destination. Pastor Poul still had the splendour of the Copenhagen spires and towers in his eyes on the day they sighted land. But that ghastly morning when he glimpsed Tórshavn for the first time – oh, it was no longer ago than yesterday although it seemed like an age to him – it was then as though both courage and joy were drawn from his heart.

Here, he found himself in the rain among decayed and badly tarred wooden houses. He could not bear the idea of remaining in the parsonage for ever. His host and colleague, Wenzel Heyde, was a master of theology and a learned man, but when Pastor Poul started discussing theological matters and revealing that he, too, was at home in learned subjects, it had been as though Pastor Wenzel had been put off. He was not unfriendly, but he did not say much and there were always shadows to be seen in his water-blue eyes, as though he was constantly being offended and wronged by concerns visible and invisible.

Pastor Poul wanted to meet his superior, Dean Anders Morsing, but he was over at Nes in Esteroy. Pastor Poul talked of going over to see him, but everyone assured him that that would be a waste of time, as the dean would probably be in Tórshavn within a few days.

What on earth was Pastor Poul to do, then? He had already paid his respects to the judge and the law speaker; the bailiff was a self-important former customs clerk, the judge an old fogey, an oddity and an atheist with whom he disagreed in every way, the law speaker, on a visit to Tórshavn, was a gentle but thirsty, bull-like man who quietly went his own way; the storekeeper a young pup, old Armgard and old Ellen Katrine with her crutch – oh, heaven preserve us! And what else? Oh God, oh God – in Tórshavn. Or Havn, as everyone called it.

And yet, every time Pastor Poul put on his soaking black hat and went out in the everlasting rain, this was done with a quiet hope that he might in time be granted something bright and smiling, a joy in the darkness. For he knew that here, too, somewhere or other in this labyrinth of narrow passageways, yards and middens, there must be a corner where beauty and something to delight the eye resided. There was no denying that he would like to see her again – the widow living in his own benefice. Not that he had any special intentions. God preserve him. He could already see what a dangerous constellation fate had brought about between him and her. But at the same time as it worried him, it was also a tiny source of joy to him in the midst of all this wretchedness. His thoughts played around Barbara. Perhaps she was not all that glorious. But, when the sun has set, the stars shine.

It was Anna Sophie, Pastor Wenzel's wife, who unexpectedly came to his help. When he was preparing to go out later in the day, she asked him whether he had paid a visit to Mrs. Salling, his predecessor's widow. For she thought after all...

This was one of the many things that Pastor Wenzel came up against in the course of a day. His cheeks grew red and his eyes shone helplessly and as though aggrieved.

"Pastor Poul," he said, "must decide for himself what he thinks suitable. As for Barbara... Mrs Salling, nothing has been hidden."

"For Magdalene's sake," said Anna Sophie quite uncon-cerned. She added, "Well, Magdalene – Mrs Stenderup – is her mother. I think you should go for her sake at least. She would feel hurt if you ignored them. Good Lord, *she* can't help..."

Pastor Wenzel capitulated and looked even more offended: "Oh, I suppose not. Mrs Stenderup is in truth... is in truth someone for whom one can only feel pity."

Pastor Poul let Madame Anna Sophie explain which way he should go. It was quite straightforward: through Gongin to Nýggjastova, as it was called, just opposite the bailiff's office and then you were *there*.

She smiled just slightly as she said this. There was something intimate and as it were artful in her entire behaviour. It was as though she knew his thoughts better than he did himself. But Pastor Wenzel continued to look hurt. Perhaps *he* was more aware of his wife's frivolous quality than she herself was. Perhaps he simply knew her far too well.

In Nýggjastova, Pastor Poul was received by Madame Magdalene Stenderup, but he did not receive the impression that his visit had been anticipated with any special sense of anticipation on her part. She received him rather with a kind of half bitter resignation to fate. He could not later recall what words were spoken, but they were uttered with a weary customariness as though she wanted to say that seeing a new priest in her home was rather like encountering a verse of a hymn that had been sung far too many times.

But he immediately forgot this in the unconcealed delight shining in Barbara's face when he entered the sitting room. Indeed, she made not the least effort to hide it. There was a child-like triumph in the warm, glittering falsetto of her voice, as though at last, at long last, she had won a protracted and exciting game that others might have doubted that she could win – for instance Gabriel, Mr Gabriel Hansen, who was also in the room. But perhaps most of all Pastor Poul himself.

And he felt it. Was it not actually as though she said to him, "Oh, you simply *couldn't* keep away any longer now." But he did not feel in the least put out by this. For at the same time it was as though she was saying, "It was good you came. Can't you understand that?" She was so natural and so seemly that he immediately felt comfortable and at ease and as it were infected by her good nature. Everything was so amusing and straightforward.

But Gabriel, whose watchful eyes had been observing this meeting, was not amused and was the last to find Barbara natural and seemly in the way in which she was throwing herself at this stranger. Not that it was the least bit surprising. Yesterday morning, he had already taken the measure of the new Vágar minister and seen that he was quite a distinctive man, rather dark and thickset, very unlike the late Pastor Niels. So it was quite easy to foresee how Barbara would behave... and in any case what the men looked like seemed to be a matter of indifference to her, provided they were... good lord, it was difficult to see what she had seen in several of them. It was enough for her that they were males!

They seated themselves around a white-scoured table, all except Magdalene, who with a disapproving look made an excuse to leave the room. Barbara was sewing. But her lively eyes were not so much directed at her sewing: their quickly shifting, greenish sheen was everywhere and for the time being mostly on Gabriel. Perhaps she did not know what he was thinking, but she knew what he was feeling. She was so perceptive. When she sat between two men in this way, she could hear the beating of both their hearts. She could play each of them like an instrument – in different keys. And now Gabriel must be consoled and redressed a little. She talked to him, asked him about something and listened very carefully to his answer. During all this she only thrice directed her eyes at Pastor Poul and on each occasion she quickly lowered them again.

Pastor Poul, who throughout the day had felt as though he were already lodged in ultimate darkness, suddenly felt himself bathed in a powerful light. This was not only on account of the white table top, Barbara's sewing and her very white and warm hands. It was especially these eyes, which shone so powerfully that she had to lower them each time they had lighted on him. It was as though they had been far too intimate and were then ashamed of themselves.

Pastor Poul at first took pleasure in these looks until he noted that they were directed far more at Gabriel than at himself. He also saw how she several times smiled with pleasure: the corners of her mouth were long and red and when she smiled they brought dimples to her cheeks. Pastor Poul did not quite understand what they were talking about – there must be veiled insinuations in what Gabriel was saying, taunts that Barbara was quite happy to hear. But he himself gradually began to feel in the way.

But his time soon came when Barbara seriously and very attentively began to ask him about his journey, about his studies, his first sermon and all sorts of other things regarding his pastoral duties. It emerged that she knew the names of several of the professors. Aye, there was no limit to her impudence, thought Gabriel. For what could Barbara possibly know about such things? Nevertheless, she went on talking as though the only thoughts she had ever had in her head were those of a parson's wife, and finally she asked Pastor Poul whether he had ever met her late husband, Pastor Niels.

"Bloody shameless, that's what she is," thought Gabriel. It irritated him that there was no one else present to witness her hypocrisy.

But for Pastor Poul, it was as though for the first time in this country he had met anyone who bothered to show any interest in him, and he expressed himself freely and honestly and in his heart of hearts he felt flattered. For although he was well aware that this sort of subject could scarcely in itself be a subject of interest to a woman like Barbara, he could nevertheless see from her face and eyes how engrossed she was and how she reacted to his slightest change of expression, and at that moment he had the thought that seemed right to him, that in a conversation with a woman the subject was only an excuse, while the real matter was the delight of standing face to face, to be able to let their eyes meet, their voices mingle and their souls touch. And Barbara's soul, which spoke through her greenish golden eyes, touched him and was occasionally ashamed and withdrew, but immediately returned and played for him and sunned itself in his powerful, eager gaze. The corners of her mouth happily turned up again now; she listened as though to a rare musical performance, and what he told her now was only apparently about parsons and parishes, but was in reality a long solo aria arising from the depths of his male soul. And the aria was heard.

It was at this point that Barbara's eyes suddenly began to wander in the direction of Gabriel. She lowered them, glanced at him once more with lightning speed and gave a little giggle. The words seemed to stick in Pastor Poul's throat: what had happened? Had Gabriel done something or said something. Was he intervening in the recital? Barbara looked determinedly at her sewing and worked quickly.

"It's a bolster," she said quietly.

But it was obvious that she was filled with hidden laughter. Gabriel gave her a caustic look.

"It *is* a bolster," she repeated insistently. Her voice rose into a falsetto and ended in that wheezing sound that was mid-way between a sigh and a laugh.

Pastor Poul had started to feel very uncomfortable indeed. He did not understand a word of it at all. At first, he thought it was he himself who was being laughed at, but then he realised this was not the case. Nevertheless, he did not at all like this mischievous new game between Barbara and Gabriel, which had quite definitely interrupted his own account and made it superfluous.

Suddenly, Gabriel tugged at the sewing. Barbara defended herself a little and rapped his fingers, but she was unable to prevent him from pulling all the white material up on to the table top. Then she suddenly gave in and said in a voice that she tried to make sound angry: "Oh, you fool, Gabriel. Yes, *of course* it's a shift. One would think you'd never seen a chemise before."

Gabriel's fat face was highly expressive of both amusement and insolence.

"Yes, of course," he replied, "but never *such* a fine one. Who's going...?"

But Barbara had suddenly flushed scarlet right down to her neck. She had chanced to glance at Pastor Poul, just for a second, and never had she been so quick to look away again. Gabriel sensed that something had happened and suddenly understood where they had got to. Damn! He had bungled things again. Pastor Poul and Barbara were both speechless; he was the only one to be saying anything and yet he understood that at that moment he was less than nothing. It was more than he could stand. He said that he would have to go now.

"Are you going?" asked Barbara.

"Yes, I'm afraid so," Gabriel said; he needed to go to the store. He was very busy at the moment.

Pastor Poul had also made signs of making a move. He murmured something to the effect that it was perhaps also time for him to go home. But then Barbara suddenly found the power of speech again and in a loud voice started to talk her way out of her confusion: No, no! Surely he needn't go. Her mother was just making some coffee for him. She hadn't been able to have a talk to him yet, as she surely, *most surely* wanted. There was simply so much for her to do in the house. Whatever he did, he mustn't go yet.

Gabriel was outside in the vestibule; he poked his head inside and pointing in the direction of the sewing, said: "Goodbye. It's nice to see you doing a chemise fit for a bride."

Barbara laughed. A little laugh that at the same time was a sigh that caught in her throat: "Oh, you do talk nonsense, Gabriel."

She went with him to the door and stood out in the rain for a moment and was full of joy. Then she went inside to rejoin Pastor Poul, the new Pastor Poul. And as it was now beginning

58

to turn dusk, she lit some candles.

After this visit, Pastor Poul's melancholy was transformed
into a quiet gaiety. When he came from his visit to Barbara
he wandered through the dark town like a man liberated and
wanted only to be alone for a time with his joy. There was just a
break in the rain. He turned off along a windswept passageway
leading down to the water. There he stopped in the shelter of a
boathouse to gather his thoughts and try to explain to himself
the source of his new-found happiness. But it was not long
before he sensed that others had made their way down to the
shore with their thoughts. A lone figure appeared out of the
darkness. They greeted each other. It was Gabriel.

He was not at all unhappy that it should be Gabriel.
Although he had been a considerable nuisance to him during
his conversation with Madame Barbara, he had nevertheless
been one of the participants in the pleasantest scene he had
experienced since arriving in this country. And although he
might appear to be something of a rascal, he was nevertheless
probably something of a cheerful Scapin to whom it might
well be worth chatting.

Gabriel also turned out to be friendly, familiar and blessed
with the gift of the gab. They discussed all manner of things
concerning Tórshavn and the country, and Gabriel retailed
some quite amusing things about many people, making Pastor
Poul laugh. But the fact that they avoided discussing a certain
person made it increasingly clear to them both that it was she
who was at the centre of their thoughts, and when they finally
reached this subject, Gabriel's voice became quite soft and
emotional.

"A charming woman, you say. Yes, but then you should
have seen her when she was eighteen and quite innocent.

Barbara was really sweet in those days."

"I can imagine that," said Pastor Poul.

"Aye," said Gabriel. "It's a pity that she was so blemished. It's galling. My God it is."

"I've heard a good deal about her already," said Pastor Poul. "So there must be something in it, although I find it difficult to make it fit in with her character, which seems to me to be decent and respectable enough and not such as one would expect of a woman like that."

"Oh, she's full of... If you knew her properly, you'd think she was terrible... She's up to her tricks as soon as she sees a stranger."

"Tricks?" asked Pastor Poul dubiously. He thought of Barbara's glances, which had been so radiant that she had constantly had to look down. "On the contrary," he went on, "she seems to me to be so completely natural."

Gabriel snorted a little. "Those eyes! Oh yes, how fine! Let me tell you something, and by God this is true: I am often ashamed of being related to her. Because at times she lives as though she was nothing but... nothing but... well, a whore."

"Well, I can't judge that, of course," murmured the priest. "I hear that's what people say. But I thought it was mainly the older people who said that kind of thing about her."

"But it's bloody well the young'uns who know first hand what she's like."

"Well, as for me," said the clergyman, "I haven't had a sense of anything on her part but what is decent and beautiful."

"Oh, good heavens. She can't tempt me," said Gabriel seriously. "I know her too well for that... Everyone knows her tricks and what she gets up to. It's really only something to laugh at... If I wasn't related to her."

"But," he concluded, "one thing I will say to you: she's as

lecherous as they come."

"Ha, ha," thought Pastor Poul after they had parted. "Gabriel here is probably not quite as indifferent as he makes out." Pastor Poul himself had to admit that he was certainly not unaffected by this conversation. And his new sense of delight at Tórshavn and all this dreary country had not diminished. He was very surprised, for Gabriel had not said anything but what was likely to spoil his sense of pleasure after his visit to Nýggjastova. Yet it seemed to him that this pleasure had now only increased.

During the following period scarcely a day passed without his seeing Barbara, and every new encounter only helped increase his happiness. He did not himself know what to think of it. He could be in no doubt that she was a woman with a bad reputation. He did not need Gabriel to instruct him in this – he could draw his own conclusions. The effect she had on all men was quite obvious. She neither did nor said anything worthy of censure. And yet! It could not be otherwise. Perhaps she simply could not help it. She pleased everyone and no one knew her ways.

So what in heaven's name could he, a man of the cloth, a man whose task it was to be an example to others – what could he have to do with such a woman? He could already clearly see the trap that fate was setting for him. But he did not fear it.

He already knew that he *ought* to avoid her, but instead he rather sought her out. His heart was thoroughly flattered. His senses were dazzled by the looks from her green eyes and titillated by her scintillating voice. And this black, wet village with its storehouses and hovels, this place that at first had been to him but a source of melancholy, he now saw as through a radiant spectrum.

Never mind, then, that this joy was only on account and

that every day that elapsed in this way only increased its cost. He would know how to pay when the time came for settling. He did not doubt that he would be solvent, whatever the price became. He had so far never doubted himself, and he was accustomed to going with all sails set.

The fifth day saw the arrival of the dean, Anders Morsing, by boat from Nes. Pastor Poul had heard that this man had once been betrothed to Barbara but had broken with her before the wedding. This latter fact struck Pastor Poul as being likely enough when he saw him. He was a man with a commanding figure, tall and stern faced. What eye games could he ever have had with Barbara? His eyes were like steel, piercingly blue and determined, so that anyone he spoke to would feel that he was being examined deep down into his conscience. But a little smile at once both grim and sweet played around his mouth.

Pastor Poul felt he had been called to order the moment he saw him. He was suddenly back in the past. The dean sat with the bishop's letter open in one hand, measuring him up.

"Hmm," he said. "As you know, a great deal is *expected* of you. Things in this country are not like they are elsewhere. The position *ought* to be that it is the clergy who serve their parishioners as models of piety and Christian living, but the contrary is often the case. I will not name any names, but we – that is to say you and I – have a couple of brethren whom one could only wish were half as pious as their parishioners. And so we hope to see our younger clergy made of different stuff."

He looked straight at Pastor Poul's face: "You see, it is scarcely a matter of having devoured so and so many big books or of being familiar with so many of the Christian movements that are to be found all over the place these days – all this skilful whining and subtle pseudo-religiosity. I will say to you once and for all what I have actually already said: that in matters of unshakable faith and true dedication to the Lord we have more to learn from these people than these people can learn from us. I mean mainly the people living out in the villages. You cannot really count the people living here in Tórshavn. For us clergymen at the moment the important thing is not whether one of us can proclaim our message, one louder than another, but quite simply that in our lives and manners we should be worthy of our calling and that we should humbly and faithfully serve, teach and guide our flocks to respect the law and to lead a sober life so that we can in some measure be worthy of the inexplicable confidence they show in us."

The dean had tapped the table a couple of times; his mouth was serious but smiling, but his eyes were fierce.

"And then," he went on, "you yourself have eyes to see. You will probably soon discover what needs to be done."

All Pastor Poul could do was express his full agreement. He tried to find the right words, but found them insubstantial and insignificant.

"And now you can go to your parish at your earliest opportunity," concluded Dean Anders.

Pastor Poul replied that he would be able to travel with the law speaker, who was preparing to return to his own farm.

"Hmm," said the dean with a smile: "Then you will be arriving in your benefice in good company. Aye, aye. I have nothing but good to say of Samuel Mikkelsen, but he is rarely in a hurry to get away when he is here on a visit to Tórshavn. Oh well, *you* must see to that. I am sure that you will take care of yourself in *every* way."

Dean Anders gave him another penetrating look and left.

Pastor Poul was quite overcome. He felt almost as though he had been baptised and confirmed all over again. This dean was like a large, sharp, spiced dram. Oh well, the time had come. In a feeling almost of elation he thought that he would be tearing himself away before long, taking leave of Tórshavn and starting to work. And that would probably not be all that burdensome. He went to the law speaker to arrange the journey with him. It was a Saturday.

Throughout the rest of the day he remembered Dean Anders' sharp, probing eyes that had thrown their light far down into his conscience and called him to order. But occasionally he also saw Barbara's radiant greenish yellow eyes, which she constantly had to drop because they knew far too much about a secret that could not be talked about, indeed scarcely thought about, but which nevertheless made her mouth turn up in a sweet, pleased smile that created dimples in her cheeks. That artful and everlasting secret that Barbara had with all men.

Farewell, Oh World, Farewell

The church bells out on Reyn were calling people to divine service. Their gentle tone fluttered above the housetops. But the tower in which they hung was sombre and rickety with age. It shook beneath the movement. The bells heaved and squeaked in the woodwork, and this piteous secondary sound mingled with chimes as light as birdsong and could be heard everywhere in the town.

The gale and the rain had set into a static cold. The dirt in the streets had become hard and sharp, and the puddles had frozen to tinkling ice. The sun shone hazily on this twenty-sixth Sunday after Trinity.

The church was small. There were thirteen pews on either side in addition to a small gallery above the entrance. It was bitterly cold among the bare timber walls. There was no loft; you just looked straight up at the heavy rafters and laths in the roof.

The impoverished people of Tórshavn began to arrive. The women wore black shawls and scarves. They came tight-lipped and with the Kingo hymnbook in their hands. The men followed, a little hesitantly and with a sombre urge to remain in the background. A few individuals among them found their way up to the gallery. They were only the heroes of everyday life – Samuel the Hoist and Niels the Punt. Here in this sacred place the women had better take the lead.

The better off and the *fine* folk also came to church. As was their right, they had their regular places, which none of the common folk dared violate. Bailiff Harme came and spread himself beside his daughter Suzanne. They sat in the front row. There was also the judge's pew, which was still used by Mrs Stenderup, the previous judge's widow, and a pew for the clergyman's family, in which the two sisters Armgard and Ellen Katrine were allotted seats as Pastor Wenzel's relatives and guests. Pastor Poul Aggersøe was also given a seat in this pew.

There were in addition many others who had their permanent pews despite not being among the elite: Mrs Dreyer, Sieur Arentzen and old Miss Kleyn. They were solid folk who paid for their seats. This was their pride and their token of distinction in the eyes of the ordinary folk, and their faces betrayed just a little awareness of this as they seated themselves.

But one feature all the churchgoers had in common was that their breath rose as grey clouds in the bitterly cold air.

Pastor Poul sat thinking of all the times he had attended service in the cathedral in Copenhagen, all the courteous commotion outside the west door of carriages, hansoms and servants banging carriage doors. He thought of the well-dressed throng of distinguished and ordinary citizens who with pleasure and dignity strode down three equally lofty aisles between the columns as the organ played a solemn voluntary and growled beneath the vaulted roof. Alas, here in Tórshavn there was only a poor, bent parish clerk hoarsely stammering his way through the *introit*. And meanwhile there was a deathly silence beneath the roof beams and not the usual coughing and spluttering.

Immediately after this, Barbara hurried quietly in and sat

down beside her mother in the judge's pew – as a final living glimpse of the world before the start of the sombre hymn.

Judge Johan Hendrik Heyde had on this day come to church together with the bailiff and his daughter. He had greeted them, exchanged a few words and smiled, but when they had entered the porch he had not accompanied them up the floor of the church to his pew. Instead, he had made his bulky way up into the gallery.

Why did he do this? He had nothing against them, but there was nevertheless something keeping them apart at that moment. They were speaking Danish. Well, of course, that was their language. And Johan Hendrik had nothing against things Danish – he had himself spent much time in Denmark, and his own family was Danish. Indeed, he would have thought it unreasonable if people such as the bailiff or the storekeeper had spoken Faroese. And yet, here on home ground among ordinary Faroese people, this easily flowing language was in conflict with the right tone. It irritated him a little, as when he heard someone nearby playing a badly tuned instrument. He was himself attuned to the people. So it was against his nature to go forward into the front row. He preferred to remain in the background in the gallery. Here, he could sit quietly and think about agricultural improvements, new fishing experiments and other useful subjects serving the interests of the country.

Some time after the judge had taken his place, there was a heavy creaking on the stairs, and up came his cousin Samuel Mikkelsen, the islands' law speaker. He was big and ungainly, but he, too, preferred the gallery. Not on account of any subtle ill will towards other good people, but purely out of discretion. He proceeded so carefully; if he made a joke it was an elegant one, and when he took a drink during the service he did so with great delicacy – not secretly like some scoundrel or schoolboy, but with imperturbable dignity. Johan Hendrik felt refreshed by his presence, but, perhaps not without reason, Bailiff Harme thought that His Majesty's Faroese-born officials misunderstood their position by hiding themselves from view among the riffraff in the six free benches in the gallery.

Things were completely different with the commandant, Lieutenant Otto Hjørring. He did not hide his light under a bushel, but strode into the church in his red dress uniform, with rapier, moustache, pigtail and everything that could be required of a military personage. But admittedly, he made a mistake and blundered into one of the common pews. Beach Flea was both honoured and concerned and directed a great number of anxious glances at the overwhelming proximity of such splendour and delectable perfume.

This was how they came, all the people of the parish, high and low. Gabriel in his Sunday best, pious and unrecognisable. The staff of the Store and the gunners from the Redoubt, the owner of the home farm with his workers and the village farmer who had come on foot from afar. The congregation worked their way through the first long-winded hymn. There was no organ. The cold, shivering voices hardly kept time with each other. Some sang splendidly and with a sense of artistry; for instance Sieur Arentzen, on whom it was plain to see that he saw himself as the main singer. Others sang with no sense of music whatsoever, and their wives simply wailed from beneath their black scarves. There was a great deal of coughing and sniffing when the last, endless, asthmatic verse had finally been sung. Hanging beneath the roof, the model of the East-Indiaman *The Lion of Norway* turned slowly on its cord. Its bowsprit started to point south.

The minister, who had been standing turned towards the altar, now addressed the congregation: "*The Lord be with you.*"

A cloud of steam emerged from his mouth. A hundred clouds of steam from the congregation replied: *"And with thy spirit."*

Pastor Wenzel was a little too small for the red chasuble, and it looked as though he at any time could stumble and fall in the folds of the alb. He glanced at the congregation. The Royal Store manager had not come. That was unfortunate. No, that man regrettably only had a mediocre record for attending church. It was particularly annoying today. The clergyman felt a sudden sense of disappointment. The sermon for the day had a message for everyone, though mainly for the great and those with temporal responsibilities, those who were most inclined to forget the church and to ignore its servants. The bailiff was there. But as soon as he turned towards the altar again, Pastor Wenzel noticed that his own wife was absent. Anna Sophie had not come yet!

"Let us pray."

He started to feel a vague sense of unease. He hesitated in the midst of the ritual. Then he swallowed hard and chanted the collect in a voice that trembled slightly. No one thought that unusual. Pastor Wenzel often spoke as though something or other had upset him. The whole of his small, red-bearded figure always gave the sense of having been slightly insulted.

The service took its course. They reached the Epistle. Pastor Wenzel, who had been feeling strangely outside it all, pulled himself together. He turned to the congregation and in a powerful voice intoned: *"The Epistle for the twenty-sixth Sunday after Trinity is taken from the First Epistle of St Paul to the Thessalonians."*

Anna Sophie had not come.

"And we beseech you, brethren, to know them which labour among you, and are over you in the Lord, and admonish you. And to esteem them very highly in love for their work's sake. And be at peace among yourselves. Now we exhort you, brethren, warn them that are unruly..."

Some time after he had finished the Epistle, Pastor Wenzel could still hear his voice echoing within his head. He had not associated any meaning with a single word of what he had read out. His heart was uneasy, his mind empty. Nor had Pastor Poul, sitting in the pew reserved for the clergy, been listening. His thoughts, too, were wandering restlessly on other paths. Indeed, in the entire church there were scarcely many who had noticed the words of the Apostle. Some were too worried, others too sleepy. And so the service progressed like a game that had been started and must go on. Unnoticed, the *Lion of Norway* had again turned and was now heading towards the south west.

As soon as the minister had gone up into the pulpit and started to speak, Johan Hendrik up in the gallery could hear that his brother had been upset by something or other. There was a certain quality in the tone of his voice that he knew so well. He had known it ever since they had both been boys.

Pastor Wenzel began hesitantly, but soon found the sure thread he had planned and followed it determinedly. It was this sermon he had prepared with such zeal and which the store manager should have heard, although it was equally aimed at the bailiff, indeed fundamentally at everyone in the congregation, right down to the most humble.

"And we beseech you, brethren, to know them which labour among you and are over you in the Lord..."

It was not every year there was a twenty-sixth Sunday after Trinity, and it was not every minister who during the service was allowed to preach on the text of the Epistle instead of the Gospel. But Pastor Wenzel, who had a master's degree, was so permitted, and at last, on this Sunday which so rarely occurred, he had the opportunity to say what had burdened his heart for so long.

Anna Sophie had still not come.

She, too, could benefit from hearing what he had to say. Although it would presumably be like water off a duck's back. No, that was not why he was missing her. He did not allow himself to think more deeply about it. But his heart knew better; it was beating strongly.

He started by rendering unto Caesar the things that were Caesar's. The king's officials and servants and all the temporal authorities – they should all be respected and obeyed. For the authorities were placed there by God. But what of God's servants? Should they not be honoured and respected in the same way? The Apostle Paul explained it in his Epistle to the Ephesians. "Pay heed to yourselves," he writes to the leaders of the congregation, "and to the entire flock, among which the Holy Ghost appointed you bishops to feed God's people, which he achieved through His own blood."

He looked around for the first time and raised his voice: "But when bishops and priests give you your spiritual food, take care of your souls and justify yourselves before God, ought they then not to be seen as equal to those – indeed at least equal to those who provide you with food for the body, ensure there are provisions in the country (this was something the Royal Store manager should have heard!), take care of your temporal wellbeing and maintain justice and righteousness among you?"

Pastor Wenzel had worked himself up: "The spiritual and the temporal are two concepts, but the spiritual is not inferior to the temporal. If you observe the laws of the land, which the authorities impose on you, ought you not to obey God's eternal commandments, which I also proclaim?"

He looked appealingly at the bailiff, and Harme nodded.

"And when you pay your land dues and taxes to the office established for the purpose by the king, ought you not to pay your dues to the Church established by God?"

The bailiff nodded again, conceding the point. Pastor Wenzel worked himself up still more: "And when you do service and pay rates to the military and its officers, are those above you in the service of the Lord not of such value that you will pay them a tithe?"

His eyes wandered over to the lieutenant, who was sleeping soundly in his scarlet dress uniform.

Then his eyes turned back to the bailiff; indeed, it was almost as though this sermon was developing into a conversation with the bailiff. And the bailiff again nodded graciously.

"For the priest," continued Pastor Wenzel, "the *priest* is your spiritual superior, appointed by the Holy Ghost – and, by the way, also by His Majesty the King – in the same way as the bailiff and the law speaker, the Royal Store manager and the judge..."

He gave his brother a look in the hidden depths of which lay a kind of mild reproach. But then he quickly looked back at the bailiff and continued: "...errh, in the same way as these are your high-ranking temporal superiors, whom it is your duty to honour and love. Do not be angry with your minister for telling you the truth. Even the most high-ranking should not be deaf to his exhortations, if not for the sake of his humble personage, then for the sake of his lofty calling."

Now it was said. Pastor Wenzel paused; his watery blue eyes wandered around rather uncertainly as though he was trying to fathom the effect of his words. Then he went on: "Furthermore, the Apostle says to us today: 'Now we exhort you, brethren, warn them that are unruly..."'

It was suddenly as though he was unable to go on. Anna Sophie – now he could see her! And he could see the Royal Store manager as well. Through one of the open windows in the church he could see over to the parsonage, and there, in the small sitting room, he could see both his wife and the manager of the Royal Store...

He swayed as he stood there, understanding nothing and feeling nothing. It was almost as though he were dreaming. Anna Sophie and the Royal Store manager! What was it... he did not remember immediately... there had always been something about this; he had known it all along.

He wanted to go on where he had left off, but he had a pain in his heart. It was growing. He was overcome by an ache that paralysed him. His heart beat slowly like an iron knot; his throat was tightened and burned, his entire figure radiated pain.

Anna Sophie!

He heard his own voice, still stammering: "Warn them that are unruly, warn them that are unruly..."

The entire congregation saw him standing there rocking on his feet, helpless, deathly pale with a tiny blood-red patch on either cheek. A few thought he had been taken ill; no one understood the true reason for his terrible distress. Some time passed. The lieutenant's easy snoring started to become restless, and he uttered a few words in his sleep.

Then it was as though the minister himself started at the great silence. He realised he was standing in the pulpit but not preaching. The congregation was sitting in the church and not listening. A ray of sunlight fell on the windows and he saw all the faces quite clearly. High up at the back of the church sat his brother with a look of surprise in his face. The *Lion of Norway* was slowly rocking in its cords, pointlessly. And the entire church was like a ship that was sailing out of control on the ocean's waves, full of people, but without anyone at the helm.

Pastor Wenzel pulled himself together. The unruly – now he had it. He spoke out loud in a voice trembling with hurt. If he had had anything on his mind before, he had no less now. The unruly, they were those of high rank! He envisaged the Royal Store manager's smooth, well-fed face. Like a flash of lightning all was made clear to him. He had admired this face, taken care of it as of a plant when the Royal Store manager sat at table in his home to enjoy a good roast. Now he saw his own happiness being devoured and himself being trampled on with the same matter-of-fact look of satisfaction. He gasped; his soul and his mind turned on the mighty and snapped at them like a dog that has been kicked without reason. He suddenly envisaged them as an eternal host of the powerful and the replete. The judge, and behind him a succession of judges who had despised the peasants in the country. The lieutenant and behind him a succession of lieutenants who had mercilessly drilled decent lads. The Royal Store manager, and behind him a host of Royal Store managers who had cheated his honest and innocent forefathers. Did he not know the great figures? King David, who stole Urias's wife. Herod, who had St John the Baptist beheaded. And behind them all Pontius Pilate, who washed his hands. The great ultimately all washed their luxurious white hands. Did he not know them? They had been the maggots eating away at his life. No more than a few minutes ago, he had stood here applying to be accepted as one among them. And now he had been stabbed in the heart.

Trembling with bitterness, Pastor Wenzel had started his confrontation with the unruly of this world, but as he gradually dug deeper into his own soul and became aware of the beam in his own eye, he himself grew with his message. No secret corner of the human heart, no selfish hidden thought, no earthly desire, no foolish vanity did he allow to remain hidden. He recognised clearly that the world and only the world was the goal and objective of the human mind. For all were born bad and sinful and did not themselves know *how* great sinners they were. No one could be just by virtue of their own strength or deserts, and all lacked honour before God. Every time a human being had performed some good act, it was followed by self-righteousness, the great flatterer, reaching out its hand to him and thereby turning good to evil. Nothing good was said or done without the world being behind it like some grubby hidden thought. So endless was mankind's *inability* to achieve true goodness. Everything was fundamentally desire, falseness, self-justification, selfishness, folly and vanity. Vanity!

"Hmm," said the judge to the law speaker; "so that's the direction he's taking today. Aye, then something or other has gone wrong for him."

But, amazed and horrified, the congregation down in the church listened to Pastor Wenzel's words and thought that he was after all a great preacher and chastiser. For it was to all of them as though he were showing them their own image in a mirror and looking deep into their hearts. They did not think that he was only looking into his own heart.

Pastor Poul, the new parson bound for Vágar, had like so many others to bow his head. For he felt that he himself was walking on the same path of vanity and was never completely happy unless his heart was flattered, his ambition fostered and his desire fired. It was the world and only the world that played before his eyes, and he had not himself the ability to look higher.

But Pastor Wenzel, who saw that he had carried the

congregation with him, went further and further down into the ways and byways of the human heart, and when he could go no further and had quite revealed humankind's complete inability to achieve goodness and its unworthiness to see God, he suddenly allowed the miracle to take place. And this miracle was grace through Jesus Christ, who took away all our sins. Indeed through grace and only through grace was it possible to rise, to relinquish the burden of this world and despise it as the worthless rubbish it is, and finally with a pure heart to turn our thoughts to heaven.

"Amen!" He concluded in a loud voice, and before he began the prayer his pale eyes wandered quickly around the church, though without getting too close to a certain window. This was a moment of grace for the Tórshavn congregation.

When they came to the hymn, Pastor Wenzel said that they were not going to sing the hymn ordained for the day – he was a master of theology and could decide this on their behalf – but another. It was by Thomas Kingo and was familiar to them from *The Spiritual Choir* or from the book called *Thousands* and known as *Tired of the World and Longing for Heaven*.

Most of them knew it by heart. Sieur Arentzen led the singing with great skill and with the loud support of Pastor Wenzel himself:

> *Farewell oh world, farewell*
> *No longer will I live in thrall*
> *The cares with which you burdened me*
> *I now cast off and from them flee.*
> *And from the sin I'll now be free*
> *Of vanity*
> *Of vanity*

The hymn fired everyone, and the entire congregation sang aloud the next verse:

> *And what is this frame*
> *Adorned by the world with so wondrous a name*

Beach Flea glanced at the commandant, who was still snoring with an indescribably non-military expression on his face.

> *It is but shades and glittering glass.*
> *It is but froth and clinking brass.*
> *It is but gross profanity*
> *And vanity*
> *And vanity*

Aye, that was probably right. Samuel Mikkelsen had a slight headache after a quiet evening of festivity yesterday. It was the fifth on the run and he was gradually beginning to feel sickened by all the jugs and glasses that were to be found on a table by midnight. No, there was surely no earthly joy without a sour aftertaste.

> *What then are my years*
> *That vanish now amid my fears?*
> *My worries then? My thoughtful mind?*
> *My sorrows? My joys? My puzzled mind?*
> *My labours now? Urbanity?*
> *'Tis vanity*
> *'Tis vanity.*

The young ones did not believe this. But there was no furrowed face in the church that did not become thoughtful at these words.

Jørgen-Frantz Jacobsen

From Bailiff Harme with his great responsibility to Samuel the Hoist with his eight children. One man had to recognise that his forty years in the job was no more than writing in the sand, while another merely awaited three shovelfuls of soil as the mortal end of one who had laboured all his life. But the judge, ever doubting and difficult, was struck by the acrimonious idea that a piece of useful work carried out on earth was more gratifying than ten cries of jubilation in heaven.

He read modern books and had come to the belief that hard work and patriotism were the tokens of greater blessings than palm leaves.

> *O riches and gold*
> *You idols of Earth so fair to behold*
> *You are but a part of the world's deep deceit*
> *Which grows and then withers and signals defeat.*
> *Your nature is profanity*
> *And vanity,*
> *And vanity.*

This was a consolation to many who had lost their possessions. But Gabriel had not sufficient control over his thoughts to prevent him from that moment falling into profound speculations as to whether various sums of money that had recently been transferred from others' pockets into his ought not to be invested in four rods of land that were for sale in Mikladal.

> *Ah, honour, what now?*
> *What are all the crowns and the wreaths on your brow?*
> *Black envy is ever now ready to chafe,*
> *In secret you hurt and so seldom feel safe*

And often you wonder at others' profanity –
Aye, vanity
Aye, vanity.

Who could deny all this? Who was not eaten by the worm of ambition – big or small? From the rented pews of the finer folk to the benches of the poor there was no soul who did not secretly glance at a competitor or a superior. Envy rode on the backs of them all. Who was without arrogance? Who had no hidden wounds?

Sorrow and a strange sense of consolation moved in great waves in Pastor Wenzel's mind. The hymn comforted him. There! Thomas Kingo had felt and experienced everything in the same way as he himself.

Ah, favour and fame,
You mightily longed for, you urge for acclaim
You flatterer false, you fast blowing wind
With eyes as of thousands and yet blowing blind –
What other are you then when examined in sanity?
Than Vanity
Than Vanity.

What on earth has come over Wenzel today, the judge wondered again. Something or other must have upset the little man and hurt him to the depths of his innermost clerical soul. Could it be that the bailiff had not bothered to listen to his sermon? Something had gone wrong, that was obvious, and now Wenzel was standing there, God help him, wallowing in every earthly passion, but with his face turned to the light of divine grace – of course, ah rubbish. This hymn would soon be a source of false comfort, a kind of brandy in which to find consolation when folk burned themselves on the porridge of life. If someone did no more than lose three marks at cards, then farewell, oh world. A fat lot of help that would be.

But when they came to the next verse, everything collapsed completely for Pastor Wenzel for a moment: he forgot divine grace and wept and sang in his sorrow:

> *Ah, friendship and faith,*
> *Who know that good fortune is merely a wraith*
> *O beauteous deceiver, o fortunate knave*
> *Treacherous ever, you never will save*
> *When ere you are close no more we find amity*
> *But vanity,*
> *But vanity.*

And fired with righteous fury and zeal, he continued:

> *Ah, fleshly desire,*
> *So many your kisses of death-bringing fire,*
> *Your matches, your kindling, your fast flying spark*
> *So many have sent into ne'er-ending dark...*

The invisible halo around Barbara's head started to glow. For it was to her that most people's thoughts were directed in envy, in lust, in condemnation. Gabriel was suffering as he lusted for her; even the judge up in the gallery sat looking at her. But she herself sat there as devoid of reflection as a bird on a fence, oblivious to the fires of Hell by which she was surrounded. The new parson from Vágar, Pastor Poul Aggersøe, loved her and was terrified.

> *...Like honey your draught, but foul is the drink,*

Ah, vanity,
Ah, vanity.

Armgard was so small and so old in her black dress. She nodded as though in confirmation of this. All she felt this hymn lacked was a verse on brandy. For that was the Devil's drink and had been the downfall of many. But her sister Ellen Katrine looked ahead quite happily as she sat there in the grip of her memories: – The World!

Then fare thee now well, now farewell,
No longer deceit shall you heap on my soul,
O world of deceit, you shall ne'er me enslave
I'll dig you deep down in oblivion's grave
I'll mend now my soul in sorrow and grace
In Abraham's embrace
In Abraham's embrace

And everyone shook off the yoke of earthly life and sang aloud of heavenly bliss. They had settled their accounts with their hearts. While the congregation rose and the bells started to resound in the wooden tower, the woeful sound of the hymn lingered in everyone's ears.

Vanity, vanity.

Pastor Poul walked slowly down the aisle. He was remembering the Sunday in Copenhagen Cathedral when he had thought he was bidding farewell to the world. But the world had come here with him. There were no columns and arcades here, no organ and no vaulting, merely a mean wooden church. And yet the world was just as powerful and difficult to say goodbye to.

Pastor Wenzel came and took him by the arm, red and

flushed and as if he were not quite himself. He came as though with authority from on high, humble and yet trembling with triumph.

"Well, Johan Hendrik," he enquired out in the entrance to the church, "what did you think of *that* sermon?"

"Well," said the judge, taking his time to put his hat on his head, "the end was different from the beginning. *Otherwise*, it was just like you at both ends."

Samuel the law speaker, who by now had emptied the first bottle of the day, paid his kindly and clear-eyed respects to his old aunts Armgard and Ellen Katrine.

A little snow was falling. The ringing of the bell sounded freer outside, fluttering among the tiny flakes of white. Everyone had a strange sense of elation. They had seen themselves and each other in the seductive mirror of the world and were fascinated and shocked at everything on this earth. But thank God! The world had no power over them; they had torn themselves away. Relieved and liberated, they hurried home. They did not know that it was the anticipation of dinner that lent them wings.

But in the empty church the East-Indiaman *The Lion of Norway* still hung in its strings, adorned with guns, pennants and flags, slowly rocking around all the points of the compass, now in one direction and now in another.

The World

It was blowing down every alley and passageway and there was a raw smell of seaweed. The weather had turned dull again. A south wind was blowing in from the sea and lessening the biting grip of the frost.

The town had fallen into a state of lethargy. People were sitting in their houses and hovels in their best clothes. They were sated with food and Sabbath and were gradually starting to be bored. Out in Reynegaard, Samuel the law speaker was playing chess with his cousin the judge. A long time elapsed between moves and even longer between words. Armgard and Ellen Katrine sat talking about the old days and every now and again disagreed about their family. It was a great lack to Armgard that she dared not knit – knitting permitted her to let off steam when she was overcome with anger, but the quiet of the Sunday must not be disturbed by worldly labours.

The minister and his wife only put in a brief appearance that afternoon; they had probably had a talk in the small sitting room. The old folk did not think it had been right of Anna Sophie to miss the service. But of course, they said nothing.

Pastor Poul had gone out. He met no one in the deserted streets. As he approached Nýggjastova he slowed his pace. In the midst of all the cheerlessness it was a profound joy to him to know that Barbara lived in this house. Was she in there, perhaps? Perhaps it was more likely that she was at the bailiff's home together with Suzanne.

On the sand, where the river ran out into the East Bay, the ducks lay with their beaks hidden beneath their wings. They uttered some alarmed quacks as he went by, but they were far too lazy to be bothered moving. They were the ducks that belonged to Springus and Whoops and Katrine the Cellar. Every family had its own, but they were without artificial markings – the local people knew the town's ducks as well as they knew each other. Well, it may be that Bailiff Harme did not know the ducks so well, although he lived quite nearby, but he had greater things to see to. As for Pastor Poul, he simply did not see the ducks he walked amongst. He was solely concerned with the thought that at that very moment it might be that he was being observed from a window. And so he was; he was being observed from a large number of windows. All the womenfolk in Gongin were very interested and for the following hour that afternoon, the great subject of discussion was that they had seen the new minister jump the stones across the river and go up into the outfield.

The southerly wind continued to blow a greyish mist in across the town. The ducks sat there, huddled together in the wind. But then, suddenly, something happened.

No one knew who first raised the alarm. It was not the lookout in the Redoubt, although he was the obvious one.

Someone or other, who had been out on some errand, had been the first to see the sight... and three minutes later all Tórshavn had seen it: crowds of people could be seen behind the corner of every house looking down towards the shore.

"Oh, Jesus have mercy on us!"

Large sails had appeared on the horizon. They stood out there like an evil and far too obvious sign. The old women were the ones who wailed loudest. These ships must mean trouble. They wailed and they wept, their teeth chattered, and they tried to warm their cold hands beneath their Sunday aprons.

Aye, there was nothing else to be expected. The last trading ship of the year had been there and left. Besides, *such* huge sails: it was obvious to everyone that this was no ordinary ship.

A moment later and another ship appeared on the horizon.

Terror was already tensing its back in preparation. It was at first like a little smoking fuse, and then suddenly it was like a blaze that was reflected in everyone's eyes, and finally it broke out in a wild confusion of shouting, weeping and cursing.

There was no real hesitation. There was only one thing to be done. Save what could be saved – household appliances, bedclothes, a little wool that had been put aside, anything at all! – And then up into the mountains. Tramping Englishmen and drunken Scots had often come ashore, broken their way into chests and cupboards, slaughtered the cattle and dragged folk away to fish off Iceland. This was something everyone had heard about. And that was not even the worst thing. On one occasion great hoards of heathens – Turks or black men it was said – had laid waste and burned on Suduroy, slaughtering to obtain food and dragging over thirty women and children off from their quiet homes to unknown devilish slavery. That was the most dreadful thing anyone could talk about. Nor had Tórshavn always escaped. Some years ago a French crew had destroyed the Redoubt and plundered the town.

The Faroese, who were themselves the descendants of pirates, had over the centuries been tamed by poverty and isolation. They had turned into a shy and faint-hearted people. Faced with foreigners, they knew but one defence – flight up into the inaccessible mountains. Now the whole of Tórshavn was on the move at the sight of three large sails on the horizon.

Someone had started beating a drum somewhere in the alleyways. There was someone there who had not lost courage. Otto Hjørring, that dull dog, was perhaps not just a loud mouth after all. But he was so drunk. With one hand he was holding the more than half dead drummer by the collar and with the other he was waving his drawn sword. He hit out at Beach Flea's dilapidated gable so that the chimney almost fell down. But Beach Flea was not at home; his wife had sent him down to the Sands to fetch the duck. And as for *her*, she had always feared the commandant, but today she only feared the pirates. And so it was with all the women. With their arms full of spinning wheels, infants and dried fish, they streamed in terror through Gongin, wept, fell down, got up again and forever implored God's help. The huts were deserted and left with their doors open, and the fire in the hearth was left to go out.

The men fled rather more slowly, indeed there were those who wondered whether it was necessary to flee straight away. But that was one thing; another was to have to don a red uniform, white gaiters and tall grenadier hats, face the enemy and defend oneself as a soldier of the king – that was probably more than Otto Hjørring, the drunken wretch, could persuade them to do.

Gabriel had spent that afternoon together with Magdalene, the judge's widow, helping her to go through the old bureau. His chubby hands eagerly slid back and forth across the woodwork, searching; he tapped gently and indomitably here and there in order to find hollow places. There was not the least little thing, not a single thing, no yellowing mortgage deed that had not seen the light of day. But the treasure in the secret compartment still refused to materialise. But there was no doubt about that – *if* it was there, he would find it all right. This was quite a different search from what Magdalene with her withered fingers had ever been able to carry out, and she was very grateful to her nephew for the strength and determination he revealed. The bureau actually groaned beneath his hand. He had started to deal with it very firmly. It looked extremely shabby and as though its dignity was offended with all the empty pigeon holes and their contents spread over tables and chairs.

Gabriel tried and tried and thought and thought. But his thoughts were as much on Barbara as on the bureau. Aye, if only he had known *her* innermost pigeonholes. In recent days it had been almost an obsession. This new minister for Vágar – was it to be his turn now? Could it be that there was already something going on between them? He kept watch as much as possible, but the store occupied him every day. He was in Nýggjastova each evening. He mocked, he insinuated, he paid court, but Barbara merely smiled secretively and protested when he went much further than was acceptable.

Barbara enjoyed him. She was so musical. There was not a shade, not the slightest intonation in his voice that escaped her. She heard his heartbeats. She heard the pitiful dog deep down in Gabriel howling and asking her to say it was all a lie. And how she played with this dog! But her kind heart often ran away with her, and then she said it was not true. But every time she said that, she secretly thought, "Suppose it were true." And then she smiled, and Gabriel's dog howled again.

She could finally scarcely do without his chatter, and when Gabriel turned his attention to the bureau, she was not far from sulking. She went out and before long returned with Suzanne.

When they heard the shouting and the din outside, Magdalene was afraid. But Gabriel had his wits about him.

He grabbed old Judge Stenderup's telescope and went up a stepladder to the top loft. Barbara and Suzanne hurried after him. But Magdalene continued to go around moaning, "Oh, Jesus, it's a pirate ship."

"Of course it's not," shouted Gabriel, staring out across the sea with a knowledgeable expression on his face. But there was just a touch of fear in his voice.

The three of them stood in a group around the little window in the gable and took it in turns to look through the telescope. Barbara was flushed with excitement and almost hopped about on the rickety floor. Suzanne said nothing.

Gabriel said he believed they were warships.

"Are they? Are they? Let *me* see."

"Even if they are warships, it may be too early to feel pleased," said Suzanne. "Men from warships can also ransack a town and burn it down. We've seen that before."

Gabriel was anything but pleased. It looked as though the ground was beginning to burn beneath his feet. He slowly descended the ladder. But Barbara and Suzanne could not tear themselves away from the window. They stared and stared, spoke breathlessly, both at the same time, interrupting each other, fighting over the telescope and all the time shouting, "Let *me* see. Let *me* see."

Barbara was far too careless about her skirts. She gave not a thought to the ladder below. Gabriel could see her legs.

"Oh, Christ have mercy on us," Magdalene went on complaining. She looked around irresolutely at all her things that lay scattered around all over the sitting room.

"Yes, we'd probably better get all that out of the way," said Gabriel in a flat voice.

Magdalene started haphazardly gathering her papers together.

"Good heavens," Suzanne's voice was heard from above. "Suppose they are pirates and they come and rape us both."

Barbara suddenly laughed in a warm descant; her eyes were radiant: "Yes. And fancy how sorry everyone will be for us afterwards. That will be the most amusing thing of all."

Gabriel could still see her legs.

"Don't just stand up there and get randy," he shouted. It was supposed to sound jaunty and playful, but it was a howl of pain. Then he tore himself away and rushed out.

He had regained his strength. Like a wounded whale, he worked his way forward through Gongin against the crowd. When he had reached Reyn, he encountered the last fugitives. He rushed into the empty apartment to carry his belongings to safety.

But Barbara and Suzanne had scarcely noticed his disappearance. They were becoming more and more entranced by the ships.

"I can see one of them quite clearly now," shouted Barbara: "There are three rows of cannon on it and a gilt figure on the prow." She clapped her hands.

The law speaker came walking through Gongin. He could hardly be said to be hurrying, but alert observers would nevertheless have noticed that he was raising his heels rather more quickly from the ground than usual. His face was also strangely tense.

Bailiff Harme was quite beside himself. His wig was askew and he was waving a long Dutch chalk pipe in the air. He had started to shout for Suzanne and looked rather apoplectic. When he caught sight of the law speaker he calmed down for a moment. This huge figure was like a rock in the maelstrom. If Samuel Mikkelsen was dispirited, it could at least not be seen in his face. He looked as thoroughly kind and quiet as usual. But he was not in a position to give any advice to the frightened bailiff.

"I don't know, I don't know," he said. "I'm so undecided, but I think I will stay where I am. But the rest of you can get away if you like. There is no knowing. For of course, they *could* mean trouble."

Several people had gathered outside the bailiff's house. They were unwilling to let themselves be seen to be too afraid. It was worth seeing what the top dogs decided to do.

But the bailiff was quite incapable of deciding on anything at all. He bustled to and fro. Now he had three ledgers under his arm. The law speaker simply stood there. Just stood.

The judge appeared. As usual, he stroked his chin.

"It will be a cause of shame to us all," he said, "if they turn out now to be friendly warships and the people on board find no one here, either in the town or in the Redoubt."

"That is my feeling, too," said Samuel Mikkelsen quietly.

And there they both stood.

Pastor Wenzel came struggling through Gongin with a huge burden on his back. He was almost ready to drop beneath silver, fine garments and bedclothes.

The judge's lips twitched a little. He could not resist it: "Oh riches and gold, – you idols of earth so fair to behold."

The minister glanced at him from under the eiderdowns, but he maintained a furious silence.

But the ordinary people were simply horrified. This man of God! They had never seen him like this before. Anna Sophie came along with the two old women. They looked so small and withered in the crowd here. The wind blew in Ellen Katrine's silvery white hair. It was a wretched sight.

People were again gripped by fear. The crowd started to

move, while the bailiff with his ledgers continued to call out: "Suzanne. Suzanne."

Something caught the light somewhere higher up. Barbara opened the gable window in Nýggjastova and leaned out: "They are not pirates! Can't you see that?"

Her voice was somewhere between irritation and laughter. It sounded as though she had been interrupted in the midst of something very amusing and was irritated that people could not understand it was all a joke.

Everyone started. Barbara's arms were resting on the window ledge, round and calm. She was wearing a blue dress, pale and flushed and with warmth in her voice. She was a picture of good humour and roguishness in the midst of the cold terror.

"Can't you understand?" she continued, "big ships like these can't be pirate vessels. They must be warships."

There was general hesitation. The law speaker shaded his eyes with his hand and stared out across the sea. Then he turned and with a little smile said, "I really think Barbara is right."

Barbara was radiant. "Yes, don't you think so? They have a white flag."

"A white flag with golden lilies?" asked the judge.

"Yes, I think so." She took the telescope: "Yes, a white flag with some gold in it."

"Oh, that's a quite different matter, quite different." The bailiff began to adopt his official deportment again. "Then they're French, and we are not at war with them."

"As far as I know, Denmark is not at war with anyone," said the law speaker sarcastically.

There was a general discussion and conversation. People went down to the water's edge again to take a look. Curiosity started to replace fear.

"My good men," said the law speaker to a couple of the soldiers, "go over to the Redoubt. We must fire a salute. Let us not be a complete laughing stock in the eyes of the foreign visitors."

They went. Order was returning. People were carrying their poor belongings back home. The air was full of joy, relief and expectancy. Only a small number of wives refused to believe and went on moaning about enemy ships. But the young people all wanted to go out to Tinganes to see the foreign sailors arrive.

When Barbara and Suzanne came down into the street, they encountered Gabriel. He appeared not to have the least idea of what was going on.

"Oh, how fat you are!" said Barbara.

"Yes, why are you so fat?"

They prodded him. And then they burst into laughter. Suzanne started pulling out red silk material from his waistcoat. But Gabriel struck out at her and went off, troubled and upset. He had eight yards of material tucked inside his trousers.

Half an hour after this, all the windows in Tórshavn shook as the cannon fired a salute. There was a dense crowd on Tinganes and at Skindersker. Anchor chains rattled; foreign voices gave orders and shouted, and out of the gunpowder smoke there appeared masts and sails, bowsprits and shrouds, carved galleries and long rows of gun ports. The sailors were swarming in the rigging, busy furling the heavy sails. The Redoubt also fired a fitting salute.

There was life and festivity. Never had Tórshavn seen anything like it. Three huge warships! When you stood on the Sand, you could see the topmasts on one of them high up above all the roofs on Reyn.

The three French warships, the *Néréide*, the *Amphitrite* and

the *Fleurs de Lys,* were returning from the war in America.
Gales and storms had driven them too far north. Now they
were looking for a harbour in the Faroes in order to repair
various bits of damage to the ships and to take on fresh water
before continuing their journey home.

But Tórshavn was not a safe harbour. As long as the wind
was in the south west, the ships were certainly shielded by
the Kirkjubø Ridge, but if it turned more to the south or east,
the waves would blow straight in on the open roads. The
law speaker, the bailiff and the judge had been on board and
explained this to the admiral. They had advised him to go to
Kongshavn or Vestmannahavn, where he would be safe from
all winds. However, the law speaker was of the opinion that he
should wait until the following day, for darkness was falling
now. It was not easy to navigate between the islands at night,
and it would be a very strange misfortune if a south-easterly
gale should blow up that very night.

Samuel Mikkelsen had never been of an irresponsible
nature, but neither had he ever been one of those quickest to
move, especially when the wine came on the table. He was
now sitting in a golden cabin, the likes of which he had never
seen before and although he was outwardly but a man dressed
in homespun, he soon had such a sense of inner wellbeing that
he felt completely at home.

Strange to think that these Frenchmen had come to take
on water. That was not much of a drink with which to show
hospitality. There was plenty of water in the Faroes, especially
when the French were providing wine in exchange.

The judge translated his thoughts, and the officers on the
ship were surprised that this clan chieftain or Finn or whatever
was able to express himself so elegantly. They had all the
time been polite to the three Faroese, and now they became

exceedingly so.

They were not themselves inclined to set sail that evening. They had been at sea for two and a half months. Kongshavn and Vestmannahavn were as dead as ditchwater as far as they could understand, but here in Tórshavn there must at least be a few people – were there no girls, so they could have a dance? The judge was most inclined to say unfortunately not. But Samuel Mikkelsen was reluctant to miss the opportunity of repaying such splendid friendship on the part of their guests, so if the officers could derive just a little pleasure from a dance, that was the least they could do for them.

And so it was agreed that a dance and some sort of celebration should be arranged in the Royal Store warehouses, and boats were sent ashore carrying lanterns and flags and barrels of wine and other articles that could serve to give a festive air to the stone cellar beneath the outermost of the buildings on Tinganes.

As the hour approached, most of the citizens of Tórshavn gathered on Tinganes to see the foreign gentlemen come ashore. There were rumours of the splendour on board. The admiral, Count de Casteljaloux had admittedly neither actors nor actresses on board, as it had been heard was the case with a small number of French marshals when they went to war. But he had an orchestra and a library, a librarian, a butler and numerous valets. Never before had there been such a distinguished man on the Faroe Islands.

The ships turned their high, carved sterns to the shore. Candles had been lit on board, and through the glass windows it was possible to see into the cabins. The sea roared noisily around the point. People stood in the stiff evening wind and stared out there. They talked about big ships that had visited the islands before, the *Lion of Norway* that had been wrecked on New Year's night off Lambareidi and the *Westerbeech*, the Dutch East-Indiaman which came to grief at the foot of the mountains of Suduroy. There were some who wanted to pass the time by singing the ballad of the *Lion of Norway*, but that was far too sad and far too ridiculous an idea for this great evening. And what would their foreign visitors think?

When the sloop with the French guests came rowing towards land, they were carrying flaming torches, and every house and every hovel in Havn suddenly shone red in the darkness. All minds were transformed, and no one knew either themselves or the world any more. Widow Oluva's miserable shop down near the whipping post, something to which no one had ever paid any attention, was clearly illuminated and grinned out towards the bay. It was as though in a dream. It was as though the widow herself had thrown off her thirteen years of mourning, let herself go and drunk herself silly. Indeed even the old church tower stood out dark red against the heavens like a symbol. No one had ever seen the church tower like that before.

But no eyes dwelt long on the heavens that evening. The Frenchmen were already shouting as they rowed through the breakers. They swung the mooring ropes with great energy and poured ashore, agile and laughing to reveal their white teeth. The women of Havn no longer knew what to do with themselves. Their cold, everyday eyes greedily drank in the fierce sunshine in the strangers' eyes and the summer in their tanned skins. It was as though they were filled with fire. Their ears were gorged with the tramping of boots and the rattle of sabres, and they were carried away by a living rhythm of men.

When the animal voice of the oboe began to shrill inside the stone cellar soon afterwards, madness took possession of every heart.

Except Gabriel's. That heart could not rejoice. His eyes never left Barbara. She was dressed in the stuff he had sold her. Alas, she no longer remembered who had provided her with her splendour, and there was not the least trace of gratitude in her thoughts. Gabriel was unknown to her, unseen by her. Her eyes opened wider and were radiant beyond recognition; she had no sense of where she was, but she simply became ever more beautiful. She should be ashamed of herself, the hussy, a harlot if ever there was one!

One of the French officers went past. Oh, of course, that had to happen, just as inevitable as tinderbox and spark. Gabriel turned away. Ugh, he did not wish to watch.

It was Captain Montgaillard, who asked Barbara for a gavotte, and with this the ball was opened.

Before long, there was not a single girl, indeed not a single younger woman, who was not on the floor. But the men of Havn turned eagerly to what they had been dreaming of all afternoon. The barrels of wine were over in one corner, and there they congregated while the admiral's men poured vast amounts of golden liquid for them. Samuel Mikkelsen, the law speaker, had seated himself by one barrel, and there he remained, quiet and Olympian, helping himself.

But Gabriel went around thinking. He calculated and calculated, but however he calculated, he came to the same damned result. There was no doubt about it. He saw the way in which Barbara's eyes admired Montgaillard's eyebrows. Faugh and faugh again! His heart burned in his breast.

There was also someone else who was not happy. That was Pastor Poul. All this had taken him completely by surprise. He had accustomed himself to the idea that he himself was a star in the black Faroese sky and in an interesting constellation with Venus; indeed a moment ago he had imagined himself dancing together with Barbara. Alas, vanity was punished as was its due. Now he saw Barbara's golden head slowly turning among white wigs and plaited hair that were turning just as sedately while he himself stood leaning against the wall and watching like some student of theology.

"Hello, brother! What sort of a face is this you are pulling on such an evening?"

He received a hearty slap on the back. It was no other than Pastor Wenzel, who had turned up, flushed and in high spirits. "No, we're going to have a good time now; and we need to, by Gad," he went on, dragging Pastor Poul over into the corner where the drinks were.

All the elite were there toasting each other. The bailiff was as red as a lantern on a ship's stern, but he was not really happy. He had imagined it different from this. Honestly! Here stood the cream of society, but the guests were not the slightest bit interested in them. Just look at that lieutenant – he didn't think himself too good to pay court to and even caress Sara, the daughter of the chap who fished stones up from the sea.

The Royal Store manager made no comment as to how he had imagined things. He was pale grey, and the sweat sat in thousands of tiny pearls all over his face; his leaden eyes shone sombrely across the dancers. If anyone was following the direction in which he was looking, they would have seen his wife, Mathilde. She was strangely vivacious in the arms of one of the French officers.

The judge was leaning against a beam, bent and amused. But Pastor Wenzel was in quite high spirits and said to the law speaker, "Well, if the store manager is cuckolded this evening, I shan't have to be bothered about being a cuckold's cuckold, ha ha ha."

The law speaker hardly commented on this. He sat there

like some deity by his barrel and had enough in himself as the dance swirled around him.

Pastor Poul was not really in the mood for drinking. The music was making a meaningless din in his head, and the wine tasted of nothing. He heard a voice close to his ear: "Just look at Barbara. She's dancing with another now. It will be interesting to see who finally gets her this evening."

He turned round. The speaker was Gabriel, and his voice was full of contempt and indignation, but he suddenly switched to a gentle, solemn tone: "Aye, just you study her carefully this evening. You will learn a great deal from that."

He went away, almost on the point of tears. He had drunk several cups, though that was not customary for him. He usually left that to those less able to keep account. But the world was all in disarray this evening and there could be no thought of doing any business.

Barbara danced with her head held high; she knew the steps and figures, then she made more steps and figures – a quite different kind of arithmetic. The madness of the dance suddenly caught Gabriel. His heart was bursting, but in a funny way. He heard the oboe, constantly telling the same little story, while the bassoon chuckled and made a frivolous contribution. He felt gloriously crazy; he felt dizzy and he had to chuckle.

Faces known and unknown were whirling and turning around him. The stone walls screeched and resounded with music. His maid Angelika was over there being kissed by a count – was that not ridiculous? Over there in the doorway stood Whoops and several others of her sort, the saucy nymphs from the Royal Store – oh, God have mercy! Their eyes stood on end; they were full of gestures, but they only had each other to flirt with for they were far too down at heel. And behind them, right out in the darkness, the men were standing like wolves, the light gleaming in their eyes as they stared hungrily at the Promised Land. Beach Flea's sorrowful features could be seen in a hatch right up under the ceiling. His sullen eyes were as though nailed to the wine. And over there sat the law speaker, immovable at his barrel. But both the law speaker and the barrel by which he sat and the cask on which he was sitting and Beach Flea in the hatch and the women in the doorway and Angelika and the count were spinning round in a huge circle. And the bows on the musicians' violins were going slowly up and down.

Gabriel had tears in his eyes. His heart was burning, but never mind, never mind! He suddenly understood everything, even the meaning of life itself. Beauty, too, he understood; he had never understood it before, but now there was a ringing in his brain and a sobbing in his breast.

Things were very different with Pastor Poul. He could not drink; he heard nothing and saw nothing; he was filled with ever increasing distress.

The hall suddenly fell silent. The music died away and the dancing stopped. Something was happening outside. One word was whispered from mouth to mouth.

"The Admiral."

Within a few seconds a lane had formed; rapiers flew from their sheaths and Admiral Count de Casteljaloux entered. He greeted people and smiled all around, and all the foreign officers stood there ramrod straight.

The townspeople watched in great solemnity. They had never imagined that such a great man could be so ugly. The light fell on his huge pockmarked face. His nose was big and twisted, his eyes protruding, and his broad lips were constantly in motion as though all the time he were remembering some fine sauce he had tasted. But he strode with such merry dignity that it was a great pleasure to observe him, and afterwards everyone had to admit that they had never seen a finer gentleman.

Some of the officers gathered around him, talking and laughing. Captain Montgaillard made some suggestion, but the admiral looked sceptical. Then the admiral began to give him assurances and became quite serious.

Gabriel had gone across to Barbara, who suddenly found herself on her own, and said something foolish to her. She smiled and only appeared pleased to hear it. At that moment, Montgaillard came and led her to the admiral, and Barbara curtseyed as elegantly as she was able.

Orders were given to the orchestra. The musicians bent over their music and turned the pages. Wax candles burnt on all the music stands, the yellow glow from them shining on white wigs, blue velvet coats and huge lace cuffs.

Then the conductor struck up. A complete silence fell over the cellar. Outside, the waves broke heavily.

The tone of a flute began to tremble in the room and another replied; it was like two lonely birds talking to each other; then, suddenly, the beautiful voices of the violins joined in with a flowering melody. This was the admiral's minuet, and he danced it with Barbara.

A moment later, it was all over, and it was not repeated. But the elegant sun of Versailles had shone on the salt cellar out on Tinganes, where breakers were wont to lash the windows of a winter's night.

Pastor Poul went outside; he was completely superfluous. Fancy that he had ever been able to flatter his heart with the idea that there should be any link between him and this woman. He now saw the chasm that existed between them. God had taken the veil from his face and shown him his own

100

foolishness.

But he felt no gratitude to God. His body was on fire.

He walked and walked. The night was not completely dark. But everything he saw, houses and gables and windows, only reminded him of the joy that had been his when he last came this way.

Finally, he had returned to the festivities. Most people had gone down to the point to see the admiral go on board again.

At that moment, Barbara came across to him, warm and radiant, and whispered in his ear: "Should we two not take a little walk together?"

Her voice was close and childlike.

They went. But Gabriel was left behind. He turned pale and completely sober. This was more than anything he could work out. The bitch!

The houses, the gables and the windows in town reminded Pastor Poul of a joy that had been lost, but which was now found again. They spoke but little.

Suddenly, Barbara said: "You are not enjoying yourself at all this evening."

She almost sounded a little humble.

Pastor Poul felt her hand. He grasped it passionately, but she merely played with his fingers. She looked at him, briefly, with uncertain eyes, and then she slowly lowered her gaze.

"No, but the Frenchmen are having a wonderful time," he replied at last. He was not in control of his voice.

A little smile spread over Barbara's lips. She still stood looking down: "Yes... but..."

Suddenly, her voice rang out: "They'll be gone tomorrow, won't they."

She looked at him. There was again an almost comical uncertainty in her eyes. She pressed his hand quite gently and said it again: "Won't they?"

Pastor Poul was quite dizzy. When Barbara said that she wanted to go home, he went with her. Then he, too, went home. Instinctively he kept away from the festivities. He had to take care of his happiness; he felt it was made of extremely brittle glass.

But Barbara went straight back to the ball.

The entire cellar was a dark confusion of drunken folk. The oboes were still speaking their strange seductive language, but no further seductiveness was needed: it was all breaking up; the law speaker alone was sitting immovable in the place he had made his own. He once put his hand to his forehead as though to wipe something away. That shawm! His head reverberated with the unpleasant sound it was making.

Johan Hendrik, the judge, came staggering towards Barbara. Never before had she seen him so humiliated. She avoided him and made for Montgaillard, who was leaning against the wall with his arms crossed. His powerful lips broke into a smile; he took her arm and spoke. Barbara did not understand the words, but she understood the melody. She looked at his face, quite close to hers; his smiling eyes were golden and as it were full of light; she felt his lips, he kissed her powerfully and passionately.

Gabriel saw it. He went outside and without beating about the bush told Beach Flea that he had now, once and for all, abandoned all hope of making a decent person out of Barbara, for she was simply not worth it.

Then he went in again. He saw Barbara in Montgaillard's arms. They sat down together by a barrel and started to drink.

It was all a cauldron of shouting and tramping. Some fresh air came in through the door. The lanterns swung slowly in the air, the shadows from their frames crossing each other and dancing on the walls. Gabriel went down into the storage cellar nearby. It was almost dark, but the entire cellar was alive. All around, between hides, barrels of tallow and casks of butter the couples all sat. He felt his official dignity rise – he was responsible for this cellar – he staggered around on a tour of inspection. But who cared about Gabriel this evening? All around, he heard gasps and sniggers, murmuring in French and howls in Faroese. He saw his girl, Angelika, blind drunk and sinfully naked among a chorus of Frenchmen. He recognised a skirt. He had himself sold it to Suzanne Harme. It was incredible what that proud Suzanne was allowing a young French officer to do to her. But what did he care about Suzanne? She was only Suzanne after all. He was drunk; he was tired; he was in despair; his eyes were extinguished, his hands were numb.

He went back, again passing Montgaillard and Barbara. He pulled himself together. He could say something to her, of course. Of course – what was more natural? But he could simply not find his own voice, and when he finally did manage to control it, he did not recognise it. Nothing at all came of it. But then the judge arrived and he was better able to express himself.

"Well, Barbara," he said, "are you sitting by a barrel? I thought you had had enough of *barrels*."

"It depends what's in them," blethered Gabriel coarsely.

Barbara stared at them, tipsy and scornful. Montgaillard did not understand what the drunks were saying.

Gabriel and Johan Hendrik walked out to the point. They suddenly discovered they were the best of friends. They had otherwise not been able to stand each other.

No. Who the hell should be bothered about Barbara? They were both agreed on that. They confirmed this with numerous embraces, and they looked deep into each other's eyes. And the new Vágar minister. If he had any ideas, ha, ha, ha. Gabriel had to laugh. He was in the middle of Tinganes, laughing at the top of his voice at the new Vágar parson. The bloody fool.

And thank God that neither of them – Johan Hendrik or Gabriel – was married. Thank God for that. They were just about the only ones here in Havn this evening who were not being cuckolded. So thank God for that.

But then Johan Hendrik said that that was all right, but that in the eyes of God he was nevertheless a miserable cuckold. And Gabriel admitted that if he was to be honest, so was he, in his heart of hearts, into which God could see, a miserable, pitiful cuckold. Even if he was Gabriel on the outside.

They were both very down, and the night was long.

When they returned to the cellar, the festivities were over. The candles had burnt down and one of the lanterns in the ceiling had started to flicker. There were no musicians and no dancing. Only a few people were wandering around like shadows on the deserted floor. Someone came up from the cellar store. It was Captain Montgaillard and Barbara. She was staggering as she held on to his arm, unbuttoned and in shameful disorder. The red silk ribbons on her dress hung there, crumpled and dead like crushed roses. There was the sound of wine squelching in her shoes.

Suddenly, she stopped, threw back her head and laughed. She took off one shoe and poured its red contents over the floor. And at that moment she caught sight of Johan Hendrik. She quickly hid her hot face on Montgaillard's shoulder and uttered a prolonged sound half way between a laugh and a sigh. Her wet, shiny stocking foot sought the shoe that had fallen on the floor.

Gabriel and Johan Hendrik stood watching this. But then

Montgaillard lost patience. He wrapped his cloak around Barbara and carried her out. One of her stockings had slipped down to her ankle and her bare leg hung there swinging to and fro. Wine dripped from her feet.

Johan Hendrik had collapsed on a wine barrel with his face hidden in his hands. He suddenly looked up. In a dreadful falsetto he suddenly sang out:

> *And what is this frame*
> *Adorned by the world with so wondrous a name*

Gabriel leant against the wall in a violent fit of drunken tears. He joined in at times. In his hand he held a garter. He had found it on the floor. It was one of the pair he had once sold to Barbara.

The singing continued its uneven progress. At times they were on the point of coming to a standstill, and at times it unexpectedly progressed well. It was like sailing a ship in heavy seas. But they helped each other out, the two of them, often looking deep into each other's eyes – they understood each other so well, and their souls wept together as they sang and confessed:

> *Black envy is ever now ready to chafe,*
> *In secret you hurt and so seldom feel safe*
> *And often you wonder at others' profanity –*
> *Aye, vanity*
> *Aye, vanity.*

But Gabriel held on to the garter. It was *that* to which he often addressed his singing. He grumbled at it and punished it:

Your matches, your kindling, your fast flying spark
So many have sent into ne'er-ending dark...

The plaintive tones slowly died away in the stone cellar. Gabriel and the judge went home. Everything was deserted now and the last lanterns were burning down. There were sounds of gentle movement in a corner. It was the law speaker, Samuel Mikkelsen, rising from his barrel. He was so ungainly – even a little more than usual. But there was a tender smile on his face. From up in the town the singing could still be heard:

Then now fare thee well, now farewell,
No longer deceit shall you heap on my soul...

Rain

The big boat from the Redoubt had been launched and was now close to the Hoist, waiting for the law speaker and Pastor Poul, who were to be conveyed to Vágar.

It was a long and difficult journey they had before them. On the first day they were to go by boat to Kollafjord and then by foot through the valley to Kvívík. The following day they had to go over the sound to Futaklett on Vágar and then across the mountains to Sandavág. The law speaker was not keen to choose this route; he was not fond of walking and preferred to sail all the way. But it was wintertime and sailing south around Kirkjubónes was not to be advised.

The ten soldiers in the boat from the Redoubt had a long wait. This was something to which they were accustomed when they were to convey the law speaker. They sat there saying they hoped not to miss the favourable current. That was a regular subject of conversation. For the current did not wait for the law speaker's tardiness even if everyone else did. They had discovered this on a couple of occasions.

It was two days after the visit by the French ships and everyday life had returned in abundance. The town had slept throughout most of the Monday. People had talked and talked that evening, and many curious things had been revealed. But today it was Tuesday and the skies were overcast.

The minister came walking along. Shortly afterwards the

law speaker appeared, obviously in no hurry.

"Oh, by the way," he remarked as though referring to some very unimportant matter, one almost designed to awaken the other's sympathy: "Barbara has asked if she could come along. I'm sure she'll be here soon."

He turned away and it looked as though he had not said anything at all.

A hint of exasperation could be seen on the men's faces. "The east flow will soon be over," commented Niels the Punt in a surly but irascible voice.

Samuel Mikkelsen made no reply. The crew mumbled discontentedly. Waiting for the law speaker was one thing. But waiting for a woman! They knew this one. There would be no end to it. In general – women and boats! Women shouldn't be allowed in boats; women were a nuisance in a boat, a bother to all with their scarves and shawls and their endless cackling. Worse than a cartload of poultry.

Gabriel came out of the store, pasty and rotund. Nothing to do today. He chatted with the law speaker and the minister. There was something or other he ought to have told Pastor Poul, but the law speaker was there. Besides, Gabriel didn't care; if Pastor Poul wanted to make a fool of himself, then let him. He *had* been warned.

It was half an hour before Barbara came. The east flow had probably finished ages ago, and there had been a lot of spitting in the East Bay on that account, some of it deep and philosophical and some truculent and angry. There was no doubt now that they would have to row against the west flow. But Barbara came along quite cheerfully. She held out a hand to Niels the Punt and asked him to help her down into the boat. Her voice was bright and light-hearted.

The Redoubt boat lurched heavily when the law speaker

stepped aboard; it rocked vigorously after the shock, but the law speaker's face was completely unaffected. He settled in the stern. Then they put off. Gabriel was left alone on the jetty, becoming smaller and smaller as they moved away.

The oars creaked and squeaked against the thole pins. The boat moved forward quickly and jerkily. The river, the judge's residence and Nýggjastova disappeared behind the tongue of land holding the Redoubt. Gongin followed; then came Reyn with the black church tower and after it the Royal Store buildings out in Havn and then the furthermost area where the festivities had taken place and finally the low spit of land on which Tinganes stood. The town was gone. They were rowing along a desolate coast.

When Pastor Poul saw Tórshavn for the first time, he had thought that he had arrived at some underworld town. But now he felt as though it was the world itself of which he was taking leave. He sat in the stern of the boat together with the law speaker and Barbara. They were constantly rocked up and down. The law speaker was steering. One moment his figure could be seen high up against the grey sky, and the next moment he was deep down between walls of foam-tipped water towering above his gentle head.

Pastor Poul had sailed the long way from Copenhagen, but he had never experienced the sea as it was today. He was so close to it; he felt its power trembling in the boat's timbers, indeed he even felt it right up his own back. He only needed to reach out a hand and it was in the waves; he looked down into them and saw the green refractions of the light.

But not a drop came into the boat. The men sat there cheerfully and comfortably and chatted with each other. The sail was hoisted. It spread out like a bird above their heads.

"You're not going to be seasick, Barbara?" said the law

speaker.

"No... Barbara?" shouted Ole Atten in his hoarse voice: "I've never seen another woman who could manage the sea so well. No one has ever seen her seasick, no one at all."

"No, she will soon be used to the sea," added the law speaker. He gave Barbara a kindly look. But his kindly eyes betrayed just the flicker of a smile.

"And she's not afraid either," Ole Atten continued his chattering.

"Oh yes, God knows I'm afraid," exclaimed Barbara suddenly. "I hate Holmesund."

She had grasped Pastor Poul by the arm. He felt that she really was afraid. A black, rocky islet lay before them. The sea was breaking heavily around it, generously donating of its abundance and never giving the rocks time to run dry again. Between this islet and the mainland there was a narrow sound, full of reefs with the sea seething over them. Pastor Poul, too, felt he shuddered a little as he saw the boat turn into these difficult waters. He looked at the law speaker, but Samuel Mikkelsen just nodded back; "The weather is fine." Shortly afterwards he added, turning benevolently towards the crew: "Your east flow is lasting well today. It hasn't turned yet."

All this talk about the east flow had been something of an exaggeration. Niels the Punt admitted that there was still a bit of it left. They had just managed it.

In reality, the current was still flowing almost like that of a river north through Holmesund. The boat was dancing on top of it like a cork. It was so close to the cliffs on the port side that that the blades of the oars almost touched land. Pastor Poul could still feel Barbara's nervous grasp on his arm. But the law speaker sat at the rudder as immovable as though he was playing chess.

Suddenly the water became calm. They were out of the sound. To the north, the mountain tops of Eysturoy stood out black and sharp. But the men expected rain. The clouds were low over Nolsoy.

It was past noon when they reached Kollafjord.

"I take it you are going to row us as far as Oyrareingja," said Samuel Mikkelsen innocently to the crew. "It's such a long walk along the fjord."

"It's a long way home," mumbled Niels the Punt. "And the wind's against us... and the west flow won't simply wait for us."

"The west flow – good lord, Niels," said the law speaker. "The west flow will surely last a long time yet. It's hardly begun."

No one made any answer to this. It could be that the oar strokes became a little resentful. The law speaker sat there looking deadly serious, but perhaps he was smiling a little, deep down inside. They made land at the end of the fjord. The men took the baggage up from the boat. It was the law speaker who had brought least – he had only a small chest. But he asked them to be very careful with it. It contained some stoneware for his wife. Then he started on his dignified way. Pastor Poul and Barbara followed him.

The farm of Oyrareingja was a little way away, in the middle of a small area of flat land but overhung by enormous rock faces. They towered up and disappeared in the clouds. There was the rushing of the river, but otherwise no sound was to be heard other than that of the pale grass rustling at their feet. The farmer came to meet them. Would the crew not come inside, too?

"I don't think they'll say no to that," said Samuel Mikkelsen.

The hearth room was somewhat crowded with the arrival of

all these men. They were so diffident and shy on land, standing lined up to receive a dram that the farmer poured for them. Niels the Punt came last with a warm look in his eyes. Aye, aye, that was very kind of you, but the west flow...

"The west flow will last until six o'clock," said the farmer. "Surely you'll have a bite to eat before you leave?"

Pastor Poul felt the need to go outside for a moment. He found an enclosure between two outhouses. It was infinitely quiet and delightful here. The law speaker was already there.

"Oh, this is a fine place," said Pastor Poul.

"Yes," replied the law speaker, smiling rather uncertainly: "Particularly if the right use is made of it."

He offered a bottle to Pastor Poul. But the clergyman wondered at the fact that in a country where there was so much occasion to drink, there was so little provision for taking the consequences of drinking. He took a small gulp and continued restlessly along the walls of the house which consisted of loose boulders and turf. But the law speaker appeared not to have any concerns of such an earthly character. He pursued his relationship with his bottle.

Rain had started to fall. The farm of Oyrareingja lay resting on its stretch of level land. The grass covered it like a carpet right up to the roof ridges, and up through the louvre the peat smoke rose in rings of blue. The cattle were lowing in the sheds. But in the kitchen the pans were suspended over the fire. The men from Havn watched with shining eyes – it was not every day they had the prospect of farm food.

When the law speaker returned, he started to discuss horses with the farmer. Could he not borrow a horse? He was so awkward and slow at walking. It would be a pity for Barbara and Pastor Poul if he held them back on their way through the valley in the rain. But if he had a horse to sit on, they would better be able to go all at the same pace.

Yes, he could have a horse with pleasure. The farmer asked if Barbara and Pastor Poul would not also like to have horses, but Barbara did not want one, she was not going to sit and get cold. And Pastor Poul agreed with Barbara.

They finally set off in miserable rainy weather.

Was *that* a horse? Pastor Poul had never seen one like it. Nor did it look particularly happy. It stood there with its eyes closed. Its tail hung straight down, its mane hung straight down and its ears hung straight down. The rain was also falling straight down.

The law speaker asked the crew to be careful with his box. There was a bit of stoneware in it, he said. For his wife. Then he climbed into the saddle, almost causing the horse to capsize. A secret smile spread from mouth to mouth. Perhaps there was also a touch of one in the law speaker's own eyes. He could presumably almost imagine what it looked like. But his voice was gentle and quiet as always when he said goodbye, and the people from the farm took leave of him with great respect.

The tiny horse put one leg in front of the other; the law speaker's enormous body swayed slowly on its back, and in this way he meekly disappeared into the wet mist.

Pastor Poul and Barbara followed after him; the grass swished gently around their legs, and they immediately got wet feet. Barbara turned her heavy outer skirt up over her knees and walked in her striped underskirt. A spirited woman she certainly was. Her face was wet, but her eyes were radiant.

The two men from the boat crew followed a little way behind with their burden. They were not happy about having to make the trip in this weather.

The rain poured down. All that could be seen in the dense mist was the wet outline of heather-covered mounds and banks of peat. So as not to lose their way, they had to keep to the river all the time. Its waters rose and rose and gradually became increasingly filthy with soil and mud. They kept encountering streams running down from the sides of the valley to the river. The law speaker's horse tramped through thick and thin, but Barbara jumped over the streams. Pastor Poul often stood and hesitated before daring to follow her.

"Jump," she shouted to him with a laugh.

He was not used to such ground as this, full of stones and hummocks, marshy patches and peat banks. He could only admire Barbara's feet, the way in which they unhesitatingly always found the right place to step on, and the elegant way in which her legs carried her. She was quite statuesque, the way in which she went over all uneven surfaces; her bosom was held high, and she looked straight ahead. But there was a constant smile on her lips as though she was straining to reach some happy objective.

Pastor Poul suddenly felt water running down his back. He was wet to the skin.

The law speaker sat there in the pouring rain, rocking and nodding, but his face was quite serene. "I'm sure you are soaked to the skin now, Barbara," he said from his elevated seat.

Barbara laughed blissfully through the water; she chuckled, "Yes, right to the skin... just look."

She drew her skirt aside; it was stuck to her knees.

"You ought to dress like a man."

"I don't know. I think it's more fun to be a woman." She laughed again and took Pastor Poul's arm, but immediately let go again.

They had been walking for an hour and could now not become wetter than they already were. It had gradually started to grow dark. They had crossed a watershed. The river they were following now ran the other way down through the valley. The surfaces of two small lakes glistened ahead of them. The boatmen told them that they were now half way.

The law speaker himself was no fiery horseman; he just quietly allowed the horse go on as it wanted. But it was nevertheless starting to tire – it was smaller than he was of course.

They had made their way forward to a bigger lake; this was Leynum. The rock walls projected across the water, but below them the path twisted its way along the lakeside. The oarsmen explained that they must not shout or speak in loud voices here as it could cause the rocks to loosen and fall down. But there was no need to warn them; no one had spoken a word for a long time.

Pastor Poul and Barbara, who throughout had been walking fairly close to each other, sometimes in front, sometimes alongside the law speaker, had now moved very close to each other in the dusk. Sometimes, on reaching some small obstacle, they gave each other a hand. They were wading in mire; their shoes were filled with mud, and they slipped and slid on the soggy ground. The rain was falling straight into their faces; it was hopeless to try to talk to each other, and sometimes they could scarcely catch their breath in this appalling weather. But Pastor Poul was in a good mood and felt refreshed. It was as though he was being drawn into a splendid new life founded on something sweet and precious.

Some way down in the intense darkness they caught sight of a couple of faint lights. Barbara shouted to him that these were the houses in Leynum. They stopped for a moment to wait for the others. Samuel Mikkelsen emerged from the gloom like a huge, tame centaur.

"We'd better go to Ole Jacob's in Leynum," he said. "He will give us shelter. The rivers are so full this evening. It will be impossible to get across them and reach Kvívík."

The oarsmen joined them. They agreed, and Barbara also thought this was a splendid idea. It was always so boring to spend the night with the parson and his family in Kvívík... whatever people might say. But Pastor Poul suddenly discovered that he was sorry that this expedition would soon be at an end. He would have been happy to go through great rivers together with Barbara.

A quarter of an hour later, they were in the croft at Ole Jacob's farm in Leynum. The law speaker gently raised the latch and slid in through the low door huge and gentle. The others followed one after the other and remained just inside the door. They all looked as though they had just been brought up from the depths of the sea. The fire was burning bright in the hearth, and the room was full of people all staring in silence at the new arrivals.

"Good evening," said Samuel Mikkelsen at last, gently and slowly.

The farmer's wife took a step towards him: "Good heavens, is it the law speaker out travelling in this weather?"

"Yes, there are five of us," said the law speaker with a slight smile.

"Bless you... come in."

Ole Jacob, the farmer, had risen and came across to shake hands with the new arrivals.

"Had we known we could expect such fine guests this evening, we would have prepared the best room," said his wife.

But Barbara laughed: "It's far cosier in the hearth room."

The saucepan containing the supper was hanging over the

fire. The girls went to and fro and were suddenly busy. But the farmhands were for the most part sitting on the benches along the wall. Some of them were carding or spinning and a couple of the older men were knitting.

The strangers were all seated. The warmth came to welcome them, and their clothes gradually began to steam.

"I imagine you need some dry clothes," said the farmer's wife.

The law speaker gave a wry smile. There could be no doubt that he was much in need of a change of clothes, but it was a fairly well known fact that there was only one single man in the country whose clothes would fit him. And this man lived somewhere far away in the north.

"I'm not really very wet," he said. "I can quite well sit here in my clothes. Perhaps I may be allowed to go to bed soon."

The farmer's wife came with her arms full of woollen clothing. She kindly started to undress Barbara.

"Oh, that's lovely," said Barbara. She smiled contentedly and relaxed all her limbs as though they were tired.

But Pastor Poul suddenly fell into a state of extreme agitation. It came all of a sudden. He jumped up and went across the floor; he was not himself aware that he was doing it.

Barbara was soon almost naked; she was like a white sheen in the hearth room. She was not in the least embarrassed at the extremely natural way in Leynum; she was herself quite natural and free. But though seemingly oblivious, she all the time ensured that no one saw anything improper or secret or sufficient of her bare skin to become dazzled by it. On one occasion she was a little unfortunate. She covered her breast again like lightning. But Pastor Poul had seen it. She suddenly blushed deeply. Those who noticed this were a little surprised – according to all they had heard, they were not under the

117

impression that Barbara was the type to blush.

Pastor Poul had sat down again. His heart was beating so powerfully that it almost hurt, and he was trembling a little all over. Two of the servant women started to help him out of his wet clothes. He scarcely knew how he managed to change.

By then, Barbara had long been dressed – in thick, heavy peasant garments. But her face was small and bright and cheerful.

The law speaker thought he would rather go and lie down if no one minded. He had a box that it was best he took with him; there was some cough mixture in it that was good to take at night.

They asked him whether he was ill. No, he was not. He was shown into the best room and a candle was fixed in a candlestick and lighted.

The conversation, which had died down for a time because of the arrival of the strangers, had started to pick up again. They had all been amazed to hear of the French ships that had been in Tórshavn, but in reality it seemed to them to be a far greater event that they themselves had received such distinguished guests this evening. The law speaker was the most important man in the islands. His enormous trousers were at that moment hanging to dry up under the roof. They were swaying to and fro majestically. But a brand new parson was also worth seeing, although attention centred most of all on Barbara.

She sensed it, and she was radiant. She knew how to talk to everyone and had a special ability to find the meek among them and encourage them with a couple of words. She delighted in their gratitude and admiration. It was not long before she had discovered that old Tormod had been interrupted in the midst of a story when the guests had arrived. She sat down on a stool in front of him and asked him to go on.

Old Tormod sat by the fireplace. His clothes were covered in peat dust and ashes, and his white head, the head of an old man, trembled slightly all the time. He excused himself at first. It was only an old wives tale, he said, which no one could be bothered listening to, least of all a parson and a learned man, who doubtless knew far better. But he was easy to tempt, and bit by bit he started telling about the little people whom men and women could encounter out in the field when least expecting to.

The farmer's wife was busy. She shouted to Tormod and told him to stop all that nonsense. He must remember he was going into his second childhood. How could he think the visitors could be bothered to listen to such rubbish?

But Tormod did not hear her. He sat with a distant look in his half-closed eyes and told how Pastor Rasmus Ganting came along the shore at Sørvág one summer's day. There was a green mound there and it was open. There was a woman standing in the doorway, and she invited him inside. Another woman brought beer in a silver cup and gave it to him to drink. But before drinking, Pastor Rasmus blew all the froth from the beer straight into the face of the elfin woman.

"That was a wise thing to do," she said.

"If I were not wiser than you, I would not have entered this mound," replied the parson.

The fire glowed hot beneath the saucepan. The shadows danced black along the walls. Up in the roof there was the huge shadow of the law speaker's trousers. Tormod told story after story. The knitting needles clicked and the spinning wheels hummed. He told about the man in Gásadal who had an elfin woman as his friend. She came to him at night. His real wife knew nothing of this, but one night while she lay on the inner side of the bed close to her husband, she suddenly felt a cold hand. It was the elfin woman who was lying on the edge of the bed at the other side of her husband.

They all sat listening in silence. A few had had various experiences that they could not quite explain. Their thoughts went out among the mighty fells to dark heaths and huge boulders, where the departed lived their silent lives... But the farmer's wife brought them all back to reality, for now supper was ready.

Pastor Poul was in a strange mood. He almost felt as though he himself had entered some mound. His heart was full of great disquiet and a strange feeling of comfort. As soon as he had eaten, he asked permission to go to bed. He wanted to try to gather his thoughts.

He was shown into the best room and asked to share a bed with the law speaker. The candle was lit in the frame again. It was placed on a white scoured table standing between two windows. The walls, the ceiling, everything was of wood that had been scoured white. On one side wall there was a cupboard and an alcove. On the other side wall there were two alcoves in line with each other. The law speaker lay snoring in one of these.

While undressing, Pastor Poul read the inscription on the stove:

When I did grasp a stronger foot, he carried me away,
So my advice to you my friend is mirror yourself in me.

The relief represented an eagle flying away with a man in its claws. What the reader was to mirror himself in was the man's backside. Ole Jacob explained that the old folks had said that this was Griffenfeld, who had suffered such a sorry fate.

Barbara

Pastor Poul crawled up into the alcove. The law speaker took up a great deal of room, but there was still a sufficient, warm space for the parson. He came up against something hard and smooth... and it turned out that they were two pint bottles. And they were empty. It seemed to take some time for a law speaker to get over a visit to Havn.

The light from the hearth room came in through the chink in the door. There was still plenty of life and talk out there. Barbara's laughter could be heard occasionally, happy and contented. Pastor Poul lay in the warm darkness and vainly tried to gather his thoughts for prayer. Good heavens, in what state was he arriving in his new benefice? His blood was fired with desire for Barbara.

He began to go through the day's events again. He felt the rhythm of the boat and saw the islet with the surf washing around. He leapt over all the streams in the Kollafjord Valley as the rain poured down. Barbara took him by the hand; she was so wet that her clothes clung to her and flopped around her. She was saying "jump", "jump", jump", in a different tone of voice each time. She invited him inside and gave him beer, and he forgot to blow the foam off it.

He awoke to hear something moving close to him. Someone or other was going to bed in the adjoining alcove. He saw an enormous confused shadow on the wall. It suddenly dawned on him that it was Barbara. He heard her lie down and pull the sliding door to, but there was still the sound of her rummaging around quite close by. His heart hammered in his breast.

Others came in. He heard the farmer and his wife talking quietly. They were probably sleeping in the bed opposite. The house had fallen silent. People were fidgeting about and settling down. There was now only a single maid left busy in the kitchen, baking bread in the warm ashes in the hearth.

Pastor Poul felt something scratching quite gently at his pillow. He thought it was a mouse and caught out at it. He got hold of a hand. He turned towards the bed head and looked straight into Barbara's eyes. A couple of boards were missing in the panel between the two bunks, and her head was no more than two feet from his. The final remains of light from the chink in the door fell on her face. She was desperately serious and silent; he could see that she was just as excited and affected as he was himself.

They silently caressed each other's hands and arms, staring at each other as though afraid. The light from the door became weaker and weaker, and finally they lay there in complete darkness. And there was no obstacle between them. The law speaker simply snored.

Coloured Stones

By ebb tide, the whole of the Midvág sands were white and dry. It was at this time that Barbara had the habit of coming across to Pastor Poul in Jansegærde from her dower house at Kalvelien on the other side of the bay. For then she could take such a lovely shortcut, she said. It could often sound as though she only came for the sake of this short cut. The sand was so flat and so white! And when it was such a short way to come – well then why not? She was always radiant as she said this.

Barbara had many radiant explanations for the ways and byways of her life; indeed she had a whole bag full of excuses that always shone like coloured stones and twinkled just like her own greenish yellow eyes. But although Pastor Poul well knew that it was exclusively for his sake that she came across the sands every day, it always hurt him a little when she spoke like this. For there was great turmoil in his heart.

His life was not days and nights; his life was flood tide and ebb tide. Throughout the long summer days he sat at his table and read the *Garden of Paradise*, *The Treasures of the Soul* or *The Rare Jewel of Faith*. But his mind was empty and only resounded like a shell's rush of waves as they scurried in and collapsed on the beach. His heart was on the white sand down there as it grew or shrank, and as the waters receded, the final remainder of his devotions also ebbed from his mind. Then he could only wait and wait.

He had two brass candlesticks before him on the table. There was a big chip in the foot of one of them. He knew perfectly well that this had happened once when Barbara in fury had thrown the candlestick at his predecessor, Pastor Niels. But he never thought about that. He only longed for Barbara to come as she did yesterday and the day before, to play with the inkwell and *The Spiritual Treasure*, to lay her gentle hands down on his wretched learned belongings and illuminate everything with her sparkling yellowish green eyes. During one of these painful times he spent waiting for her, he had started to write a few verses about her.

> *My fair one,*
> *My dear one*
> *My joy and delight,*
> *My angel so bright*
> *You have me now captured.*
> *I am simply enraptured*
> *My heart is in thrall*
> *To your gestures and all.*

But he could not even concentrate on these verses about Barbara. His eyes were all the time down on the sand, where he expected to see her.

When she came, she could be seen as a tall, elegant figure among all the children running around and playing down there. She was always this upright figure as she walked. But he had once seen her bend down to tie a shoelace that had come undone. Like the other women in the village, she usually wore shoes of pale, soft skin with red ribbons tied around her ankles. Her walk was so light that she left no traces; the sand was firm and ribbed in the shape made by the waves as the tide had left it. Pastor Poul often thought how it must hurt her feet to walk on this bumpy terrain and how the gravel and the small stones must cut into her heels and the soles of her feet. He loved her feet, which every day took all these steps to come to him, and which sprang so nimbly across the river. When she reached the house, he always saw her face the moment she went past the window. Her expression was deadly serious; her eyes were afire, and she was hurrying.

And yet he was every day afraid that she would not come, that the ebb would run out like an hourglass and flood tide again cover the entire stretch of sand. But did he have the least reason to fear this? It had so far never happened that she had not come. On the other hand it had happened that she had come unexpectedly, having walked the long way around the bay and had taken him unawares with her vehement expressions of love. And once, when she had not found him at home, she had left a brief letter on his table saying, "*My dearest frend, I could not wait so long so came strait here, for I like best to be were you are, but you weren't here. All my love, Barbara Christine Salling.*"

It was written in a terrible, restless hand. But Pastor Poul became quite dizzy and almost horrified when he read it, for he felt that this was a trembling declaration in flesh and blood and not just a glittering stone from Barbara's fairytale bag.

But it had also happened that he himself in the middle of the morning had gone up the hillside and said, "I so long to be with you." And in an unequivocal voice she had replied, "That is *good*."

When he left her again, she was standing straight, high-bosomed and rosy cheeked like a goddess, and her eyes were like glowing embers.

People in the village believed that Pastor Poul and Barbara

were betrothed, and the rumour of this had long since reached Tórshavn. Everyone shook their heads and said that it was only to be expected. But in reality, betrothal and marriage had never been mentioned between the two. They had never had time for that, for they were always much more than betrothed and married if only they saw each other.

But in lonely times it happened that the minister had misgivings that horrified him. When he turned to the heavy volume entitled *Spiritual Treasure* in search of Christian words and thoughts for his sermons, he most often only found things condemning his own way of life. It said that chastity was a necessity for a believer, that it could not be separated from the fellowship of Christ and that it was the fruit of faith. And the means to achieve it were 1) a sacred, genuine intent, 2) immediately to smother evil desires, 3) to avoid all occasion of sin, 4) to shun laziness and idleness, and 5) to mortify the flesh by fasting. Alas! As though he did not fast. His flesh would often scarcely allow him to eat, so sick and filled with longing was he for Barbara to appear. And when he had eaten it could happen that he brought his food up again.

No, he was a miserable priest, and it was only a poor consolation to him that all it said about chastity was that few could boast of it. For he was a decent man and did not know *how* few they were.

He often read until the sweat broke out on his forehead as he searched for some brief passage suggesting that God might have some slight ground for satisfaction in him and Barbara. For they loved each other so deeply and so genuinely. But he failed to reconcile Barbara and God. How could he even speak to God about Barbara? And how could he talk to Barbara about God?

He could in no way defend his actions, and yet it was

impossible for him to act differently. He had no power over himself.

But of course he could enter into a marriage with Barbara. Then everything would be different. For woman was also a most useful creation with which to combat adultery, fornication and loose living. He read this in an ancient little book that he found among the things Pastor Niels had left. It was called *A Mirror for Pious Women* and in many ways was a charming book in all it had to say about the married woman. "It is irrefutable," it said, "that it is impossible to find such good tender friends who mean so well and are so faithful to each other as God-fearing husbands and wives, who are one flesh, one body, one heart and have one will with which they share happiness and sadness, good and evil with each other, and especially the woman with her beauty, charm, love and kindness, her sweet and life-giving word is to her husband the supreme fortification in his troubles after the word of God."

When Pastor Poul read this, his heart was filled with sweetness, but at the same time with a terror that made his head whirl. He knew Barbara's history, of course, and he knew her far better than his heart would admit.

Woman is compared to a hind, which has an extremely sharp and quick sense of hearing, especially when it pricks up its ears. But when it sinks its ears, it is said to be almost deaf. Like a hind, woman, too, must open her ears when she hears the word of God or when her husband admonishes her and she must pay careful attention to what people say of her. On the other hand, she should be deaf to all Epicurean mockery of God and to the shameful words and deeds of a fool that encourage unchaste thoughts and foolish living...

But oh, Barbara. Were there any words of Epicure that were not immediately caught by her ears and caused her senses to tremble? Was there any subtle remark that did not immediately bring life to her eyes? Was there any game that she was not immediately willing to play?

Pastor Poul was like the fowler hanging on his rope and daring to look neither up nor down.

For if he raises his eyes to heaven, the line is lost to sight in the distance, and it seems he is hanging on a thread that has been cut. But if he looks down, he realises the horrors of the pit.

He scarcely dared to think. He only dared to live. His happiness drew him mercilessly on through the summer days; his happiness was a trembling, fleeting hind whose ears were always raised and alert.

Except in church. But Pastor Poul's sermons were not good.

Barbara, who noticed everything, also noticed that her beloved was not entirely happy, and she felt that as a profound affront. One day when they were talking about their love, she said, "Every time I give you all my hand, you only give me your little finger."

Pastor Poul was so amazed at this that he remained silent for a long time. That was not as he had understood it, no, far from it, the contrary in fact.

"You don't give me your whole hand," he said. "You don't because you can't."

Now it was Barbara's turn to be amazed. She flushed a little and hurried to counter, "I give you everything I have to give you."

She looked rather upset. Pastor Poul walked up and down the floor. Then he suddenly exclaimed, "Barbara. You know I have my calling."

"Yes, but can I not help you a bit?"

She ran over to him, flung her arms round his neck and asked with such intensity: "Can I not help you a little?"

Pastor Poul remembered the little note from Barbara and how terribly badly it was written. It was as helpless as a prayer; it was the most touching thing he knew about her – he treasured it like a piece of her own soul.

Barbara looked at him in child-like enthusiasm. Her eyes were quite comical: "I can write all right when someone dictates to me."

The parson was as though intoxicated by it. Christian Scriver's *Treasures of the Soul* lay on the table and was so delightfully sweetened. Barbara clapped her hands. She suggested that they should write a sermon straight away – now, immediately. But Pastor Poul said no. He wanted to think about it first. They could start tomorrow.

Barbara said she would come early the following day. She was so blissfully happy; she kissed him again and again when she went.

"Now I am sure we shall have a wonderful time together. For, you see," she added in a quiet voice, "I can now be part of everything you do. Don't you see?"

Pastor Poul walked around for a long time and knew neither what he was doing nor what he was saying. He caught himself reciting two lines of a hymn:

Hallelujah, God is great
And heaven replies: Amen.

Barbara came the following day ready to write. She had so many quills with her that the minister had to laugh. He asked whether the geese up in Kalvelien were completely naked now that Barbara was going to write a sermon. But she explained that she had spoiled her pens so because she wrote so quickly.

She sat down enthusiastically at the table, placed the paper obliquely in front of her, put her head on one side and, as soon as Pastor Poul started to dictate, set about writing eagerly, her tongue protruding just a little from her mouth. Her hair fell a little down over her forehead; her face became more and more flushed as the pen scratched and sputtered.

Never had Pastor Poul imagined anything like this – that this beautiful woman should become his obedient and eager assistant. His happiness increased like a bubble and grew light and unconstrained. Suddenly, all his emotions deserted him; he thought of other things and had ideas. Barbara's bookish qualities, God help her, were probably not exactly outstanding. But as she sat there she could presumably be of help to him. Yes, even those simple geese were the instruments of the spirit and learning, for they were the source of the quills. For a moment he was filled with elation. Then he became disheartened. In his relationship with Barbara he had never had any sense of superiority, only of devotion. He felt a deep want and went over and stood by the window and made himself a peephole through the condensation on it. All was green and luxuriant outside, and mist was drifting across the grass.

Barbara put in a full stop, ceased writing and looked up: "What more?"

She brushed her hair from her forehead and was flushed with excitement.

"Let me see what you've written."

She handed him the sheet. It was adorned with big letters, dancing about enthusiastically, untidily and all rising towards the right top corner of the paper. The spelling was indifferent, but readable.

Then he discovered something and in a voice full of pain exclaimed, "Jesus."

Barbara did not at first understand what he meant. She suddenly blushed scarlet.

"Barbara. Oh, you can't even spell Jesus."

"Oh." She quickly snatched the sheet from him, sat down again and with the tip of her tongue between her teeth and with a scratching pen she quickly and determinedly crossed out *Jeses* and wrote the word properly above it. Then she handed him the paper, happy and almost triumphant.

But Pastor Poul did not take it. He sat on his chair, pale and staring at her. Barbara grew confused. It looked at first as though she was searching in her bag for some brightly coloured stone with which to gladden him again. But her heart was too wise. She suddenly understood who Jesus was and grew unhappy.

She went across to Pastor Poul, but he held his face in his hands. She was embarrassed and fiddled uncomfortably with his shoulder and then she gently touched his hair and his cheek, finally whispering quite softly in his ear: "You mustn't be angry with me."

He made a fierce movement.

"Get away, you... you... it is not me you have to ask for forgiveness."

Barbara went over to the window and drew some helpless signs and lines in the condensation. She was miserable, overcome with shame and despair. And the clergyman was filled increasingly with concern. He sat there slumped in his chair. This was the first time there had been an angry word between him and Barbara. He quite forgot his anger. And yet he could not persuade himself to go across to her.

"Of course," Barbara finally murmured in a broken voice, "of course this was a terribly silly idea of mine. For I am not worthy... I'm a sinner."

And she drew an array of long lines in the condensation. It looked as though she was undertaking some very important task.

Pastor Poul sat in silence for a time. Then he asked her: "Are you... are you a very great sinner?"

Barbara turned towards him. Her eyes were intensely fearful as she looked at him.

"Yes."

Then she ran across and knelt before the priest and embraced his knees and hid her face. And so she knelt for a long time without either of them saying a word. But this time it was he who played just a little with her hair.

He was fundamentally embarrassed. What had he done? He did not know what it was that this reminded him of. Perhaps it was some dream. But it was at any rate something very shameful. He began to see himself as a tiny man, an insignificant man with the pointing finger of a Pharisee. But here was a great sinner, a woman weeping before him.

Suddenly, he came to think of Simon the Leper's house and his heart was delivered. He had it. He got up and leafed in the Bible to the seventh chapter of St Luke.

"Barbara, will you listen?" he asked.

She nodded, sullen and silent.

"And behold. A woman in the city who was a sinner, when she knew that Jesus sat at meat in the Pharisee's house, brought an alabaster box of ointment, and stood at his feet behind him..."

Barbara sat in total silence while he read to her. She gave Poul an occasional stolen, frightened look. But he read on to her about the woman's humility and about the Pharisee's self-justification, and he reached Jesus's parable of the man who had two debtors. "The one owed five hundred pence, and the other fifty. And when they had nothing to pay, he frankly forgave them both. Tell me therefore, which of them will love him most?"

Barbara started. It was as though something suddenly dawned upon her and she was on the point of making an exclamation.

But the parson continued to read more of Jesus's words: "And he turned to the woman and said unto Simon, Seest thou this woman?"

Now Barbara was trembling and she became very embarrassed. For she was the woman, of course, and her heart had turned into an alabaster pot of ointment. Never had she given and never had she received as now.

"I entered into thy house, thou gavest me no water for my feet; but she hath washed my feet with tears and wiped them with the hairs of her head. Thou gavest me no kiss, but this woman since the time I came in hath not ceased to kiss my feet. My head with oil thou didst not anoint, but this woman hath anointed my feet with ointment. Wherefore I say unto thee, her sins, which are many, are forgiven; for she loved much, but to whom little is forgiven, the same loveth little."

As these last words were read to her, Barbara started to brighten up. Her golden eyes shone, afraid and happy. But Pastor Poul sat motionless and silent. He was completely taken aback. He had learned something quite new about God's infinite mercy.

"Thank you, Poul," said Barbara. She was dreadfully ashamed. "I thought God had rejected me long ago," she whispered, embracing him blindly and passionately as never before.

But Pastor Poul had to say to her, "Dearest of all, *I* am not the one to be thanked. I will go outside for a time so you can be alone here as in a closet and thank God for His words."

How she managed to thank God, Barbara scarcely knew herself. But if it was sweet – and that it undoubtedly was – it was also short. For one two three, she was outside in the open with Pastor Poul, chirping like a bird.

The fog was dispersing and was now illumined by the sun's rays. A gentle warmth was weaving its way in through the drizzle, gently burning their skin. And the green infield of Midvág lay smiling among the figures created by the rising mist. Buttercups and cowslips shone golden in the grass. But every blade was still heavy with dew.

It was ebb tide now, but that was of no significance.

Barbara was happy; she took Pastor Poul by the arm and said that they should go up to the lake, to Sørvág Lake.

When they reached the brown heath, the sun was shining in all its splendour, and the heather and the earth became dry and good to walk on. Pastor Poul walked along pondering at what had happened. It was such an inconceivable joy to him that he could scarcely believe in it. The pearl had been found now, for God and Barbara had become reconciled.

But Barbara was not thinking so much. She was walking quickly and dancing about. She was a great sinner and Jesus was her friend. She was merely thinking that Pastor Poul was not happy enough. She walked close to him and held on to his arm and interlaced her fingers with his. Then she gave him a consolatory smile and said as though to a child, "You are a sinner as well, aren't you, Poul? Yes, of course you are. We are both great sinners."

Pastor Poul did not know whether to laugh or cry. He said "Alas!" and was both burdened and happy. And Barbara smiled and consoled him still more and was not far off turning to lies and saying that even if he didn't owe 500 pence, the figure was rapidly approaching 450. But then she held back and gave him a sympathetic look. For in her heart she knew that he did not even owe 50. Poor, good Pastor Poul, she so loved him.

Pastor Poul had a feeling that her Christianity would not stand a theological test. But he merely smiled at the thought and remembered the words of the Scriptures: unless you turn and become like children... That tinder-dry book *The Treasures of the Soul* at home on his table had only confused his mind and hidden God's true love from him.

They reached the water. There it lay, black and shining, and the green and brown ridges surrounding it were reflected in it. Pastor Poul had often visited these places. When visiting his parishes of ease at Sørvág and Bø or going out on the lonely island of Mikines, this was the way he took. And he had walked out here in lonely, troubled hours. But he had never been out at Sørvág Lake together with Barbara and he felt it was a new, serious world into which he was introducing her. He had had a host of beautiful ideas regarding this area, and he longed to tell her of them.

There was a cluster of tiny huts by the lakeside. They were not houses for people to live in, but peat stores and boathouses. But it nevertheless still looked like a small village. And just at this time there were a crowd of busy people there. The people of Midvág cut their peat in the summer in the Sørvág fields on the other side of the lake, and this was just the time when the first peat was dry and ready to be transported across the water.

Pastor Poul and Barbara sat down in the heather. A single, heavily laden boat was approaching land.

"When I come here," said the parson, "I always have to think about Lake Gennesareth. I don't know why that should be. The first time I saw this lake it was like an old dream coming back to me. But then I realised that it was simply the idea of Lake Gennesareth."

Barbara hardly replied to this and perhaps she did not entirely understand it. But her bright eyes showed how she admired Pastor Poul and how her heart clung to his every word.

"These houses over here," he went on, "strike me as being just like Capernaum."

"Capernaum," shouted Barbara happily. It was now as though she better understood and suddenly felt she could take part in the conversation. "Capernaum! Was it not in Capernaum that... that..."

But then she turned to eagerly pulling heather up and looking down into the ground: "Wasn't it there that thing happened, you know...?" And she was again embarrassed.

The minister thought for a moment and then replied that St Luke said nothing about where it happened, but it could well be that it was in Capernaum, for Jesus often went there.

Barbara said that it was *probably* Capernaum. Her face was radiant and she became very engaged for now *she* had a role in the story told by Pastor Poul. This was a splendid big stone that she presented to herself, and her eyes shone golden in the sun.

"In general," said Pastor Poul, "Jesus went around in all the small villages by Lake Gennesareth, and sometimes he was over on the other side, out in the desert, preaching. I always think of that place as being over there where you can see people working."

Barbara sat for a time, chewing a blade of grass. Then, all of a sudden, she said:

"You remind me of Jonas, my first husband."

Pastor Poul did not know what to think of this and he made no reply.

"You *always* remind me of Jonas," Barbara went on. "I thought that straight away – the very first time I saw you."

"Oh, that time in the entrance to the Royal Store?"

"Yes, I had simply gone down to see what you looked like."

"Were you very fond of Pastor Jonas?" asked the priest.

"I've never been as fond of anyone as I was of Jonas. We always talked to each other just like you and I have done today, about all kinds of things, and we were never tired of being together. That was at Vidareidi... it was wonderful. But then he died, and I missed him terribly. I always, always wished it could be like that again when I was married to Jonas. But it never was."

She threw a sprig of heather down.

"What did you talk about then, you and Pastor Jonas? About God?"

"About God as well. About everything. I don't remember all that well; I was so young in those days, but when Jonas talked about God it always made me happy. It was not like when..."

She suddenly stopped.

"Like what?" asked Pastor Poul excitedly.

"Like when Anders started on his everlasting reproaches and sermons and..."

"Pastor Anders? The dean from Næs?"

"Ugh yes; he's a dean now. I suppose people have been kind enough to tell you that I was once betrothed to him? But I couldn't stand him. Always full of... retribution and condemnation... and he was always seeking to improve me."

"Were you so much in need of improvement?"

Barbara looked down: "I needed a husband like Jonas; that was all I longed for and the only thing that could keep me away from... from sin."

This last word she only managed to utter after what seemed

to be a great effort. It sounded entirely alien to her lips. But then she suddenly pulled herself together and added: "He gave me stones for bread."

"So did you tire of the word of God?" the minister asked.

"Yes," said Barbara. "I grew tired to death. But I didn't forget Jonas, and I kept on thinking that perhaps another might come... one who was like Jonas and could make everything well again."

"And then Pastor Niels came?"

"Pastor Niels!" It was as though Barbara had forgotten that she had ever been married to someone called Pastor Niels. But then she suddenly burst out: "Poor Niels! Aye, it was dreadful. And it was Dr Balzer who was responsible for it all. He made such a mess of that leg. I hate that fool."

The minister fell into deep thought. Then, at last, he asked: "Yes, but was Pastor Niels not able to lead you back to the Word of God?"

Barbara seemed at first to pull a face, but then her features softened and she said quietly, "I was terribly fond of Pastor Niels. You must believe that even if I was often a beast to him. We were terribly good friends. But... but... you know: he had such a dreadfully dreary, squeaky voice."

The minister turned away and looked down at the ground and felt quite dejected. There he saw a tiny spider busy between heather and blades of grass.

But Barbara got up, brushed something off her clothes and exclaimed:

"Come on; let's go down to the water. Perhaps we could get across to the other side on that boat."

Pastor Poul followed her. She took his hand again and intertwined her fingers in his; then she looked up at him and said, "Now we are at Lake Gennezareth and going into

Capernaum, aren't we?"

And when they entered Capernaum, she embraced him and said, "You mustn't die, you know. I can't do without you."

She was very serious, and she was trembling.

When they reached the water, the boat was unloaded and ready to set out again. Pastor Poul and Barbara were allowed on it. They sat down on the narrow thwart in the stern, close to each other. The boat was full of peat litter and the oars creaked and squeaked against the bone-dry thole pins.

All around them lay the vast shiny surface of the lake, and the reflection of the afternoon sun glittered on it and dazzled them. But over on the shore there was the dark shadow of the mountain, and in the waves as the boat cut through them there were also cool, black patches. Barbara held her hand down in the water and let it run through her fingers.

The peat lands were a dark area with black peat bogs. They looked like wounds in the earth. But the air was clear and echoed with the voices of grown ups and children working round about. There were the cries of curlews and golden plover standing on piles of heather, and here and there, where people were preparing food, smoke was rising into the air. It was a smoke that tore at their eyes and burned them, but it was sweet and strong like some kind of brandy. There was thyme in it.

Barbara said that walking in the peat like this was one of the things she liked best. She dragged Pastor Poul round from one family to the other and wanted to know how far they had got and when they thought the last peat would be dry enough to take across. They were given something to eat by one of the families. These were poor people, but Barbara praised the food and persuaded the minister to do so as well.

There was an old woman helping to carry the peat down to the water. Like all the others, she bore it in the Faroese manner

139

in a *leyp*. This was a big wooden creel carried on the back and held in place by a woollen band around the forehead. The old woman was on the point of collapsing beneath the burden. Her neck was strong and tough enough and her face showed great determination. But her legs could scarcely carry her.

"Let me try to carry that leyp," said Barbara.

"Oh no, no no," said the old woman. "Of course not."

But Barbara was clever and managed to get the leyp from her, and before anyone knew what she was doing, she had the coarse woollen band around her forehead and had bent her slender back beneath the heavy burden. She managed to get down to the water without staggering, unloaded the peat and ambled back with the leyp hanging over one shoulder. Now Pastor Poul also decided to carry something. They loaded the leyp for him and put the band around his forehead. But no sooner had he taken up the entire burden than his knees started to shake. His neck was not strong enough, and he suddenly fell over backwards and sat down.

"I knew it," shouted Barbara in delight.

But people were polite and explained that no strangers could carry a leyp because their necks were not trained to do it.

Then Barbara set about it again. There was no stopping her; she laughed and everyone admired her. But each time she put down the empty leyp she stood as upright and high-bosomed as ever. Her eyes shone, and she was like a lighted candle among them. She was as though filled with strength and benefaction, for God had accepted her heart today.

Only when the work was done did she brush the peat litter from her neck. She said that she had also got peat litter down her back and she laughed and shook herself. Then she went on with Pastor Poul and was still glowing and full of warmth.

They went south and reached the end of the lake. But there

was no River Jordan here. The quiet, shining water cascaded mightily into the ocean. All was blue and foaming deep beneath them. Thus ended this Lake Gennesareth – not in a narrow valley, but in a never-ending rush of water.

They leapt from stone to stone and reached the other side of the brief stretch of river between the lake and the waterfall. It was evening now, and all the heath's birds were silent. When they reached Midvág it was approaching midnight. But it was high tide, and so Barbara found an excuse to stay with Pastor Poul a little longer. They walked in the dewed grass, and the northern sides of everything – the houses, the boulders, the wooden crosses in the churchyard – were illumined by the great beacon in the sky above the mountain tops. It was so deathly quiet that they only dared whisper. They sat down and talked and talked and were agreed about everything, and meanwhile the light in the heavens moved further and further to the east.

When Pastor Poul lay down to sleep, he was still immersed in the grandeur of nature. His senses were slow to release the dark earth, the scintillating heavens and the bright voices that had sounded across the heath. But the sudden waterfall down to the sea was the end of everything. Yet God's mercy and God's goodness were so great and so remarkable that it could well be imagined that the angels *spelt* the words a little wrongly in their heavenly hymnbooks. Indeed, it was hard to imagine anything else.

Barbara, too, went to bed renewed by this great day. She did not quite have an exact recollection of everything, but her heart continued to cling to the words: "Her sins, which are many, are forgiven; for she loved much."

And she did love much.

Brandy

The turf on all the roofs in Tórshavn stood out green and luxuriant in the mist. It was a dry, gentle mist which did not even manage to dampen the stones in the alleyways, but it was so dense that it shut out everything and everybody as though in a cupboard filled with white darkness. The sound of boys playing noisily on Tinganes and the screeching of gulls above their heads was damped down and strangled in the impenetrable atmosphere. But other sounds coming from far away could be heard quite clearly. The rhythmical sound of oars out on the fjord had been heard repeatedly during the day, and each time this happened, the boys had stopped their game and listened and watched until a fully manned boat glided out of the mist and came alongside near the Hoist or one of the other landing stages in the East Bay.

It was St Olaf's Eve. The streets in the town were filled with quiet crowds of villagers. They had come to Havn to meet their friends and see the opening of the Assembly. They strolled up and down in their heavy buckled shoes, meeting on street corners, standing in groups and exchanging news. A dawning merriment to be seen in the eyes of many, but their talk was subdued and they made no great noise. They radiated a sense of solemnity and dignity.

The women of the town had a bit of fun opening the windows a little and watching the village men as they secretly congregated around a bottle in some corner or alleyway. But they were less keen on meeting the St Olaf visitors face to face. The villagers had a curiously simple way of *asking*. They could sit there so innocently and look as though they were not able to count to three. But just watch them! They could count both to three and to nine, and no one needed to be in any doubt as to what gossip they were interested in today. The town's great scandal was already known throughout the country, and all they wanted in every single village was to get to know it in greater detail.

Aye, it was a hell of a scandal, unlike any other. It affected not only individuals, it affected the entire town. Gabriel had been the first to set the story going. Already several months ago he had been telling the farmers who visited the store all about the *French brats* that would soon be appearing in Tórshavn. Just wait until August, he had said, and then they would see how busy the midwife would be all of a sudden. He had had a good laugh and the villagers had all gone home bursting with this news.

It was also said that Barbara was soon to marry the new parson from Vágar. Aye, she was an unusual woman. She never seemed to have had enough of parsons, the farmers said. But Gabriel was not quite so sure that her appetite was so great this time. There could well be other reasons than desire. Let's see, he had said. He knew what he knew. And before long everyone thought they knew that Pastor Poul was about to lumber himself with a French baby.

"Aye, isn't it a bloody scandal," Gabriel would say to his customers. He never tired of talking about Barbara's boundless guile. While holding a weight from a pair of scales or a grain measure in his hand he would often stand and actually be lost for words at her behaviour, and he shook his head and snorted,

"What a bloody scandal!"

Throughout that summer there had been a rare delight in going to the Royal Store, and this twenty-eighth of July the shop was also the first place the St Olaf's Festival visitors made for as soon as they came ashore. The first to come was Niels Peter from Leirvík. He was a great joker, but most people were inclined to smile a little at his curiosity and lack of discretion. He blurted things straight out, and the expression French kids was out of his mouth almost before he got inside the door. But Gabriel simply told him to shut up and go to hell. Niels Peter was so crestfallen that he simply slunk away again. He did not understand a word of it and could only thank God for there not having been anyone else to hear him when he put his unfortunate question to someone in authority. This was an experience he did not want to share.

Other village folk came into the shop later. They were better able to observe the niceties. They were slow and ponderous and they wasted time on all sorts of talk about the weather and the way the harvest was coming on. But Gabriel said not a word about the great human harvest in Havn. It was remarkable; indeed it was a disheartening and disappointing start to the Feast of St Olaf. The odd visitor went so far as to ask whether there was any news. But they went no further. They were respectable farmers, who could sense which way the wind was blowing. And they obviously felt that the air in the Royal Store was not favourable to many questions today.

When they left, they were none the wiser. They were bursting with curiosity. They went up hill and down dale in the town, peering all over the place and staring in at every miserable window. They hailed other St Olaf visitors at random and asked them straight out whether *they* knew anything about these blessed French children. But no, no one knew anything;

even Niels Peter knew no more than a vague rumour about this person and that person, a rumour that the others had all heard already. And yet this was to know far too little in view of the fact that they were now on the very scene of the crime. Whoops went past, and she was quite obviously expecting; aye, she was indeed. But Whoops had been like that so many times before.

They were not enjoying the brandy. No, all the signs were that this St Olaf's Festival was going to be a dull affair. No one invited them inside, and you could not see a hand in front of your eyes in this fog. They could not find anything better to do than to go back and forth through Gongin – out to Tinganes and back again.

"Can't you have a word with Gabriel," someone suggested to Niels Peter.

He shook his head: "No, I can't."

"Oh yes, it's easy for someone like you."

"I could have asked him all right," said Niels Peter, "but I don't think he's going to tell me anything. He probably won't tell anybody except his closest friends. You could ask, Hans Lavus, you're his cousin."

Hans Lavus slowly turned his head, stared thoughtfully into space and closed his eyes a couple of times. He had white eyelashes.

"Aye, aye," he finally nodded, but it sounded as though he were talking to himself rather than to any of the others.

"Aye, 'cos you are his cousin, aren't you?" Niels Peter continued.

Hans Lavus was not Gabriel's cousin at all; he was a feeble-minded vagabond known throughout the country and tolerated on account of his affability. He thought he was someone important – he usually referred to himself as a member of the

Assembly. But his was a gentle, melancholy superiority that only had one fault – that he was susceptible to flattery. And now they all maintained that he was the only one of them to whom Gabriel would condescend to talk, he was not the one to deny it. His eyes began to come to life, and he looked around in delight: "Hm, well, my good men. Hmm, yes. What is it you want me to ask him about then?"

Niels Peter told him what to say. He was to say: "Well, Gabriel, my good man, what can you tell us about the French kids today?" And then he should offer him a pinch of snuff. Like this. Niels Peter straightened up and showed him how a great man would offer a lesser man a pinch of snuff. The farmers exchanged secret smiles. The devil of a man, this Niels Peter. But never mind, St Olaf's Day was approaching. They all went into a corner. Hans Lavus was given a dram as well, and then they all made for Tinganes.

Gabriel took little notice of the procession, headed by Hans Lavus, that started to fill the shop. He stood weighing some corn for Whoops and was silent and official. Only when he was finished did he deign to cast a glance at the newcomers.

"Hmm, Gabriel, hmm, my good man," were the words uttered by Hans Lavus in a voice that was gentle but stupid: "What can you tell us about the French children today?"

He smiled foolishly and rummaged around to extract a ridiculous snuff box from a filthy red handkerchief.

Gabriel almost blew up, but he managed to control himself. His quick brain had in a trice recognised the conspiracy stamped on the far too numerous and serious faces of the villagers. There was especially no mistaking Niels Peter's face at the back of the crowd. A great laugh was ready, waiting for every word. For several seconds, no other sound was heard but that of Whoops's asthma. Then, finally, in a tired and calm voice, Gabriel said, "Be off with you, Hans Lavus. I haven't time to stand here fooling around with you all day. Here, take this."

He flung a sugar lump across the counter. Hans Lavus greedily grasped the white cube and examined it with sticky, enchanted eyes. The village men stood watching helplessly. All their plans had gone awry. They felt foolish and had no idea how they were to get away with their dignity intact.

But now Whoops spoke. It started with a wheezing sound in her tight chest, but then her voice broke through:

"Aye, I think you should get out, Hans Lavus, and the rest of you had better go with him. Perhaps you don't know that things have changed in the Royal Store now. But let me tell you that Gabriel's not going to talk about French children any more. He's been like some avenging angel all summer, mocking and telling lies about us ordinary people and accusing us of all having bastards. But the biter's getting bitten now. So you can go home to your villages and tell everyone that. Because Gabriel's got a French baby to look after himself. You can tell them that from Whoops. He's going to marry the bailiff's daughter on Sunday. And the baby's expected already next month. And you can guarantee that the bailiff's daughter isn't a woman ever to have been to bed with Gabriel. No it was a far superior chap, a Frenchman, even if Gabriel is registered as husband and father twenty times over."

Gabriel had stood throughout this pale and silent. When Whoops had finished, he said in a gentle, commanding voice, "I will go in and fetch the Store manager, so I will."

"Yes, you just go in to him," Whoops started all over again. "I don't think he'll be too keen on coming out and talking about French kids either. The fine folk have become ever so meek and mild recently. Whoops's not the only one; there are both fine married ladies and fine daughters who are going to give birth in August."

"You foul-mouthed witch," said Gabriel. The idea that it was not merely he himself, but all the official class that was being scorned gave him renewed strength. "You watch your mouth," he said ponderously, "for otherwise I'll make sure you give birth in the Black Hole – understand?"

Whoops was by now closer to the door.

"Aye, you can have me put in the Black Hole a thousand times or laid on a bed of sharp stones," she screamed, "but turn a French babe into a Gabriel babe – that you can't do. Goodbye."

The village men's eyes had gradually grown bigger and bigger. They were almost horrified, and when the Black Hole was mentioned, they began to feel very uncomfortable. They slowly trooped out of the shop, weak-kneed at the sensation. Niels Peter stood bent over on the steps; his shoulders were shaking slowly as though he were sobbing. The village men at the front of the throng also began now to squirm a little. But there came not a sound from them. They simply got a move on, the entire crowd got a move on, indeed they were actually in a hurry to get away, and only when they reached a well-hidden corner did they stop and start to grin. They were so excited that they could hardly drink, and it was a long time before they found their voices again. But then a mighty sense of ease began to spread among them; the news and the wine filled them with warmth, and one of them started to sing a ballad. And during the course of the day it became more and more frequent that chance bits of ballads could be heard among the tarred wooden walls. The milky white mist blotted out every alleyway, and they couldn't see a hand in front of their eyes, but the town was filled with invisible hilarity.

Gabriel was left behind alone in his shop. He went round with an old bag gathering up all the remains of corn and sugar and tobacco that had been spilt here and there on the counters. This confrontation had been worse than expected, and he realised that he could expect a couple of difficult days. But there was nothing for it. He had made up his mind, and it would be all right. It was only a question of keeping himself under control. The only trouble was that he was so unaccustomed to keeping himself under control when faced with this crowd of monkeys. But the more he controlled himself, the less they laughed and the fewer the costs.

The actual prize was sure enough. He had carefully considered it, debit and credit. Suzanne Harme was a good match, the best match in the country. It was a given thing that promotion would come along with her, and he had straightaway made the condition that the bailiff would appoint him his head clerk. This also gave him the almost certain prospect of being Harme's successor. Admittedly, the bailiff had not taken upon himself to die in the near future, but he had nevertheless had one apoplectic fit.

That was the most important entry, but to that could be added the fact that Suzanne was both a beautiful and sensible woman. Gabriel never tired of repeating this to himself. She was no Barbara – thank God she was no Barbara! Admittedly, she was not untouched. But when you take over a piece of damaged goods just because it is damaged, you cannot at the same time demand that it should be undamaged. And Suzanne was only a *little* damaged, and it was also a lasting advantage that no one in *this* country would be able to boast of being the father of her child. That would have been confoundedly unpleasant.

Finally there was the advantage that although she was not

exactly Barbara, Suzanne was still almost Barbara. There was after all something of Barbara about her, a Barbara without Barbara's faults. Could it be better?

On the debit side, however there was the fact that in marrying Suzanne, he precluded himself from marrying Barbara. He did not really understand this question. For had he ever wanted to marry Barbara? Certainly he had not. Was it not far better not to be married to Barbara? Certainly it was. This account was in a bit of a mess. Why should it be an entry on the debit side that he was not to marry Barbara, when this same fact entered into several factors on the credit side? He thought about this more and more and was simply not sure of either himself or his accounting. Finally, he consoled himself with the thought that it was all only a question of how items were entered. Exactly, it was a question similar to that of profit and loss. Or the cash balance. That was put on the debit side as well. Curious, that.

The other entry on the debit side was the laughter. It was in reality only a small item that could not be compared with the others. But there was the confoundedly unfortunate quality to it that it had to be paid in cash, straight away. But after that it would admittedly be a thing of the past. What might be added to it later was probably not of any significance. So it was only a question of getting over it. Outlays were of course always embarrassing, but when you knew what you were getting for your money...

Neither did Gabriel tire of repeating this to himself; he comforted himself with it and so he remained bravely in his redoubt. It was not always easy to look the enemy in the eye; people were drunk and awkward today... That confounded Whoops had lit the torch of revolt, so to speak, and fired the rabble with disrespect. Were decent men from the villages not coming into the shop and making all kinds of snide remarks? Aye, he had a feeling that there was some kind of secret gathering round the corner where people were laughing at him and whence spies were sent now and then into the shop to test the atmosphere.

There had not been such a merry St Olaf's festival for many years. The people of Tórshavn had enjoyed themselves during the winter, when the French ships were in port. Now it was the villagers' turn. They had nothing to drink but brandy and the only dance they knew was the traditional one of the Faroes. But that, too, had its advantages; it had great advantages and was well suited to the occasion.

It was Niels Peter who started the dance. His great success out in the shop had made him the man of the day, and he was not one to hide his light under a bushel. With a strident voice he started off with:

> *The king he asked his daughter dear –*
> *Matrori, matrori*
> *Who's your eldest son so fair?*
> *Turalulu quack, quack, quack,*
> *Turalulu quack, quack, quack,*
> *Turalulu quack.*

There was nothing wrong with that. But it was disrespectful and out of the ordinary that they should be dancing outside in Havn, just in front of the Royal Store. More and more joined the ring, and the high spirits and exuberance increased by the minute. A few more restrained men thought it was dangerous to taunt Gabriel in this way. They could see that he was a man who would advance in power and glory and who would be able to avenge himself when his hour came. But the younger ones refused to be told. They were drunk now and only thought of making mischief. When a pale and angry Gabriel came out on the steps and asked them to bloody well shut up, Niels Peter looked him in the eye and sang:

> *The bailiff said to his daughter dear –*
> *Matrori, matrori*
> *What's become of your honour clear?*
> *Turalulu quack, quack, quack,*
> *Turalulu quack, quack, quack,*
> *Turalulu quack.*

And then Gabriel went back inside. But Niels Peter started changing the verses now to be more and more audacious and personal. He sang out at the top of his voice:

> *The bailiff he said to his daughter dear:*
> *Who will be your husband here?*

This was too much for Gabriel. He rushed down the steps and swore that he would put a bloody end to this insubordination. He was off now. He would send for the authorities, the commandant and soldiers. But he did not get that far. Two of the strongest village men took him between them, grasped his wrists and forced him to join the chain and dance along with them:

> *To his son-in-law the bailiff quoth*
> *Matrori, matrori*
> *Your kids they'll be of noble birth*
> *Turululu quack, quack, quack*

Barbara

Turululu quack, quack, quack,
Turululu quack.

The men danced around and flung Gabriel's arms around, looked deep into his eyes and sang like mad. But suddenly they all stopped; the words died on their lips, and no sound was to be heard but the gull's cries in the mist. The law speaker had appeared among them. He was walking so modestly, and if he had not been so big they would not have noticed him. Behind him, in the mist in front of the gate to the store, came Barbara, walking up the ramp together with Pastor Poul and the bailiff from Vágar. They had just come ashore at the Hoist.

"Mercy me," said the law speaker in his gentle ox-like voice, looking around in amazement: "What's going on here?"

They all looked rather sheepish. Gabriel had hurried back into the shop. Hans Lavus, too, had slunk away. He was the only person in the whole country who could not stand the sight of the law speaker; it always upset him. But otherwise there was usually only a sense of security wherever Samuel Mikkelsen appeared. The immense calm he exuded was a pleasing inspiration for every heart. Nor was it long before Niels Peter pulled himself together sufficiently for him to be able to give a sort of explanation.

"I suppose we can all take pleasure in this," he said boldly. "It's not every year there is such a splendid wedding in Havn."

There was the brief shadow of a smile in the law speaker's eyes. It was clear that he had understood the implications, but he betrayed not the slightest change of expression.

"It would be better if you went up into the assembly room and danced a decent dance suited to St Olaf's Day," he said. "This is a most peculiar place to be dancing."

A moment later, the shop was full of good-natured, agreeable talking. It was a relief to Gabriel once more to be among well-mannered people who knew how to congratulate him in the right way. The law speaker had learned of the coming wedding through a letter from the judge, and on the way to Havn he had given the news to Pastor Poul and Barbara.

"How nice," said Barbara to Gabriel. Her voice was perfectly honest. "Fancy your marrying Suzanne. Well, you will almost be a brother-in-law to me."

"I hear you are going to be married as well," said Gabriel lamely. There was no possibility for him at this moment to make a malicious remark. No, in every respect Barbara could have plenty of reason to smile. He had measured her up quickly. There was no question of *her* expecting.

"Yes, isn't it fun," said Barbara. "We are both going to marry."

She was happy, and there was no malice in her words.

The law speaker spent that evening with Bailiff Harme. The bailiff had visibly aged. During the winter, he had been seriously ill and had lain sick in bed for a long time. He had been told of his daughter's condition far too late. She had been so caring as not to wish to cause her father this emotional shock before he had gained his strength again. But it was difficult to know how to act. It was summertime, and he might perhaps have been able to get his daughter out of the country on one of the merchantmen. But unfortunately, he had no relatives he believed he could confide in. In addition, there was of course the child. It would be the best thing for everyone that it should have a father. He had actually thought of the judge, but to have suggested it to him would have been an insult. Then there was Gabriel... No, it was in truth not because the bailiff had a great opinion of this Gabriel. And he thought even less of him after recently having got to know him better. But something had to be done.

"Aye," said Samuel Mikkelsen. "I can't say but that I would have liked to see your daughter with a husband other than Gabriel. To tell you the truth, I have never had much confidence in him. But what does Suzanne herself say?"

The bailiff smiled a rather unhappy smile. He sat there for a time lost in thought.

"Perhaps," he said, "perhaps you ought to have had a talk to Johan Hendrik after all. I don't really know, but when all is said and done, he is a sensible man and not one to have refused in any unseemly manner. And if he had agreed, it would have been so much better for all concerned. Nor do I think that *he* would have been less esteemed for that reason. People are so different and they are respected in different ways.

At that moment, Gabriel entered. He was very agitated and took little heed of the law speaker's presence in the room.

"The lower orders are in an unruly mood today," he said. "It's as though the Devil's got hold of them. I think it's bad enough that I have to go around taking on myself the results of Suzanne's confounded wanton behaviour."

The bailiff looked up and almost forgot to hide his amazement. What kind of a tone was this? Had this lad already started talking about "the lower orders"? He had to smile a little. No, no, he thought, when the poor gain control, there's no knowing what they will get up to.

"I want Niels Peter in the Black Hole," Gabriel went on. "He's insulted and scorned all authority today. It's all right sitting in here and taking it easy. Why do *I* have to suffer for it when I've done nothing but good? *I've* had to stand there today and listen to a scurrilous song all about the bailiff and Suzanne."

"If the song was not about you, Gabriel," said the law

speaker gently, "surely you should not have been so upset by it?"

Gabriel stared furiously at Samuel Mikkelsen's imperturbably placid face: "About me? About me? Of course it was about me as well... what the hell...?"

"Was it?" said the bailiff. His eyes were so kind and so beautiful.

"And now I want an arrest order for Niels Peter," said Gabriel angrily to the bailiff. "Then I can go over to the commandant or to Gunner Hans and have it put into effect."

Bailiff Harme shuffled a little. He was uneasy and in doubt. He was breathing heavily and fiddling with a pen. Then he started to walk up and down the floor and was very flushed.

The law speaker had all the time sat in exactly the same position. Now he slowly rose, thereby actually darkening the small room. He stood for a moment looking out of the window. Then he said:

"Well, this matter doesn't concern me, at least not for the moment. But if you will take my advice, Gabriel, you will not make anything of it. You can't put all the St Olaf visitors in the Black Hole after all."

Samuel Mikkelsen left. He was not happy. "Good heavens," he thought, "there are going to be a lot of people in the Black Hole in times to come."

Here and there in the town, he could occasionally hear the refrain:

Turululu quack, quack, quack.

He wished they would stop.

People greeted the law speaker with happy faces. His figure was the huge sign that the St Olaf Festival had really begun.

But the law speaker went straight to his lodgings and lay down. Of all the strange things that happened during these St Olaf's Day festivities, this was perhaps the most unusual.

A Clerical Convention

St Olaf's Day came with sunshine and bells ringing.

As the newest cleric in the country, Pastor Poul led the service in the church, and everyone was there to hear what admonitory words he had to say to the members of the Assembly. Later, the law speaker went to the Assembly with the book of laws under his arm, and the church bells rang out anew. The law speaker was followed by the bailiff, the judge, all seven of the country's clergymen and the six sheriffs and finally the forty-eight assembly members, their necks adorned with their white ruffs. The farmers were solemn and no longer sang Turululu quack. Gabriel had recovered his composure and was no longer demanding that Niels Peter should be thrown into the Black Hole. The town's womenfolk looked inquisitively out of the windows and no longer shouted insults at the passers-by. All that was to be heard was the ringing of bells and the tramping of solemn buckled shoes.

The law speaker entered the Assembly Chamber followed by all the dignitaries and assembly members. The ordinary populace remained outside in Gongin. Through the open windows they could just make out the dark paintings of King Frederik and Queen Juliane Marie.

The law speaker rose and cleared his voice.

"May the peace and blessing of our Lord Jesus Christ," he started in his deep, gentle voice, "be with us and all who are present at this good Assembly now and evermore. Amen."

From a book he read the lengthy passage with which the Assembly was opened. The words were difficult to distinguish, and his voice sometimes sounded weak and indistinct. But finally, he put the book down and concluded:

"Upon these words, be seated in the peace of Our Lord."

The Assembly was now in session, and the discussions began. Bailiff Harme was the first to speak. He supported himself a little on the table, and his head shook a little. It was clear that he had gone considerably downhill since last year. His voice, too, was weaker. It was almost pitiful to hear him clearing his throat and saying "erhh – ehmm" in this way, for there was no power or dignity there any longer.

As was customary, the bailiff asked whether anyone in the Assembly or among the people had complaints to make regarding the country's provisions or against the staff of the Royal Store for their behaviour, measurements or weights. There was a general murmuring. Over the year, various people had sworn that come the St Olaf's Day Assembly they would complain about the good stockings the Royal Store had rejected and refused to take as payment, or about the Royal Store having run out of brandy. The chewing tobacco had also been poor and mouldy for a time. Not to mention Gabriel's frequent malicious behaviour. But now, on being asked and with the bailiff surveying them, they were all silent. It was not easy to rise in this Assembly; it was difficult to put things in the right way, and if you made a foolish error you were sure to be a laughing stock throughout the country. No, it was in all respects best to stay quiet. As the old saying had it: *If you are silent, you suffer only one injury, but if you speak out you suffer two.*

This first day of the Assembly was usually only quite a

brief event, really no more than a formality.

There was to be a clerical convention after the Assembly. Pastor Poul was extremely unhappy as he went out to Reynegaard along with all his colleagues – Pastor Severin from Suduroy, Pastor Marcus from Sandoy, Pastor Wenzel from South Streymoy, Pastor Gregers from North Streymoy, Pastor Anders from Eysteroy and Pastor Christian from the Northern Islands. As for Barbara, he had only caught a glimpse of her today. Heaven only knew where she might be. Pastor Poul was always on edge when he did not have her with him, and here in Havn, her lively goings on were sheer torment to him. The dean, Anders Morsing, congratulated him on his sermon, but Pastor Poul scarcely heard what he said. He went around looking left and right to see if he could not see a trace of her in the crowd. But he only saw unfamiliar farmers.

"Well, if you will be content with my modest dwelling," said Pastor Wenzel as they entered Reynegaard. He was small, red-haired and unctuous as always.

"Modest dwelling? Indeed." These words were spoken by Pastor Severin. He uttered a long, asthmatic sigh and burst out in a hoarse laugh: "Verily, verily, I say unto you... well, God forgive me. No, what was I going to say... modest dwelling! My dear colleague, which of us has a house like this? I must say!"

He rubbed his hands and walked quickly up and down the floor. He was a very small, fat man with a gentle, happy face.

Reynegaard was no modest dwelling, and the hall they entered was a large room with four windows. The sun threw brilliant squares of light on the white scrubbed floor. Outside there was the church, the churchyard, the *Corps de Garde* and the Black Hole.

"No," Pastor Severin continued, "suppose you and I had

houses like this, eh, Pastor Gregers?"

He went across and made to slap Pastor Gregers on the shoulder, but he could only reach part way up his back. "What would you say to that? Eh? Eh?"

With each word, he slapped Pastor Gregers on the back, and each blow sent up a cloud of dust like the smoke rising from a canon being fired; it rose in thick swirls from Pastor Gregers cassock and performed a dance in the sunlight. Pastor Gregers lost the drop hanging from his nose and started in alarm. He was a thin, rheumatic man with a lined face and a threadbare wig. He tried to speak, but only when Pastor Severin stopped slapping him and had burst out laughing violently did he manage to say anything.

"We have the dwellings to which the Lord has called us," he said in a plaintive, hollow voice.

"Oh well, I suppose so," said Pastor Severin. "But I just wish the Lord!" he was overcome by violent coughing, "What was I going to say... oh no. Have the moths got into your wig as well?"

"No, in my case it's the mice."

"Really? I must say..."

They had both taken off their wigs and now embarked on a serious discussion of domestic trials. A new clear drop was gathering beneath the tip of Pastor Greger's nose. Many things had been sent to try him.

And that was the case with all of them. The tall, bony Pastor Marcus from Sandoy complained to Pastor Christian from the Northern Isles at the large number of children God had given him. They were a true blessing, but they were a large number to cope with."

Thank God, one of his sons had married a girl from a good farm in Skálavík, another, with the help of the bailiff, had managed to lease a good farm on Suduroy, and three daughters were also well married. But there were nine children left. Life was not easy. No indeed it was *not* easy.

Pastor Christian had no children and was not married. He would far rather talk about the Moravian Brethren. He said he *understood* the Moravian Brethren, and he had to say that he sympathised with men like Zinzendorf and Spangenberg.

"Well," said Pastor Marcus, his daughter Elsebeth was nineteen now. He had brought her with him to Havn, as she was getting nowhere just sitting out there in Todnes Parsonage, so if Pastor Christian would talk to her a little about spiritual matters...

"Yes, Spangenberg," said Pastor Christian, stroking his chin with long sensitive finger movements. He pronounced the name in a quiet, solemn voice as though he were whispering some sacred word. His face was pale and passionate, but otherwise he was a tall, handsome man with a mass of curly hair that was powdered and flattened at the back to form a modest pigtail that projected across his ruff.

Pastor Wenzel had left his guests for a moment. He went into the parlour and was aware of the sound of many voices and the scent of chocolate.

Madam Anna Sophie showed up in the doorway, flushed and pale, with her mouth full of cake.

"Well, I must say," said Pastor Wenzel, looking very aggrieved. "There is plenty for everyone, I see."

"Yes, why not," said his wife. "It is only once a year that all the clergy's wives are here, so... I actually wondered whether I ought to have invited Barbara as well, but they are not married yet, of course."

"Oh, that too. That too." Pastor Wenzel had developed a little red patch on each cheek and went away hurt. His wife stood for a moment, chewing her cake and watching him. Then she went back to all the parsons' wives.

In the hall, Pastor Anders had embarked on a discussion with Pastor Poul. He had caught him by the folds in his cassock and dragged him across to one of the windows. He spoke to him with a very authoritative look on his face, and his eyes were blue and sharp beneath his bushy eyebrows.

"Aye, I have been in your situation as well," said Pastor Anders. "As you probably know, I was once betrothed to Barbara... Barbara, Pastor Niels' widow, so I know what I am talking about."

"Yes, I know," said Pastor Poul tersely and courteously.

"I expect you will not take it wrongly if I speak to you as an older and more experienced man," the dean cleared his throat, "and as your superior."

Pastor Poul bowed his head.

"So I am turning to you *fraterne*, but also *serio*, and I must most earnestly beg you to consider what it is you are about to take upon yourself."

Pastor Poul looked up.

"I have given it my most serious consideration throughout the summer," he said. His voice was trembling and on the point of breaking.

"Yes, I, too, once had to consider all that," said the dean. "And I have never regretted the decision at which *I* arrived."

Pastor Poul felt uncomfortable in the extremely firm stare from the dean's blue eyes. He thought briefly of the dean's wife, of whom he had caught a glimpse that morning – she was fat and had a pointed nose and a piercing voice. He was surprised that he could feel so mischievous at such a serious moment that he was on the point of smiling. He was suddenly reminded of his school days and his headmaster and was still as unpleasantly affected by the blue eyes. But he had nevertheless to think of some answer. And so he said:

"I neither can nor will break a promise I have made."

"Oh," said the dean and looked away.

Pastor Poul was simply amazed at the effect of his reply. He almost felt as if he had uttered an untruth and was just a little ashamed though he did not know why.

"Oh, I see," said the dean again. He was rather lost as to what to say, but it was clear that he was not beaten. After a moment or two, he asked: "Are you convinced that the woman you are going to marry takes her vows as seriously as you take yours?"

It struck Pastor Poul that he ought to be furious at this question, but he refrained. He did not even manage to affect anger, he said merely:

"I know that Barbara means it very, very seriously. But of course, she is a weak person, and I know that as well."

The dean made no reply. He merely turned his disturbingly blue eyes straight on Pastor Poul.

"But perhaps one might also have faith in God," Pastor Poul suddenly added.

The dean looked away, and Pastor Poul again felt a little ashamed. But the dean stood up straight and said in an authoritative voice: "No, you just listen to me. You must not imagine that God can be bothered to lend you a hand in the confounded risk you are taking with yourself and your sacred calling in a marriage that... that... are you crazy, man?"

"I know it is a risk," said Pastor Poul, "and I know as well as anyone that Barbara is... a sinner... of course..."

He caught himself about to draw on the window pane, but it was shiny and completely free of condensation. "Well," he went on in a calmer voice, "we mustn't forget that Our Lord himself did not feel He was too good to consort with sinful women and..."

"No, by Gad, but He didn't marry them," said the dean.

"No, of course, He didn't marry anyone – that is to say he was the bridegroom of all sinners, and that being so, we human beings ought to beware of considering ourselves too good to... I simply mean that one ought to beware of any kind of self-righteousness."

"Hmm," said the dean, nodding a couple of times. "Perhaps it is for her sake that you are going to marry her?"

"It is my hope to God that it will be a blessing."

"Oh, like that. Even so, it is presumably not a platonic – I mean a purely spiritual marriage you are thinking of."

There was palpable scorn in the dean's voice. Pastor Poul countered quickly:

"No, indeed, miserable sinners as we both are. But everything is in God's hand."

"No, by God, it isn't," the dean said brusquely. "I mean..." he corrected himself in a loud voice, "thou shall not tempt the Lord thy God."

"Oh, is this the young man?"

It was Pastor Severin who had joined them. He slapped Pastor Poul heartily on the shoulder, inhaled long and asthmatically and burst out in a loud laugh: "No, really, is he tempting the Lord? Tempting the Lord? Is it not he himself who has been a little tempted, eh? eh? Eve and the serpent, eh? Be careful of the snake. Marry her? A foolish idea, my dear friend, a foolish idea, I say. No, you just take a lesson from the dean; he was too clever for her, so he was... too clever, I believe..."

Pastor Severin turned round now and started to slap the dean's shoulder: "He chose a better woman, indeed he did. The dean's wife."

Pastor Severin was quite out of breath and suffered a long bout of coughing: "What was I going to say: There's a lovely smell here of... of chocolate, I do believe."

He looked around delightedly.

"Yes, my wife..." said Pastor Wenzel solemnly and reservedly.

"Well, this is what I call a clerical assembly," shouted Pastor Severin, rubbing his hands.

"Well, yes," said the dean, giving Pastor Severin a severe look. "We have not arrived at the chocolate yet. There are a few things..."

He went across and started a discussion with Pastor Wenzel, and it was obvious that the Tórshavn minister felt comforted by this. He had until this juncture been completely alone in this gathering.

"*The Rare Jewel of Faith*," Pastor Christian was heard to say. He was tenderly caressing a book that he had just taken out of his pocket. "Do you know it?"

Pastor Marcus gave the back of the book a near-sighted glance. Hans Adolf Brorson, he spelt out laboriously. "No," he said with no sign of interest, "I don't know it. No, you see," he went on, "those two bits of land up in Depil are just inside your benefice, and it would be a good idea for you if..."

"What?" shouted Pastor Severin. "Good heavens. Has my dear colleague been acquiring land right up in the Northern Islands?"

"It's only about two roods," said Pastor Marcus. "It isn't all that much. But it's better than nothing, better than nothing," he added with a glance at Pastor Christian.

"But of course, as a bit of a dowry," said Pastor Severin shrewdly.

"These are the fruits of the burdensome and difficult task

of preaching two funeral sermons," said Pastor Gregers with a hint of bitterness in his hollow voice.

"Well I got them for *one*," said Pastor Marcus glancing first at the dean and then up at the ceiling.

"For *one!*" Pastor Severin burst out in a loud laugh. "For *one!*" He started slapping Pastor Marcus's shoulder. "You mean two birds with one stone? Eh? Eh? Well done. Aye, the rest of us ought to learn from that. To take land as payment for our funeral sermons, eh? From earth you are and to earth you shall return and with earth your funeral must be paid! Ha ha ha! Not only *one*, but *two* roods for a funeral sermon."

"Well," said Pastor Marcus, looking at the dean and Master Wenzel. "It is only in certain cases, you know. Unfortunately, there are many who do not pay anything at all for a funeral sermon."

"No, it isn't easy for those who don't own any land," said Pastor Gregers in a hollow, dry voice. "Where there is nothing, even Caesar has lost his right."

"I have nine children that are not provided for," said Pastor Marcus gloomily.

"Tell me, what do you charge for a requiem mass?" asked Pastor Severin.

"I'm not a papist," said Pastor Marcus angrily, "and what I own I have acquired by honest means and had it duly registered. Things are not so easy for me. My parishioners are not as generous as yours. I am told that no one gives less than a *sletdaler* in your parish.

Pastor Severin burst out in a terrible laugh. He put up his hands and coughed and protested and almost choked. "That is a lie," he shouted. "A lie as black as they come. God knows I was paid three *marks* for the last wedding I conducted. Plus an eight *skilling* piece."

"Oh, did you get it at last?" said Pastor Gregers in an unpleasantly dry voice: "That was the last eight *skilling* coin on Suduroy. You will never get any more of those."

"No, damn it," said Pastor Severin, suddenly serious, "no, then there are perhaps no more of them. But *mark* coins still turn up," he added regretfully. "There seems to be no end to them yet, although I have exchanged quite a few."

"Such things," said Pastor Marcus in a matter-of-fact voice "could never have happened on Sandoy. It is because Suduroy is so far out of the way that it can go on. The people of Sandoy wanted to man boats to Havn to exchange their copper straight away. But then Suduroy is so far away.

He stroked his chin: "Fancy, only getting silver in the collection. But today the people of Suduroy have probably filled their whole boat with copper. Of course they have. And then you'll see. It will all be evened out. Now you will not see anything but *skillings* in the collection for ages..."

"Well, let's see," said Pastor Severin, rattling his pockets. "For the time being I am all right... oh." He caught sight of the dean and suddenly became rather more subdued. "But," he added with a wink, "this is something in which we could help each other."

He burst out laughing and turned to Master Wenzel. He was the only man in the gathering whose shoulders he could manage to pat without stretching.

"I consider myself too good for that sort of thing," said Pastor Wenzel in his wounded voice.

He drew back a little from Pastor Severin and remained close to the dean.

"Well, what about *you*," said Pastor Severin, turning to Pastor Poul: "Listen to my advice, young man. Keep hold of the copper coins and don't let go of them. Take care of the *skillings*, and the *dalers* will take care of themselves. You'll see, you will have need of them."

"Hmm," said the dean, "I suppose we shan't be able to get a proper convention out of this gathering?"

He looked around with his authoritative eye, but at that moment caught sight of Pastor Marcus, who came along together with his daughter.

"Now, Elisabeth," he said, "curtsey to the gentlemen as your mother has taught you, and say good day politely to everyone in the room."

"Oh, indeed," Severin came rushing up. "I must say indeed that *this* is quite a young lady, eh? Eh?"

He set about slapping Pastor Christian's back, and Pastor Christian's head rocked in time with the blows so that his little pigtail went to and fro like a pendulum. "Now that's what I call a real young lady."

Elsebeth blushed deeply. Her clear eyes were a little slanting, and she had the innocent look of a young kid. Pastor Severin chucked her cheek several times, and, scared stiff, she stared at the floor. Pastor Christian also blushed a little. He was still standing there holding *The Rare Jewel of Faith* in his hand and his face had adopted a polite and apprehensive expression.

"Well, talk to her, do talk to her, for heaven's sake," shouted Pastor Severin. "Is that any way to go about things? Good heavens. When I was your age..."

"Now, don't spoil it all; it had begun so well," said Pastor Marcus in a concerned voice.

"Aye, Severin, be off with you now. What are you doing around the young people?"

It was Pastor Severin's wife who had entered the hall. She was small and plump and resembled her husband in every way.

The dean sat down in despair and stretched out his legs. Master Wenzel walked quickly up and down the floor.

"Shameful," he whispered. "Shameful."

He had again developed a red patch on each cheek. A powerful scent of chocolate filled the hall. The parsons' wives were already in the parlour, approaching like a wave of noise, sweat and coloured shawls. Madam Wenzel Heyde plump, tired and replete; Madam Anders Morsing portly, pinched and shrill-voiced, Madam Gregers Birkeroed merry and mannish and Madam Marcus Faroe small and worn.

Pastor Gregers turned his red-rimmed eyes and his bent hands towards the ceiling. "Oh, Lord, have mercy on us."

A new group of people had filled the hall, taking it over like a flock of cockatoos taking possession of a tree. It was as though all the clergymen paled and disappeared. Only the dean remained behind like a hawk with watchful, cruel eyes.

Pastor Christian tried to smile. It almost looked as though he was about to faint. He was surrounded by a cloud of feminine beings and feminine chatter. But he gradually grew increasingly sure of himself. All the questions that were put to him were so heartfelt and ordinary, so easy to answer that he felt quite relaxed. It was as though he were being encapsulated in a warm cloak of care and maternal tenderness. And everything proceeded so naturally. The dean's wife had put her arm around Elsebeth and was gently rocking her to and fro as though she were a child in need of being comforted and calmed. Elsebeth herself had begun to smile. She raised her shiny doe-like eyes from the floor and looked into Pastor Christian's handsome, dreaming face.

"Well, you see," whispered Pastor Severin to Pastor Poul. "As for womenfolk, it is, when all is said and done, a matter to be treated with thought and consideration. You would not have been cheated if you had been in Pastor Christian's place. And what a beautiful lamb!"

"*De gustibus et coloribus non disputandum*," said Pastor Poul.

"I beg your pardon? What? Oh-h no," said Pastor Severin, starting to laugh. But his laughter was less loud than before. "What was I going to say was that of course it is never nice to have a widow in the benefice. You are right in that."

The dean had risen. He noisily cleared his throat: "As for the betrothal, that can perhaps wait until later..." He looked Pastor Marcus sharply in the eye and added: "For, let me remind you, this is a clerical convention."

The ladies were a little hurt and stalked out of the hall; they really did not wish to disturb. Pastor Christian was left there on his own, red and pale and still holding his Rare Gem in his hand. Master Wenzel, Pastor Gregers and Pastor Severin again adopted their customary sizes. The dean sat down at the table and snapped open the minutes of the clerical meetings.

"We must presumably see about arranging a Christian conclusion to this meeting," he said.

"Yes, of course," said Pastor Gregers, suddenly folding his hands, "we must also allow for the things of the spirit."

The dean gave a severe smile. All the clergymen took their seats around the table and started to cough and sneeze and unfold huge, red handkerchiefs. They also took out some large sheets of paper. These were the church and clerical records from their parishes for the past year.

"Has anyone anything more to add in this gathering?" asked the dean.

No one had anything.

"Dear brethren," said the dean, "then I will close this meeting by reminding you of some words that I called to your

171

attention last year, and, if I remember rightly, the previous year and the year before that."

He smiled again surveyed the gathering with a sarcastic look: "It is really only the admonition directed to the clergy by the Royal Synod in Rendsburg, in which it is said, "Then it is surely our bounden duty seriously to consider that God established the task of preaching and gave that task to us, not for the sake of things temporal," and the dean raised his voice, "but so that through us He might be glorified to mankind."

There was a pause. Dean Anders rested his blue eyes for a moment on each individual clergyman, dwelling especially long on Pastor Poul.

"Those words are truly not superfluous," said Master Wenzel solemnly with a meaningful look in the direction of Pastor Severin.

"Alas no, no indeed," said Pastor Severin, shaking his head. "We are all weak and unworthy beings... indeed we are. God knows we are."

"Yes, indeed," agreed Pastor Marcus. He held his hand to his mouth and glanced up at the ceiling.

Pastor Gregers said nothing at all. He merely nodded. But Pastor Poul and Pastor Christian appeared to be lost in thought.

"Incidentally," said Dean Anders suddenly, starting to leaf through his book. "There is another point in the same exhortation that perhaps also deserves to be remembered."

He smiled again, almost cruelly: "It is about observing the dignity of one's station," he said, allowing his eyes to stray in the direction of Pastor Poul. But then he suddenly looked at Master Wenzel and read: "This is truly not achieved by the acquisition of numerous honorary titles and marks of distinction, not by insistent, ingratiating, flattering and worldly intercourse with the distinguished and wealthy in the congregation, with obvious children of this world, thereby to gain advantages, temporal honours and benefits, not by showing ourselves to be commensurate with the world in free, unrestrained language, costly dishes and clothing."

Master Wenzel had turned as white as a sheet; he sat gasping for breath. His blue, rather watery eyes had taken on an unpleasant sheen, while the red patches in his cheeks had adopted an unhealthy glow. He said nothing, but merely looked as wronged as an innocent dog that has received a beating.

Nor was there any doubt that the dean had been aiming at Master Wenzel in his last exhortation, and it obviously seemed unjust and exaggerated to everyone. Heavens above, Master Wenzel was decency personified, the most Christian of all of them.

"Alas," Pastor Severin said without further ado, "if my sins were not greater than Master Wenzel's." He was on the point of bursting out in his customary laughter, but he refrained.

"Alas," said Pastor Marcus in harmony with him, again looking up at the ceiling.

Master Wenzel sat fiddling with the clasps on a book. His hands were trembling violently. But suddenly, in a strangely broken voice, he said, "He who cannot see into a person's heart knows not his sins. Many are openly guilty of minor sins, others sin mightily in secret."

They all started and gazed at Master Wenzel. He sat looking down at the table. It was impossible to determine whether a thin and apprehensive halo fluttered momentarily over his thin hair.

"We have all sinned," he added, "and we are without honour in the eyes of God."

The dean looked angry.

"Well, perhaps we should close with a short prayer," he

said.

Master Wenzel suddenly started eagerly leafing through the book that lay before him. Pastor Christian, too, came to life. "I would like to suggest a hymn from *The Rare Jewel of Faith*," he said.

"No," said the dean in a sharp voice, murmuring some scornful words about jewels.

"Here, in *Hymns and Spiritual Songs*," said Master Wenzel, continuing to leaf through the book, "there must be some suitable brief verse."

"Well," said Pastor Gregers Birkeroed in his careladen voice, "some verse or other. For instance: *Ne'er am I without a care, but yet am never without grace; I am ever full of sorrow...*"

Dean Anders Morsing looked as though he was about to say, "Shut up." He took *The Spiritual Choir* from Master Wenzel and started to look through it himself: "We're not going to have any sighing of that kind here. Far better to have a penitential hymn."

He pronounced the word in a voice full of retribution and scorn.

"For instance, there is one here: the second hymn is one of confession and remission. He flicked through a few more pages: it is quite unending, but never mind, we need a desperate remedy..."

He looked up, his eyes shining with a kind of grim merriment beneath his bushy eyebrows.

The clergymen coughed, sneezed and unfolded huge handkerchiefs. Master Wenzel distributed *The Spiritual Choir*.

Pastor Severin was the first to start singing. He had a mighty voice:

Come soul, now let us weep

And flesh, thou shalt weep, too.

Now Pastor Gregers' hollow, plaintive voice could be heard:

> *Let us now for sorrow weep*
> *With eyes and mind and spirit.*

And now all joined in the singing:

> *Cleanse your unclean heart*
> *Of evil, shame and fault*
> *Replenish it with sigh and pain*
> *Throw off the cloak of sin*

The clergymen sang loud and slow, lingering tremulously on certain notes.

It was like a boat full of penitents, rowing hesitantly and uncertainly over treacherous waters. Only the dean sat there as a kind of steersman, with sharp, commanding eyes. Occasionally, he beat the rhythm on the table.

By the time they had reached the twelfth verse, tears were pouring down Pastor Marcus's cheeks. But Pastor Severin was singing with excited voice and transfigured face.

The twentieth verse was the last. It was sung with undiminished power and a confident sense of liberation:

> *And I will make my prayer,*
> *Confess before your face*
> *And seek forgiveness fair*
> *From you the Son of Grace.*
> *Ah let me now be told*
> *You sin-free are, go hence!*

Then shall my lips tenfold
Your praises e'er dispense.

The clergymen rose and wiped their noses.

"Aye," said Pastor Severin. "It seriously does one good to occasionally have resort to the saving arms of God's grace."

"Yes, grace," said Pastor Marcus. "Where would one be without it?

The dean gave him a sardonic nod.

"Well, I don't think you need to ask that question, Pastor Marcus. Incidentally, I don't think you should think yourself too safe."

"Nor should any of us," he added in a louder voice.

"God will not be mocked."

Pastor Severin was busy pushing snuff up into his broad nostrils. He directed a gently reproachful look at the dean and gave a huge sneeze.

"Well," said Master Wenzel, opening the door to the parlour. "If you would be so good as to..."

The scent of chocolate and the sound of women's voices again made their way into the hall.

"Aye, yes," exclaimed Pastor Severin. "It's so good... what shall I say... earthly things also demand attention."

And he burst out in his usual laughter and slapped Pastor Christian on the back.

In a Garden

Barbara was that day wearing a green silk dress with a white gauze fichu. She was irritated that Pastor Poul was taken up all that morning; she said that the clergymen were wasting their time on a lot of rubbish. They were not discussing anything but tithes and wool and wool and tithes. For that was what parsons were always like when they got together. And that, of course, was something Barbara knew all about. She was in the bailiff's house with Suzanne, listening to her sad story. She didn't know what to say to her; she herself was so happy and had know idea what it was to be unhappy.

"You are all right," said Suzanne with a sad smile. "You have always just fallen in love or just got betrothed. You don't know what it is not to be at all in love and yet betrothed."

"Yes, by God I do," Barbara exclaimed suddenly and with conviction. "If there is one thing I know, it's that."

She sighed happily and in relief. "I have been married for years without being in love."

"Yes, but not to Gabriel."

Barbara's face became pensive for a moment. It was true enough: she had not been married to Gabriel. Then in a knowing voice, she said, "Gabriel!... You'll manage him all right."

Suzanne shook her head gently: "You have no idea of how I loathe him."

Barbara's face still looked as though she was estimating Gabriel. She didn't loathe him. He was always so full of mockery and so sure of himself, but it could surely not be difficult to throw him off balance. Curiously enough, she had never tried to do that. She had never had time.

"Gabriel," she said, "...you can probably have everything your own way with him. All you need to do is tease him."

"Yes, but I can't stand him. I simply can't abide him."

"Oh-h," said Barbara. "But then you simply don't need to bother about him, do you?"

That was the remarkable thing about Barbara. Suzanne had always admired her and believed that she was equipped with all the experience in the world. But all she was doing now was talking like a child. She was sitting in the sunshine over by the window and looking out and was most interested in talking about things of no import. And when she suddenly saw Gabriel approaching, she became radiant and shouted out to him:

"Hello, Gabriel."

As he entered the room, Suzanne felt that Gabriel was different from usual. There was a delighted, almost benevolent smile on his fat face. He rubbed his hands: "Well, Barbara, how goes it?"

That was all he said. His eyes said everything else. With friendly insolence he considered her slender figure. The well known titillating laughter could be heard in Barbara's throat and an expression of great delight illuminated her face. Gabriel became hot under the collar as a result, but at the same time he felt a little stab in his heart.

"Aye, Barbara," he said, "you are all right. You always get away with things."

Barbara gave something between a sigh and a laugh. She

tried to look serious. "What do you mean?"

But she was far too happy to be able to hide anything. She blushed and was very beautiful. Gabriel's insolent face almost broke. His heart hurt him. Damn it. What did he want with this rose on which he always scratched himself?

But Barbara had suddenly had second thoughts and hurried across to Suzanne. She kissed her and embraced her time after time.

"Good bye, Gabriel," she shouted and went.

Gabriel stood and thought for a while. He kicked a footstool and then went across to the window. "Good God," he said, shaking his head. "Now she's gone out to look for him – the parson. Ugh, that lecherous creature. I hope you won't have too much to do with her in the future, Suzanne; she'll not do you any good."

Suzanne had got up. She tossed her head; her eyes were small with scorn: "At least Barbara is in love with the man she's going to marry, and that's more than can be said of me."

She went out and slammed the door.

"Now then," shouted Gabriel, throwing himself down in a chair. He crossed his legs and was completely at home in the bailiff's sitting room.

When Barbara emerged into Gongin, she met Johan Hendrik, the judge.

He greeted her with his usual sarcastic smile: "Well?"

Barbara laughed contentedly.

"Ah, when you look like that, we all know which way the wind is blowing," said the judge. "Tell me. Is he very much in love?"

Barbara laughed back at him. She liked Johan Hendrik; she often actually felt an urge to confide in him.

The judge stroked his chin. "This man Gabriel," he murmured. "Hmm, I don't know. It's a bad business."

"Why on earth have *you* never thought of marrying her?" said Barbara with a laugh. But she immediately blushed slightly.

"I? Who do you think could be bothered with an old man like me?"

"Oh, stop it, Johan Henrik." Barbara laughed aloud and was by now quite red in her face.

"What do you really think I would be like as a husband?" asked Johan Hendrik.

Barbara looked down. Then, kicking gently at a stone: "I don't know. I once dreamt you were married."

"To Suzanne?"

"No. To me."

"Now, now," said Johan Henrik, "are you sure I can stand hearing that sort of thing?"

Barbara's face was quite pale. She tried to look straight at the judge, but finally had to close her eyes. There was something both comical and touching about this.

"No, what was I going to say," she finally managed to mumble: "I think that Suzanne would be a thousand times happier with you than with Gabriel."

The judge stroked his chin.

"The law speaker said the same to me this morning. Have you two been getting together?"

"No, not at all. *Not at all*." Barbara laughed: "It was just something that struck me the moment I saw you. And so I thought I might just as well say it to you straight away. Fancy the law speaker having the same idea!"

She was flushed and happy and had quite recovered her composure.

"Aye, it's a curious thing," said Johan Henrik. "This is the only time in my life that I have had the impression that the law speaker really wanted something. He certainly didn't *say* much, as you can well imagine, but..."

"Well, won't you, then?" shouted Barbara. She stood there shuffling about, and her voice radiated both eagerness and expectation.

"Well, of course. As far as I am concerned... I have always thought very highly of Suzanne, and even if they should write a song about me... though I don't think they will do. But, you understand, I don't think there is much to be done about that now."

"Oh, but you must try, Johan Hendrik. Won't you?"

"We'll see," said the judge, adopting a meditative expression.

But then he brightened up and glanced at Barbara:

"But then it will never be us two."

Barbara dropped her eyes like lightning. Her throat tightened.

"Goodbye, Johan Hendrik," she exclaimed and hurried off in the direction of Reyn. Joy radiated like a sun in her voice.

The first thing to meet his eyes when Pastor Poul left Regne-gaard after the clergymen's dinner was Barbara in her radiant green silk dress. He felt a dull sense of satisfaction as so often when he had hoped but not expected to see her. She came towards him with a smile, took his arm and was full of gaiety and tremulous spirit. The falsetto in her voice tickled his ear like a rainbow of sounds. He went with her; she was vivacious and relaxed, while he himself was burdened with agonizing joy.

"Where shall we go?" he asked.

They wandered through Gongin right down to the river outside the town. Pastor Poul told her about the meeting, about Pastor Christian and Elsebeth, and Barbara laughed and said that it was a cruel way to treat Pastor Christian.

"Didn't they say anything about me?" she asked suddenly. Her voice sounded rather humble and she looked down.

"No. That's to say, Pastor Severin said something ridiculous, but you know what he's like."

"What did he say?"

"Oh, he simply laughed loud and said something to the effect that it was all madness and so on."

Pastor Poul felt a little pressure on his arm. Barbara shot a quick look at him. There was something both worrying and grateful in her look. There was a pause. Then she quite casually asked:

"Did the dean say anything?"

"No," replied Pastor Poul firmly. "But Pastor Severin," he added quickly, "Pastor Severin thought that it would have been far better if *I* had married Elsebeth Marcusdatter from Sandoy. He said she was a sweet lamb."

Barbara looked like a child that has been ill treated. But it was merely a shadow that passed over her face. She laughed straight away and said, "You know, I think Elsebeth's a very sweet girl and she suits Pastor Christian *perfectly*."

Barbara continued lost in thought. Then she added, "But Pastor Severin is and will always be a fool. He usually addresses speeches to me and calls me Chrysillis and Amaryllis."

They had stood for a time down by the river, had turned back and again reached Reyn. They didn't know where to go. Barbara suddenly had an idea: they should go into the headmaster's garden and sit down. It was so quiet and secluded there.

182

The sun was shining straight down into the headmaster's garden. It was behind the school on a steep slope on the best side of Reyn. There were no trees, but several decorative bushes and everywhere the angelicas stood as high as a man with clusters of white flowers. Nowhere in the Faroe Islands had Pastor Poul seen such a luxuriant plant growth; he was almost anaesthetised by the heat and the spicy scent from the plants.

Barbara sat down. She was at home here as she was everywhere else in Havn.

"Have you got a knife?" she asked.

He handed her a knife. Barbara cut one of the tall angelicas off, trimmed the leaves and flowers off it and handed him a piece of the thick stem. "There," she said, "just taste that."

Pastor Poul bit the stem. It was extremely green and juicy.

"Doesn't it taste good?" laughed Barbara. She had started eating.

The angelica tasted strong, burning and fresh and darkly spiced all at the same time. Pastor Poul did not immediately know whether he liked it; he was quite surprised, and it burned his mouth.

"It tastes of summer," said Barbara. She sat with the greenish white flowery sunshade in her hand, turning it with her fingers.

"It tastes as it looks," said the parson, thinking of the plant's fierce, luxuriant green. Everything around them was green. They were sitting as though at the bottom of a bottle.

"Can you imagine," said Barbara, "I've proposed to someone today, proposed to a man."

"Proposed? What do you mean?" asked Pastor Poul. "Who have you proposed to?"

"To Johan Hendrik, the judge."

Pastor Poul's heart had started to beat. What was this? He was always full of apprehension, never felt completely safe.

"Oh Poul. Don't look like that," exclaimed Barbara. She took his head in her hands and looked him straight in the eye: "Do you hear? You mustn't look like that."

"No, but..." he murmured and was quite confused.

"Did you really believe what I said?" Barbara went on, refusing to let go of his head. Her voice was both happy and indignant.

"Of course not," said Pastor Poul, gently disengaging himself. "You just... gave me a fright."

"You are so silly, you know," said Barbara. "You mustn't be like that. It's not nice of you. It's really horrible. I didn't propose on my own behalf, of course. I proposed on behalf of Suzanne. Can't you understand that?"

And then Barbara told all about Suzanne and Gabriel, how horrible he was and what a pity it all was, meanwhile twisting the big, greenish flower parasol she was holding.

But Pastor Poul thought of that Sunday evening when the French ships were in port.

"And what did the judge say?" he asked idly.

"Well, of course, he said... that he would rather have married me."

"Oh," said Pastor Poul.

Barbara's eyes wandered a little and then she tried to catch his, but he was looking down at the ground. So she took a blade of grass and tickled his neck with it.

"Silly, silly, silly," she whispered in his ear.

It was a moment or two before Pastor Poul raised his head, but the moment she could see into his eyes, Barbara flung her arms passionately around his neck, kissed him long and fervently and finally sighed affectionately. At last she, looked him in the eye and asked: "Did you really think that?"

But at that moment she held him tight again, moaned and was almost as though she would never let him go. Pastor Poul sat there in the burning air, quite confused; he could still feel the sweetness from the angelica in his mouth, and his heart was burdened with agonizing joy.

Gabriel was in the bailiff's sitting room as Pastor Poul and Barbara went past. The sight of them struck him like a blow between the eyes; he was perfectly well aware that they must be together at that moment. Nevertheless, the sight of them was more than he could stand; it hurt him, not only in his heart, but in his stomach as well, indeed right down into his legs. This was the very devil. He wandered restlessly up and down the floor. Then he went out. He didn't want to go too quickly, for he was frightened of catching up with them and seeing them again. Why did he go out at all? He couldn't prevent the lower part of his body from bearing him away through Gongin.

He stopped in the middle of Reyn. He couldn't see them anywhere. The sun was burning down on his head, and he had forgotten his bonnet. He was completely confused and at a loss and had a dull sensation in his thighs. He wandered around among the houses, but kept returning to the highest point of Reyn, the part known as the school ground. His nostrils were palpating. Suddenly, he heard Barbara's laugh. It struck him like a tiny sharp, shiny arrow somewhere in his body. No, this was more than he could stand. He went straight into the headmaster's garden and made his way through the red currant bushes. He stopped and listened for a moment. The flies were buzzing and the sun burning. He could now hear Barbara's voice quite close at hand. And there she sat in her green silk dress and great fichu.

Barbara and Pastor Poul.

The very moment he saw Gabriel approaching, Poul adopted that dark, tense expression suggesting that he would now have to hold on tight again. But Barbara was surprised; she laughed and said, "Gabriel! Are you here?"

Gabriel gave the two an embarrassed smile and took up a position in front of them. Pastor Poul felt as though a cloud had passed before the sun. He stared bitterly at Gabriel's powerful legs and said not a word. He had a sense of disgust at the sight of him, just as he would have had at the sight of a bluebottle on a fresh berry.

It was Barbara who spoke first. "Would you like some angelica, Gabriel?" she asked quite unconcernedly.

The clergyman gave her an angry look. But Gabriel, too, was incapable of showing any kind of polish. Perhaps he was put off by something in the exaggeratedly natural tone of her voice; perhaps he was provoked by a glint in her friendly eyes. Hell! He knew perfectly well he was standing there looking foolish.

"Angelica," he snarled angrily. "I don't eat churchyard plants.

Barbara looked as though someone had hit her. She was completely unaccustomed to people speaking to her in that harsh tone.

"But, Gabriel," she said, "this isn't..."

"They are corpse plants," said Gabriel. "Don't you know there's been a plague cemetery here?"

"Rubbish," shouted Barbara. "The plague cemetery wasn't here; it was right down there in the corner."

"Even so, it's still horrible," said Gabriel.

His anger was actually directed at the clergyman though

he refused to see him or to acknowledge his presence here in the garden.

So it was Barbara he was scolding, and he felt a kind of sweet satisfaction as he observed the effect of his words. He laughed quietly without smiling and went on, "Surely you know, Barbara, that angelica's a filthy plant. You can get leprosy from it. Ha, ha, ha. Aye, otherwise where the hell should all that leprosy come from that is all over the place here in Tórshavn? It's horrible – *horrible!*"

Barbara was really upset. Never had anyone told her that what she was doing was horrible. She spun the big bunch of angelica round quickly and suddenly threw it away.

"You do talk rubbish, Gabriel," she said with a brief laugh that was anything but happy.

Gabriel was so pleased with his victory that he sat down beside Barbara.

"Oh well," he said in order to say something, and he groaned a little. He ignored Pastor Poul. Nor did Pastor Poul look at him; he was so angry that everything went black before his eyes.

Gabriel gave a gentle laugh again and was sufficiently appeased to add, "No, of course it's never been proved that it's the angelica that causes leprosy. But, everyone knows that Hans, Niels the Point's son, who was put in the leprosy hospital in Argir last year had gorged himself on angelica just before he was taken ill."

Barbara made no reply to this, but suddenly she said, "Are you pleased you're going to get married, Gabriel?"

She wanted to talk about something other than angelica.

"Pleased?" said Gabriel. "What the hell have I got to be pleased about?"

"Well, pleased about Suzanne for instance."

"Hmm. Am I supposed to be pleased about the baby, do you think? Hardly."

He sat with his elbows resting on his knees and staring down into the grass. Suddenly, he looked at Barbara and laughed: "No, it must be admitted that there was someone who managed things a lot better that evening."

Barbara gasped.

"You've got it absolutely wrong," she exclaimed vehemently. Laughter and indignation struggled for supremacy in her voice, and she gradually showed signs of blushing. But she did not manage to become angry.

Gabriel sat there laughing silently and watching her. He had the same gently offensive look as he had had that morning. He gave the minister the occasional searching glance. It was the first time he had turned his eyes on him. Pastor Poul had the same withdrawn expression that said he was keeping a grip on himself.

But Barbara hurried to talk of something else.

"Are you really so unhappy to be getting married to Suzanne?" she asked Gabriel.

"Aye, God knows I am," he gave an honest sigh. "There's no denying I had other ideas."

A delighted smile lit up Barbara's face. Again a little laugh escaped her.

"Yes, but Gabriel," she said, blinking several times, "perhaps... perhaps you don't need to?"

Gabriel's face took on a quite remarkable expression. An enormously arrogant idea flickered across his mind for a moment. His lower lip became quite limp.

"Don't need to?" he said uncertainly.

Barbara continued to look at him, still blinking quite slowly. "Well, I mean that it might not be necessary," she said a little hesitantly.

"Of course it's necessary, damn it," said Gabriel hesitantly. But all at once his face became pale and tense: "Tell me, what do you really mean by that?" he shouted.

"I simply mean that you can probably get out of it if you want," countered Barbara.

Gabriel bounced up.

"Who the devil says I don't want to? I mean... who the hell says that I... that I can get out of it?"

"No one is saying that yet, but the judge might perhaps be willing to marry Suzanne if she will have him. Both the law speaker and I have discussed it with him, and... and..."

Barbara shrugged her shoulder and looked mischievously up at Gabriel. "And when you are so upset about it, well..."

"Thank you very much, Barbara," said Gabriel solemnly, "I am most grateful," he went on in a voice that was almost a roar, "for telling me this in time. I will bloody well never forgive you for a dirty little trick like this."

He was already out of the garden. His feet knocked away bits of turf, which rolled down the slope. Barbara stood scornfully watching the huge play of muscles in his backside. Perhaps she was at the same time a little angry that he had left her in such an undignified manner. She noticed that his trousers were made of some thick, very solid material.

But suddenly a yellow butterfly flew up from the bushes and started fluttering around the garden.

"Oh, look!" she shouted.

Pastor Poul slowly rose. The sun was baking down on them. He still had in his mouth the acrid sweet taste of luxuriant flowers and black earth.

Tides

Pastor Poul awoke. The sun was shining in through the window and casting its light on Barbara's clothes, which were lying in a pile on a chair.

He was married now. Barbara was asleep beside him.

Some of Barbara's clothes were white linen, and some were coloured materials – it was her apparel from yesterday lying there, quickly taken off and thrown down, untidily, but not without beauty. Pastor Poul lay a little, looking at these garments. Perhaps she would have arranged them a little differently if she had thought about it. But did Barbara think of anything? As the clothes lay there they represented one of the deeds of her heart, captured and preserved in its powerful, thoughtless nature and grace.

Pastor Poul was filled with tender admiration and gratitude. These clothes lay there like a statement made in confidence, a kind of moving declaration to him. He turned over towards her. But her face when asleep was different from when awake. He had not noticed this before. When she was asleep her features seemed almost to express a kind of grief; there was something helpless and tormented about them. This, too, she showed him. But was it the *intention* that he should see it? Was this confiding something in him that she would not have admitted to when awake? His heart beat for her.

Who was Barbara? Was she the woman who yesterday

190

evening had undressed by the chair over there, or was she the woman sleeping here with suffering expressed in her face? Suppose everything he knew of Barbara was only a guise, a parti-coloured container like her clothes?

Her eyes opened, and she was immediately another. She smiled at him as though she had suddenly found him again after he had been away from her for a long time. She was warm with sleep and put her arms around his neck. Then she looked at the sun and said it was time to get up.

Barbara got out of bed. As natural as a flower in bloom, she went around in her bare shift; only her feet shrank some insignificant amount on contact with the cold floor. Pastor Poul lay wondering. Here, outside Nýggjastova he had gone trembling at the mere thought of Barbara less than a year ago. And there she was now, standing before him as his legally married wife, naked and radiant with warmth from the bed they shared.

He was suddenly overcome by a sense of disappointment. Was this really all? A bed, an embrace and a curiously sweet atmosphere to which, however, he had long ago grown accustomed – was there no other content to this phantasmagoria by which he had been possessed for some nine months.

Barbara slipped her shift off and stood quite naked on the floor. Pastor Poul felt a huge surge of desire, but then the sense of emptiness crept over him again. So that was how Barbara looked. She was beautiful: he realised that. But he felt nothing as a result.

He met her flaming eyes in the mirror and heard her excited voice: "No, my dear. I must hurry today. We have to leave."

"That's a pity," he heard himself say. He was quite amazed. Never before had he needed to tell such a lie to her. He remembered how incredibly wild he had once become one winter's night on having caught a glimpse of her naked body in a hearth room. Now she was standing in the morning sunshine sprinkling her blushing body with eau de cologne. And he was so cool-headed that he simply felt the lack of his torment and pain.

Barbara blew him several kisses and laughed. But suddenly she started: "What's wrong, my love? Are you upset? But I simply *haven't* time."

She ran across and just touched him with her lips in a kiss. Her body was fragrant and cool. But Pastor Poul felt it as though a huge soap bubble had burst. He was filled with painful sympathy for Barbara and reproached himself bitterly.

But Barbara did not know his thoughts and started to dress. She buttoned her slip above her hips, took a quick look at herself in the mirror, sat down and drew her stockings on. Already by now, Pastor Poul started to feel different. But Barbara was simply now conscious of him. She quickly tied her garters around her knees. Then she took a comb and started to do her hair.

He sought to catch her eyes in the mirror. But she looked only at her own image and smiled to herself as she arranged her hair. He tried to talk to her, but she only replied in monosyllables and enveloped herself in a cloud of fragrant powder.

"May I kiss you?" he asked.

He saw her smiling mouth, red and white in the mirror. She carefully fixed a tiny black patch on her cheek.

"May I kiss you?"

She rubbed the patch away and put a new one closer to the corner of her mouth. Then she suddenly turned towards him, her bosom fragrant and swelling, her eyes burning in her powdered face. She gave him a quick, preoccupied kiss and immediately turned back to the mirror.

"You really are doing yourself up," he said. "I had no idea that you painted your faces so much in the Faroes."

She made no reply. He could think of nothing better to do than put on his trousers. Then he sat down on the edge of the bed and thought about love. It was like sunshine and fleeting shadows.

Barbara had put on her blue dress. She tied a silk scarf around her neck and was radiant and fragrant. Then she opened the window. A gentle breeze cleared away the clouds of powder. Tórshavn's cockerels were crowing and its ducks were swimming out on the smooth waters of the East Bay.

"There goes Gabriel," she said.

Gabriel was walking through Gongin dressed in a wig and a three-cornered hat. He had become a fine man. Even his shadow was as sharp and *distingué* in the morning light as any of the silhouettes on Bailiff Harme's hessian-covered walls. People greeted him respectfully and he replied by raising the silver knob on his ebony walking stick up to his hat. It was one of the bailiff's walking sticks.

Gabriel was married and on the first morning of his marriage had been presented with a son. The child had come into the world rather early; he was sickly and had had to be baptised immediately. He had been called after the bailiff and his name was Augustus Gabriel Harme.

"Goodbye," said Barbara, blowing a kiss, "I have an awful lot to do today."

Pastor Poul ran after her, but she dodged him and was off like a frightened bird. He was left behind in his stocking feet like some half-dressed wretch. The usual vague unease again began to trouble him. He wished back the moment a short time ago when he had not been the least interested in her. He looked out of the window and saw her go in through the door to the bailiff's house from which Gabriel had emerged a short time before. Well, so he knew after all where she was for the time being. Fancy his having had the absurd idea that he was not keen on Barbara. He lit his pipe and slowly dressed.

He felt the need to talk to someone or other. But who on earth could he talk to about Barbara? His colleague the Tórshavn parson? Master Wenzel would give him some airy-fairy answer to any down-to-earth question. The law speaker? He envisaged Samuel Mikkelsen's kind face. He would smile sympathetically and benevolently at the subtleties of love. The judge? He would consult a book on philosophy and throw light on the question with examples and parallels. But when it came to the point, was that not to be preferred? He had heard the word of God so many times, and what he needed now was a secular sermon. The judge was a man he had always found it good to talk to. He liked this bony reasoner. He had simply never had time, never had a breathing space.

There was something strange in his having started to reflect today. He had not reflected for the past nine months. Was it not after all as though the fever in his heart had become less? He was glad of that and yet he did not like it.

When, half an hour later, he entered the judge's sitting room, he immediately sensed an atmosphere he knew. It was something from Copenhagen; he came to think of Regensen and of the halls of residence in the university district, and suddenly he remembered the soaring, golden spire of the Cathedral Church of Our Lady. He felt as though he had been thrown back into an earlier, forgotten time when many things had not yet happened.

The judge received him. He was not fully dressed and he was holding a book in his hand.

"Forgive me," he said. "It isn't that I am a lazybones. But I often become so engrossed in my books that I forget to get up.

"Aye," thought Pastor Poul: "Regensen!" He spoke first a little about the weather, and the judge talked about the harvest, which he believed would be good after the favourable summer.

"You are a man who takes a sensible view of everything, Mr Heyde," said Pastor Poul without further ado.

"I do my best to do so," said the judge in his quiet, deep voice.

"Well," said Pastor Poul, looking as though idly out of the window, "then you presumably think I am a very foolish man?"

"Why?"

"I am thinking of my marriage."

The judge sat down, threw his right leg over the left, leant forward and buried his chin in his hand. Then he changed legs and leant back, and finally, digging his silver snuff box out of his pocket: "He who lives without committing foolish acts is not as wise as he himself thinks."

Pastor Poul looked at him in amazement. The judge rose, waved his hand dismissively and laughed: "No, you mustn't think I invented that saying myself. I am not as wise as that. No, they are by *La Rochefoucauld*."

"Laroche... oh, one of these new-fangled philosophers?"

"Well, new-fangled... no, but he will never become *démodé*. I often read one of his sayings, rather like when I take a pinch of snuff. It is so healthy."

He offered his little silver snuffbox to Pastor Poul: "It is so good occasionally to hear the truth about yourself and about people in general." The judge gave a loud sneeze. "It's a subject which I never tire of considering."

"That was the impression I had of you," said Pastor Poul.

"All the more surprising I find it that you recommend to me what you yourself call foolishness."

The judge sat down and laughed. He again crossed his legs and rubbed one of his socks.

"Well, putting it bluntly, I mean: just you jump overboard. Someone has to live life, and he who avoids foolishness also avoids life, believe you me. Do you know, I will happily admit to you that I not only admire you, but I envy you. Now, don't misunderstand me. First of all, I am very well aware what a daring game you are playing, and you will probably find that life is not simply a bed of roses. But to express my thought quite precisely: I envy you the experiences you are going to have."

"Even if I lose the game?"

"Precisely if you lose the game. If you win, there must be something wrong with you."

"I don't really understand you."

"You will understand me afterwards – provided you survive."

The judge suddenly rose and went across and gave Pastor Poul a slap on his shoulder: "I hope you can appreciate a joke – of course you will survive. You must not let yourself be influenced by any superstition. So, have courage. But you surely already know beforehand that you are embarking on an adventure."

"You say you envy me the game I have come to play. So it is an obvious question why you yourself are not risking an adventure of any kind."

"Ah," said the judge: "I am far too sensible. Reason prevents the acquisition of wisdom. Don't reflect yourself in me; I am just a pedant. Here I have been for years and years, dying from curiosity to understand mankind, and for that purpose I have read God knows how many books. Do you think I have become wiser?"

He paused for a moment and laughed. "I will tell you something: What one understands from a book is only what one approves of, and what one approves of is only what one in one way or another knows beforehand. Or what fits in with one's own ideas. The rest is smoke."

The judge had made a pause. He sat there apparently far away in thought and whistling with half his mouth. Then he got up suddenly and started to walk up and down.

"Do you understand? Here I am reasoning and studying the chart of the ocean called human life. And then you suddenly come along and put out to sea with all sails unfurled."

"Towards my own shipwreck of course, you say."

"Well yes. But understand me aright: a philosopher never suffers a total shipwreck. And so it was just this that I wanted to say to you: since you have got yourself on this vessel, go on like a philosopher. Make your philosophical and moral observations of everything you see and hear, and every day measure the strength of the wind force of foolishness. Then you will make shore one day, perhaps robbed of your vessel, but in return you will be able with an omniscient smile to shake your head and say, 'this world, this world,' just like my aunt Ellen Katrine."

Pastor Poul still felt confused.

"It's something new for me to hear," he said, "that foolishness should be a means of achieving wisdom."

The judge stopped and laughed. With his thin fingers he made a gesture as though he were a preacher: "For a man of God such as you this shouldn't be so difficult to understand. Just as you have doubtless discovered that the road to salvation goes through sin, so the road to wisdom goes through foolishness."

Pastor Poul thought he recognised something in this train of thought. He felt ensnared by it, though it helped him through a difficulty.

"I thought you were a disciple of Baron Holberg and men of that kind," he said, "whose moral stance is said to rest exclusively on reason."

The judge suddenly sat down. He looked as though he had a pain in his stomach; he grimaced and was as though in pain:

"Well, what am I to say? The only thing you have to hold on to is your poor reason. That is why one reads Holberg and Bayle and Locke and all those men. But if, in my ignorance, I can take the liberty of criticising these writers a little, it would be to say that in all their reason they forget that Man is fundamentally unreasonable and can simply not live without foolishness. I am not far from sharing my brother Wenzel's belief in original sin."

"Original sin?"

"Yes, or original unreason. Sin and foolishness are only two names for the same thing. My brother Wenzel encounters it with a vengeance and calls it sin and for that reason pesters Heaven with a tedious correspondence concerning the miserable and perverse state of his own heart. I do not feel myself to be one iota better than he, but yet I cannot see myself as anything but laughable and foolish. Viewed correctly, my dear Pastor Poul, we are all of us nothing but monkeys. We are ravaged by jealousy, greed, covetousness and vanity. Especially vanity."

He shook his head and laughed: "But that is because of our natures, whether it is the Devil or someone else that has planted this monkey nature within us."

"How true, how true indeed," said Pastor Poul. "What would we all be if God in His love had not given us the grace that makes all our sins as white as snow?"

"Grace," said the judge, "bah. Grace... rubbish. What is grace but smelling salts to sniff at when the foot sweat of sin becomes rather too pungent?"

Pastor Poul could not help smiling. He thought of the hymn sung by Pastor Severin and Pastor Marcus. But all this was dreadful; it was heresy; it was unlawful.

"No," Johan Hendrik went on, "smelling salts can perhaps take the smell away, but the sweat remains even so, damn it. You are only stifling one piece of foolishness with another."

Pastor Poul shook his head and said, "What you are saying only applies to the orthodox. Modern Christians do not believe in grace unless with an honest heart you repent your sins and try to improve your life. If you don't do that, then you do not *receive* grace."

"What do you mean by 'an honest heart'? Aye, you must forgive me for asking you like another Pontius Pilate."

The judge rose and again started to walk up and down. Pastor Poul thought of his own heart. It could not be entirely honest. In relation to Barbara that morning it had been shamefully inconstant and erratic. He did not know whether he had loved her at all at that moment or whether it was not all some enchantment. He had no answer for the judge.

"Well, there you are," said Johan Hendrik. "We cannot escape the monkey in our own hearts, whether we are Christians or atheists. Have you read Pascal? No, of course not. My brother Wenzel has not read him either, and that is a mistake. But he has read Kingo, and he says, 'Farewell, oh world, farewell.' Well, does he the blazes. But never mind, he is only a monkey like all the rest of us. I really don't know how God is to differentiate between us. My own poor reason has not taken me any further than recognising my foolishness, but it has never persuaded me to try to improve my unreasonable heart. It has not helped me more than grace. And yet I cannot find any other way of worshipping God than with the light I have been given to examine the fool within me and try to be of use in the world in which I have been placed. In my circumstances there is little to learn and less to achieve. But you, my dear friend, you must know that the people who encounter true grace are those whom fate has grasped to play, as though they were an instrument. But whether these people can be bothered to learn anything from it is another matter."

"I consider you a heretic, Mr Heyde," said Pastor Poul. "But I must confess that I have learnt something from you."

The judge made no reply. He stood by a small table and was busy screwing a flute together. When he had finished, he put the instrument to his lips and blew a long cadence.

"Well, see," he said. "This is one of *my* follies. I cannot refrain from playing the flute even though there is nothing rational or moral in it."

He again blew a long, trembling trill and then stood thoughtfully holding the flute in his two hands: "Even that old fogey Holberg had a passion for music. You wouldn't have expected it of him. Have you ever seen him?"

"No, he was dead before I started at the university."

"Oh yes. *I* once heard him playing... one evening when I passed his house in Copenhagen."

Johan Hendrik played a few short pieces and talked in between them. He told about his nephew Andreas Heyde, who was an excellent violinist. Andreas' father was dead, and he himself was now studying economics in Copenhagen.

"Economics?" asked Pastor Poul in surprise.

"Yes," nodded the judge. I saw to that. "Then he might perhaps be of some use to his native land. Wenzel, of course, wanted him to study theology. He thought the other was far too

200

worldly a subject."

"And then he argued that theology was at least a subject on which you could earn your bread and butter."

Johan Hendrik grimaced. "Oh, this world, this world," he added, shrugging his shoulders.

"You are no great lover of the clergy, I can understand," said Pastor Poul with a smile.

"Not as great as Mrs Aggersøe!"

The judge suddenly lowered his instrument and made a deep and very affable bow in the direction of the open window.

"Good morning, Johan Hendrik," came the sound of Barbara's voice outside. "Your playing has drawn me here."

"Hmm," said the judge. "You can easily kid me with that. I know why you are here. But it is only a good thing that you miss your husband."

Pastor Poul had immediately risen. His wife blinked when she saw him and then laughed, though unconvincingly.

"Actually" she said, blushing, "I really came because of the music. I didn't know Poul was here."

"Well, come in," said the judge. "And I will play for both of you. It ought to be on an *oboe d'amour* now."

Barbara looked at the judge and laughed. It seemed to Pastor Poul as though there existed some understanding between the two of which he knew nothing.

"An *oboe d'amour* – do you know what that is, Barbara?" the judge went on. "You don't understand the word, perhaps? But you always know the melody."

"No, I must get on," said Barbara. "I simply haven't the time to stand here; I have *so* much to do. By the way, there's a ship in the offing. They say it's the *Fortuna*."

She waved goodbye and smiled once more at the judge. But when she had gone a little way down the alleyway, she turned round and blew a kiss to her husband. By then, the judge had retired to the middle of the room.

"Yes," he said, "you have a lovely wife. I have paid court to her since she was a little girl, and she has always been so charming as to pretend that she has not known how old I am."

Pastor Poul gave him a dubious look. These careless words pleased him, but they did not quench his thirst for reassurance. He wanted most to open his entire heart to the judge, to implore at least this man to be his ally. But he feared to have truths revealed to him that were too devastating. He had already discovered that Johan Hendrik was a surgeon who used the knife without mercy. So he turned the conversation on to more ordinary subjects, and it was not long before he took his leave.

"Goodbye," said the judge. "If there is any way in which I can be of service to you, I hope you will come again. I shall be following you with interest."

Johan Hendrik did not know whether he should appreciate this interest. He felt as though he was a boat made of paper that had been pushed out to sail in a great river. For the moment, the current was gentle. He lay turning this way and that in the tidal waters of love.

Fortuna

At that moment, a certain movement could be sensed in the streets of the town. Windows were opened, people were looking out and a few hurried off down the narrow stepped alleyways leading down to the shore. When Pastor Poul came down to Nýggjastova, he saw that a ship was approaching. He recognised it as the *Fortuna*, the ship which had brought him to the country one dark November morning nine months ago.

Neither Barbara nor her mother was at home. He had the impression that the entire town was on its toes. The sun was shining and the flags were raised on the Redoubt. The mood was as on some public occasion. On the way to Tinganes he caught up with the law speaker and joined him. He asked him if they were not soon to be leaving.

"My dear friend," Samuel Mikkelsen replied, looking at him with a smile. "Just when the ship has arrived! No, I don't think we shall be getting away today after all."

Pastor Poul had all along had some indeterminate feeling of antipathy towards this ship. Now he was quite irritated as a result of its arrival. He was suddenly keen to get away as soon as possible; he was on edge and worried at having to remain in Havn any longer. His concern increased when he arrived at the Hoist... here he found Barbara at the centre of the crowd. She scarcely heeded him, but went around without having her eyes on anything but the ship.

"Good Lord," he thought. "Am I now to be jealous of a ship?" He had to shake his head at his own foolishness. This was not a great problem with which to burden his heart.

When the ship soon afterwards dropped anchor in the East Bay, an unfamiliar figure could be glimpsed on the deck. It was presumably a passenger, but no one was able to say who it was, for no one was expected. People stood around in inquisitive groups chatting and making guesses. They had a long wait, a wait filled with excitement. But when the boat was at last on its way towards the shore again with the skipper and the unknown stranger on board, there was suddenly a cry of recognition from the quick group of women right out by the Hoist:

"Andreas. It's Andreas."

And now everyone could see that it was Andreas Heyde, the student, who had come back home.

The Reverend Wenzel Heyde, who had also come down to Tinganes, suddenly acquired two flushed cheeks: "That was not the idea... that was not the idea."

Even the judge looked as though he disapproved. He had always imagined that his nephew would finish his studies before coming home. He had to admit that this did not suggest very serious study. But otherwise it appeared that the people of Tórshavn were happy to see Andreas again; they crowded together down by the Hoist and surrounded him as soon as he set foot ashore.

Andreas Heyde quickly made his way through the crowd, greeting people and laughing. He had a fair, manly face and very big, cheerful eyes. His clothes were those of a gentleman, well tailored, but he wore them in a careless manner of his own. His hat was skewed, and there was tobacco dust in the folds in his waistcoat. The bottom buttons were not even fastened, so that his shirt ballooned a little over his waistband. He made straight for his uncles and greeted them cheerfully, after which he was so busy shaking the hands of people both high and low that he simply had no time to answer questions.

Not until things had calmed down around him and he had brushed a little snuff away did he suddenly turn his head to look at his two uncles and say, "Well! That was a surprise for you, wasn't it."

There was a light and cheerful, perhaps a slightly challenging tone in his voice.

"Your uncle and I..." Pastor Wenzel began in a serious and solemn tone.

Andreas interrupted him with a little laugh. He stood with both hands in his pockets and, to the sound of a slight click, sank first one knee and then the other. "See here," he said, taking out a paper: "Resolution of the Royal Exchequer! You hadn't expected that, had you!"

The Tórshavners stood around exchanging quite loud comments on the new arrival. They all knew him; he belonged there, and they were proud of him. Someone commented that it was a man like him who ought to have got the bailiff's daughter instead of that oaf Gabriel.

"I don't think you had better say that," said another. "Andreas is probably used to finer young ladies than the bailiff's daughter."

"Bah," said a third one. "Finer than the bailiff's daughter! If Suzanne isn't a fine lady..."

"Aye, she's fine here in Tórshavn, but what about out in the rest of the world?"

"Tórshavners are never too fine for Tórshavners," concluded Whoops. "Suzanne, poor thing, it was not prophesied at her birth that she would have to marry some great local hulk, and

I've told him that to his face."

"You're mad, so you are. He'll soon be manager."

"I don't care, even if he..."

"You should be a bit more careful – the law speaker's just over here."

"I'm not afraid of the law speaker. He's such a kind and gentle person to be in that position. If only they were all like him."

Samuel Mikkelsen had stood for some time quietly amused at this conversation. Now he turned his bearded face towards Whoops and said with his kindly smile: "You seem to forget that I'm a Tórshavner as well."

"Oh," she said, "that makes no difference. You, Samuel, and the judge and the lot of you. A lovely family, God knows you are, and you never forget ordinary folk."

The law speaker smiled again. He knew it all. It happened that Whoops and other poor folk turned up in the town to beg for a little wool, a little tallow or any other of the country's products. They never left a farm belonging to him or to a member of his family without having received a little help. Good God, the people of Tórshavn had so little to live on. You had to take pity on them even if some of the things they said were occasionally a little rough.

The judge and Pastor Wenzel had with growing surprise read that Frederik the Fifth, by the Grace of God, King of Denmark and Norway, the Wends and the Goths, should via his Exchequer have recommended that the student Andreas Heyde be permitted to undertake a journey to the Faroe Islands in order to carry out research and to report on the country's geography, its flora and fauna, its inhabitants and its economy.

Pastor Wenzel was dazzled and silent. The judge stood there gesticulating enthusiastically. But suddenly he put a dubious hand to his chin and asked, "But do you really think you can do that?"

"Can?" laughed Andreas.

"It will be difficult," said Johan Hendrik. "But by God it's a wonderful job. How the devil have you managed to get it?"

"Professor Oeder has worked it for me," said Andreas. "He is my patron."

Johan Hendrik looked around in some confusion. What he would most have liked at this moment was somewhere to sit, somewhere where he could settle down quietly and consider this amazing thing. But there were crowds of people everywhere. Andreas himself was like quicksilver. It was impossible to obtain any proper information in the midst of this confusion. That would have to wait.

Never in his later life did Pastor Poul forget this moment. The very second that Andreas Heyde stepped ashore, his heart was filled with terrible forebodings. He saw straight away that a dangerous bird had flown in, one against which he would never be able to defend himself. He knew that from now on he was at the mercy of a play of unpredictable forces.

His eyes sought Barbara. She was standing a little way away from him, up by the entrance to the Royal Store, on the spot where he had seen her for the very first time. She appeared tó be engrossed in a conversation with Madame Anna Sophie Heyde. She would turn her head occasionally and glance first out across the water and then, on the way back, across the group of people standing together. Then she resumed her conversation. He could hear her voice and her laughter. Her entire being was radiant.

He felt that at that moment she was his enemy. It would be a hopeless undertaking to go up to her and seek to tempt her away from this place. He had no power over her; she did as she wanted in every single thing. She was cat-like and terrible.

Andreas Heyde came closer and closer to the entrance, still chatting and laughing. He had perhaps not noticed Barbara so far. Pastor Poul observed him at closer quarters, noticed the authoritative manner in which he was ambling along, examined his friendly and at the same time indifferent features. He was attracted by the vivacity of his character. And at the same time he was aware that this meant his own ruin.

The inevitable was approaching. Andreas Heyde looked up suddenly and adopted a vigilant expression. Barbara had the side of her face turned towards him and saw nothing. But Anna Sophie started to jest and ask Andreas if he no longer recognized the old aunt who had come down to receive him. Throughout this welcoming scene, Barbara stood there with a preoccupied but polite expression and held her head in a quite dignified manner. Then Andreas quickly turned to her with an open and slightly arrogant smile. His stance was careless, but the moment he saw her face he became serious and quickly prepared to pay her a compliment.

"Well, I suppose you know...?" said Anna Sophie.

"Oh yes," said Andreas with a bow. "I remember you well from my time at school... Mrs Salling."

"Mrs Aggersøe," Anna Sophie corrected him with a smile.

"Mrs... Mrs Aggersøe?" Andreas asked in surprise and bowed again. His fair face was quite stiff with confusion.

Barbara suddenly blushed.

"I remember you well," she hurried to say, finishing her sentence with a little laugh.

Pastor Poul heard it. This familiar sigh ending in a falsetto, oh, he knew her. The game was on now.

Both Andreas and Barbara were a little embarrassed, but it was she who was the first to find a few matter-of-fact words to say. She also came to his assistance, listening attentively to what he told them, and applauding his words with brief bursts of laughter. It was not long before he was as relaxed and cheerful as before. Yet he did not quite become himself again. In everything he said, there was now a somewhat gentle tone of gravity and courtesy.

"I suppose you will be content to stay with us, Andreas?" asked Anna Sophie. They moved off. Pastor Wenzel, the judge, Andreas Heyde, Anna Sophie and Barbara. Everyone was on their way home. A broad flow of people moved slowly between the Royal Store buildings up along the path between the churchyard and the Corps de Garde. Pastor Poul went with them and managed to walk alongside his wife. She looked at him, as though a little surprised, but she said nothing.

"We are not likely to be leaving today," said Pastor Poul.

"No," was her indifferent reply.

"Perhaps it is not all that important to you either?"

"What? Oh, leaving. No, of course we can't leave now the ship's arrived. Tomorrow, my dear. Or another day."

She spoke to him as to a pestering child, kindly but with her mind on other things.

"You will come in, won't you?" asked Anna Sophie. "You must come and meet our nephew, Pastor Poul."

Pastor Poul would have liked to find an excuse, but Barbara said, "Oh, do come, Poul."

Pastor Poul went along as the last of the guests, unhappy and plagued with misgivings. He felt completely out of it. It all reminded him too much of the evening when the French ships came to town.

Andreas Heyde was not a man to sit still on a chair in the parson's living room. He was all over the place, talking to everyone at the same time, about economics one moment, opera the next and occasionally the slaughter of pilot whales. He had with him a new book, he said, that would interest the judge – he had it here in his chest and would dig it out straight away. Unceremoniously, he took off his morning coat, hung it over a chair and started unpacking. Meanwhile he sang in his clear voice: "La la la la la la la la!"

Then he rose and looked at Barbara with sudden courtesy.

"Oh, Mrs Aggersøe, forgive me for being so *sans façon*. I forget to put away my bad student habits. I will try to remember..."

The judge thought that Andreas looked less like a student than a *petit maître* with his exaggerated shirt sleeves and his lace. These were perhaps bagatelles that could be attributed to his youth. He was reluctant to make a hasty judgement. But he had expected his nephew to be rather different from this.

So had Pastor Wenzel, very much so. He was by now deeply upset; the red patches glowed like geraniums in his cheeks. He did not know who he was most angry with, Andreas or his wife, Anna Sophie, who was bouncing about and making a fool of herself for this empty-headed fop they had got in the house. But Johan Hendrik was here reaping the rewards for his great plan of making the lad study such a vain and worldly subject.

"La la la la la la la la," Andreas was already singing again.

"Aye, la la la la," thought Johan Hendrik. There was no denying that he was annoyed. "La la la – bah."

Pastor Poul watched his wife. She was sitting straight up on a chair and saying nothing, but there was a slight smile on her lips. Andreas did not address her or even look at her. He looked at anything but her. And yet she was the pivot around which all his excitement revolved. Pastor Poul saw this with devilish clarity, and he saw that Barbara saw it. She was enjoying it all, both the economics and the opera and the dolphins and the chest and the shirt sleeves and the singing, as though it were all a comedy being performed in honour of her. What was it the judge had once said: that no dog could admire her from its corner without her noticing it and taking pleasure in it! But this was a young Apollo making himself into her monkey.

Andreas Heyde soon started digging out all kinds of things from his trunk. He was impatient and swift and spread it all around, stockings and waistcoats, books and music, buckles, pistols, small caskets with miniatures on the lid and many other manly and masculine possessions. A sweet, fiery perfume rose from the chest. Finally, he took out an instrument; it was a lute.

"Good heavens," Pastor Wenzel exclaimed in a bitter voice. "I must say you have gathered some worldly goods."

"Yes, indeed," said Andreas. "But I still haven't got one of those," he made a circular movement, "one of those millstones, you know, uncle, that priests wear... I mean a ruff, one of those you would have liked to see me turn up in."

He pulled a comical, innocent face and threw a hidden glance at Barbara. Pastor Poul saw that she quickly bit her lip and stifled a laugh. She suddenly flushed and looked serious. Pastor Wenzel turned around and quickly went up and down the room. Shortly afterwards, he went out.

The judge smiled to himself. He stood watching the battle.

"I actually thought you played the violin," he said.

"So I do," replied Andreas. "But I keep my violin separately, in a box constructed specially for the purpose. I only take this lute when I am going to sing."

"Do you sing as well?"

"Well, just a few short ditties."

"Hmm," said Johan Hendrik, putting his hand up to his

chin.

"Well, sing a song for us," shouted Anna Sophie and Barbara almost as one voice.

They had suddenly become restless; they could not sit still; their eyes were shining with excitement. Andreas started thrumming and screwing on his instrument. A thoughtful wrinkle had developed between his eyes, and he sat down on the edge of his chest, one leg dangling in the air and the other supported on the ground. He stared ahead for a few more moments, and then he suddenly looked up in his eager manner, thrummed a powerful chord and sang:

> *Oh Columbine, oh Columbine,*
> *Oh Columbine, sweet love of mine,*
> *Your lovely face I long to see,*
> *Oh, do you never long for me?*

He laughed and looked at Barbara with comic despair in his great eyes. Then he continued sobbing over his lute:

> *In days gone by, you loved me dear*
> *But love has left you now I fear*
> *So dear to me you aye have been*
> *No longer I to you, I wean.*

Pastor Poul wished he were far away. He felt as though his heart was an open book, which everyone was reading and laughing at. In despair he tried to put on a merry face, but he knew he looked miserable and wretched. But suddenly, the judge slapped Andreas on the back: "All right, Harlequin, I think that's enough. Think of your uncle; I don't think he appreciates this sort of thing. And I thought you said you had a book for me?"

Andreas put the instrument down. It was as though he had suddenly forgotten song and music. He quickly bent down over his chest, rummaged around a little in it and extracted a book: "Here it is, uncle. I hope you will accept it as a little present. It's quite a new book, and one that has been much discussed."

"François Quesnay," read Johan Hendrik.

"Yes, he is one of the new economists known as the physiocrats. They want everything in the world to go according to a quite new melody, one that is quite new and more natural. They say that agriculture and the exploitation of the earth are the true source of all wealth, and of course ought also to play first fiddle in the economy of any well run land.

The judge stood with the open book in his hand. He looked with shining eyes at his nephew, who became increasingly eager as he explained how everything in the world would work of its own accord if only the peasantry, from the sweat of whose brow everyone lived, could be enlightened, skilled and industrious.

"*Pauvre paysan*," he said, "*pauvre royaume. Pauvre royaume, pauvre roi*! Aye, we see that here, too. If our farmers were skilled enough themselves to grow all the corn they use for their bread, the king would have no need to sell the corn here in the Royal Store at a great loss to himself, and our country would save a great deal thereby."

The judge made several times to stroke his chin, but he forgot, and his hand stopped half way there and sank down again – this was far too interesting. Barbara was the only one not to be interested in the discussion. It was as though a shadow had descended on the area of the room in which she was sitting.

"Well, we must be going," she said.

Andreas suddenly came to a standstill. He didn't really know which way to turn, and it looked as though he wanted to address everyone at the same time.

"Going?" said Anna Sophie. "Surely you will stay and have something to eat? The food is almost ready. Andreas, come along and I will show you your room."

"My room," said Andreas. "I had thought of asking for a room that is not up in the attic. I might need to get up, you see."

He went out together with Anna Sophie. The judge stood there deep in thought and then he joined his brother in the study.

Pastor Wenzel was walking up and down in some agitation.

"I don't know what you say to that young show-off," he muttered. "Now you can see what's come of those pointless studies. He's eaten up the whole of his inheritance, indeed he has. And my money and your money. And otherwise all he's done is learn to sing some dubious ditties."

"Well," said Johan Hendrik, "he has his faults. But what the devil has that got to do with his studies? The lad knows his economics."

"Yes, you can see that by his showy clothes," came the bitter reply.

The judge suddenly turned towards him: "Never mind, I'm damned glad we haven't got him home as a pedant or a bookworm." He bleated angrily: "Or as a sanctimonious hypocrite. Now he's come for the good of the country. We have to help the farms to prosper. I don't think you understand that. But let me tell you something you will understand: That will produce more tithes for you as well. Goodbye."

Pastor Poul and Barbara had been left alone in the living room.

She avoided looking at her husband, and she jumped when he suddenly was standing before her.

"Oh, my dear," she exclaimed. "What is wrong with you, Poul?"

She got up and stroked him, and her voice was one of great tenderness: "What is wrong, my love?"

Pastor Poul made no reply and did not move. His face showed no emotion, but his eyes turned black with anger. He was not far from striking her. But suddenly he crumpled and simply said, "Barbara."

She hurried to embrace him and she looked at him. There was some terrible fear in her eyes.

"Will you leave with me today?" he asked dully.

"Yes" she replied, still frightened. But suddenly her face brightened: "Yes, let's go." She kissed him several times: "Of course. We will simply leave."

"But what about the law speaker?" said Pastor Poul suddenly. "It is hardly likely he will want to leave today."

"Never mind," said Barbara. "We'll go without him. We'll get someone to row us there on our own."

Andreas was radiant when he entered the room a few minutes later.

"Did you get a comfortable bedroom?" asked Barbara.

"Couldn't be better. In a parsonage one ought always to stay on the ground floor... strange when it is my Uncle Wenzel who is the minister."

"Yes, then you can come home in the middle of the night when you feel like it," said Barbara.

"Exactly," shouted Andreas. "You understand me, Madam."

"Yes," Barbara went on. Her eyes were full of life: "And then you can..."

She broke off.

"Exactly," said Andreas. "That as well."

They both laughed. Barbara was a little flushed. But she suddenly reached out her hand to him and said, "Well, goodbye, monsieur, and enjoy yourself. We are leaving now."

Andreas Heyde's face was suddenly like a candle that has burnt out.

"Are you leaving?" he stammered. "I thought..."

A tiny delighted smile spread around the corners of Barbara's mouth: "Yes," she said in a tone that was both teasing and apologetic. "We really do have to leave now."

"You can't leave today," said Anna Sophie, who had entered the room. "All the men are unloading. You won't find a team to row you."

"No, you won't get anyone," repeated Andreas eagerly.

Barbara looked a little dubious. "What are we going to do, then?" she asked. "It looks as though we shall have to stay." She gave her husband a look that was at once one of laughing and weeping: "That's a pity, Poul."

Pastor Poul was desperate. He felt it was a matter of life and death.

"We'll walk to Velbestad," he said, "and get a boat there. And that will be a lot quicker as well."

"Yes, that's a good idea," said Barbara. "It's both quicker and a lot more fun. How foolish of me not to have thought of that straight away."

"But what about all your luggage?" objected Anna Sophie. "You can't take it with you that way."

"No, that's quite impossible," said Andreas in an effort to persuade them.

"No, so we are no further," said Barbara.

"The law speaker can bring the luggage when he comes," said Pastor Poul.

"Yes, of course," said Barbara. "The law speaker can bring the luggage. Then we had better be off."

She gave Andreas a look that was both smiling and apologetic at the same time.

"Well, then, goodbye monsieur."

Within quite a short time all the arrangements had been made. The luggage prepared and Barbara dressed for the journey. As they passed the westernmost houses in the town, she suddenly took her husband's arm and gave him a warm smile. "Oh, it's so exciting. It's almost as though you are carrying me away."

She pressed herself close to him before letting go of his arm. Before them lay the broad landscape in the light of the midday sun. They walked across stretches of green and over brown heaths and were more and more alone amidst nature. The rivers rushed and the golden plover sang in the heather. It was a beautiful afternoon, warm and fresh. When they had reached the ridge above Velbestad, they had a view west over the open sea. The islands of Hestoy and Koltur stood out, surrounded by foam and with the afternoon shadows on their east-facing slopes. The mountains of Vágar rose bluish in the north west. Pastor Poul and Barbara looked at each other and laughed as though they had escaped some great danger.

Christmas Festivities

The first months Pastor Poul spent as a married man in the Jansegard Parsonage were the happiest in his marriage. During this time, the days became shorter and shorter and the weather increasingly rough and stormy. In the few hours around noon when it was light, they could see men carrying baskets on their backs as they went across towards the lake to fetch fuel from the little group of peat stacks that looked like Capernaum. But it was a desolate and wet Capernaum, and when the men returned with their burdens in the dusk and in the cold light produced by the showers, they looked grey like cats against the dark earth.

The winter was a burden to many minds. But for Pastor Poul, the darkness was only like a warm nest into which he burrowed deeper and deeper. His days were good and sweet. Wherever he was, wherever he went, whether in the servants' hall, in the pulpit or in the huts tending the sick, he knew in his own mind that he was a man who had just left a good harbour and was about to return to it immediately. Barbara was always waiting for him, always looking forward to his coming home. She made clothes for him and tried them on him, and she was in a bad mood only when he had to go away for any length of time. Then, she could hardly bring herself to pack his chest and give him food for the journey. But occasionally, he had to go to the distant parishes such as Sørvang and Bøur and to

218

spend a few nights there, and a couple of times a year he even had to go as far away as the island of Mikines.

He could perhaps simply have felt that he was too happy, as had happened a couple of times before, but he knew now how fragile happiness was, and the uncertainty following from this made him spry and alert.

He now realised something that he had been unaware of as a younger man – that love is like a flame that cannot burn clear and bright without fear, like a draft of air, keeping it burning. But this fear, which had once been erratic and unpredictable, had now become a gentle, steady draught. He knew there was only one danger threatening him. He always remembered Andreas Heyde, but he never mentioned him. Nor did Barbara mention him.

And yet it happened that they spoke about him. In their happiest moments, Pastor Poul could feel it like a stitch in his heart, and then he would ask: "Do you think you can always be with me as you are now?"

What Barbara answered to this varied. When she was at her giddiest, she made no reply at all. But otherwise it could happen that she looked uncertain and in a deeply emotional voice said: "I hope so."

When this upset her husband, she tried to console him. She said that he should stop asking such foolish questions, that it was nasty of him especially now that they were so very happy together. And when she could not think of anything else to say, she would finish with these words: "Good heavens, Poul, one doesn't have to think of such things. There are just the two of us at the moment, aren't there, Poul. Can't you be content with that?"

Pastor Poul saw the wisdom in this. They were both helpless, defenceless human beings.

He knew Barbara, good God he did! Her intentions were no less good than his, and her heart was many times better than his. But she was not in control of her heart; it always went its own way. They both trembled before this heart, which was so untameable and so blind, and the only thing they could turn to in their human weakness was the Grace of God.

In this way, Pastor Poul learned to accept every new day as a gift from God. In the dark mornings, he read morning prayers for the servants in the light of a tallow candle, but afterwards he usually went down to the sands to say his own prayers. And while the day burst forth from the south east like a blood red rose, he wandered back and forth on the dark shore and remembered the words of the morning hymn:

> *Each morn He fills my cup*
> *With mercies beyond count*

There were frequent golden mornings in December and this was the source of great joy to Pastor Poul. But for most people, the days were only like more or less confined pools of light in the harsh confines of the dark months. Everyone was now looking forward to the joys of Christmas and the sense of liberation they would bring, and they were preparing for it by slaughtering sheep and baking. A couple of boats had been in Tórshavn to fetch Christmas drinks, and one of them brought a letter for Barbara from her friend Suzanne.

It was quite a cheerful letter, a happy letter. "If you had been here," wrote Suzanne, "you would hardly have recognised Havn again. Things are quite different here now. We have had a ball, and we are soon to perform a comedy in the Assembly House. It is called Herman von Bremenfeld, and all we young people are going to take part in it. As you might imagine, it is

Andreas Heyde who is the driving force in all this."

Barbara was at first very enlivened by this letter, but then she lapsed into thought. Pastor Poul did not get much out of talking to her that day, and she answered him as though from a different world. That evening, he asked her if she was sorry she had not been to the play in Tórshavn. But she embraced him and said that she would far rather celebrate Christmas with him in Jansegard. He dared not tell her that it would only be a very brief Christmas that they could celebrate together. On Christmas Day itself, immediately after service, he had to go to Sorvág to celebrate Evensong, and if the weather was good, he would have to go to Mikines on the second day of Christmas. He hoped very much that the weather would not be good.

Among those travelling by boat to Tórshavn was the law speaker. He was the last to return. Only on Christmas Eve, after dark, did he return to Sandavág. By then, the holiday, was with them, and there were not many who noticed that he had a guest with him. No one had been expected in the law speaker's home, but as soon as the sons in the house saw the stranger, they guessed it must be Andreas coming to celebrate Christmas. We thought as much, they said as they shook his hand. Andreas could surely not come back to the Faroes without also visiting Stegard! And Andreas laughed and was immediately just as he had been as a boy when he had regularly visited his relative Samuel Mikkelsen and been guilty of countless mischievous tricks together with Samuel Mikkelsen's four boisterous sons. He remembered everything and everybody and went through the room greeting each individual farm servant.

Old Armgard was spending that Christmas at Stegard. Andreas was a little nervous when he was about to enter the formal room to greet her. He grimaced to his half-cousins as he took hold of the door handle.

"She is in a good mood this evening," they said. "She'll be nice with you, you can be sure of that."

Armgard was indeed in a good mood. Her face melted in tenderness and pride when she recognised her nephew. She held his hand for a long time between her bony hands.

"Oh, Andreas, is it you? So you are home again, God bless you. I can't tell you how pleased I am. But now, Andreas, sit down and tell your aunt what you have been doing. Let me hear all about it."

Andreas sat down and told his story, breezily as usual, but in a polite tone. He had occasionally to repeat himself, but that did not happen often. Armgard was not deaf: she just wanted to be sure she had heard everything.

"I am glad," she said, "that you think about this poor country. Let's see how your potatoes, or whatever you call them, will grow. You are like your great grandfather, Poul Caspar, the law speaker. He was the first one to introduce real gardens here, as you know. He brought all those berry-bearing shrubs outside here. But dear Andreas, you won't take it the wrong way if your aunt gives you some good advice? You must also think a bit about yourself. Don't miss the chance of getting a good job in time."

Andreas was quite touched to see his aunt's face. It was so old and so affectionate. When she smiled, he could see the stumps of her teeth in her mouth.

"So," his cousins asked him, "she didn't read the riot act to you today?"

Andreas felt a little embarrassed. The law speaker's wife, Birita, hushed her sons: "Be quiet with you. You make a dreadful row. Samuel, you ought to have a word with them."

Samuel Mikkelsen smiled: "Andreas doesn't take them seriously," he said. "He knows them of old."

"I'm afraid he knows them only too well," said Birita.

The law speaker had four sons, but the oldest of them, Peder, was now married and was working for his father by running the old family farm on Eysteroy. The other three, Mikkel, Jacob and Samson, were all unmarried and lived at home with their parents, spending a lot of their time fishing and helping in the running of the farm and were otherwise among the keenest participants in all the weddings on Vágar. There was also a daughter, Armgard Maria, a beautiful, dark-haired girl. But she rarely said anything. It was always the brothers who talked and played games in the common room.

"Tell me what we are to do with them, Andreas," said the law speaker's wife. "Their father and I would have liked them to have had an academic or administrative training, but they can't be bothered. And, God help them, they can't all become farmers. Not unless they could marry into a farm. But what do you think? Do you think there is any honest farmer's daughter who could be bothered with these shameless lazybones?"

Mikkel laughed: "What do you know about that, mother? I've not so far noticed that the girls avoid me. I had actually been thinking of finding a girlfriend this Christmas."

"Yes, I'm sure," said Birita. "Ladykiller that you are. Your Christmas girlfriends are rarely your girlfriends by Easter. When are you thinking of getting yourself betrothed to a decent girl?"

"I don't care a damn about your Christmas girlfriends and Easter girlfriends," said Samson, the youngest of the sons. "I'm going to go to sea now. I want to take part in a war, let me tell you. I'm sure you'll be able to take me along with you and get me on a warship, won't you, Andreas."

The law speaker stopped in the midst of his work. "You shouldn't talk like that, Samson."

Samson had risen and was standing there, enormous and enormously lively in the middle of the room. He was swinging his arms about.

"Aye, you are one on your own," said Birita. "I don't think Andreas will want to have you with him in Copenhagen to make a laughing stock of yourself."

Samson made no reply. He closed his eyes, started to rock his shoulders and in a loud voice broke into the ballad "Now sail the nobles of Norway".

"Aunt Armgard will be after you, Samson," shouted Mikkel to him.

But Samson took no notice. Like one going berserk he lumbered around the entire room, waving his huge arms in the air and singing all the time.

"You should have a serious word with him, Samuel," urged Birita.

The law speaker smiled benevolently in his great beard. His beautiful, clear eyes followed his son's great gestures with secret delight. But finally he cleared his throat and in a deep, half plaintive, half admonishing voice exclaimed, "Good lord, Samson, this really isn't fitting behaviour for the hours just before we celebrate Christmas. Do quieten down, Samson, please."

Supper was ready soon after this. Silence descended slowly on the room, and all ate the abundance of good food with solemn faces as they sensed the approach of the great festival. The law speaker read the evening prayers, as was his custom. His deep voice was rather hoarse and, although he read very slowly, he stumbled over the words a couple of times. But he was tired, having just arrived from a visit to Tórshavn, and he was longing to get to bed. The members of the large household started to prepare themselves for the night. Everyone had to be up early the following morning, for it was Christmas Day.

The law speaker's sons and Andreas went out onto the croft for a moment. There was a light frost. The jagged silhouettes of the mountains cut out huge, sharp sections from the starry sky.

"Shall we have a drink now?" asked Samson quietly. He had opened the door to a barn. A heavy, sweet scent of hay met them from the dark.

"No, better wait," said Jacob. "It's not Christmas yet."

"You and I, Andreas, we ought to stay up until midnight," suggested Samson. "Then we could have a drink together."

"Don't bother Andreas," said Jacob. "He's tired after travelling."

"Well, what the hell," said Samson. "Then we can presumably sleep in the hay. And then we can get up all the earlier. Shame on those who lie snoozing on Christmas morning. I don't know whether you will be satisfied with that, Andreas? You are probably used to a different sort of cushion in Copenhagen."

Down in Regensen, Andreas has often dreamt of being at home and sleeping in a scented hay barn. He accepted readily; his blood was restless and he, too, was impatiently longing for the night to be past. But he had not only come to Stegard in order to celebrate Christmas; he also had another little objective in coming to Vágar.

They could sense the warm scent of the cowshed. The cows were standing in the darkness and chewing the cud, occasionally lowing and breathing deeply. Andreas found something familiar in this sound; he felt at home in Stegard again and he was filled with gratitude for this place, where he had spent so much time in his childhood. He saw before him the imperturbable, heavy and steady shape of the law speaker. He had the same gentle and slow voice as the cows; he was a farmer through and through. But he was a farmer of the great type, generous and hospitable, and the slightly diffident smile that was always to be seen on his dignified face was affectionate, humble, ironical and tolerant. It was part of everything that went on; it was like a flame that flickered with every word that was said, indeed almost every thought that was thought. Such was the wisdom, the sensitivity and the fun that dwelt in this giant. Andreas felt a little ashamed. What face would Samuel Mikkelsen have adopted if he had known the real objective of this visit? There was no knowing. He lay down to sleep in the law speaker's sweet hay. Through a hole in the stone wall he could see a star twinkling.

He woke, shivering with cold. Outside, the stars were still twinkling.

"Happy Christmas," said Samson in a hoarse voice. "Have you slept well in the hay? I know you need something to put a bit of heat in your body now." He handed him a small barrel from which a gurgling sound was to be heard: "Cheers."

"Cheers," said Andreas. "And happy Christmas." He put his lips to the hole in the flask and drank a couple of mouthfuls. They made his stomach burn.

They both got up and shook themselves. It was still night, and there was not a single candle to be seen in Sandavág.

"We must have something to eat," said Samson. He opened the door to a slatted shed. The door creaked on its hinges. Inside hung dried sheep's carcasses one after the other, and there was a raw, sour smell of meat. Samson took out his knife and with an assured movement he cut a leg off.

"Meat's a good thing," he said. "It's good when you're hungry, when you're cold, when you're tired and when you're

226

in a bad temper."

"And when you're in love?" laughed Andreas.

Samson pulled a manful face. They ate and carved and ate. Andreas felt a fiery pleasure in this meal; the hard dried mutton broke between his teeth; its acrid juice exhilarated him; his stomach cried out with delight and hunger. "Eat," said Samson. "We'll make do with the rest of this leg for the time being... you can be sure that father will be pleased for us to have it."

They each sat on a bucket. On the floor between them a tallow candle provided some light. Suddenly, they heard footsteps up on the road. Samson listened. "That's Ole the Gate," he said. "I know his walk. He's usually one of the first to come and wish us a happy Christmas."

They went outside and listened to the steps as they came closer and closer. There were just a few lights to be seen in the village now and there were also signs of movement in the law speaker's house.

"Well, all the Christmas visitors will soon be here," said Samson.

The dignified farmers who came very early in the morning to wish the law speaker a happy Christmas were all shown into the best room, where Samuel Mikkelsen himself poured a drink for them. The younger visitors came no further than the parlour, where the sons acted as hosts, and a few unfortunates could hardly be persuaded to go further than the hearth room.

They were all nevertheless entertained generously and finally seated at table around splendid haunches of dried meat. The candles burned in the candlesticks and the men's shadows flickered like trolls on the whitewashed walls. But there were no loud voices to be heard; all were sedate and decorous in their Christmas celebration.

However, the young were not content to sit there and soon embarked on other Christmas visits. On the other hand, the older people were soon engrossed in all kinds of memories and spent a good deal of time around the law speaker's silver tankard. He frequently poured for them and finally invited Farmer Halvdan and Farmer Justinus to stay and hear the reading of the Christmas Gospel. By this time they both had rather stiff eyes and were full of profound, Christian thoughts. They did not refuse to stay and hear the Word of the Lord.

The guests and the people of the household slowly gathered in the parlour, where they devoutly seated themselves along the walls.

"You are a learned man these days, Andreas," said the law speaker. "I think I will ask you to read the Gospel for us today. I am sure you will do us that favour."

Andreas was confused. This was not exactly what he had intended. He wanted at first to say that he was going to Midvág to attend the Christmas service, but he quickly realised that the law speaker was doing him an honour. He felt like a renegade as he settled down at the table with the candles and Jesper Brochmand's great *Book of Homilies*. Armgard sat over by the stove, her cold eyes half closed, her pale, bony face with the hooked nose immovable as a mask. The last of the servants came in and sat silently near the door.

"Since it is such a solemn feast today, perhaps we should sing a hymn," said Samuel Mikkelsen as he started to flick through his hymn book. They started to sing quietly:

> *For us the blessed day now dawns*
> *Then let us all this day rejoice*
> *Our Christ is born this happy morn*
> *Now let us sing as with one voice...*

The law speaker led the singing. His voice was not particularly melodious, but there was a resonance in it that moved Andreas and made him think of a bassoon, a horn or some other innocent shepherd's instrument. He was overcome by a moment's devotion, but woke up to cold reality when the hymn came to an end. The book lay open before him. Brochmand's sermons were renowned for their length.

"And it came to pass in those days that there went out a decree from Caesar Augustus..."

He read in the light, lively way he had acquired and immediately heard that the tone was wrong. This was not the heartfelt, halting and naive Danish he had heard Samuel Mikkelsen sing; it was a profane language, a dreadful language. He paused on finishing the Gospel. All his listeners sat motionless, most with their faces hidden in their hands. Farmer Halvdan sat there with glassy, running eyes, pulling at his white beard.

"I think I will go into my room," murmured the law speaker to himself. "I can hear just as well from in there..."

At that moment Andreas chanced to look at Samson, who was sitting entrenched with the stove between himself and Armgard. He thought he saw the flash of a smile cross his face. He felt humiliated and made to look ridiculous in this dignified seat in which he had been placed contrary to his wishes.

"Come O Children of God," he began, "and weep at the world's neglect in failing to receive Jesus Christ, Saviour of the World and King of Kings. Behold, now that thing is being fulfilled that Elijah so clearly prophesied: 'The ox knoweth his owner, and the ass his master's crib: but Israel doth not know, my people doth not consider.'"

No, the law speaker ought to have read this. Andreas was

unable to strike the right tone; he blushed at the priestly dignity conferred on him and merely wished that it should have an end. He could already have been half way to Midvág by now. He read without thinking, he no longer understood the words, he thought only of how he could shorten this torment. But all around him his listeners sat intent with their faces buried in their hands.

Then a sound was heard from the bedroom, at first a slight sound, but one that rapidly became louder. It was all too obvious that someone was snoring. Andreas glanced into the room and at the foot of a bed he could see Samuel Mikkelsen's crossed legs. He wanted so much to laugh; his voice became weak and unrecognisable; sweat broke out on his forehead; he read and read while the house was shaken by the law speaker's snoring. But the congregation still sat there piously with their faces hidden. Only Armgard looked straight ahead – her face looked as though of stone.

Andreas gabbled away; he was himself almost insentient. He was constantly overcome by an urge to laugh; it was a sickness, an attack of cramp. He had already read numerous pages, but there was still no prospect of the word amen. He felt like a disabled ship, out of sight of land and without a compass, being tossed on the wild ocean of Brochmand's eloquence. The next time he had to turn a page, he turned several. He did not himself know whether it was two or four, and it made no difference for there was still no amen to be seen.

Then Armgard spoke: "Wait, Andreas," she said. "Turn back a page."

Andreas turned back a page and to his delight he discovered an amen. He looked gratefully at his aunt and made to read the remainder of the sermon.

"No, Andreas," said Armgard. "You have not got back to

Christmas Day yet."

Andreas looked at the book in some confusion. At the top of the page it said Lesson for the Feast of St Stephen. He understood not a word of it.

Armgard had risen. She gave a resounding bang on the table. "Turn back, turn back, confound you. God forgive me for what I say. Sitting there and reading page after page about St Stephen on Christmas Day! What are you thinking of? Turn back to the place where you cheated the first time."

Andreas turned back, page after page, all of which he had read. And finally he found the amen to Christmas Day. It was on one of the pages he had jumped.

Armgard had sat down again. "Read from the place where you cheated," she repeated brusquely.

Andreas started to read again, as obedient as a small child. There was a painful silence when he finally said amen. But at that moment the law speaker appeared suddenly in the doorway to his bedroom, refreshed and smiling.

"Thank you very much indeed," he said, "for taking that on. If only we could read Danish as fluently as you can."

"Aye, my friend," agreed Farmer Halvdan in his old man's falsetto. "Your reading is heavenly, just as good as a Danish pastor's. But you read it a little too fast for my old ears."

Andreas was still a little embarrassed. The listeners came one after one to shake hands with him and thank him for the reading. Last of all came the law speaker's sons, dignified and silent like the others, but inside illumined with laughter.

Farmer Halvdan and Farmer Justinus had begun to take their leave. The law speaker asked them to stay and said they were letting Christmas in.

"Dear friend," they said. "Are we not letting Christmas out? We have had everything we could wish for. Both the gospel and the sermon."

They left, dignified but merry.

Andreas stood out on the croft. His heart was light; he was already getting over that slight mishap of his. When all was said and done, it was not in order to read prayers and sermons that he had come to Vágar.

Samson emerged. He slapped his shoulder: "You are not exactly the emperor's friend now," he said with a laugh.

"I wonder whether I would have been in any case," thought Andreas. He could hear the church bells in Midvág in the distance.

Pastor Poul's dinner on this Christmas Day was a rather hasty affair. The service at Midvág had dragged on, and he had scarcely arrived at Jansegard before the crew arrived that was to take him to Sørvág. The day was so short, they said. It was best to travel by daylight. But they had to wait for a time in the hearth room, which was perhaps something they didn't mind.

Barbara was a little sulky.

"You have to admit," she said, "that it's no fun for me to have to celebrate Christmas in this way. And then that you are going to Mikines. I assure you that there has never been a priest on Mikines at Christmas before. If you get there you can risk the sea turning rough so you can't get away for months. This idea is sheer madness."

"Yes, dearest of all," said Pastor Poul, "but you wouldn't let me go out there last summer or during the autumn. It can't be put off any longer now. The folk out there haven't seen their minister yet although I have been in the parish for over a year. Their children are running around unbaptised like heathens. Some people can't get married and others are lying in unsanctified ground and have never had a funeral ceremony.

They have plenty of reason to reproach me out there, so you must understand I was forced to promise this."

"To go at Christmas?"

"Something had to be done. To make up for my negligence, you understand."

"There has never been a minister out there at Christmas."

"For that very reason, Barbara. And by the way there is no guarantee that the weather will be good enough tomorrow for me to leave. And in that case I will come back to you, you know..."

But Barbara was not to be mollified and remained sullen, and the meal ended as it had begun, in a bad atmosphere. The minister had just put on his travelling clothes and was ready to go when he chanced to look out of the window.

"We have visitors," he said. "Or more correctly, you have visitors. If I am not mistaken, it is the law speaker's sons coming across the sand."

Barbara brightened up. She hurried over to the window.

"Yes," she said. "It's Samson... and Mikkel... and..."

"And Jacob, I suppose?" said the parson.

"No," said Barbara. "It isn't Jacob. It's..."

At that moment, the minister saw how her face was completely transformed. She went away from the window, speechless and extremely confused. She looked almost as though she had received an unexpected blow to her face.

The minister quickly looked out again. A terrible presentiment had struck him. He immediately recognised Andreas Heyde's careless gait and his fair face. He was the one leading the three.

Pastor Poul turned to his wife. She was still in turmoil, and when she started to speak, she was not in complete command of her voice.

"That's too bad," she said. "Those men are not going to find anyone at home. I'm coming with you... as far as the harbour. Then they can wait if they have the time."

She was in a great hurry as if she was afraid. She quickly found some warm clothes to put on and hurried out together with Pastor Poul. The oarsmen, in some surprise, followed them.

The weather was calm and cool. There was hoar frost on the ground, and all the small pools were covered with ice as clear as glass. Barbara repeatedly took her husband's arm and held him tight. As they moved further away from Jansegard she slowed her pace and finally walked quite slowly.

"You must come back to me soon. Promise?"

She said it in a low voice and as though afraid. Otherwise, she had said nothing. She was very serious and gave him a look that was full of pain.

"I will come as soon as I can," said Pastor Poul. "I might already be here tomorrow if the weather shows signs of changing."

"Yes, it will. I'm sure it will," Barbara insisted.

"Oh, God help us, Barbara," exclaimed the minister. "Can you forget me in three days?"

Barbara did not immediately reply, but finally she said, "Dearest Poul. You know what I want most of all. That's all I can say. Hurry back home."

And while the oarsmen were well ahead for a few moments, she flung herself on his neck and embraced him passionately. Then she stroked his face and looked at him with sadness in her eyes. They had passed the ridge. The great expanse of water lay before them. When they reached the small group of houses they had once called Capernaum, the oarsmen dragged a small boat from a boatshed and pushed it into the water. The thin ice close to land was splintered with a shrill sound. Pastor Poul took his leave.

"Come back soon," was the last thing Barbara said. She was quite emotional.

The boat slid silently away from land. The cold winter light lay on the surface of the lake. Barbara went home. Pastor Poul sat watching her as she moved up through the heather, quick and upright. She did not look back.

Weatherbound

Pastor Poul was awakened early by his host the following morning. The weather was calm and the sky was bright with stars. If he wanted to go to Mikines, said the man in Sørvág, conditions could not be better at this time of the year. They offered to row him out there straight away.

He asked them whether they thought they could also row him back the same day. Their reply was that this was in God's hand, but if he finished quickly at Mikines they would try to wait for him at the jetty. Provided the sea didn't turn rough. It all depended on that. For if the weather was not good at Mikines it would be just as impossible to come alongside as it would be to put off.

After this, Pastor Poul could not but keep his promise to pay a Christmas visit to Mikines. But he shuddered to think of all the stories he had heard about people who had been stranded for months out there simply because of high waves at the landing stage, and he knew that he would not feel safe again before he was well away from that island.

It was still dark as they rowed out through the long Sørvág Fjord. It was a demanding journey they had before them, one that was hardly ever undertaken during the winter. Mikines was so far out to sea, the most distant of all the Faroe Islands. And the village and the landing stage were right over on the western end of the island. Altogether they would be rowing some eleven or twelve nautical miles from Sørvág.

The men looked up at the starry sky and thought the good weather would probably last all day. They pulled at the oars and rowed with a will. Dark promontories and frost-covered fells slipped past on either side. When they came to the mouth of the fjord, they could glimpse the distant island of Mikines in the starlight, rising like a single mountain from the western sea and with its peak shining white. But its slopes were black and steep and left no room for the snow.

It was not long before the stars gradually began to grow paler, and by the time the boat reached the open sea, day had dawned. Mikines grew before the prow in the early winter sunshine, fiery red and raw in its wild, rugged splendour. It was at once a revelation and a nightmare.

It was still early in the day when they arrived in the little village on the western tip of the island. There was great excitement when the boat appeared, and no sooner had Pastor Poul set foot ashore than the bell up in the pitiful little turf-covered church started ringing merrily and launching its sounds in the light morning. It was a happy day for everyone on Mikines.

The path up to the village was long and steep. Pastor Poul went into the churchwarden's house and allowed himself a hasty breakfast and then he went straight on to the church, where everyone had gathered. Everyone except the men from Sørvág, who had gone down to their boat again.

Pastor Poul held a service, a brief service, but one without unseemly haste. The sun shone all the time in through the small windows, confirming that the weather was holding. Four children were baptised afterwards and a young couple entered the married state. Then there remained nothing but a couple of graveside ceremonies. Pastor Poul went out among the withered grassy mounds of the graves, and the little church bell sang out once more over the entire village. When this was done, the clergyman's errand was finished. The weather was unchanged. Pastor Poul went back to the churchwarden's house and prepared to leave. He had feared that the people might delay him with a meal and refreshments, but it was as though his host understood him and knew he wanted to get away again as soon as possible.

He was already on his way down to the landing stage when a man came running after him and stopped him with some confused words. He wanted him to come back and baptise a child.

"Baptise a child?" asked Pastor Poul. "Why was the child not at church?"

"Well, because it had not been born yet."

Pastor Poul was annoyed. He understood from those accompanying him that they were irritated by this man and were most inclined to send him off. But he did not want to look difficult.

"Then let me baptise it quickly," he said and turned to hurry back.

"You ought perhaps to have refused," said the churchwarden. "That idiot ought to know that you haven't much time... on a winter's day... and so late in the day as well."

"Where is the child then?" asked Pastor Poul harshly as he entered the unknown man's house.

Its owner made a ridiculous, pleading gesture: "The child... the child isn't born yet... that's to say not quite... not quite born. But I assure you," he continued in a pleading tone, "that my wife is very quick. It will be there in no time."

"For God's sake, Hanus, are you completely crazy?" exclaimed the churchwarden. "Are you trying to make a fool of the minister? What are you thinking of?"

"It'll be here so soon, in no time," Hanus Elias assured them.

At that moment, Pastor Poul considered going. He was sufficiently angry to do so. Why he still did not leave was something he was always unable to explain to himself later, although his thoughts in later years often turned on this disastrous moment.

They had waited for something like a quarter of an hour when a sudden gust of wind shook the house. Pastor Poul looked out and noticed the wind briefly move the withered grass on the neighbouring roof. The sun was no longer shining.

Hanus Elias came in at that moment, pleading and beseeching. "Oh please, don't go. The child is born. It only needs to be washed a little. Oh, please... surely you don't have to hurry like that?"

"Come on then. Bring the child, damn it!" said Pastor Poul, stamping on the floor.

He started wandering furiously backwards and forwards in the room. The churchwarden had gone outside to look at the weather. He came back and said, "There is no time to waste."

"It'll be all right, it'll be all right," wailed Hanus Elias.

The wind blew again through the grass on the neighbour's roof. There was the sound of a child's shrill cry. Three breathless men came running along: they came to fetch the minister. At that moment the child was brought out. Half an hour had been wasted.

Pastor Poul baptised the child like lightning. When he asked its name, the godmother hesitated a little. The child was to have five names. Pastor Poul gave it three, and the moment amen had been said he was out of the door. All the men present ran with him.

Once they had a clear view, they could see the boat far below them, fully manned and rocking violently just off the landing stage. But otherwise the sea looked quite calm, and a touch of sunshine could still be seen over its surface.

Pastor Poul ran for his life down the cliffs. The entire village was on its feet, and everyone had but a single thought: would the minister manage to get away?

He reached the furthermost flat rocks. The boat was rocking only a couple of yards from him – a bold leap was all that was needed. Pastor Poul knew that it was his happiness that was at stake, and his heart was in his mouth. Time after time, the boat approached land, but each time it had to withdraw hurriedly to avoid being smashed against the rocks. It rocked more and more violently in the rough water. Perhaps he might have leapt on one occasion if he had been an experienced seaman. But he was not. But now the best of the Mikines men gathered around him. They were ready to help him in any way possible, and they shouted to the men on the boat that if necessary they would throw the minister on board to them if they would make sure to catch him. But no opportunity presented itself. It was too late. The sound of the waves falling and rising against the coast was already beginning to drown the men's voices: it was the surf that was taking over. Once more the Sørvág boat made a daring attempt to come close, but it was little more than a polite gesture. It was hopeless.

Then the accident happened; one of the men from Mikines who had been among those gesticulating and shouting the most slipped on the smooth rocks and fell in the water. He was quickly grabbed by the others and pulled ashore again, dripping wet. It was Hanus Elias.

The churchwarden rebuked him severely: "That served you right. Now you've gone and ruined everything, you misery.

You just can't behave like other human beings. Go home and be ashamed of yourself. You can see now what a lot of trouble you've caused."

Shameful and dripping wet, Hanus Elias went back to his house. Caused? What had he caused? Just caused the minister to stay on Mikines. Was that such a catastrophe? When you were a clergyman and could be given hospitality by a man like the churchwarden. And at Christmas time as well!

But the minister stood as though paralysed and with despair in his heart he watched the boat row away. When it had got some way out, it raised the sail and moved off quickly.

"Aye," someone said: "they will have a good wind and the current's in their favour as well."

The churchwarden turned to Pastor Poul. "That was most unfortunate," he said. "Perhaps you would accept my hospitality and stay at my house now?"

Pastor Poul spoke few words after this. Twenty-four hours ago he had still been a radiantly happy man, and even an hour ago he had been full of confidence and hope. Now he was helpless in a trap. His misfortune was so great that he could scarcely conceive of it.

Farmer Niklas, the churchwarden, thought to himself that the minister was more upset by this misfortune than was reasonable.

"The weather is not really bad," he said, "and as far as I can see, there is no sign of a gale coming. It's just the direction of the wind that is so confoundedly unfortunate. But if the delay isn't more than a day or two? Let's hope for the best."

Pastor Poul gave Niklas a kindly look but at the same time shrugged his shoulders as though he nevertheless considered it all to be pretty hopeless. He went across to the window. The weather still looked quite good; there was no movement to be seen on the endless, grey surface of the sea, where glimpses of sunshine could be seen glinting here and there.

He felt as though he had been placed under some sort of spell.

Farmer Niklas had the table laid and put on it the best food the farm could boast of. Pastor Poul was friendly and polite, but he had no appetite whatever, and early though the dusk was falling, he asked Niklas to show him where he was to sleep.

It was some relief to him to be left entirely to himself. A kind of dull calm gradually came over him. He consoled himself by asking, when it came to the point, why should he fear the worst? And even if the worst did happen! Should it break him completely? Surely he was both a man and a priest?

But at all events, this was a test, a hard test. He prayed that God would support him. It was a long and fervent prayer, and he felt that it gave him strength. "We must see how it goes," he whispered to himself. "Time will tell. God alone must decide."

When he awoke the following morning, he did not, as he had expected, feel his heart pierced by despair. On the contrary, he felt consoled and collected. There was no particular change in the weather. There was a little wind, but otherwise the same silver red dawn as yesterday. Pastor Poul embarked on a conversation with the churchwarden. After breakfast they went round the village together. The minister wanted to visit the sick and the old people. It passed his time. He gradually grew accustomed to the thought of this misfortune, which, when it came to the point, was perhaps not a misfortune at all, but merely a test for him and for her. He imagined his arrival home. Barbara coming to meet him, smiling, and his being as it were already able to see in her smile that all was well.

Aye, perhaps Barbara had really changed in the course of these deep, happy winter months that they had spent alone together in the parsonage. Perhaps she was not the old Barbara, but a new Barbara, a transfigured and loyal Barbara filled with longing.

Eleven days passed before the weather was such that the minister could leave. On the other hand, it then turned as beautiful as if it were midsummer. The wide sound between Mikines and Vágar was only disturbed by choppy sea and by the quick-moving flashing tracks of the wake bearing the boat along at great speed. Sørvág Fjord was as calm as an inland lake and full of reflections of clouds and steep mountain sides. In Sørvág the leading oarsman found a horse for Pastor Poul and rode with him as far as the lake. A small group of oarsmen were already waiting, ready with a small boat. The minister had said that he was in a great hurry.

Pastor Poul had at first felt grateful and relieved on this journey home. He had felt he was being helped by God and by human beings. But the closer he came to Midvág and Jansegard, the more his spirits sank. The image of Barbara coming to meet him gradually gave way to another picture, which was not really a picture at all, but a void. Void! Empty rooms! And a void that blankly told him that Barbara was not at home. That Mrs Aggersøe had gone to Tórshavn... on a visit.

Barbara is not at home!

Barbara is not at home. The certainty struck him like an icy shudder as he hurried down towards Midvág. There, the village came into view, and the sands, and Jansegard. No, Barbara was not at home. That really was the situation. It was the old, half deaf maid Kristine, whose voice was to give him this news in the everyday and thoroughly dutiful voice

243

of a servant. Barbara had gone to Tórshavn. She had left no message.

Pastor Poul went backwards and forwards in the empty rooms for a moment, still clad in his travelling clothes and with a blanket over his arm. "Barbara," came the sob deep down inside him.

He went into the hearth room to ask Kristine whether Barbara had left alone or with someone else. But he could not get the question across his lips. Suddenly he thought of the law speaker. Samuel Mikkelsen... Samuel Mikkelsen must surely be on his side! He surely could... he surely could not have allowed that thing to happen that now had happened.

Pastor Poul threw down the blanket, loosed his travelling clothes a little, but did not take the time to take them off. He was quickly out of the door and on his way to Sandavág. He felt that talking to Samuel Mikkelsen would be the saving of him. He ran most of the way, and when he reached Sandavág he was drenched with sweat and so out of breath that he could hardly speak.

He found Samson on the Stegaard croft. He said that his father was down at the boathouses. He would be home before long.

Pastor Poul sat down on the boulder nearest to him. He was tired out.

"Won't you come inside?" asked Samson. "You are not very comfortable there."

"I'm all right," said Pastor Poul, brusque and preoccupied.

Samson saw the look in his eyes. He left him in peace and went indoors. There, he merely said that the minister was outside. "He wouldn't come in," he added. Not much was said about this. A couple of curious eyes peered out. They saw the minister sitting there in the dusk with his elbows supported

244

on his knees, hiding his face. No one ventured to disturb him.

Down on the shoreline a dot had appeared; it rose and grew slowly out of the ground, first a head and then a pair of shoulders, and then gradually the full figure of a man slowly approaching and growing bigger and bigger in the twilight. It was the law speaker on his way home. The clergyman suddenly saw him as a big shadow in front of him and jumped up. Samuel Mikkelsen wished him good evening.

"Barbara has left me," said Pastor Poul.

The law speaker made no reply. He stood there looking unhappy.

"Won't you come inside?" he asked at last in a quiet voice. "Come, let us go this way."

They went through a special door into the law speaker's study.

"I am furious about this," were Samuel Mikkelsen's first words after they had sat silent for a while. "It was not with my blessing they went to Tórshavn together, but I couldn't prevent them. I tried to reason with them, but as you can imagine... it is pointless to try to talk to people when they are in the grip of such madness."

The law speaker spoke gently and hesitantly. Nevertheless, it tore at the parson's heart, and when he heard the words in the grip of such madness he was overcome by a sense of deep dismay.

"Andreas is so impetuous," continued Samuel Mikkelsen. "I ought not to have invited him out here to the west... but it didn't for a moment strike me..."

"He would have come sooner or later in any case," said the minister. "This had to happen."

"Let me give you a dram," said the law speaker, almost pleadingly persuasive.

He opened a cupboard and filled a silver goblet to the brim. Pastor Poul pushed it away. "No thank you. Not now... I... no thank you."

"You are perhaps like me," said the law speaker. "I don't much like the strong stuff unless I'm feeling happy."

"I'm not in the mood," mumbled the priest.

They sat for a while in silence. The goblet stood on the table between them.

"You could drink it as medicine, you know," suggested the law speaker.

The parson made no reply. Suddenly, he emptied the goblet.

"That would do your heart good," said the law speaker.

The minister felt it did his heart good. Suddenly, he smiled. He smiled like a dog; his eyes were glazed and hungry.

"Aye," he said. "I'm not in the least bit surprised, not a bit. For I knew it already."

The law speaker perhaps also smiled for a split second. He was thinking that he, too, knew it beforehand. If not exactly this, then something like it. Then he went for the bottle again and once more filled the goblet.

Pastor Poul sat mumbling to himself. He repeated in a dull voice: "But it had to be like this. Although I knew it so well all the time, I couldn't act differently."

"No," said the law speaker. "I suppose not."

"Aye, aye, that's how things are."

Pastor Poul drained the goblet again. His eyes were like those of a blind man, and he drank avidly. "Oh, yes," he said.

The door slowly opened. Armgard came in with a candle; she was rather bent and slow in her movements when she walked around. She screwed up her cold eyes as she looked at the parson.

"Good evening, Pastor Poul," she said slightly ironically.

"And how are you?"

"I'm all right, thank you," said the parson. "And you?"

Armgard had sat down with her knitting.

"How can one live when one's relatives...?" She broke off.

The knitting needles were in motion; they went like a machine. Her eyes half closed.

They all sat for a while in silence. The minister had not eaten since that morning. He felt that the law speaker's cognac was beginning to dull his senses. There was something like black snow in front of his eyes; the fierce pain in his breast had lessened just a little.

"When I come to think of it," he said, "it's perhaps not quite so overwhelming... I mean, well, one must be able to rise above one's own fate. I can see the ludicrous element in it. Ha ha ha! Besides, cuckolds are always objects of ridicule."

He laughed again, and the tears came to his eyes. He drank a further goblet and said, "Oh yes, oh yes."

"Well, let us see," said the law speaker. "I imagine things will settle down again. Of course, Barbara is often so... often so... unpredictable."

He glanced at his aunt. Old Armgard's eyes had almost closed. If she had not been knitting so intently, it might well have been thought that she was dozing as she sat there. But he knew her better and was aware that she could be expected to make some comment at any moment.

"Barbara!" said the minister, his face suddenly taking on a completely foolish look. It seemed as though he was having a vision. Suddenly he exclaimed, "Do you really think that? Do you think she will ever come back? Do you? Do you?"

His voice was quite outside its usual pitch, wild and pleading like someone suddenly shouting out in sleep. Then, more calmly and almost as though talking to himself: "Could

I simply just once, one single time in my life... aye, then I wouldn't ask more. Oh Barbara, I do so miss you."

Armgard had looked up. She cleared her throat, but interrupted herself and continued knitting. There was a scornful expression around her nose and mouth.

"You see," said Pastor Poul, turning confidentially towards the law speaker, "You understand... I have to explain myself... You have the right to expect an explanation from me. I have known perfectly well throughout that this had to happen; I've always been aware of it."

"Oh, of course," Armgard interrupted him ironically. "That's why you were so intent on marrying her."

The parson ignored her with the superior stance of a drunken man. He merely turned further away from her and grasped the law speaker's sleeve.

"Well, I've been expecting this all along. Like a punishment, one could say, for it was all far too good, it was far too... epicurean, too voluptuous, too blissful." He stumbled seriously over the words: "You understand. It had to come. It was expected. Even so, it came unexpectedly. I mean it came unexpectedly on that day. I wasn't prepared; it was too sudden. If I can just once... I must at least be allowed to... I won't try to avoid the punishment, but first, first... I will do that," he shouted and struck the table.

"Aunt Armgard," said the law speaker: "Pastor Poul needs something to eat."

"That has been seen to," said Armgard.

Pastor Poul leant back and stared ahead. "Barbara," he mumbled. "If she knew what I'm thinking and feeling for her now; if she knew my heart now, she would come to me. Cheers. Cheers, Barbara, can't you hear me?"

He had raised the silver goblet and sat there weeping.

Armgard turned her chair away with an expression of disgust. A girl came in and laid the table for Pastor Poul.

Pastor Poul himself was sitting slumped in his chair, looking as though nothing of all this concerned him. The law speaker had got up and put his bonnet on a shelf under the ceiling.

"There we are," he said. "Come, my dear Pastor Poul, have something to eat. I'm sure you need it, you know."

He spoke in a gentle, almost plaintive voice and smiled quite helplessly. Pastor Poul took a piece of flatbread and put it on his plate. The table was not set for the law speaker and Armgard. They both sat a little way from the table, as was the custom when entertaining guests.

Pastor Poul hardly touched the food. He sat there with a dried leg of mutton and made a couple of indifferent and feeble attempts to cut some meat from it.

"Do have something to eat, my dear friend," said the law speaker. "Meat will strengthen both heart and soul."

But the minister did not touch the meat. It looked as though he was already beginning to fall asleep. He suddenly sat up, clenched his fists and, waving his arms wildly, sang:

Oh Lord, Thou madest me both great and wise,
I pray Thou wilt my sinful self chastise

Armgard gave him a surprised look. "That sounds like a new hymn," she commented.

Pastor Poul looked quite idiotic. "Isn't it good?" he asked. " 'Oh Lord, Thou madest me both great and wise, I pray Thou wilt my sinful self chastise.' Aye, that's how it is. Now I've found it. Ha, ha, ha. One suddenly finds it."

"Listen, Pastor Poul, you poor thing," said Armgard in a sharp, didactic tone: "You are a simple man, and I am sure God would never think of punishing you. No, no," she continued in a mocking falsetto tone sounding rather like a gull's laughter: "You who cannot even look after your own wife. But she, who continues to corrupt the youth of this country, God help me, now she can't even leave our family alone... When she is subjected to divine punishment one day...!"

And old Armgard struck the table with her clenched fist so that the silver goblet resounded to it.

Pastor Poul sat for a moment open-mouthed. Then he said, "Aye, to Hell with her. The Devil take her, the way she's behaved. Bloody woman. Confounded bitch she is."

And with this, he fell asleep. The law speaker smiled unhappily and discreetly called his sons. They carefully carried the minister to his bed. They were not completely ignorant as to what had taken place in the law speaker's room.

"You should have seen," said Samson with a wry smile, "you should have seen when he drank to Armgard. I think he thought it was Barbara."

Tempo di Minuetto

Pastor Poul woke in the middle of the night and at first could remember nothing at all. But suddenly he recalled everything that had happened. It came to him like a great blow at the root of his heart. After this, he slept no more, but lay there filled with the greatest presentiments and with a desperate pain in his breast. He longed avidly for the people of the house to awaken and for day to come.

He was the first up that morning, and the first thing he did was to ask the law speaker's sons whether the weather looked as though it was likely to be good enough for him to get to Tórshavn that day.

He went out and in and then out again, held out a hand in the half light and felt a fine drizzle; he looked at the sky and tried to guess the direction of the wind. The idea that he could see Barbara again that evening was almost enough to choke him.

But the law speaker's sons were slow to leave their bunks, and when they finally emerged under the eaves they said that they thought the strong wind would probably rule out the possibility of reaching Tórshavn that day. There was at all events no question of going south around the promontory now that the days were so short, but it might be possible to make land near Velbestad. They said they would discuss this with their father.

The law speaker had never been an early riser. When he finally turned up, there was something slightly concerned about his profoundly phlegmatic person. It could be imagined that he would have looked like this if Stegard had been burning down around him. He was bordering on being in a hurry.

During his long wait, Pastor Poul had been wandering ceaselessly in and out of the house. He had in turn stared at the weather and stared at the people. He was like a dog, wretched and unable to speak, pleading for human interference in some desperate affair. Now, finally seeing the law speaker approaching, he rushed straight over to him. A sense of irrepressible impatience emanated from the clergyman; his will was so strong that it had the effect on the others of some uncontrollable force.

"The weather isn't good; it certainly isn't," said Samuel Mikkelsen. He leant forward over a dry stone wall and studied the heavens intensely.

A short time passed.

"I think it would be wisest for you to go by way of Futaklet," was the tentative suggestion of the law speaker's son Jacob.

Pastor Poul made no reply to this. But perhaps he made some slight gesture or other. His entire being radiated the most intense dislike of the idea. He knew that this would be a journey taking at least two days. And was he now to have that dreadful journey back to Futaklet, to Kvívík, to Leynum, to Oyrareingja, all that long way that in happy days he had travelled together with Barbara? And which she had now travelled together with Andreas! His heart tightened into a knot in his despair.

"Of course," said the law speaker with conspicuous gravity, "we have to realise that Pastor Poul might be in rather a hurry today."

He looked enquiringly at the minister: was that not so? His eyes only expressed kindness and courtesy.

"This is the devil of a gale," exclaimed Jacob. He was a little short of breath, as was his habit when he became excited.

Samuel Mikkelsen made no reply. Pastor Poul stood shuffling apprehensively. He was quite beside himself; indeed it was as though his spirit wanted to wrest its way out of his body and fly alone across the Vágar Fjord.

The law speaker gave another look appraising the clouds: "The wind is very strong," he said. "But then its direction is as favourable as we could wish for as long as it stays in the north east. And there was a half moon yesterday, so the current should be favourable... though it isn't exactly gentle when the moon is so close to the earth."

He stood considering for a while; his face betrayed no feeling. "If we wait until the west flow lessens a little, it will probably be possible," he added.

It sounded almost like a chance remark. Only when the law speaker and his sons were on their way back into the house did Pastor Poul understand that these were the last words to be spoken and that the matter had been decided. He stood there alone and could hardly believe he had got what he wanted. He was to see Barbara again that evening.

But in the law speaker's home there was a considerable commotion that morning, as the minister could not fail to notice on the expression of the law speaker's wife. And Samuel Mikkelsen once had to silence his son Samson, who was otherwise never accused of being a coward, but who nevertheless swore roundly at the prospect of undertaking this bloody trip just for the sake of a baggage like Barbara. But the law speaker said they would go for the sake of Pastor Poul, out of pity for him. And Armgard banged the table and her face looked like flint as she said they must go for the sake of the family to ensure that that whore should not be the complete ruin of Andreas.

It was getting on for midday when Samuel Mikkelsen and ten men rowed off from Sandavág. He himself sat in the stern, steering the boat, and Pastor Poul sat with him. The wind gusted and took them out towards the gap. The sail was hoisted and the great boat was blown along, and all the houses in Sandavág and Midvág quickly receded into tiny, insignificant groups while the mountain peaks above them started to reach their black fingers up above the steep sides that had been hiding them. The knot in Pastor Poul's heart gradually began to loosen; he was sailing, flying towards his goal. This evening... he did not know whether he should be filled with fear or joy.

It was not long before they reached Klovning, a sharp promontory, the outermost part of which had been split off from the land and stood out there brooding over the sea. Here, they turned out into the open Vágar Fjord and rowed east along the high-rising land. The wind came from above in unpredictable gusts, and they lowered the sail. The water was smooth and black, the towering rock known as the Troll's Wife's Finger rose like a dark spire a thousand feet above their heads, and behind it the perpendicular mountain was still much higher.

The men rowed. They dipped their slender oars in the waves in short, quick movements, and the boat progressed jerkily and resolutely, the law speaker and the minister nodding involuntarily with each movement. The men spoke in hoarse voices and spat quids out into the water. They kept a close watch on the clouds above them. "The sky's like a pot of soot," said one of them.

He was right. The sky was very dark. And at the foot of the

mountain the water was boiling gently. But the law speaker was smiling from the depths of his kindness, his hand resting excitedly on the rudder. His redhead son Samson was rowing like a giant. "So sail the heroes of Norway," he sang and gave the clergyman a great look and winked. And Pastor Poul smiled back at him. It was as though a healthy current of air was beginning to fill his heavy heart. He wished he had been a man like Samson.

They had been rowing for an hour and had long been clear of the Vágar coast. The wind was blowing slightly against them from the Vestmanna Sound, but the water was not particularly rough. Then, suddenly, one of the men said: "Listen, isn't the wind turning more to the east?"

"Yes, I've noticed that," said Samuel Mikkelsen. "So it's all the more important to row in close to the Streymey coast. Then we shall be sheltered all the way to Velbestad and even have the east flow with us."

But it was still far to the shielding coast of Streymey, and it was both wet and salty, for the wind blew more and more against them, and the water splashed regularly into the boat so that one of the men occasionally had to bail out. But the high prow went doggedly up and down, up and down, and forced its way east yard by yard, while the oars snapped at the waves.

"So sail the heroes of Norway," sang Samson once more, laughing through the salty water that was running down over his brow. But Pastor Poul no longer felt happy and was impatient at the slow progress.

"The wind's changing, the wind's still changing," said the men, concerned that the east wind had now started to turn south. Their senses were alive to nothing but the weather and the current; they looked and looked and took note of countless signs in the flight of the clouds and the movement of the waves. But over the restless surface of the sea, the islands rose like roughly carved blocks. To the south west, Koltur raised its wild head, rearing towards the heavens, and the current before them was like a long row of battlements and chasms.

When a snow shower suddenly blocked out everything the boat all at once seemed terribly cut off. All that could be heard was the falling tops of the waves between the oar strokes. The law speaker fumbled to take out a compass and guided the boat according to it. The wet snow whipped him angrily in the face, but he showed no sign of concern.

"It's changing, it's changing," he was thinking as he watched the trembling compass needle.

"Barbara, Barbara," thought the minister, desperately peering out into the snow.

It had been Samuel Mikkelsen's idea that they should make the entire journey in the lee of the high mountains of Vágar and Streymey, which would shelter them from the strong north-easterly gale, and at the same time he would let them drift south on the east flow through the Hestur Fjord. Now he saw this plan come to nothing. In the course of half an hour, the wind had turned to the south east and was now blowing up along the Streymey coast, exactly in the opposite direction to the flow of the waters. This was the worst thing that could have happened.

When the snow shower had passed, they could all see it. They were below the mountains of Streymey, but out in the fjord the gale had already taken a fierce hold of the rough waters of the east flow. They themselves were moving against a strong wind, but close to land the current was not so strong. Few words were spoken. They all knew it would be risky to turn round; it was just a matter of creeping slowly forward and keeping close to the coast in the teeth of the gale and hoping they could land at Velbestad. But that village was still three miles away.

They had now been rowing for over three hours. The huge Konufjall suddenly appeared out of the clouds like a petrified roar. Remains of mist were still flying past this mountain ruin, hiding the gigantic rock faces and revealing them again, wrapping themselves around cliffs and releasing them again, dancing, fuming and rising like smoke up through wet chasms and abysses. It was like looking up into some gigantic organ playing silently but with tempestuous, visible reverberations.

The law speaker kept the boat as close to land as possible. They rode over the tops of the waves on the edge of the surf, and it often looked as though they were about to be thrown on to the rocks. But on the other side of the boat, the east flow was foaming, whipped up by the gale blowing against it.

Pastor Poul sat looking at the wet shoreline. Its brown seaweed was bared deep down in the gaps between the waves. This is the island Barbara is on, he thought; it is only a couple of yards away. If only I could get ashore, I could hurry over to the place where she is. He thought no further than this. He did not know what would happen subsequently. And so he thought much too far ahead. The law speaker was thinking no further than Lambatangi, which they were soon to pass. It was renowned as the pincer-like meeting point of two currents.

"Aye, aye," thought Samuel Mikkelsen, "the east flow is certainly at its highest now. But there was a half moon yesterday. That means the current is at its weakest. Although... the moon is at its closest to the earth at the moment. It's not likely to be entirely smooth."

Samson was rowing like a wild man. A vein in the middle of his forehead stood out. It was swelling like those in Roland's neck as he blew the horn Oliphant at Roncesvalles. All ten men rowed and clenched their teeth. The boat crept forward, yard by yard.

"We're like a fly on a tarred stick," sighed one of the men.

"Aye, just like a fly on a tarred stick," groaned another. And they worked their way forward at that moment in the great cleft immediately north of Lambatangi.

"A bit breezy today," commented the law speaker calmly to Pastor Poul.

Immediately afterwards the first wave caused by the meeting of the two currents rose before them, its foaming crest rising above their heads. The law speaker grasped the rudder and said rather louder than was his wont:

"Keep going."

The men dipped their oars in the water. It was as though they were whipping the boat on towards a foam-capped death.

"Now – now – now – row – row – keep going – row – now," groaned an old man in time with the oar strokes. The law speaker steered the boat straight into the middle of the surf; it reared up in the turbulent waters, veered and took in water on both sides while everything disappeared in foam and froth, and salt water descended on them in torrents. The minister sat there deathly pale and held tight. A melody was going round in his head all the time. Suppose he did not find Barbara this evening?

Suddenly, all was quiet. They lay rocking on an expanse of foam. The two men at the rear of the boat were bailing out, and the rest were pulling on the oars for all they were worth. It was only for a brief moment. Suddenly, the law speaker shouted:

"Row all you can!"

This time he did shout, and his voice was quite broken. A green wall of water was rising in front of them, arching and cautiously starting to burst into a broad and elaborate crown of foam lacework at the top.

"Mercy on us," said one of those in the prow.

The wind dropped suddenly. They were in the shelter of the wall of water; it hung over them so they could see the green daylight through it; the oars complained bitterly against the rowlocks. Then the boat rose and reared until it was almost upright.

They were surrounded by a prolonged rumble as if of thunder. Pastor Poul felt a rush of icy water against his thighs and was blinded by the foam. The furious profile of Koltur and the Konufjall, like some gigantic organ issuing steam and foaming clouds, was the last thing he saw. He felt a scintillating, icy pain and a delight as though of immeasurable quantities of splintered glass, and he thought: Is this the end? And he went on to think, relieved and free, that this was what it was like. And at that moment he saw the prow rise defiantly out of the water and saw all the men with the sea pouring from their beards.

They tore the lids off their food boxes, tipped the contents out and started to bail as though possessed. Samson bailed out with such energy that the water formed something like a thick jet out from the boat, and when a young man from Sandavág complained, "Jesus, we are finished. And all for this," Samson even had time to shout: "Shut up, you chicken, and keep bailing."

And they all bailed and rowed and bailed again like mad. Even the law speaker bailed, little though his body equipped him for it, and Pastor Poul also found a tin with which he could bail. The water washed around their legs; flatbread, legs of lamb, knives, sheaths and other equipment from the boathouses floated about, but the boat, which for a moment had rested as though dead, came back to life; the prow rose and again attacked the waves, and the law speaker now told them for God's sake to row and they would soon be out of danger. It was not long before they escaped the current, just as a fresh chalk-white wave burst into flower and spread right over the black waters.

"Oh, you were scared this time," laughed Samson putting his hand gleefully on the shoulders of the young man he had been scolding. But a farmer by the name of Justinus, who was one of those in the boat, spoke in a quiet and very subdued voice when he said to the law speaker: "I thought we were going to be wrecked this time."

"So did I," replied Samuel Mikkelsen. "Lambatangi is a terrible place."

"God won't take us until He is ready for us," commented another.

But Pastor Poul noticed that the same melody continued to circulate in his head. It had been there all the time. It was a minuet. He remembered it from the day when the Frenchmen had danced on Tinganes.

A shower came on and hid all the mountains and inlets. The boat struggled its way along the coast of Streymey. Like a fly on a tarred stick.

The breakers on the submerged rocks near Velbestad shone through the dusk as they finally reached the place. The waves were breaking right up into the grass, and there was no possibility of landing there. The law speaker tried to approach the coast in various places, but had to give up. They could see there were men on the shore shouting to them, but they could not hear them. They spent over half an hour at this place, and it gradually became quite dark.

"I can't see any alternative now but to try to make it to Kirkjubø," said the law speaker.

This expression "try to make it" had an ominous sound. It was something you only attempted when you were in serious trouble. To land twelve men on a spot where no one ought to have been did not appeal to the mariner Samuel Mikkelsen. And what about their mission! What would the people of Kirkjubø think of them splashing around here like monkeys on such a stormy day – the law speaker himself! – in order to row a desperate parson whose wife had left him? Would it not be better to wait for the west flow and a calm sea and then to raise the sail and hurry home with both current and wind behind them? No, there was nothing else for it. This poor man had to be put ashore somewhere on Streymey, otherwise he would surely go out of his mind.

It was two miles by water from Velbestad to Kirkjubø, still directly against the current. The law speaker's men rowed, groaning on their oars, biting their teeth and pulling back in their seats with all the weight of their bodies. And the boat had to be bailed all the time. The veins stood out on Samson's forehead. He made one more attempt: "So sailed... the heroes... of... Norway"

But his voice was hoarse and his eyes lifeless. They rowed on in silence. Only a minuet continued to play in the parson's inconsolable mind. Then – far into the evening – the law speaker suddenly turned the boat into the shelter of Kirkjubø Holm. Through the darkness, they could just make out where they were – the great farm and the ruins of the cathedral. Soon, the boat was safely drawn up ashore, and Samuel Mikkelsen and his men, who were all wet, went quietly to the farm, almost as though they were a little embarrassed.

The Kirkjubø farmer received them with generous hospitality and immediately explained to Pastor Poul that in former times this had been the seat of the Bishop of the Faroe

Islands. He pointed to the great cathedral, the empty windows of which stared out at them, black and eerie. But Pastor Poul had no sense for antiquities; he refused even to dry his clothes, and he scarcely had time to have a bite of food. The farmer did not believe he was serious in his intention of reaching Tórshavn that evening in this dreadful weather and with night approaching. But the law speaker quietly drew the farmer aside and told him that there was no point in talking to people when that madness was upon them.

That madness – the farmer understood that. Aye, what was that woman not capable of bringing about! Now, today she had almost been the cause of twelve men's deaths; there was no getting away from that. The Kirkjubø farmer pulled at his white beard. He said nothing. Nor was that necessary: men like Samuel Mikkelsen and him could well exchange thoughts without saying anything.

However, there was no discussing this: if Pastor Poul insisted on reaching Havn that evening, he should be provided with a good guide. The farmer sent his best fell guide with him. They had to go across the fell known as Kirkjubøreyn, the Kirkjubø Ridge. For, there were no rivers in flood there, no bogs and no marshes.

They started on their way shortly after this, both carrying small horn lanterns, the dim ring of light from which glided across greensward and rock. Pastor Poul walked quickly, hurrying restlessly up the steep path. Only on reaching the most difficult passages on the steep mountain side did he let his guide go first. A minuet was playing constantly in his mind, though he was not aware of it; he was not thinking; he was only longing. Short of breath to the very extreme as a result of the steep climb and constantly being interrupted by hindrances, he moved on still with this melody playing in his head. It became the theme of his suffering; it led him on; and like a sleepwalker he clambered over the cyclopean rock faces up to the edge of the great, rock-strewn expanse.

"Now we must make sure that we don't lose sight of the path," said his companion, "Otherwise we shall be in trouble in this darkness."

The path was an insignificant trodden track that twisted its way over gravel-strewn surfaces and between piles of boulders. The guide wanted to go forward carefully, taking note of each tall cairn they passed, but Pastor Poul was running ahead all the time, and they only found each other again thanks to the light from their horn lanterns. Then it happened that the minister's lantern was blown out by the wind. This was in the middle of an open area strewn with huge boulders. Pastor Poul did not immediately notice his misfortune; he merely went on, grim and dull. Then he heard his guide shouting and saw him swinging his lantern. He had obviously clambered up on some boulder. Pastor Poul turned around and made for the place, but the light suddenly disappeared. The shouts continued, and Pastor Poul also shouted. But he ran as though he was lost. And in this way the two men wandered around in the pitch darkness of the evening, each with an extinguished lantern, hopelessly shouting for each other among great boulders and smashed rocky fastnesses. The sound of their voices blew away in the powerful gale. They did not find each other again. But Pastor Poul followed the course that his sleepy mind prescribed for him, and he walked and he fell and he got up again and tramped on through jumbles of stone and great rocky screes without being able to see a hand in front of his eyes.

Once, when he had reached a smoother region, he suddenly heard a strong, constant whistling sound. Slowly, this great, sorrowful sound penetrated his consciousness; he stopped, and the fear that he had so far not felt, gradually emerged in his heart. He ran for some way, but he could still hear this sound of seething sorrow to his left. When it became a little lighter, the moonlight turning the clouds white, he saw he was standing beside a mountain lake. Its waves were hurrying towards the desolate, stony shore and breaking against it. This was something living he had found here in the desert: a troubled lake, and its sole passion was isolation.

He hastened on; it grew lighter and lighter; a half moon was rushing through the clouds, and in sharp, hesitant patches of light, Pastor Poul could see where he was: in the midst of a congealed ocean of boulders with great waves, mighty breakers of rocks and foam of receding gravel. And the stones were laughing at him and the cliffs had such terrifying shapes that he was gripped by panic, and he ran as though for his life.

He ran for a long time. But finally it was downhill on softer ground, and when he stumbled he no longer hurt himself, but immediately felt the moisture seeping in through his clothing. He waded through sumps and at last found himself outside a lonely house in which candles were burning. When, breathlessly, he knocked on the door, he suddenly heard the minuet in his head again and it dawned on him that it had been going round and round in his mind all the time he had been running and groaning and complaining and – who knows – perhaps howling.

As soon as he was inside, he asked if he was on his way to Tórshavn, but the words stuck fast in his throat. For around him in this hearth room he saw nothing but appallingly ravaged or crazed faces, all gaping and staring foolishly at him.

"God help you," finally said one man with a face as white as chalk. His voice was unreal in its melodiousness. "God help you," he repeated. "This is the lepers' hospital. The Argir hospital."

"The lepers' hospital," exclaimed Pastor Poul and sank to his knees.

"Yes, sir, the lepers' hospital," came the words from a man squatting like an animal and eating from a trough of food. There was a foul smell in the room that caught his breath. It was like a nightmare.

The pale man with the melodious voice said he would go a little way with the minister. The river was not easy to get over this evening, so he would show him the best place to cross it.

"There's a play on in Tórshavn this evening," he said. He seemed to know everything and spoke at great length in his gentle voice. They met someone in the dark. "He's one of the inmates," he explained. "They are allowed to wander around out here, but they are not allowed to go indoors near other people." And he explained that it was no fun for him to be counted among the inmates. But no one would have him at home although he was only slightly ill.

He went on talking, full of knowledge and melancholy until they came to the rushing Sandá river, the rushing waters of which were swirling there in the moonlight.

There, Pastor Poul thanked him for accompanying him and managed to cross the river in safety.

His heart started to beat violently, for he was now quite close to Tórshavn. He could already see the odd light, and yes, now he was to see Barbara again. He could think no further than to that event. She was presumably at the play... so he would not even be able to talk to her. Breathlessly, he went on his way. And the minuet!

He went past the first houses and remembered the afternoon only five months ago when he had run past here with Barbara. Everywhere was closed and deserted. Nýggjastova was dark, too; no one was at home. Pastor Poul tramped on through Gongin with his dead horn lantern.

But in the Assembly Hall there were festive lights and a crowd of people. The first thing he set eyes on as he entered was the judge, who with an earnest face was stroking his violin and playing some gentle music. He was sitting towards the back, and somewhere else at the back there were several others standing and laughing, including Gabriel, big and heavy, wearing a bright red dress coat. And Pastor Paul gradually realised that all this was something he somehow recognised, but he was on the point of dropping with fatigue and from that murderous beating of his heart. Of course, this was *Holberg's Jeppe of the Hill*, and Gabriel must be Baron Nilus. For in a huge bed in the middle of the floor lay Andreas Heyde, carrying on something dreadful and saying in a drunken voice, "Surely I am dreaming? Yet I think not. I will try to pinch my arm; then, if it doesn't hurt I am dreaming, and if it hurts, then I am not dreaming..."

At that moment, Pastor Poul caught sight of Barbara in the midst of the crowd. She went out of the hall, and he thought she was running away from him and went after her. But she stood waiting for him in the entrance hall.

"But my dear," she exclaimed. "Are you mad? Are you completely mad?"

Her voice was on the point of tears, so tender was she. She felt his torn, wet clothing and stroked his cheek. "Are you completely mad?"

"Barbara, I've come... to you," stammered Pastor Paul in a broken voice.

"Have you come to me?" She spoke as though to a child, and delight began to bubble up in her voice. "But how on earth have you got here in this weather? Dearest Poul. Walked from

Kirkjubø? Are you mad?"

She took a firm hold on his arm: "Come on. Come home, my dear."

And she twisted her hand down into his and clutched it and patted it tenderly with her other hand and led him through Gongin, supporting him and being close to him with all her body, time and time again, glancing briefly and shyly at him, radiant with joy. But Pastor Poul still bore the extinguished lantern in his left hand.

She got him into Nýggjastova, lit candles, helped him out of his clothing and gave him something to eat, doing all this silently and willingly, eager to serve him, such as he had never seen her before. It was a source of great comfort to him. But while he ate slowly and as though sleep-walking, he had nevertheless to ask her: "Do you love – him?"

Barbara suddenly became serious. She looked down and quickly replied: "Yes."

That is to say she really whispered it; she hardly said it; she simply breathed it suddenly... it certainly was a yes, but it could almost sound like a no. Her eyes were filled with regret.

There was a slight pause, after which she asked, "Poul, may I drink a little of your beer?"

She took the tankard, drank from it, handed it to him and said, "You have a drink as well. You must be very thirsty."

And Pastor Poul drank and was again as though refreshed. He felt it like a caress through his insensate weariness.

"I'm glad you are with me again," said Barbara suddenly and humbly. She looked down.

Pastor Poul was no longer in despair. But it was simply all as though he were dreaming it. He ate calmly, ate his fill.

"I'm going to make sure you have some sleep now," said Barbara.

Pastor Poul lay down on his bed.

"Shall I sit with you until you go to sleep?" asked Barbara persuasively. "Would that not be good?"

Pastor Poul felt his will awakening within him. New unhappiness, new unease.

"What is to become of me, Barbara?" he whispered.

"Well, my dearest love," she exclaimed in her tenderest descant voice, weeping and laughing at the same time. Her throat tightened. She sat down on the edge of the bed and bent over him. "You mustn't be so upset, you know." Her voice now sounded as though she were telling a secret: "I must tell you something. There is no reason why you should be. No reason at all. My feelings for you are exactly as they were before. As always. That's the truth... really."

She kept glancing at him. Her look was still one of nervousness, of regret and sudden fear. She had put her hands in under his shoulders and was convulsively playing his back with all ten fingers. She was sombre and ridiculous, flushed with shameful expectation.

Pastor Poul was tired, and his thoughts moved only slowly. But he took hold of her and drew her close, and he suddenly felt she was quite submissive. His breast was filled with joy; a mighty wave rose slowly within him and filled him with delight. Good heavens. Everything was permitted to him; indeed she even came to his aid, drew off her clothes humbly and speedily and lay down beside him. Close to him he saw her eyes as green as the ocean depths every time she glanced up at him; her face was unrecognisable, unlovely, even ridiculous with delight.

Aye, aye, aye, everything he had suffered, endured and battled with, it had all only happened so that they should experience this moment of inconceivable union. Oh, she rewarded him for Mikines, for the cold ashes in Jansegard, for the great sorrow of Stegard, for the danger at sea by Konufjall, for the terrible wasteland of Kirkjubøreyn, for the lepers at Argir and for the minuet, pling, pling, pling. Ha ha ha! Barbara rewarded Pastor Poul; she gave herself to him, she was gracious to him, she rejoiced senselessly with him as the people of Tórshavn went home from the play... indeed throughout half the night.

Like a man drowning in heavy waves of joy, he fell asleep, and Barbara's eyes were still sparkling with the green of the sea when he let her go.

China

Pastor Poul started to wake, but lay for a long time without being aware of anything. He suddenly came to himself with a violent shock to his heart, but then he immediately remembered Barbara. He was lying there beside her. Yes, that was right, everything was well; it was not the catastrophe he had imagined. And he sighed, released and freed; his heart was again beating at walking pace. Indeed, it was strutting along like a tired horse that has suddenly been let loose in a luscious meadow. He turned over and fell asleep again.

When he awoke, it was almost light. Barbara opened her eyes, stared at him at first in some confusion and then recognised him with great delight. She put her arm round him and kissed him.

"I'm glad you've come," she said, looking shameful and rather stupid. She fiddled in some embarrassment with the button on his shirt.

Pastor Poul said that he was happy as well, that he did not remember ever having been so happy as on the previous evening.

"No, never," was Barbara's enthusiastic response. "Never ever have we both been so gloriously happy. Do you know what it reminds me of? Do you remember that time at Leynum?"

She quickly looked down and pressed herself close to him.

"But now, what about...?" said Pastor Poul, immediately

breaking off. His mind was filled with laughter, enormous laughter; indeed the horse of his heart ran a joyous lap around its green meadow. "Oh, Andreas Heyde," he thought. "Ha, ha, ha." But he refused to betray his joy, and not a sound escaped him.

And yet, Barbara had understood him so well that she hastily and almost in fear exclaimed, "You mustn't say that to anyone. Do you hear? It's a secret between you and me. Oh, I can't imagine how desperate he would be if he got to know it."

She stared ahead, lost in thought and no longer took any notice of her husband.

Pastor Poul lay long in silence. His heart's horse stood still and behaved as though he was afraid. This was the first time he had heard her mention Andreas Heyde, and the tone in which she was speaking was quite unknown to him.

"Barbara, do you regret it?" he asked.

"Oh no, dearest," she said, smiling at him. But directly after this she again started to stare out in the air as though she had a vision.

"I'm so afraid he has got himself drunk," she said suddenly. "He was probably drunk yesterday evening."

She was trembling a little.

"*I* was drunk yesterday evening," said Pastor Poul.

"Were you?" said Barbara absent-mindedly, still staring in the air.

Pastor Poul did not know whether he was angry or unhappy; he turned away from his wife. She was in love with Andreas Heyde. But this was nothing but what he had known all the time, indeed no more than she herself had said. Had he for a single moment thought things could be different? Had he really come here to take her back home to Jansegard? Had he really been so foolish? No, he remembered of course what he

271

had thought. If only he could win her once more, one single time.

Well, his undertaking had been carried out. Carried out with enormous force and intensity. What more did he want? Yet once more?

"Why have you turned your back to me?" asked Barbara. There was just a hint in her voice that she felt she had been wronged. Pastor Poul felt a little happier and made no reply.

"I think you're angry," she whispered in his ear.

He turned towards her again and smiled.

"I'm not angry," he said. "I was merely thinking. You are in love with someone else, and I am merely in your way. I won't try to prevent you from doing anything, and it will be no use in any case. So I shall have to put you out of my mind and quite forget you. Don't you agree?"

Barbara made no reply; she shook her head hopelessly, almost imperceptibly, just enough for Pastor Poul to see it. She was very serious, and her eyes were filled with great sadness.

"But Barbara," Pastor Poul continued, "if you... if it isn't me you are fond of."

"But you know how much I love you," said Barbara. "You must surely have understood that. Otherwise all that yesterday evening would have been unthinkable. There is no reason for... everything between us is as it always has been. Don't you understand?"

She spoke urgently and forcefully; she held on to his wrists and let her hands glide up his sleeves. Then, in a lighter tone, she suddenly added: "You should simply never have left me. Then nothing would have happened."

She smiled happily at the discovery she had made here, this little coloured stone. She believed in it herself: "We two ought simply to have lived here together in Tórshavn, shouldn't we?

I didn't thrive in that village. You'll stay here for a few days, won't you, my dear?"

Rather more than an hour later, Pastor Poul was on his way to the judge's home, satisfied but scarcely consoled. His wife had gone to Andreas Heyde. He was probably in need of a visit from her, poor man. Pastor Poul was happy at the thought. One must be noble to one's enemy. Now he had fitted him with a good horn in his forehead. But why should he be a unicorn? One horn was no horn. No, there must be at least a couple. Pastor Poul caught himself thinking thus. Was he already such a – libertine? Aye, thoughts were flashing through his mind today; he was in a strange mood, unhappy and ardent and proud. He sat down in one of the judge's chairs, threw his hat down and said, "Well, now I've experienced being my own wife's lover. There's another man who has managed to become his own coxcomb's coxcomb. Which do you think is the worse?"

Johan Hendrik Heyde's good-humoured, lined face lit up; he was at once all attention; he sat up, put his book down, rubbed the tip of his nose with a finger and said, "Well, that's what I call an amusing way of looking at things."

Then he twisted round and supported his chin in one hand.

"Well, It's usually said that the husband is the only person who can be a real coxcomb, as he is the only person married to the woman in question. You can never be coxcomb to your own coxcomb, for..."

"No, you are applying far too legalistic a mind to it," interrupted Pastor Poul. "It is only in the eyes of God and man that Barbara is my wife. In her heart of hearts she is another man's woman. So in reality this other man is the coxcomb as he is the one who...? Don't you yourself agree... that they are much in love?"

"Alas, far too much in love," sighed Johan Hendrik. "Andreas makes no attempt to do anything useful at all, although he could achieve great things. Just imagine, sent by the Exchequer! It is all wrong."

"Aye, I think so, too. It really is all very wrong," laughed Pastor Poul boisterously with a sharp stab in his heart: "Very wrong indeed, ha, ha."

The judge looked at him attentively.

"Aye," he said, "you are now in the embrace I knew you would be in. You seem to be taking it well... hmm, how shall I put it? You seem to stand the sea well."

"I'm in a furious mood," said Pastor Poul. "A desperately furious mood, and yet an ecstatic mood. I had never imagined I could encompass so many powerful emotions at once."

"Ha ha. I thought as much. Then perhaps God hasn't deluged you with all those misfortunes in vain. But you are still only at the first stage."

"I remember what you said to me the last time we saw each other. That people who encounter true grace are those whom fate grasps and plays like a musical instrument."

"Yes, assuming that these people are instruments at all and not reeds or pieces of firewood or heads of stinging rays."

"Good heavens, I am an instrument," said Pastor Poul. "A wind instrument. And God is playing me mightily. Like a shawm, a pitiful shawm."

"Well, you are perhaps not a trombone, and, by the way, take care not to become a trumpet." Johan Hendrik smiled satirically: "But woodwind. Aye, let's say a woodwind instrument. That might sound a bit uninteresting, but it is really the most beautiful of all instruments."

He suddenly rose and started energetically walking up and

down.

"The main thing," he continued, stopping in front of Pastor Poul, "the main thing is that one has a character that can be inspired but not broken by misfortune. Desperation and fury are the best winds to sail in if only you know how. But don't sail too close to the wind! It is possible to overturn. I take it you are about to undertake a series of foolish acts, eh? But do at least refrain from killing my nephew!"

"I assure you," said Pastor Poul, "that my feelings towards him are almost those of a colleague."

"They will scarcely continue like that."

Pastor Poul straight away felt the truth of these words. At that moment, Barbara was together with Andreas. She had promised to come home this evening...

"Will you play something?" he asked the judge.

"I will play a little piece for you. Unfortunately, it is only a solo. Alas, I am almost always reduced to playing solo. And that never becomes as *agitato* as for instance in a trio."

He gave the parson a wry smile and played a long tremolo. Pastor Poul had a sense of intoxication. He was unhappy but ardent; the music filled him with fervour.

Was he to be furious and enraged throughout the day?

Pastor Poul had detained the judge for a long time, and now he had determined to leave. Barbara had promised to come this evening, but evening was still far off. He was overcome by a terrible sense of loneliness that gnawed away at his heart as he drifted through narrow alleyways made depressing by the winter gloom. He met a man whose face he thought he had seen before, though he did not know where. The man recognised him and greeted him. He encountered several people whom he remembered as from a dream. They all recognised him and greeted him. He gave no more thought to it, but when he returned to Nýggjastova, his mother-in-law Magdalene told him: "The men from Kirkjubø have been here to enquire about you. They wanted to make sure you had got here safely. They have been out all night with lanterns and candles on Kirkjubøreyn looking for you."

Her voice was peevish and resentful as always. Pastor Poul's only reply was: "Oh." At that very moment he realised he ought to pay a visit to his colleague, the Tórshavn minister. He was not keen on Pastor Wenzel, but he was drawn to his house. You never knew what might happen in that house. It was certainly not prudent to go there. But he felt desperate.

Pastor Wenzel received him with some reservation on behalf of heaven and various reproaches on the part of his family. He made no direct comment, but it seemed obvious that he was giving Pastor Poul responsibility for the indignation emanating from his wife and now relating to the Heyde family. His expression was one of deep injustice. Besides, he had both sick parishioners and folk in mourning to attend to – there was so much undeserved suffering, and he asked his colleague to forgive him and left. But his wife stayed at home and made preparations for a modest cup of coffee.

"Perhaps you are not all that keen on coffee?" she said when Pastor Wenzel had left. "Perhaps you would rather have a glass of French brandy or rum?"

For the first time in his life Pastor Poul really discovered Mrs Anna Sophie Heyde, and he immediately felt at ease with her. She was big, fair and gentle and in everything she did she reflected an understanding that comforted him a little. Indeed, he suddenly sensed a caressing and soothing hand. He decided at once that he would also speak to her as a friend and unburden himself to Anna Sophie. He longed and thirsted for her feminine friendship. He had long been so lonely, indeed ever since he had come to this country. He suddenly realised that Barbara had not been his friend. She had been an adversary, indeed his enemy, and he had had to play against her all alone. He longed now to talk to a friend – about his enemy, about his enemy...

And Anna Sophie looked kindly and thoughtfully at him.

"You have so much power over her even so," she said. "I noticed what went on during the play yesterday evening."

Pastor Poul felt a secret joy. "I suppose there were others who noticed as well," he commented.

"Not everyone, not everyone," laughed Anna Sophie.

"Really?"

"Not Jeppe." She gave a deep sigh and shook her head. "Oh, Andreas. He was so sure of himself. And when he had finally finished playing the part of Jeppe, he was so drunk that he simply didn't miss her. Not until this morning..."

"Is he so negligent with her?" asked Pastor Poul. He suddenly felt terribly depressed.

"Negligent... I don't know what to say. Not always at any rate. Our dear Andreas can be pretty empressé. And then no one can resist him."

"Aye, aye," said Pastor Poul, his face contracting in pain. "I know it; he understands the art. Sometimes negligent, sometimes attentive. Barbara is like that as well. Don't you think I know how to deal with it?... But I just don't do it."

He stared darkly at the table top. Nothing hurt him so much as this fact, that Andreas could be negligent towards Barbara and yet loved by her.

"Cheer up," said Anna Sophie. "In this game it never goes according to the rules."

"Aye, he who can be the most negligent is the winner," was

Pastor Poul's dispirited reaction.

"Ha ha, you're a man. You have no idea how we women love to cheat. Especially Barbara. She always cheats, oh God, oh God. Do you think for instance that what she did yesterday evening was in accordance with the rules? You certainly didn't look particularly negligent when you came into the theatre, ha ha. You looked rather as though you had just been dug up out of the cemetery. Good Lord... and yet she went with you."

Anna Sophie shook her head admiringly.

"It was probably out of pity," said Pastor Poul tentatively.

"No, it was out of... well, femininity! She has a lovely nature. If only there were others like her. You know... all we other women love her... although we ought to envy her. And that's saying a lot."

Anna Sophie laughed. Pastor Poul said nothing. He sat there burning with desire for Barbara; he emptied his glass, and she was in his thoughts. He wanted her so much that every joint in his body hurt him. He had slept with her last night, and that had seemed quite improbable to him. But it was even more improbable that she would come back to him this evening. Although she had promised to. No, he did not believe it. And yet he believed it and found himself in a state of intense excitement.

"Where is she?" he asked.

"Not here – as you can imagine. She never comes here. Nor do we see much of Andreas. They have their regular spots..."

Pastor Poul felt a landslide of disappointment and horror. It dawned on him that he had all along believed that she was somewhere or other here at Reynegard. Ridiculous idea. Now it was suddenly as though she had completely escaped him. She had her secret paths.

"She's full of lies," he suddenly exclaimed.

Anna Sophie shrugged her shoulders slightly.

"So are all women. We have to be. You mustn't think badly of us for that. When a woman tells a lie, it isn't the same as when a man tells a lie. No, we are different."

"I'm losing Barbara," said Pastor Poul.

"One never loses Barbara," said Anna Sophie with a smile. "But on the other hand, one never possesses her entirely. If you simply understood that, you could perhaps take it all more calmly."

"Aye, so that's what she's like," said Pastor Poul angrily. "She wants the lot. She wants Andreas, but that doesn't at all mean that she wants to give me up. She never gives any man up. But in this case, she's going to have to make a choice."

"She will never be forced. Nothing will force her."

"I won't force her, but I might kick her as far into Hell as a hare can jump in fourteen years."

Pastor Poul got up. Everything went black before him.

"She will come back to you," said Anna Sophie quietly.

"Do you mean that? Seriously?"

Pastor Poul was suddenly a different person.

"You can be almost sure of it. I think I understand Barbara. I think you should show a little confidence in me. Meanwhile, you must take it calmly. You have your life before you. Nor should you forget that there are other women in the world."

She rose and as it were stretched a little; she was big and blonde and gentle and smiled briefly. Pastor Poul felt this gesture like a glimpse of sunshine through the mist and always remembered it, in the way in which one often remembers completely indifferent observations.

He was a little intoxicated when he finally left Reynegard. He would probably have stayed there for ever talking about

Barbara if the dusk had not reminded him that evening was approaching. A terrible tension and impatience started to press on his heart, but he was helpless and could do nothing but wait. Here he sat in Nýggjastova, in Barbara's home, and he was one of the family. But where was Barbara?

Magdalene, his mother-in-law, put some food before him and did not deign to address many words to him. When he said something to the effect that Barbara could probably be expected soon, she merely turned an indescribably incredulous face to him.

"Well, where can she be?" he asked.

"Do you think that I ever know where she is or who she is with? She is my daughter, I can't deny that, and I have tried to bring her up as well as possible. But now, Pastor Poul, I wash my hands of her; I have always told you I would, and now I am washing my hands of her."

Time passed and the loneliness was a nightmare to Pastor Poul. He sometimes thought someone was taking hold of the door catch, and at those moments he was filled with such anticipation that he both saw Barbara's figure before his eyes and heard her sparkling voice.

"My dear! Have you been waiting long? Are you angry with me?"

But Barbara did not come, and the vague click of her mother's cards from her game of patience was the only sound he heard.

Pastor Poul could not stay still. He went out.

"Say I've gone down to the bailiff's," he said to his mother-in-law.

She answered him with a sarcastic nod and sighed. And set about a new game of patience.

Gabriel was smoking a long chalk pipe and was in a good

mood. His wife Suzanne was sitting nursing little Augustus. Bailiff Harme himself had gone to lie down; he had recently become very frail. But as for his daughter, it was noticeable how well she looked; even Pastor Poul could not help noticing that. A fresh fine radiance had appeared in her smiling cheeks and teeth, and in her eyes there was a roguish look that grew into radiant sunshine every time she looked at her son. She was an exquisite, dark beauty, and Gabriel smoked his pipe and possessed her to such an extent that Pastor Poul could almost hear him say; "There, my friend. This is the way of a wise man."

But Suzanne, sitting by the window and cradling her son, started to sing:

> *Close the window tight, my dear,*
> *Wish the whole dear world good cheer,*
> *Wind and rain have brought him back*
> *And so I know I nought shall lack.*

"What is all that dreadful rubbish you're singing?" said an irritated Gabriel.

But Suzanne merely turned her roguish eyes towards her husband and went on singing.

> *Can I not sing as I will*
> *To my child*
> *As I wish*
> *And as I can*
> *And as I must.*
> *Close the window tight, my dear,*
> *Wish the whole dear world good cheer,*
> *Wind and rain have brought him back...*

Gabriel went out – rather suddenly. He left the room. It could have been the call of nature. Suzanne laughed. It was a well-known lullaby she had been singing. But Gabriel didn't know it. It had never been sung at his cradle.

His good humour was half spoiled when he returned. In a rough voice he asked where Barbara – that is to say Mrs Aggersøe – was that evening. Pastor Poul replied that she was out, but that he expected her to be home soon.

"Hmm," Gabriel burst into a snigger. "Then you'll have a long wait."

Pastor Poul had no answer to this, but Gabriel continued in a voice trembling with scorn: "Never in all my born days have I seen anything as plain stupid as your marriage to her last summer."

Both Suzanne and Pastor Poul were quite amazed at Gabriel. He was almost weeping. Malicious pleasure, fury and past suffering were intertwined in his voice.

"Let us not talk about Barbara now," said Suzanne in an attempt to put him off.

"Talk about her? Is Pastor Poul perhaps not to be allowed to talk about his own wife?"

He turned towards Pastor Poul: "I don't know how much you intend to put up with. If I were in your place then... God, what impudence! I can have her put behind bars if you wish and her gallant along with her!"

"Put her behind bars?" said Pastor Poul. "And make me a complete laughing stock?"

"You're already a laughing stock, damn it. It can never be worse. Do you want to be Pastor Niels all over again? Or even worse? She's never been as bloody randy and shameless in view of everyone just as she is now. It radiates from her everywhere she goes. She's... she's a scandal. Puh. And then... aye, God help us... going off with you yesterday evening as though there was nothing wrong. Ha ha ha, oh dear. God help me, you are more gullible..."

"Oh, you are so hard, Gabriel." Suzanne's voice was dry and sharp. Her face was flushed with anger.

"Hard! Hard! Perhaps it hasn't dawned on you that is my task and duty... and your father's... to watch over... morality. Isn't that right? But of course. Of course. Your sweet duty as a wife is as usual to take the side of the baggage, the whore, the paramour and invite her to a cup of coffee... while I am out."

Pastor Poul didn't know what to say. He was worn out, ashamed and in despair, and in images that were far too clear he saw how Barbara had lived and shone in this world of trivialities while he himself had been caught on Mikines.

Gabriel went out and returned with a bottle of brandy in one hand and a copy of King Christian the Fifth's Norwegian Law in the other. With magisterial weight he placed the heavy book on the table, told his wife to fetch some glasses, filled them and offered them round. Pastor Poul immediately emptied his glass; he did so in his distress and without any dignity. It was the only thing he could do. There was nothing he could say.

"Let's see," said Gabriel, starting to flick through the book. "Let's see what the law says... mmmmm..."

He licked his fingers and turned the pages with an unaccustomed hand. He had not been concerned with the law for many months. "Here it says... here it says... let's see. Concerning murder. On severing limbs and wounding, no. On challenges and duels. No!" He was sweating: "Regarding domestic violence, regarding keeping the peace in church, no. Regarding damage, regarding accidentally wounding. No!" He was sweating: "Regarding self-defence, no. Regarding...

loose living!"

He almost shouted it and then sniggered: "Aye, that's a bit steep. A parson's wife, too! Let's see: 'Where a woman commits adultery, a fine to the man of 24 pieces of silver and to the woman of 12 pieces of silver, and both must do public penance.'"

He sniggered again. "But if they do not have the means to pay the fines – by God they haven't, at least she hasn't – then they shall be punished by imprisonment. But if they marry, he will pay four and a half pieces of silver and she half that amount and they shall not be required to do public penance..."

The parson stiffened, and Gabriel, too, looked a little dubious. But then he said: "Oh, but this is only about single people. I thought as much – the punishments are too mild."

He emptied his glass. "There must be something about married women, that's to say about adultery, Let me see... it wouldn't be too much if she were to be given a public whipping, would it?"

Pastor Poul rose. He was in a state of wild agitation. "I don't demand any punishment at all for her, I simply do not," he stammered fervently: "No revenge, no. Although she has... cost me..."

He stood leaning against the chair back, and the chair was trembling between his hands.

"And then," he added after a time, suddenly thinking again: "I mean, she might change her mind."

These words were uttered in a tone of desperation. He started walking to and fro.

"I am sure she will. You'll see," said Suzanne with a curiously convinced tone in her voice.

"Aye, she probably will," was Gabriel's dry comment as he stopped between two paragraphs.

"No, you won't make her any better by whipping her," said Suzanne passionately, rising with flashing eyes.

"Be quiet," replied Gabriel, continuing to read eagerly. "It's not at all certain there is any authority for whipping her. There's all sorts of other rubbish here. But my God, it would do her good."

He leant back in his chair. "A really good thrashing over there at the whipping post. The day that happened..."

"All you are doing is showing what sort of a man you are, you miserable creature," said Suzanne through gritted teeth.

Gabriel looked a little ashamed and took a glass. "I only mean she needs a good beating. That's my opinion," he said.

"What concern is it of yours?" hissed Suzanne. "What have you to do with it? Here's Pastor Poul, and when all is said and done, he is the one most concerned. He can punish her himself if he wants."

Pastor Poul had sat down and slumped on the edge of his chair.

"Yes, I will," he said. But his voice sounded peculiar, and it sounded as though he was swallowing something.

"Have a drink," said Gabriel. "Help yourself. Well then, why the devil don't you give her a good hiding like all other men do when their wives refuse to behave. But perhaps you're like Pastor Niels, who preferred to have a good hiding himself."

"If only I could get hold of her," said Pastor Poul, breathing very heavily. He could feel anger growing throughout his body. Everything grew dark before his eyes.

"That's easy enough," said Gabriel.

"When I don't know where she is?"

"Hah! I can tell you that. She's up in 'China' together with her gallant.

"Gabriel," shouted Suzanne.

Pastor Poul drank another glass. His anger spread from his belly and loins up through his chest and out into his arms. He clenched his fists hard and groaned quietly. His face was as white as a sheet and as hard as stone.

"It's no good chastising her," cried Suzanne suddenly. She was weeping, complaining, persuading: "It's no use Pastor Poul; it will only harden her. I know. I know her. Her mother has beaten her – oh! When those two from Stakkenes had committed incest, she took her with her herself to see the beheading. And then – so she should never forget it – she took her home and gave her such a hiding that the whole town could hear it. And just look how much good it did. You cannot chastise her, you cannot chastise her; it's a foolish idea, a ridiculous idea. You are such fools. Such fools."

But Pastor Poul was seeing red and black. He could already hear Barbara's screams resounding throughout the town, her glittering falsetto voice falling into a whine and being splintered like a tower of crystal. He was set on violence and vengeance; he grabbed his stick; Gabriel took the bottle, and they both left.

"You fools," shouted Suzanne after them, weeping. "You fools." Little Augustus Gabrielsen Harme woke and also started weeping.

"China" was a small building where the seamen working for the Royal Store were wont to congregate when they were in Tórshavn. The place did not exactly enjoy a good reputation, less because it was a centre for smuggling than for certain other reasons. Just beside the real "China" there was another, smaller building, a kind of annex overlooking the vegetable garden on the west side of the Reyn. Andreas Heyde had rented this building in order, he said, to be able to study undisturbed.

His intentions had apparently also been more or less serious at first, but it soon turned out that the Muses did not thrive well in such close proximity to Bacchus and Venus. But since New Year, Bacchus had been less in favour, and Andreas had led a life that probably looked almost decorous to those who could not see in the dark.

Pastor Poul and Gabriel fumbled their way from Gongin into the pitch-dark, steep, stepped alleyway known as Klettaskot. They were both possessed by a terrible anger. Pastor Poul was intent on hitting hard. He was going to thrash and beat the gallant, Barbara and whoever else got in his righteous way. Gabriel had more ambitious plans: he wanted to surprise, expose and bring down the devil of a scandal and shame on their sinful undertaking; he was intent on grabbing them and showing them caught in the act, exposing them to public mockery and confronting them as the representative of the law. Nevertheless, he felt that both Pastor Poul and he himself needed to strengthen themselves a little before they set to work. They stopped, drank to each other from the bottle, wished each other all the best and found themselves on quite fraternal terms. A small, narrow flight of steps led down to "China" and the other house. But Gabriel wanted first to reconnoitre and so he proceeded into the kitchen garden behind the house. There he saw there was a light in the living room.

"Ha, we have them," he sniggered and tiptoed over to the window.

The curtain was drawn, but he could peep in through an open strip at the bottom. Pastor Poul was paralysed with fury. He recognised the curtain from Jansegard. Barbara had given it to him to hang at his study window.

"They are not in bed yet," whispered Gabriel, pallid with

disappointment.

He turned to Pastor Poul, his face half illuminated by the light from inside. He looked in again: "But he's not wearing shoes. Perhaps they are getting ready for bed now... wait."

And he moved so as better to be able to observe what was going on. But Pastor Poul was not going to wait. He went round the house to the door, and when he found it locked he started hammering it and kicking it and shouting.

"Open this bloody door!"

Gabriel was with him in three strides.

"Stop it for God's sake," he hissed. "You're spoiling it all now. We can't prove anything now."

"I'll show them! I'll show them," screamed Pastor Poul in a completely demented voice.

He smashed a small window with his stick. But the door withstood his attack.

"Let me," said Gabriel, starting to fiddle with the wooden lock with his knife.

The parson went on kicking. It resounded throughout the neighbourhood, which was deserted now people had settled down for the night. Windows and doors were partly opened and an array of people in shifts, woollen stockings and all kinds of intimate garments, with bare legs in wooden clogs, were standing ready and with teeth chattering behind anything they could hide behind, while dogs barked and cocks flew cackling from their perches. But the core, the very flame behind all this din, was still the parson's improbable voice swearing and complaining.

The door suddenly opened. Gabriel had managed to tease the bolt off. Pastor Poul rushed into the dark room and fell over something, but was immediately on his feet again. Gabriel followed, and they both went into the inner room, where a light was burning and found it empty. The window was open, and fleeing footsteps could be heard in the garden. Gabriel took a quick look around and bounced out into the garden. He was like a ball of power, and vegetable and stone crushed and crashed beneath his feet.

But Pastor Poul was left behind with the scent of Barbara in his nostrils, the well known, sweetly familiar atmosphere of her many little things, her clothes, her movements. Aye, Barbara's genius was at home here. He recognised one of her skirts, flung over the bed, a pair of her shoes, her small boxes and cases and in the middle of the table the inkwell from Jansegard, his own lovely inkwell that she had given him when he went to live in Vágar! A large quill stood fluttering in it and in front of it lay some paper with writing on it. And now he could also see other things he recognised: music paper, a lute and many of the male, gallant things that had once been extracted from Andreas Heyde's trunk.

He stood as though nailed to the spot. He was sweating with horror right to the extremities of his limbs. He supported himself on the table top, gasped for air, groaned, indeed even whimpered now and again.

"Foxes have holes," he finally stammered dully and in the voice of one intoxicated. "Foxes have holes."

There lay a piece of manuscript before him. He read it through several times without discovering the least meaning in it. "The Faroe Islands," it said, "are a small group of tiny islands situated some... nautical miles west of the coast of Norway and... miles... from Shetland. Captain... has estimated the northernmost point to be... miles of latitude north and... miles of longitude west, their southernmost point at..."

Andreas Heyde's great work on the Faroe Islands, written on the orders of the Royal Exchequer, finished here for the time being. Pastor Poul did not laugh. It merely dawned on him that these lines had been written here in this room in the light of Barbara's tender presence, and suddenly he took the paper, crumpled it up and threw it on the floor. Then he took hold of the lute, swung it round, went out into the hearth room and smashed it to bits against the edge of the fireplace. The strings sang out, rattled and suddenly fell silent. It was like a murder. Pastor Poul threw the remains of the instrument on the fire and raked the glowing cinders over it. Then he fetched all the sheets of music and set fire to them, and he quickly let Barbara's skirt, her sewing box, the curtain, the inkwell follow them.

Gabriel entered, winded and swearing under his breath. He had abandoned the chase. But Andreas had floundered with one leg in a dunghill. Gabriel sniggered bitterly: he had heard that quite clearly and it was the source of great triumph to him. He was well drunk now. It was some time before he realised what Pastor Poul was up to. But then, suddenly stern, he said: "Stop doing any damage. As an official acting on behalf of His Majesty I can't agree to that. And you are drunk."

And with this, he staggered out. But before going, he put the crumpled manuscript in his pocket. He scarcely realised what he was doing. It was more like a habit. He was fond of having official documents to hand.

Pastor Poul had wrecked the entire room. His eyes were dim and witless; his lower jaw hung down. He was carrying large bundles of bedstraw out to the chimney; fevered and sweating he went about in the red light from the fire like a harvester, harvesting the hay from the bed of indignation.

"Foxes have holes..."

The neighbours watched in horror to see the sparks gushing and pouring out of China's chimney. The crowd grew bigger and bigger, but no one dared to go in to the madman who was smashing chairs and benches and throwing them on to the fire.

"Foxes have holes."

Then the watch came. That was Niels the Watchman, the Beach Flea, Ole Eighteen, Rebekka's Poul and the Hobbler, all carrying maces and sabres, but otherwise wearing wooden clogs or ragged bootees and not very militaristic to behold. But they were all upholders of the law, and they rattled their weapons as they went down the narrow steps to China. They were a little embarrassed to find the pastor from Vágar to be the incendiary, but Niels the Watchman was a man who precisely knew his duty. Nor did the soldiers encounter any opposition from the poor troubled priest. He went with them without causing any bother.

"Foxes have holes..." he croaked as he tumbled down into the black cellar of the Corps de Gardes.

Nul ne mérite

"Let me," said Barbara. "I can reach a lot further down."

And so she did; her arms could be seen bare and flickering white through the swirling sea water. She had a knife in one hand and with it loosened a sea snail shell that was firmly fixed on the steeply sloping rock. The shell slowly rolled down through the water into her other hand.

"There you are," she said, drawing her wet arms out of the water. Her face was hot and breathless, but her hands were red and a little numb from the water.

"You're a water nymph," said Andreas. "An oceanide."

They both lay on the black rocks at the water's edge catching sea snails. They were going to use them as bait, for on these summer evenings they would often sit with a fishing rod and catch Norway haddock and coalfish to boil or fry.

"No, you'd better let me," said Barbara again, eagerly reaching down into the water. "You can't do it because of your sleeves."

She examined the rock deep beneath the surface, and the leaves of the seaweed wrapped around her arms. Her hair had fallen down over her forehead. She peeped up through the wisps now and again and blew them away.

Andreas sat listening to the grotto-like sound of the sea each time it rose squelching and clucking among the rocks. Barbara's short sleeves were wet, but she paid no attention to them. She worked in the green depths, her back tense with excitement, and when she looked up from the darkness her eyes had the same sheen as the water.

"Yes, she's a Nereid," thought Andreas. He had seen paintings of Nereids sitting on rocks and skerries, splashing in the waves with their white bodies and with a sea green light in their eyes. But here and there their bodies were red and as it were numbed by the great watery element into whose embrace they surrendered.

He sat there and was a little confused as always when Barbara was renewed in his imagination. Ah, here, suddenly, he saw her as part of nature, part of the great natural world. And truth to tell, he needed that. By now he was only too familiar with her in bed.

It had been a long winter. Not that it had been a boring winter for them; on the contrary. It had been a winter full of adventures and escapades and secret rendezvous such as not a soul could dream of in a half subterranean hole like Tórshavn. Especially while China was uninhabitable and they had not had any permanent lodgings to share, they had lived a life after his own heart. But now it was summer, and his heart had turned towards the natural world, tired of darkness and of caresses that were too genuine.

But look at Barbara, how cheerfully she transformed herself into a daughter of nature. She had given him sweet kisses and with the same gracefulness she would give him salt kisses and caress him with a wet, numbed hand. She would embrace him in the scent of seaweed and the raw substance of mussels and leave him behind blissful and with fish scales in his hair and clothes. Aye, she was an oceanide. He would make love to her somewhere on this rocky coast.

They walked far along the desolate shore that day and

in their great delight and self-oblivion they allowed nothing natural to remain secret from the naked rocks on which they sat and from the playful, capricious sea breeze.

But afterwards, when he opened his eyes and saw the shore again, and the fjord and the long, curving ridge of Nolsoy, Andreas was overcome by a strange mood that he failed properly to understand. Damn it all, he was not usually a man who regretted an undertaking successfully completed. Nor did he see anything other than that he had acted in accordance with nature. But as he observed the evening sunshine on the tiny houses on Nolsoy's familiar isthmus and the vast surface of the fjord stretching like a floor from his feet, he felt that it was after all something different he had sought in these natural surroundings of his homeland. What the hell, it was not at all Barbara he had wanted. It was nature itself he had wanted. That was what he had come to this country to investigate and to describe in a splendid and useful account. And here he had not merely wasted a valuable working winter on vain pleasures, but now, as nature was opening up again he dragged his amorous frippery out on the shore and fished for Norway haddock while other men rowed out to sea or went off into the mountains.

As they were walking home, they saw a ship in the offing. It was the *Fortuna* on the first visit of the year from Copenhagen, and Barbara involuntarily caught hold of Andreas' arm.

"Are you in a bad mood, Andreas?" she asked quietly.

"No, my love," he replied.

But later, after they had passed the Redoubt and could see the town, Tinganes and the Hoist, where people had begun to congregate, she said in a troubled voice, "I'm just thinking that you will be leaving one day."

"Don't think about that now. That's a long time away.

You know perfectly well how little progress I've made on my work. And besides," he added with a laugh, "I'll take you with me, my love."

Barbara started and a great radiance came into her eyes, but she immediately became deadly serious and in a voice that almost expressed fear asked, "Do you mean that, Andreas?"

"Of course I mean it."

He attempted to laugh, but could not quite bring himself to do so.

"I really do mean it, seriously," he said in a strong voice. "Of course. Of course."

Barbara still remained serious for a time, but then she suddenly brightened up.

"There's nothing I want more in the world. Copenhagen. And Poul, you know... he will probably... probably... have the marriage annulled, and then I shall be free, completely free. I've always simply longed to get away from here. Don't you think... don't you think I could come to Copenhagen?"

She was inspired, she was glowing with an incredible idea, and she almost danced over the rocky ground of Kragesten.

The peat smoke from all Tórshavn's supper pots was rising straight up in the air in the low evening sunshine, and the turf roofs of the town were shaded dark green in the golden haze. Voices could be heard from the Hoist, and the *Fortuna's* anchor splashed down into the silent waters.

"Aye, if Barbara left the country," thought Andreas, "I would settle here."

But Barbara was dancing enthusiastically in front of him like a large, black shadow straight in line with the red sun.

When Andreas visited his uncle a couple of days later, Johan Hendrik suddenly said to him: "Well, Andreas, I suppose you are not thinking of going back to Denmark? What is the situation, actually? I suppose the Exchequer has not laid down any limit to your time?"

"No," said Andreas hesitantly. "All the resolution says is that I should do it. It says nothing about when."

"Hmm, that's not so good. But for that matter I suppose they don't hurry about things down in the Exchequer. But..."

"I don't think that's a bad thing. For to be perfectly honest, the work is not progressing very quickly... not as quickly as I had imagined."

The judge walked around the room, rubbed his thigh, whistled through half-closed lips, drummed a little on the table and was very pensive.

"You could leave on the *Fortuna* now," he exclaimed suddenly.

"Now!" shouted Andreas.

"Yes. Have you anything against that?" Johan Hendrik gave a wry smile.

"Before I'm finished? I'd better tell you the truth, uncle. I know you are not so harsh in your judgement as other people are. Well... it is shameful to have to admit it, but I have hardly made a start yet."

Looking away, he added: "That's to say I had started. But all that work was destroyed by... that parson from Vágar."

The judge's smile twisted into a decidedly satirical grimace. He rubbed his thigh very energetically and then suddenly sat down.

"Tell me, Andreas. Suppose you were finished with your relationship and everything was otherwise as it is now. Would you then look favourably on the idea of leaving?"

Andreas hesitated a moment. His careless self-assurance had quite deserted him, and his big blue eyes adopted a hesitant look. It might seem he had been caught in a trap. But all at once he drew himself up.

"Well," he said. "I honestly do not know whether you will completely approve of my answer, but there is no point in putting on an act for you. If I could leave, I would have been delighted to do so. But I see no way out of all this. For either I must leave having achieved nothing, and I cannot do that. Or otherwise I must first achieve something, and I cannot do that either... at least not as long as Barbara..."

"But perhaps you might consider leaving her?"

"It would be difficult, but...! I had thought she was more capricious..."

"Ha ha ha ha!" The judge filled his nostrils with snuff, and his face was distorted with a sense of amusement. "Capricious? Ha! You are a couple of young fools. You are each as capricious as the other. You simply cannot be capricious at the same time. Can you not understand that? When you are capricious, she is not. And when she is capricious, you are not. I thought you realised that, damn it. How old are you? Twenty-three?"

The judge suddenly grew very serious: "And she is twenty-nine... twenty-nine. Aye. If she were sensible...! But she is not. No, she is not."

He put his hand to his chin and started considering. "Fundamentally... fundamentally, Barbara is in various respects... not particularly bright."

He sneezed and pulled a face. "God preserve us from whatever else might have happened if she had been."

He paced up and down the floor, suddenly stopped and said: "Suppose she had been able to think!... She would have been awful, wouldn't she Andreas?"

Andreas made no reply. He sat there and hung his head.

"Barbara," Johan Hendrik went on, "is ruled entirely by her heart."

He stared darkly into the air. "And it will be a sad story... a sad story the day her heart fades and she has to allow herself to be guided by her reason."

He shook his head. "Aye, I fundamentally feel sorry for her."

"I feel so dreadfully sorry for her," Andreas suddenly exclaimed. "She sacrifices everything for me and doesn't give a thought to herself."

He had tears in his eyes. "Reputation, repute, is all a matter of indifference to her; she doesn't consider her own advantage at all."

Johan Henrik hesitated a moment. Then, in a strangely sarcastic and dry voice: "You mustn't weep, Andreas. For she takes other people's advantage even less into consideration. She does what she wants to do. And you are surely intelligent enough to see what damage she does both to others and to herself. Do you never think of the parson from Vágar? He risks being unfrocked for misconduct and desperate behaviour. They say he has not been sober in the pulpit since New Year. And you haven't done an honest day's work since New Year. What are you thinking of?"

Andreas made a helpless, impatient gesture with his body.

"If only I had written that report, I wouldn't have hesitated..."

The judge went over to his bureau, whistling softly as he rummaged in a drawer. "You see, Andreas," he said, "it is not because you have deserved it. Nor is it because I consider that it would benefit your promotion in industry and useful virtues that I am doing your job for you. But something had to be done. In addition, it gave me great pleasure. Although I would wish it had been you who had this pleasure. But here you are. Here is the report."

Andreas stared at the elegantly written manuscript that was placed on the table before him.

"So you will leave on the *Fortuna*, won't you?" asked the judge. His eyes were warily trained on his nephew.

"Uncle, you don't think much of me, and there is no reason why you should. But I still have a certain sense of honour."

Andreas flared up with these last words, and his big eyes flashed. But Johan Hendrik did not bat an eyelid; he simply quickly wiped the tip of his nose and said in a dry voice: "Explain yourself a little. Honour is such a vague concept."

"Do you think I should adorn myself with borrowed plumes?" asked Andreas, standing up straight.

"Ha, you'll put a few of your own plumes among them. At least the flight feathers. The entire work will have to be rewritten, as I am sure you understand. To begin with, because it has to be written in your own hand. Secondly because the whole thing needs countless improvements, not only with a view to language and expression, in which you will doubtless find me too old-fashioned, but in the actual reasoning, too. For in economic questions and a scientific approach I consider myself to be inferior to you. So, in short, this is only the material I have gathered for you, and you must yourself work out how to interpret it. However, I believe you can do that far better down in Copenhagen than here as things now stand."

Andreas's pale face was now more helpless than ever. A sheen again began to appear in his eyes.

"Uncle, I appreciate your not thinking too ill of me and doing this for my benefit."

"That you have a bright head on those shoulders, I still do not doubt," said Johan Hendrik. "And that is why I... otherwise everything would go haywire."

"But... Barbara?" asked Andreas mournfully.

"What good do you think you will be able to do if you spend all your time with her?"

"I've told her that I will take her with me when I finally leave..."

Johan Hendrik's red, lined and as it were slightly dusty face suddenly contracted into a stony mask. "Barbara in Copenhagen! Ha, you will be able to get rid of her there at least. I will guarantee she will be in the harlots' prison within a month. Did you really mean that?"

"No."

"It was foolish, simply stupid of you to say that to her. Does she believe you?"

"I don't know. Yes, probably. But she thinks it is a long way off."

The judge stamped one foot on the floor and then started to pace up and down. "Weakling, weakling, weakling," he mumbled, "you confounded weakling. You will get away from her. Understand?"

"Yes," whispered Andreas. "But it will not be easy. This is breaking my heart."

Johan Henrik again made one of his grimaces and stood for a moment deep in thought. But then he brightened up and said in a cheerful voice, "All right. We won't mistake our feelings and persuade ourselves that our weakness is nobility."

"No," said Andreas. "But this is going to hurt her very deeply."

Johan Hendrik slowly opened his snuff box. "Listen, Andreas, let us talk this through reasonably."

He took a pinch of snuff and held it out between the tip of his first finger and his thumb.

"*Nul ne mérite d'être loué de sa bonté s'il n'a pas la force d'être méchant.*"

He took the snuff, pulled a face and sneezed. "Well, that means that no one deserves praise for being good if he has not the strength to be unkind."

The *Fortuna* was loading in the East Bay. Niels the Punt and the Beach Flea were paddling the big lighter back and forth between the Hoist and the ship. It was mostly jerseys, socks and woollen goods that were being taken aboard, the fruits of a winter's labours and diligence in all the Faroese hearth rooms, heavy hard-knitted things intended to be sold in Copenhagen, Hamburg and Amsterdam for the use of seamen all over the world.

"If I ever leave this country, I am afraid I shan't have the right clothes," said Barbara dreamily. "What do you think, Andreas? Do you think I shall look good enough?"

She laughed quietly and roguishly and her cheeks took on a red flush. They were sitting alone at the extreme end of Tinganes, close to the spot where a compass has been carved in the cliff floor.

"Clothes? You have more clothes than anyone else here," said Andreas. "And whatever you don't have you can easily find in Copenhagen. See. The sun is almost directly in the west." He pointed to the compass.

"Aye, so it's time to break off and all the men will be going home now," said Barbara idly.

He did not want to contradict her. He knew that the men would not be going home before the *Fortuna* was fully loaded. The weather was good and the wind was coming from the north, and it was the intention that the ship should be under sail late that night. But Barbara still had no idea.

Andreas' carefree heart bled that day from tenderness and shame. She was so happy as she sat with him playing with her glorious new idea, the dazzling lie about her journey to Copenhagen. He simply could not take that from her; he wanted to let her delight in the idea as long as he could; he lacked the courage to see her lonely and betrayed on this shore. Alas, every time he looked at her bright face he wanted to kiss her and weep in her arms – this woman whose happiness he was about to murder.

"Do you think I dance well enough?" she asked.

"You are by nature a better dancer than any other woman I know."

"I once danced with an admiral. It was down here, in the cellar..."

"Yes, you danced with an admiral, and then you went and married a parson!"

"Oh, you always have to...! That was much, much later. But do you think the way I dance is fashionable?"

"I'll teach you to dance according to fashion. Shall we go in to Uncle Johan Hendrik? Perhaps we could organise a little dance there."

They rose and walked up between the various Royal Store buildings. The idea of having a dance was a relief to Andreas as well. He would dance his way out of this; it was the only way; otherwise his waxen heart would melt on this beautiful, sad evening. And his uncle, the judge, was to play for it. It was not asking a bit too much of the old boy to expect him to play the music for his own comedy. Andreas had always been afraid of his rectitude and had usually had to look down when confronted with his searching and knowing look. Now he was confused about what to think of his uncle. But in his insecurity he held more closely to him. For his moral respect for him knew no bounds.

Johan Hendrik agreed. It must be possible to arrange a ball.

Sieur Arentzen would surely come and play his cello. And there were several young people in Tórshavn who would not say no to a dance.

But when later that evening, dressed in their finest clothes, they all turned up at the judge's home, the joy was contained and the guests mostly spoke together quite quietly. It was as though something or other oppressed them.

"You aren't as you usually are," said Barbara to Andreas.

Her eyes were shining in her powdered face. She was nervous. "I don't know," she said, "this is only like the shadow of a ball."

Outside the windows with their small panes, the night was calm and quite light. A rosy touch of day could still be seen atop Nolsoy, and all the turf roofs were illuminated by this reflected light on their north side. The East Bay lay deep down below like a black mirror. The ducks were asleep on the sand with their heads tucked under their wings.

"Oh," said Johan Hendrik. "Whoever arranges a ball in daylight? I ought to have thought about that."

He went out and returned with a lighted candelabrum and started lighting candles round about, on the bureau and on the bookshelves. They fluttered palely and had little effect, but the judge went outside and started closing the shutters.

"What the devil," shouted Gabriel from the steps. He was one of the few who had been initiated into the secret plan. "Is this an evening for dark deeds?"

"I don't know," replied Johan Hendrik. "Daylight doesn't seem to be suitable for this party. This Andreas is made of soft stuff. Hmm. But I can't sing my own praises... I haven't been able to bring myself to tell her either. But perhaps that is best. But we are going to have the devil of a day tomorrow."

"Hi, hi, hi," chortled Gabriel. "This is going to be one hell

303

of a comedy."

"Aye, give the devil an inch! There's nothing grows like lies."

"Oh, because you're giving Barbara a taste of her own medicine. How has she herself behaved?"

"That is true," said the judge, breathing out. "That is true. But still..."

He stroked his chin and looked thoughtfully out across the fjord. "No, no... if we say anything now I am afraid we shall not get Andreas off."

They both went indoors, and the gaiety was by now quite palpable. Sieur Arentzen was tuning his cello and trying the tone with broad strokes of his bow. Everyone was talking noisily and the candles were shining in their eyes.

"Well, there we are, there we are," said Johan Hendrik, rubbing his hands. "Now everything is as it should be."

He grasped his flute and produced a long trill.

"Yes, now it is...!" shouted Barbara. And her voice betrayed enthusiasm like warm sunshine. She betrayed a childish delight, and the whole of her body was moving.

"Aye, Barbara, we are fooling you, fooling you..." thought Johan Hendrik.

But Barbara clapped her hands and said: "I suggest for fun that we pretend this is a school of dancing. And Andreas shall be the dancing master and tell us when we are not dancing according to the fashion. Isn't that a good idea?"

Andreas stood there, pale and wearing his most gallant suit. But when the flute and cello started to blend their voices, his heart was fired and all his carefree spirit came upon him. But he completely forgot to be the dancing master.

In fact there was nothing for a dancing master to do – at least not as far as Barbara was concerned. She danced with such erect elegance and yet such relaxed delight, such measured steps and yet so much grace that there was nothing to correct in her but a couple of tiny adjustments. It was in her very nature to do everything correctly. Yet there was in her face a kind of serious watchfulness; only when she looked at Andreas did her eyes glow warm, and once when she reached out her hand to him in the dance, she asked him tenderly and seriously: "Is it good?"

The judge sat watching her; his face was twisted by a flute and no one could see in his lined and ambiguous features whether he was laughing or crying. But Johan Hendrik was not laughing that evening.

"Alas Barbara. We are fooling you," he thought, and his heart turned. Never had he seen beauty and naturalness so deceived. Here, she was dancing for Andreas. Oh dear, oh dear, that windbag, that fool. She was sending him amorous looks, and in a few hours he would be sailing away from her like a scoundrel.

Johan Hendrik blew and blew; the cello sounded deep alongside him; the tunes came time after time and the dancers filling his living room made the same steps and figures time after time, while the candles dripped and gradually became shorter. This was a large apparatus he had set going and dared not stop – a fairy tale with a dreadful ending. Once, during a pause, he fetched wine, all the bottles he possessed, and the merriment increased. Andreas, too, was enjoying himself and seemed only to be living in the present; it was a radiant, joyous occasion in this dark house in which all the shutters were closed. But, with sorrow in his heart, the judge only looked at his victim and saw how solemnly radiant she was in the midst of her ebullience, how strong she was in her joy, how devout in dance. She was nature personified, but at the same time she was blind, easy to deceive, and they were deceiving her, they were foully deceiving nature in the midst of its blind, trusting splendour.

And then this Andreas, his nephew, dancing and laughing and thinking of nothing! That lad probably resembled Barbara in his bad qualities, but not in the good. What nature was there in him? No, he was surely not worth the sacrifice she was making to him of her divinity, no, God forgive them all. Ugh!

And the ball came to an end. The judge's house was once more opened to the summer night. Its pale light fell soberly on bottles, glasses and smoking candles. It was like some fairytale soap bubble that had suddenly burst. Nolsoy lay there as clear as day and expressionless; everything was expressionless and silent, and everyone involuntarily lowered their voices as they went down the steps. The harbour was without a sign of life, and the gulls were asleep on the roof ridges.

"Then you will come back here when you have taken Barbara home," said Johan Hendrik to Andreas. "I would like to have those nets taken up before going to bed."

"Very well," replied Andreas. He was at first a little confused, but quickly understood the idea.

"Why did you say yes?" asked Barbara, deeply disappointed, as they went along the street together.

"Yes, but, dearest," said Andreas, "I could hardly refuse him. Besides, if we don't take the nets up now, it will be midday before we get the job done..."

The judge remained standing in his doorway. He would not be sure until Andreas was safely back. Alas, alas. But... *nul ne mérite d'être loué de sa bonté...*

Barbara went to bed, disappointed and rather angry with Andreas. She had also been filled with a quite indefinable sense of fear. He had recently not always been his usual self. But she was not inclined to worry. Besides, she was dizzy from the wine and the dancing, and she soon fell asleep.

She half woke to the sound of singing. For a long time she heard it through her dreams and felt deeply worried by it. But suddenly she understood what it was. It was the anchor song on board the *Fortuna*. They were weighing anchor. And almost at the same time she was overcome by a dreadful fear. Like a bird, she was out of her bed and over by the window.

There was a quite new sheen over Tórshavn now, and the sun was adding a touch of red to the north-eastern tip of Nolsoy. This glorious vista touched Barbara's sense of beauty, but her thoughts had no time for delight. Aboard the *Fortuna* she caught a glimpse of the men going round the capstan.

"Heave-ho, heave-ho."

Then they fell silent. The sails were already set and the *Fortuna* slipped silently out of the bay. And then it was that she suddenly caught sight of Andreas on the deck. She caught only a glimpse of him, standing there as he was on his arrival. But it was Andreas; that was absolutely certain.

She made a brief sound, a wail of despair, and within a second she had grabbed a skirt and was out of the door. She rushed down to the Sand... there was no one to be seen. The *Fortuna* was slowly making its way out. She ran like mad on bare feet over naked rocks along the East Bay. After the *Fortuna*.

In one place she had to wade to her knees in the water to get past. In another place, outside the store manager's house, she scraped her leg and made it bleed by clambering up a high stone terrace. She got past the entrance to the Royal Store and ran on, out to the furthermost point of Tinganes. Then she could get no further. The *Fortuna* slid away. She again uttered the same plaintive wail, and then she ran back along the empty shore.

But as she reached the Hoist, she met Niels the Punt.

"Oh Jesus, Niels," she shouted to him. "Has Andreas left? And I was supposed to be going with him."

Niels stared at her in amazement. He was uncomfortable with this meeting. He had often seen Barbara, but never as she was now, wringing her hands and with coarse marks of tears down her cheeks.

"Yes," he mumbled, "Andreas was on the *Fortuna*."

"And I was...!" sobbed Barbara. She was completely beside herself. But suddenly she changed. A sign of eagerness and cunning persuasion started to shine hopefully through her tears. She grasped Niels' arm.

"But you can still catch it, can't you? If you hurry, you could row me out to it in a four man boat. You and Ole Atten and...?"

She looked up at the entrance to the Royal Store, where three men from the town were grouped together, looking on in amazement and embarrassment.

"You could easily do it, couldn't you?"

Barbara's voice was regaining something of its customary sound, breaking into a falsetto in her eagerness, and she stood dancing on the hard rock.

Niels was immediately aware that this was a doubtful undertaking. "Bless you," he said hesitantly. "You can't just go off to Copenhagen without shoes or clothes, you know."

Barbara looked down at herself and saw how shamefully undressed she was and blushed for a second. But she had not the time, and she immediately forgot it again. She called to the other men and urged and persuaded them with her wet and wildly radiant face.

"I'll go home and put some clothes on quickly. Meanwhile, you'll get the boat in the water, won't you?"

She did not wait for an answer. She dashed away from them and in through the entrance to the Royal Store. And thus, in the very first weak rays from the sun, she ran through the whole of Tórshavn, in a shift and skirt. No one saw her. Yes, Johan Hendrik did, just as he emerged from Reynegard. But he did not believe his own eyes; only later did he realise what kind of natural eruption he was witnessing.

A quarter of an hour after this, a boat rowed by four men skimmed out over the shiny surface of the East Bay. Barbara was in the stern, completing her dress. She did not so much as turn to her mother, who, wrapped in an array of rags and tatters and with horror in her old voice was standing over on the sand and calling her name. The town had been awakened. The early sunshine was flashing in various windows as they were opened out of curiosity; indeed several people were already out in their slippers. But Barbara sensed none of this. She was only looking at the *Fortuna*, which with its sails unfurled was moving out of the fjord like some golden statue.

"There's fog to the east," remarked Niels the Punt as they passed the Redoubt point.

"Aye, that's what it's like at this time of the year," gasped Ole Atten. They put all their strength into the rowing. The boat swept forward over the shining waters.

"It's like rowing for pilot whales," shouted young Marcus excitedly from the prow: "If only the Lord would send us a whale!"

"Yes, but not now," said Barbara quickly and nervously. She had a hand over each gunwale; she was almost standing up in her seat, and never for a second did her eyes leave the *Fortuna*. The boat was not moving anywhere near quickly enough for her. The sun shone on her left cheek; she looked like a goddess driving a chariot.

"We're catching up," she shouted.

Niels the Punt was still watching the east. It was a summer morning of rare beauty. But the fog lay in great, lazy banks out in the sea and to the north of the islands. It glided so gently, mingling with the blue mountains, wrapping itself around their feet and leaving the peaks clear and sharp in the bright day. It was a good weather mist, a true sign of summer. But, thought Niels, it was not good for visibility. What concerned him particularly was the great bank of cloud behind Nolsoy. Shreds of it were already pouring in over the low isthmus on which the village of Nolsoy lay. But Barbara did not see this. She was only looking forward.

"We're catching up," she shouted again with hope and jubilation in her multi-toned voice. "Don't you think we'll catch them?"

The men looked forward over their shoulders.

"Aye," said Niels. "If it all goes as it's going now, we'll catch them."

"Oh, Niels," said Barbara. "You never make promises. I know you."

"Promises? Bless you. I don't want to promise too much." Niels was gentler and more accommodating this morning than he had ever been. But promise...

It was also curious that the *Fortuna* was not heaving to, although those on board must have seen the boat long ago. There must be something suspicious in this undertaking, thought Niels. Aye, that was what they had all been thinking. That was not why they were making such an effort; they were not expecting much by way of thanks for this rowing trip when they returned to the shore. But they had had so many tellings off before, both from the commandant and the bailiff, and now recently also from that man Gabriel. They were quite willing to accept another one on behalf of Barbara, for she had always been nice to them.

The *Fortuna* changed course and sailed more to the east. It was now at the end of the fjord, close to the southern tip of Nolsoy.

The boat was now far out. Kirkjubøreyn and Nolsoy had in some way expanded before them, blue islands, fells and peaks had appeared both to the south and the north. The boat pitched and foamed forward across the great surface of water.

"Make for the tip, make for the tip," shouted Barbara.

"The current...!" Niels the Punt objected.

"Oh, you and your current," shouted Barbara impatiently. "Can't you see we'll make a short cut if we go in close to the tip?"

Niels did partly as she asked He knew it was a wrong manoeuvre if the *Fortuna* was to be caught up with, but he was filled with increasing doubt both as to whether it could be caught and also as to whether it should be caught. It was probably a dubious business to help someone to leave the country without a passport issued by the authorities... now that he thought about it. And he did not for a minute believe that Barbara had such a passport.

Nevertheless, he rowed with all his strength, and so did the others. They could do nothing else in the face of Barbara; she was shouting to them, her eyes were shining and she was eagerly encouraging them to go on.

The *Fortuna* was now a good way behind the tip, and they themselves were approaching this long, sharp point. From Tórshavn it looked low and flat, but now it started to rise before them like a wall, wild and black. Through the furthermost stretch there was a hole through which you could see the light of day. Otherwise, the water was black and green here, close to the land. By now they were so close that they could clearly see the sheep grazing in the sunlight up on the cliff, while they themselves were in the shade.

The men put their feet hard against the boat's timbers and almost pulled themselves to their feet with every stroke of the oars.

"Now – now – now," groaned Niels the Punt rhythmically through gritted teeth. Ole Atten had lost his bonnet; his white hair and beard were blowing all over the place, and he was puffing like a pair of bellows; he was laughing and looked like both a giant and an old monkey. Young Marcus was hooting from the foremost thwart, and Beach Flea's face was so bloodshot that it looked as though his eyes would pop out sideways. Oh Lord... this was how the men of Tórshavn rowed for Barbara; they were fine fellows, splendid men. And the sea washed past them on both sides, and Barbara shouted and exulted and praised them.

But when she looked towards the land, she saw that the boat was hardly moving. They had got into a current and lay there as though in a quickly flowing river. Tears came into her throat, and she gave a cry of disappointment and fear.

"Bless you, bless you, don't lose heart," groaned Ole Atten. "We're gaining; we're gaining round the point. That's such a short way. You've got to have patience to win."

But patience was about the last thing that Barbara possessed. She rose, she sat down, she wrung her hands, she shouted at the men and was quite beside herself. It took them a good quarter of an hour to make the few metres around the point and gain the view east...

And that was when everything collapsed. Barbara's

expression was suddenly completely empty; the men glanced over their shoulders and then took on the same expression.

The *Fortuna* was not to be seen. There was nothing at all to be seen. Neither sea nor sky. There was nothing but white mist, a void and the cries of gulls. The men rowed as though possessed for a little while, but suddenly they stopped and rested their oars. Helplessly. The boat fell quite silent.

At that moment Barbara burst out in great, heartrending weeping. The men sat there helplessly and heard her terrible sobbing. But the current silently and quickly took the boat back around the point and into the Nolsoy Fjord, where there was no mist. And when, finally, the oars were dipped in the water, the prow was turned towards Tórshavn.

It was a downcast, sad sight an hour or so later as they rowed into the East Bay again. People were standing watching on Tinganes, on the Redoubt and on every tongue of land. Many had seen Barbara leave; everyone saw her return. She was in the stern, stiff and as white as chalk.

Johan Henrik, who had been standing at his window, turned into the room. He could not face this scene. But otherwise, the people of Tórshavn simply had to express their views on the gauntlet that was being run. The boat was followed by murmurs as it came along the banks of the bay.

"Aye, there's plenty as have burned their fingers on her. Now she's burnt her own fingers. And thoroughly, too."

When the boat hove to at the Hoist, Gabriel was standing on shore waiting, and a whole group, mostly young people, immediately formed around him. Nor was there a single window free around there. But Gabriel was almost lost for words when he saw the state Barbara was in. White and speechless like a sleepwalker, she came ashore and went straight past him to Nýggjastova. Only when she was out of sight did he collect himself together sufficiently to give the men a dressing down. Silent and embarrassed, they put Barbara's badly packed and as it were randomly assembled luggage ashore. Gabriel kicked the pile contemptuously.

"And she was off to Copenhagen with all that junk! Take all this rubbish up to Nýggjastova," he ordered some children. "But you," he continued to the men, "you just don't know what you've let yourselves in for. If you'd got Barbara out of the country today, you'd soon have been following her into the Bremerholm prison. Understand?"

And with that, he left. Old Ole Atten, the most loyal of all the soldiers, felt his hands trembling. But Gabriel was sniggering as he entered the bailiff's house.

"Hi, hi, I bloody well truly believe now that the gilt is really off the gingerbread. The damned bitch is really finished now."

Suzanne did not deign him a word. She merely finished the bow she was tying and went straight up to Nýggjastova. On the way there, she met the boys coming along with the wretched remains of Barbara's finery.